P9-DFQ-185
YA
Fic
Nor
34711300016666
DISCARD

WHERE I END

WHERE I END & *YOU BEGIN*

& YOU BEGIN

HYPERION
Los Angeles New York

First Edition, June 2019
10 9 8 7 6 5 4 3 2 1
FAC-020093-19109

Printed in the United States of America

This book is set in 11-pt. Adobe Garamond Pro/Adobe
Designed by Mary Claire Cruz

Library of Congress Cataloging-in-Publication Data
Names: Norton, Preston, 1985– author.
Title: Where I end and you begin / by Preston Norton.
Description: First edition. • Los Angeles ; New York : Hyperion, 2019. • Summary: As punishment for breaking into their high school to watch the solar eclipse, Ezra, his crush Imogen, Ezra's best friend, Holden, and Imogen's best friend, Wynonna must perform in the school's production of Shakespeare's *Twelfth Night*, but before the first rehearsal starts, socially inept Ezra and badass Wynonna wake up in each other's bodies.
Identifiers: LCCN 2018040278 • ISBN 9781484798355 (hardcover)
Subjects: • CYAC: Dating (Social customs)—Fiction. • Best friends—Fiction. • Friendship—Fiction. • High schools—Fiction. • Schools—Fiction.
Classification: LCC PZ7.N8253 Wh 2019 • DDC [Fic]—dc23
LC record available at https://lccn.loc.gov/2018040278

Reinforced binding
Visit www.hyperionteens.com

THIS LABEL APPLIES TO TEXT STOCK

To Jenny, who Believed in times of doubt

To Laura, who Strengthened in times of weakness

To Erin Rene, who Loved no matter what

ONE

I HAD IT FROM A very reliable source that Imogen Klutz was watching the total solar eclipse from the roof of Piles Fork High School.

I mean, *technically* I heard it from Holden, who heard it from Jessica, who heard it from Brittany, who saw Imogen post about it online, only to promptly delete it two minutes later. But Holden was trustworthy. And Jessica liked to gossip, and Brittany lived every moment of her waking life on social media, so . . . it wasn't exactly an *unreliable* source.

"Have you asked You Know Who to the You Know What yet?" Holden asked me.

You Know Who was Imogen, and You Know What was prom. And no, I hadn't. My excuse was that I was an antisocial loser with crippling anxiety who had no intention of branching out of my small, sad, pathetic world, thank you very much. I mean, my greatest strength was *math*, for Christ's sake!

I was condemned to a life of celibacy. I had accepted this fact.

Holden told me to shut my Valium hole—as best friends often

do—and then told me of Imogen's eclipse plans. And then he told me of *our* plan. We had a plan, apparently.

The plan was simple: We'd break into school, too. And then—under the magic of the total solar eclipse—I would ask Imogen to prom.

That was all fine and dandy. Except that if Imogen was watching the eclipse from the roof of Piles Fork High School, it was *guaranteed* that Wynonna Jones would be there. And Wynonna Jones's favorite hobby—aside from photography, jamming to '80s rock, and macking down on pork rinds—was making my life a living hell. It was part of who she was. A key ingredient to her identity.

"What about Wynonna?" I said. "You *know* she'll be there, too. I mean, it was probably *her* delinquent idea."

"I'll keep Wynonna preoccupied," said Holden. "You just worry about asking You Know Who to the You Know What."

"But you *hate* Wynonna."

"More than anything in the world," Holden agreed. "But I care about *your* antisocial loser ass *more* than I hate her. So are we doing this or what?"

• •

Little did we know, traversing Carbondale an hour before the eclipse—even on foot—was a low-key nightmare.

"I'm trying to decide if this is a really cool thing or a nightmare," said Holden. "Because every time I see another schmuck wearing a fanny pack, I lean more and more toward the nightmare scenario."

Holden was being dramatic—but only slightly. The tourists had descended on Carbondale like a plague of locusts. Except these particular locusts were wearing cardboard eclipse glasses, cargo pants,

Crocs, and—tragically—fanny packs. Pedestrians filled the sidewalks in droves. Automobile traffic resembled what I imagined my uncle Gary's arteries looked like on his breakfast/lunch work diet of McGriddles and XXL Grilled Stuft Burritos that he had been subsisting on for the past twenty years. Everyone and every*thing* was heading in the general direction of Saluki Stadium. That was where the biggest eclipse viewing party was taking place.

"Speaking of nightmares," said Holden, "you look like shit. You okay?"

"Didn't sleep last night," I said. My tone was flat. Unaffected. Completely resigned to my fate.

"Man, tell me something I don't know. Forget sleeping pills. You need some good ol'-fashioned chloroform."

Although the stress of asking You Know Who to the You Know What may have been a factor, the root of the problem was my chronic insomnia. I hadn't slept in the past seventy-two hours and counting. And boy, was I feeling it. I could feel the ache for sleep in my bones. I could *feel* the circles under my eyes. But I didn't dare crawl back into bed. That would be putting too much pressure on my not-so-trusty hypothalamus—the dysfunctional part of my brain responsible for shutting things down. It was like the concept of "stage fright" when you pee at a public urinal. It didn't matter if your bladder was in nuclear meltdown mode. Performance was impossible. When it came to sleep, it was best just to let things shut down on their own—*wherever* that may be. At my desk in Biology, in the passenger seat of Holden's car, in the booth of an IHOP. Wherever. On bad weeks, my chronic insomnia would build and build and build until my sleep deprivation reached criticality and I just blacked out. It didn't matter if I was standing, walking, or doing jumping jacks. My body just dropped like I was in the Matrix and someone pulled the plug on me.

I could feel the shutdown closing in. It felt like the thing holding my atoms and particles together was slowly coming unglued.

"I mean, normally the sleep deprivation works in your favor," said Holden. "You've got this unhealthy, anemic male supermodel thing going on. Like that *Twilight* vampire meets Jared Leto playing a heroin junkie. But you *really* look like shit today. I'm saying that as a friend."

"Thanks," I said. I held my hand over my heart. "I'll cherish that right here."

Holden nodded, like he expected nothing less. I returned my attention to the sidewalk ahead and the hordes of people occupying it.

And the fanny packs.

And the Crocs.

"Okay, I *get* the fanny packs," I said. "They carry the stupid glasses, right? What I *don't* get are the Crocs. Have you ever seen so many Crocs?"

"Oh, I *totally* get that," said Holden. "They're comfortable."

"No, walking around my bedroom *naked* is comfortable. Wearing Crocs is just obscene—in public, no less, Jesus!"

"Crocs are comfy as shit," said Holden. "Deal with it. If you want to get mad about something, get mad that these bastards are commercializing outer space. Next thing you know, they'll be selling real estate on Uranus. Like, who the hell owns Uranus? God, it makes me so mad!"

To demonstrate his madness, Holden clenched his fist, aiming his fury at a low-set construction stop sign—*clearly* a symbol of capitalist socioeconomic oppression. But because Holden was five foot nothing—no shit, roughly the height of a really tall hobbit—he still had to give it a running jumpstart. He bolted, jumped, reared his fist back, and unleashed it like a spring-operated can of whoop-ass. The impact of his fist gave a sharp metallic clang that seemed to echo for blocks. This earned us plenty of startled and annoyed looks from the tourists crowding around us.

Holden barely landed on his feet, staggered for balance, and crumpled.

"Shit," he said. He recoiled his fist, cradling it to his chest. "Shit, shit, shit."

"Easy there, Fight Club. You okay?"

"Shit, shit, shit," Holden continued, in worlds of pain. He brought his fist to his mouth and started sucking on it like a gigantic Tootsie Pop.

Meet Holden Durden—the biggest idiot in all of Jackson County. Also, my best friend. He technically earned this honor by being my *only* friend, but I liked to think that his merits outweighed the clear and utter lack of competition. And because his name was rich with pop-culture potential, I liked to call him Fight Club—or sometimes Caulfield—depending on his mood, which was like a Green Day album. It ranged from lost, alienated soul seeking connection to anti-consumerist anarchist reaping destruction. And I guess there was a weird middle ground that appreciated Crocs.

But despite his height—as well as his aggressively nonconformist behavior—he was actually kind of a stud. He'd had at least seven girlfriends over the course of his high school career and probably twice as many flings. He may have been short, but he carried those five feet and zero inches with Napoleonic confidence.

"Jesus Christ on ice!" said Holden. "Why are there so many fucking people?"

It was a reasonable enough question—*if* you hadn't lived your whole life in Carbondale, like Holden and me. If you *had*, then you knew Carbondale was the self-proclaimed "Solar Eclipse Crossroads of America." You see, the last total solar eclipse to hit Carbondale was only seven years ago—which *sounds* like an eternity, until you realize that prior to that, the continental United States hadn't seen a total solar eclipse since 1979. Which is older than Metallica. So basically, what we were experiencing was an impossible surplus of the rarest celestial event known to the planet Earth. Not to mention, the eclipse of seven years ago reached its "point of greatest duration" in Carbondale—a whopping two minutes and forty seconds. Which was allegedly a big deal. This eclipse business was Carbondale's entire identity. They closed school for this shit.

But Holden already *knew* this, so I resolved to change the subject.

"Jesus Christ . . . on ice," I mused. "Are you imagining our Lord and Savior as a chilled beverage or a theatrical figure-skating show?"

Holden laughed, rolled his eyes, and punched me in the arm. "Shut up, you atheist schmuck. God knows you need a fucking miracle."

• •

My obsession with Imogen ran deep. It all started in elementary school during our fourth-grade production of *Romeo and Juliet*.

Obviously, it was a kid-friendly version with a dumbed-down script. Also, our fourth-grade drama teacher, Ms. Lopez, resolved that the double suicide was too dark, so she went with an alternative, happily-ever-after ending.

Now don't get me wrong. Even in fourth grade, I was antisocial as balls. But there was something about playing a role—*being* someone else—that opened something up inside me. It felt like I was free to say or do whatever I wanted. Which was weird, because I was reading and memorizing a script, so it was kind of the opposite.

Turns out, I was a fourth-grade prodigy at Shakespeare. Even if it was a dumbed-down, alternate-reality, happily-ever-after Shakespeare. It was like a right-brain tsunami, rising to meet the incredible wall of my left-side math brain. I nailed the auditions and was cast as Romeo.

And Juliet was none other than Imogen Klutz.

Imogen was a glutton for drama and theatrics. She was born for the role.

Over the course of that fourth-grade production, I sort of fell in love with Imogen. Even though the only time we talked was when we were reciting lines to each other. But somehow, nine-year-old me was *convinced*: If I just nailed this performance, Imogen and I would be together.

I know, right? Whatever *that's* supposed to mean to a fourth grader. Jesus.

Naturally, I botched it all up.

Act 1, scene 1: Benvolio (Romeo's cousin) is having a riveting discussion with Lord and Lady Montague (Romeo's parents) about those motherfucking Capulets (seriously, fuck them), and they are also expressing deep concern over poor, emo Romeo, who has been sulking around among the sycamores lately. As Romeo sulks onto the scene, Benvolio promises to find out the reason for his melancholy.

Spoiler: Romeo is in love with Rosalind. Unfortunately, Rosalind doesn't reciprocate the feeling. Also, she has sworn herself to a life of chastity. Poor, emo Romeo . . .

Enter ROMEO.

Benvolio: *"Good morrow, cousin!"*

And that's when I forgot all my lines.

Except it was more surreal than that. It was like an out-of-body experience. I *literally* felt like I was in the audience, and I was watching the Shakespearean Tragedy Formerly Known as Ezra. I watched as he destroyed his acting career, and his future with Imogen, in one fell swoop. His eyes were wide, and his mouth was open, and he looked like he might faint at any moment, or possibly die.

I knew my lines. I *knew* them! I whispered them to myself from my out-of-body seat in the audience.

Is the day so young?

Is the day so young?!

IS THE DAY SO YOUNG?!?

But the lines never made it to the Ezra onstage.

Benvolio whispered the line to him. Offstage, Ms. Lopez whispered the line to him. Loudly. Loud enough for the first several rows to hear. Finally, in a moment of peak exasperation, she rushed onstage with a full script and attempted to shove it into his limp-noodle hands.

The Ezra onstage looked at the script like it was his own death sentence.

And then he ran offstage.

Out of the school.

I found myself curled up in the parking lot, having an actual mental breakdown.

Crying.

Ironically, our production of *Romeo and Juliet* was on the evening of Carbondale's first total solar eclipse. Ms. Lopez seemed to think it was poetic—being a tale of star-crossed lovers and all. It wasn't until later that I learned how Romeo and Juliet *really* ended. It wasn't a romance. It was a staunch, die-hard tragedy! If *that* didn't act as foreshadowing of my future with Imogen, nothing did.

That was about the time my chronic insomnia became a thing. Although technically, my insomnia also followed a minor car accident from my childhood—one that happened a night or two before *Romeo and Juliet*. But honestly, I couldn't remember a damn thing about it.

My doctor suggested my insomnia was trauma-related. I suggested it was I-don't-know-how-to-be-a-human-being-anymore-related. My doctor suggested that maybe *that* was trauma-related. I suggested that space-time was made out of spirals, known mathematically as the golden ratio, and that this ratio—1.618—was the mathematical constant that governed the universe, but knowing that wasn't going to help me sleep—if anything, it was doing the opposite—so, like, did he have anything stronger than Ambien or what?

We were at an impasse.

There was a reason Holden and I chose today for my promposal. Because it wasn't just about prom. It was about fixing me. Because clearly, I was broken. I was psychologically damaged goods.

I only mention any of this because life is a journey of spirals. Repeating patterns.

The past always has a way of catching up to the future.

• •

Piles Fork High School was desolate—a redbrick, three-story megalith from a forgotten era. Okay, so the forgotten era was last Friday. The grounds were too well kept for this to be some post-apocalyptic setting. The grass was cut, the roses were coming into bloom, and the hedges were crisp, elongated cubes. Even if Piles Fork's education system *was* a sham, at least the groundskeeper, Ziggy, kept the shrubbery on point.

As we ascended the front steps and approached the glass doors, Holden pulled a key out of his pocket. It sank flawlessly into the keyhole and clicked as he turned it.

It's maybe important to know that Holden's mom was *Principal* Durden.

Holden stole his mom's master key. I mean, it was a long time ago, but he *did* make a copy. Well, two copies. He gave one to me for my sixteenth birthday. Told me to keep it on me at all times. Maybe we'd sneak into school on a Saturday and smoke pot in the teachers' lounge.

We never did, but it was a noble idea. It's the thought that counts.

"Let's split up," he said.

"What?" I said. "Have you watched any horror movie ever? That's like the number one no-no."

"I'm sorry. Is there a homicidal sociopath in this scenario I'm unaware of?"

"Wynonna Jones?" I suggested.

"Wynonna isn't a *homicidal* sociopath. Just a regular one."

"How do you suppose they got in?"

"When it comes to the Jonesy?" said Holden. "Anything's possible—picking the locks, scaling the wall, quantum teleportation. . . ."

"That's *scientifically* impossible, actually."

"Listen, Stephen Hawking, we're on a bit of a time crunch, and we still don't know how to get on the roof. If we're gonna make this happen, we're gonna *have* to split up. Call me if you see the girls or the entrance to the roof, and I'll do the same. Okay? Okay."

Without waiting for a response, Holden turned and delved west.

I took a deep breath, flipped on the flashlight on my phone, and ventured east.

I climbed the eastside stairs to the third floor. Listened to the quiet clap of my shoes echo up the stairwell. Once I reached the top, I began scouring the main hall clockwise. Turned into each branching pathway as it came. Checked each room and closet. Kept my eyes on the ceiling, in case there was some sort of . . . hatch . . . or whatever.

That's when I heard it—a small metallic slinking sound. A clatter. A soft thud.

My whole body atrophied. I waited. Realized I wasn't breathing, at which point I made a conscious effort to *keep* not breathing.

I heard it again.

Slink—clatter—THUNK!

This time, I was sure of it.

It was the sound of a vending machine.

And it was coming from the floor below.

I hurried to the nearest stairwell, gripped the handrail, and descended with quiet, anxious steps.

It was either Imogen or Wynonna—one or the other. I doubted it was both because it was *impossible* for Wynonna not to talk when Imogen was around.

Slink. Clatter. Thunk.

Whoever it was, they were sure stocking up on some serious sustenance.

I slowed my pace near the bottom of the stairs. Lurked cautiously to the corner—knowing full well that the vending machine in question was mere feet away on the other side.

Palms to the wall, I peered around the corner.

It was Imogen Klutz.

You know that scene in high school movies where our protagonist, Awkward Social Outcast, lays eyes on our lead female character, Girl of His Dreams—the first time we, as an audience, meet her—and we see her in slow motion, and her skin glows with ethereal radiance, and her hair flows like a waterfall or something similarly flow-y, and all sound cuts out to an annoying pop song, like the Smash Mouth cover of "I'm a Believer"?

Yeah. That.

Okay, so I kind of had a thing for Imogen. And that thing may have been called "obsession." She was beautifully lanky with a long, gawky neck; a heart-shaped face with kind eyes; and sheets of sandy-blond hair that kind of frizzed around the ears. She had an affinity for sweaters and often coupled them with colorful, awkwardly fitting jeans and beautifully ugly no-name-brand sneakers.

And the eyebrows. Oh my god. Don't even get me started on the eyebrows.

Okay, I'll tell you.

On the surface, Imogen's eyebrows were big, bad, and beautiful. Unplucked and unashamed. Some might go so far as to call them "colossal" or "gargantuan." That wasn't an exaggeration. Deep down, however, Imogen's eyebrows were an enigma. Beneath the planes of their vast, follicular arcs, they contained the secrets of the universe. And the darkness! They were *sooooo* dark—practically black against the sandy blond of her hair—drawing you in like gravitational singularities. Resistance was futile. Think *Labyrinth*-era Jennifer Connelly and you're on the right track. Add a dash of black magic and a pinch of metaphysical transcendence, and SHAZAM.

Those were Imogen's eyebrows.

Of course, when I told Holden this, he told me I had a troubling eyebrow fetish, and I should probably seek psychiatric help.

Anyway, as I witnessed all of this in slow motion, with Smash Mouth singing in the background, and—*slink, clatter, thunk*—the last bag of pork rinds fell into the dispenser hatch of the vending machine, there was a hazy moment when I apparently wandered out from behind the corner of the stairwell. But I didn't say anything. Lest anyone forget, my role in this movie was Awkward Social Outcast, and it was a comedy at my expense.

Imogen turned her head slowly—suddenly noticing the human-shaped figure . . .

. . . standing six feet away from her . . .

. . . in a dark, empty hallway . . .

. . . watching her.

She screamed and threw her arms in the air—along with all the snacks she was carrying—chips, candy bars, pork rinds, and a pair of Dr Peppers. One of the Dr Peppers landed in such a way that it cracked and spewed pressurized soda like a punctured vein in a splatter film. The other Dr Pepper landed uncracked, although it caught a backspin and rolled beneath her foot—*right* as she took a frantic step backward. The sole of her shoe landed on the center of the can, wobbled unsteadily, and the rest was poetry in motion. That is to say, Imogen's leg shot up in an elegant high kick, the can of Dr Pepper launched like a ballistic missile, her entire body swung like a catapult, and she landed flat on her back.

"Shit," I said.

I immediately swooped to Imogen's aid—only to hover over her body, mirroring her paralysis.

"Oh my god," I said. My hands floundered aimlessly. "I am so sorry. Imogen, are you okay?"

There was a long moment when Imogen's eyes were like marbles—glassy orbs disconnected from sentient thought. She was dead. I killed her. I ogled Imogen to death. Death by ogling in the first degree.

Then she blinked, and there was life. Her eyes focused on me, and she smiled.

"Oh, hey, Ezra," she said. Then she winced. "Ouch."

"Where does it hurt?" I asked.

Imogen made a vague, wibbly-wobbly gesture with her hands that seemed to encompass her entire body.

"I'm gonna call nine-one-one," I said.

“No!” said Imogen. She immediately attempted to sit up. “No, no, no. I’m good. I’m fine.”

“Are you sure?”

“In a breaking-and-entering situation?” said Imogen. “Ten minutes before the eclipse? I am *so* sure. Wynonna would kill—”

“Slevin, you little shit!” said the last voice in the world I wanted to hear. “What the hell sort of perverted things are you doing to my best friend?”

I whipped around, and there she was—Wynonna fucking Jones—strolling onto the scene like some sort of deus ex machina. But, like, the opposite. A sort of *anti*–deus ex machina who fucked things up right when you thought everything would be okay.

Wynonna’s style could best be described as “military hippie-core” or maybe “’80s vomit-punk.” All I could tell you was that she had electric-blue hair and was currently wearing combat boots, a pair of very distressed jeans—shredded, bleached, and pegged to a fault—a bomber jacket covered in patches, tied snugly around her waist, some sort of boho-crochet top, and bracelets. Lots of bracelets. Like, *way* too many bracelets for any one human being. And yet, there they were—bold, overbearing, and predominantly neon. She had a pair of tattoos on her inner forearms. On her left arm was the word “dharma.” On the right, mirroring the other, was “karma.”

Ironically, it was the karma hand (rocking electric-blue nails to match her hair) that shoved me square in the chest. I staggered backward—almost tripped and fell—but landed against the wall of lockers behind me.

“Did he hurt you?” said Wynonna.

“No, no, I’m fine,” said Imogen, crawling to her feet—although this was followed by an invalidating wince.

“Was he trying to put his creepy moves on you?”

I felt myself flush red.

"What? No!" said Imogen, appalled.

"Did he try to bank-rob your virginity?" said Wynonna.

Okay, now I was fuchsia, swiftly encroaching on magenta.

"Wynonna!" said Imogen, wide-eyed. "Can we *not* talk about my virginity?"

But Wynonna was already bored with Imogen and set her predatory sights on me. I still had my back to the lockers, but Wynonna's presence was reverse-magnetic, pressing me flat against the cold blue metal.

"I'll tell you how this works, Slevin," said Wynonna. "I'm like Imogen's daddy. If you want to ask Imogen on a date, you gotta go through me. At which point I'll decide whether or not I'll kill you. Are we clear?"

We were *so* clear. Cellophane, even.

However, at that exact moment, I heard Holden calling my name. Then he rounded the corner and saw his best friend being bullied—yet again—by Wynonna fucking Jones.

"GET YOUR HANDS OFF MY BEST FRIEND, YOU BLUE-HAIRED SNAKE."

Wynonna turned her head, and then her lips twisted into an amused smirk. "Blue-haired snake?"

"You lay one more finger on him," said Holden, "and I'll . . ."

But Wynonna was already raising a single finger—slowly, tauntingly. She made an incredible display of it. She then reached it slowly toward my face. But her eyes were on Holden. Testing him. Sneering with her pupils.

"Don't. You. Dare," said Holden.

She pressed my nose like a button.

"Boop," she said.

If my nose were a button, then Holden was the doomsday device to which it was wirelessly connected. He extended his arms and screamed like a total maniac—which Wynonna thought was hilarious. But then he marched over to Imogen.

Wynonna's smile vanished.

Holden snatched a bag of pork rinds off the floor.

Wynonna's eyes widened with alarm. "Put the pork rinds down, you son of a—"

Holden ripped the bag of rinds wide open, shoving his face in them like a wild animal.

"—BITCH!" Wynonna screamed.

Holden was chomping, scarfing, *devouring* with voracious force. Wynonna all but assaulted him, ripping the tattered bag from his hands. By that point, there was nothing but deep-fried pork dust and Holden's smirking chipmunk cheeks, bulging like balloons. He didn't dare swallow, though. Like any sane human, he knew that pork rinds tasted like salty, deep-fried ass.

Both Holden's and Wynonna's heads rotated slowly, homing in on the second—and final—bag of pork rinds.

Wynonna bolted. Holden, however, dove like a baseball player for home plate. And because the vinyl tile floor was as buffed and shiny as the immortal bald head of Bruce Willis, he slid like it was a Slip 'n Slide. Holden snatched the bag and barrel-rolled, and Wynonna tripped over him. He tried to get up, but Wynonna grabbed him by the shirt and muscled him down. They proceeded to roll around on the floor.

The moment Holden was on top, Wynonna went for his throat. Bad idea. Holden's ballooning cheeks deflated, and he spewed chewed-up pork rinds all over her boho-crochet top.

Wynonna screamed with understandable horror. Holden coughed and gagged.

Imogen, meanwhile, crab-crawled away from the action on long, spindly limbs until she was right next to me. Climbed to her feet. Leaned toward my ear, although she was unable to tear her eyes away from the carnage.

"Why do they always do this?" she said in a hushed tone.

It was a very large question containing layers upon layers to unpack. Here were the facts as I knew them:

1. Wynonna hated me, but . . .
2. She loved to torment me.
3. Holden always came to my rescue, but . . .
4. He always did it in an unstable, psychotic, rage-y sort of way.
5. I think Wynonna loved that, too. I think she got a rush out of it.

It was a vicious, never-ending cycle. In fact, one might assume that it was a part of the normal balance of their lives. That if you took this away from them, their states of being might very well spiral into chaos.

Then a thought occurred: I was experiencing a rare, one-on-one conversation with Imogen. *If* you disregarded our best friends grappling MMA-style on the floor, that is. Which I did. In fact, Wynonna and Holden were inadvertently acting as a kind of strange and horrifying—but nevertheless effective—icebreaker. It was about as perfect an opportunity to ask You Know Who to the You Know What that I could hope for.

However, now that Imogen was standing next to me—clearly *not* having a 911 emergency—I devolved into my usual state of crippling social ineptitude.

Somewhere in the pandemonium, Holden managed to break free of Wynonna. He lunged to the nearest window—one of the few at

Piles Fork that you could actually slide open. This is what Holden did. Slid it *wide* open with one hand. With the other, he thrust the hostage bag of pork rinds over the three-story drop. The bag dangled in his fierce grip.

"Take one more step and the pork rinds get it," said Holden.

Wynonna froze in her oversized combat-boot tracks. Raised her hands in a slow and steady cease-fire. She was apparently taking the hostage situation very seriously.

"*Eeeeeasy*, Durden," said Wynonna. "Don't do anything we'll all regret."

"Apologize to Ezra," said Holden.

"Excuse me?"

"Or the pork rinds get it."

Wynonna glanced at me with a sort of residual disgust. Or dismissive resentment. It was hard to pin down exactly *what* it was, however, because my mind was slipping. Like the *moon* was currently slipping over the disk of the sun, causing the sky to darken with a strange, dusky hue. Although I was only vaguely aware of it in some distant compartment of my brain.

"No way," said Wynonna. "I am not apologizing to—"

Holden let his grip slide but only slightly. The pork rinds slipped half an inch.

"Okay, okay, okay!" said Wynonna. She turned to look at me. Took several steps forward until we were standing at a safe, apologetic distance. I could sense the words coagulating at the back of her throat, like a scab.

"Ezra Slevin," she said, pronouncing each syllable of my name overdramatically. "I am sorry . . . that you're a PATHETIC LITTLE CHICKENSHIT."

She lunged at Holden. Smashed him into the wall, tweaking

his "pork rind" arm against the window frame. Holden yelped. The brunt of the impact, however, went into her right combat boot, which she planted flat against the wall. A compressed spring. She fastened her arms around Holden's head, Randy Orton–style, and kicked off, launching the two of them like a WWE finishing move. I thought for sure she was gonna RKO Holden's ass "outta nowhere!"

Instead, Wynonna kicked off a little too hard, and she and Holden collided into Imogen and me.

I felt it—a cerebral *FLASH*! I felt the impact like my astral form was being knocked out of my human shell.

We were a tangle of limbs, a human blob, rolling across the vinyl tile floor—*crash!*—right into the lockers. The *kshhhhhhh!* of ringing aluminum buzzed in my ears.

"Owwww," said Holden.

"Am I dead?" said Imogen faintly. "Is this what being dead is?"

"Fuck me," I mumbled to myself, in a moment of existential quandary.

Those were the words *I said.*

Except it was *Wynonna's voice* that said them.

Somewhere in the human blob, I felt a body stiffen. As if they, too, recognized that something was cosmically wrong.

I opened my eyes. Glanced down at my hands, palms flat against the cold tile.

Except they *weren't* my hands. They were smaller. Thinner. Smoother.

Each fingernail was painted electric blue.

That's when I noticed the tufts of electric-blue hair framing my periphery.

It was then—and only then—that I realized someone in the human blob was looking directly at me. I rotated my head slowly.

The face staring back at me . . .

. . . was *me.*

It was Ezra Slevin. A mirror image of my face. A doppelgänger. His protruding head was sandwiched between Imogen's long sweatered torso and, rather unfortunately, Holden's ass.

He looked as terrified as I felt.

And then it happened again—*flash!*

Suddenly, I was in a different place, looking a different direction. Also, Holden's ass was in my face—which *should* have been an alarming situation in its own regard. However, I was too preoccupied looking at Wynonna, and she was looking at me. We both seemed to be sharing the same look, and the look said, "What the actual fuck?"

"Oh shit!" said Holden. "The eclipse!"

Wynonna and I snapped out of our Twilight Zone situation—if only for a moment. Even Imogen made an *Eeep!* sound. We all twisted, and squirmed, and pulled, and slowly unraveled from one another. Staggered upright and rushed to the open window. Everyone fumbled to remove their respective cardboard eclipse glasses from various pockets, struggling to assemble them to our faces.

By the time we succeeded, the black circle occupying the sky was already in the process of receding. A blast of white light punctured its side.

We had missed it.

Finally—whether from the disappointment, or the stress, or the Twilight Zone–level shit in between—my body decided this was as good a time as any to shut things down.

I blacked out.

TWO

VOICES DRIFTED ABOVE ME—so close, and yet, so far away—like they were standing over me in some parallel dimension.

Oh my god, oh my god, oh my god, said Imogen.

Don't worry, said Holden. *It's okay, it's okay. This happens all the time.*

What, is he narcoleptic or something? said Wynonna.

Not exactly. He's more of a hard-core insomniac who occasionally breaks from sleep deprivation.

And that's OKAY? said Imogen, incredulous.

I mean, there's no long-term damage from it. It's just a part of his disorder or whatever.

How long has it been since he last slept?

Um. Holden had to stop and think about that one. *Two or three days?*

Two or three DAYS?

Again, Holden seemed to pause and mull this over. *Three days,* he said definitively.

Oh my god.

But it's okay, Holden assured her.

How exactly is that OKAY?

I mean, it's normal.

That is not normal!

Are you saying we SHOULDN'T call nine-one-one? said Wynonna.

Oh, no, we definitely should. His body hit the floor like that Drowning Pool song.

The voices faded into dreamless sleep. A swollen pool of blackness, like an abscess in time.

• •

"You haven't slept in *how* long?" said the paramedic.

"Seventy-two hours," I said. And then, as an afterthought, added, ". . . ish."

I was rounding to the nearest day, of course. I had neither the time nor the patience to provide exact measurements for my insanity.

Even though I felt fine—all things considered—the paramedics had me lie down on a stretcher so they could determine how "fine" I was for themselves. Judging from the looks they exchanged, I was failing with prowess.

Imogen, meanwhile, was standing over me—as close as the paramedics would allow, at least—shaking her head like I was the saddest thing she had ever seen. Like a blind orphan with cancer, petting my puppy and dearest friend, Scruffles, who I didn't realize was dead.

Normally, I would've appreciated the attention—even if it *was* just pity attention. However, I was a little preoccupied with the event that I was currently referring to in my head as What the Fuck Just Happened?

"Are you seeing a doctor?" said the paramedic.

"I have a psychiatrist," I said.

"Are you on any medication?"

"Belsomra."

"How's that working?"

I glanced from him, to the other paramedic checking my vitals, to the police officer interrogating Holden and Wynonna, and back to him.

"Less than desirable?" I offered.

"But your doctor still has you taking it?"

"I mean, it's not like it's *worse* than the others."

"What else have you taken?"

"Ambien, Lunesta, Rozerem, Sonata . . ." I said, feeling a bit like a wizard rattling off magical words. "Valium—"

"Valium?" said the paramedic.

"I've had chronic insomnia since I was nine," I said. "We've made the rounds."

"And you say this is *normal* for you? Passing out like this?"

"It isn't *abnormal*."

"Was there anything about this particular instance that *was* abnormal?"

Wynonna seemed to overhear this question. She looked at me, and I looked at her. Our gazes interlocked for a staggering nanosecond before we hastily looked away, embarrassed.

"Nope," I said. "Completely normal."

• •

"It's true what they say," said Holden. "No good deed goes unpunished."

"What part of breaking and entering is a 'good deed'?" said Principal Allegra Durden. (Yes, like the antihistamine.) Aka Holden's mom. She emphasized "good deed," air-quoting with her index and middle fingers.

Like Holden, Principal Durden was small-framed—barely an inch taller than her son. Her size, however, had no effect on the sheer intimidation her presence inspired. Though she and Holden shared the same features—black hair, dark eyes, intense mouth—she wore them with a certain edge. A deadliness of sorts. Perhaps it came with the territory of employment in the public school system. It probably didn't help that she was called in on a school holiday to assume the role of Dispenser of Disciplinary Action.

Frankly, we were lucky we didn't get arrested. We were only so fortunate because Holden's mom was the principal, and her fury eclipsed that of all our parents combined. The police seemed largely satisfied by her rage and handed us over without a fuss.

Our fate was relinquished to the Wrath of the Durden.

"Ezra and I didn't break and enter!" Holden protested. "I mean, we didn't *break* anything, at least."

"Okay, I'll give you that," said Principal Durden. "You didn't break anything." She rotated her cannon-like gaze to Wynonna and Imogen sitting beside us. Together, the four of us sat in a straight line in front of her desk. Like targets in a shooting gallery. "At least you boys didn't *break the window of the girls' bathroom* to get in."

"It was an accident!" said Wynonna. "The window was already unlocked. I'm sooooooo sorry if I happen to have a *bigger ass* than Imogen. I didn't ask for this thing, you know."

"Oh, hush," said Imogen. "Your butt is fine."

"Nobody is here to talk about your butt, Miss Jones," said Principal Durden. "Having a big butt isn't a criminal offense. *Using* your big butt to break the window of the girls' bathroom, however, is. And unfortunately, Miss Klutz, you are an accomplice to Wynonna's butt."

Imogen's long, gangly form seemed to be imploding on itself in utter shame. Wynonna, meanwhile, was slouching back in her chair, arms folded, blatantly manspreading into Holden's leg room. In open defiance, Holden was attempting to manspread even farther—despite having the shortest legspan of the four of us.

"*You*, on the other hand," said Principal Durden, returning her attention to Holden, "*stole* my master key, made *two* copies, and gave one of them to your best friend for his *birthday*. And, of course, I had to be told this by the police. Am I missing anything?"

"Um, yeah," said Holden. "How about the part where we called nine-one-one and saved Ezra's life? We're basically heroes!"

Wynonna snorted. Principal Durden shook her head, probably wondering which part of her genetic code was responsible for Holden's grasp on reality. Surely this was Mr. Durden's fault.

"Right, Ezra?" said Holden. "Tell her!"

Oh boy. Okay. This was happening.

Imogen looked at me. Though I refused to make eye contact, I was well aware of her in my periphery. I *felt* her gaze. There was a soft but intense pressure to it—like Darth Vader slowly choking me with the Force.

Don't say anything stupid, Ezra. Be cool. Think cool thoughts.

"I've never known a greater trio of heroes," I said. "If it were up to me, I'd award each of them a Congressional Medal of Honor. Maybe a Nobel Peace Prize for them to share."

There was a fine line between "cool sarcasm" and "sounding like a complete idiot." I may have crossed that line.

Principal Durden dropped her head in her hands. Wynonna gave a sharp bark of laughter. Imogen imploded further. She looked like a dying daddy longlegs crumpling in on itself.

"See!" said Holden. "That's what I'm sayin'! What kind of

Orwellian world are we living in when the system punishes the heroes? If you punish us, Mom, then you're just another cog in the totalitarian machine."

Principal Durden pursed her lips. Leaned forward and interlocked her fingers. If Holden had just issued her a challenge, then she was accepting it.

"I was *going* to give the four of you detention for a month," she said. "*Now* I realize that isn't severe enough."

Holden, Imogen, Wynonna, and I straightened in our seats, each of us in varying states of panic.

"How is detention not severe enough?" said Wynonna.

"Because you don't have to *do* anything in detention," said Principal Durden. "And because you're all friends, and I would just be giving you a place to hang out. I've seen *The Breakfast Club*. I know how it works."

"What's a breakfast club?" said Holden.

Imogen looked appalled—by Holden's breakfast club comment, not the punishment situation.

"Um, we are *not* friends with *them*," said Wynonna. "I'd rather be friends with a dead opossum."

"Oh yeah?" said Holden. "I'd rather be friends with my own wiener!"

"Oh, I'm sure you already are."

"Oh snap! Good one, Wynonna. I am *totally* friends with my own wiener. We've shared the best of times, he and I."

Wynonna's face retched in response.

"Please, Holden, never talk about your wiener in my office again," said Principal Durden. "No one is impressed by it."

Wynonna chuckled. Holden's face pinched into a scowl.

Principal Durden took turns looking at each of us individually.

When her eyes rested on me, however, I noticed something weird—sympathy, maybe? Whatever it was, it passed like a glint of light on the highway. She blinked, leaned back in her chair, and it was gone. Miles away.

"There's a saying," said Principal Durden. "Hell is a state of mind. As there are varying degrees of guilt in this situation, I've decided on a hell that might not be so bad for some of you. And for others... well..." She glanced between Holden and Wynonna. "It's gonna suck."

She opened the thin middle drawer of her desk, reached inside, and pulled out a bundle of pamphlets—four, exactly—and laid them out on her desk for each of us.

The four of us leaned forward. Several pairs of eyes widened, for various reasons—Imogen out of excitement, Wynonna and Holden out of pure, unadulterated horror. The pamphlets were black-and-white, the cover art minimalist. A pair of silhouettes were standing back-to-back. Though they stood the exact same height, one was distinctly female, and the other, male. The top of the pamphlet read:

William Shakespeare's
Twelfth Night
A Piles Fork High School Production

Two thoughts occurred immediately:

1. Holden told Principal Durden about my crush on Imogen. Specifically, how it all started with our fourth-grade production of *Romeo and Juliet*. Really, this came as no surprise because Holden had the biggest mouth on the planet Earth.
2. She probably thought she was helping me.

However, fourth grade was a long time ago. Not to mention, the most traumatic event of my young, fragile life. And rather than nourish my talent as a budding actor, I had hidden it under a bushel, lit the bushel on fire, and scattered the ashes in the metaphorical Sea of Things I Will Not Do with My Life.

I had nothing against Shakespeare. At least, I thought the modern retellings were all right—*10 Things I Hate About You* (*The Taming of the Shrew*), or *My Own Private Idaho* (*Henry IV Part 1, Henry IV Part 2,* and *Henry V*), or *Romeo + Juliet* (*Romeo and Juliet* with Baz Luhrmann spilled all over it), et cetera, et cetera. What I *did* have a problem with was reading Shakespeare out loud (in front of Imogen). And performing Shakespeare (in front of Imogen). And being on a stage in costume (in front of Imogen). Really, Imogen was the root of the problem—through no fault of her own—and this smelled like all those things combined.

"What the hell is this?" said Holden.

"It's a play," said Principal Durden. "And as of now, the four of you are in it."

"No," said Wynonna, shaking her head. "No, no, no, no, no."

"I'll also be adding each of you to our eighth-period theater class."

"*Eighth* period?" said Holden, appalled. "That's a *thing*?"

"It's an extracurricular period. They meet off campus from two-oh-five to two fifty-five at the Amityvale Theater downtown."

"That's disgusting," said Holden. "I'm *disgusted*. Man, if Pink Floyd ever heard about this bureaucracy . . ."

In the midst of Holden's conniption, and as Wynonna dissolved in a vat of denial, I couldn't help but notice Imogen's eyes.

They were balloons inflating with delight.

"But . . . isn't that class full?" said Imogen. You could tell, she was exercising every bit of restraint *not* to get too excited.

The class *was* full. At least, it *had been* full. I knew this because it was the reason Imogen was rejected from the class for the third year in a row. And I knew *that* because Holden provided me with printed copies of Imogen's schedule for the third year in a row, along with a note about the one class that didn't make the cut.

I swear to god, I wasn't a stalker. Holden merely facilitated my fantasy of *becoming* one.

I also knew the real reason Imogen didn't make the cut. Why many interested students didn't make the cut. Everyone knew. It was kind of an open secret.

Principal Durden gave an uneasy chuckle. The sort of laugh that meant the opposite of funny.

"That may have been the case," she said, "but there's been a few changes and *several* openings."

"Eeep!" said Imogen. She raised her fists to her mouth in trembling balls of delight.

"And as of this moment, you four are enrolled."

"No!" said Wynonna. "I refuse!"

"*If* you refuse," said Principal Durden, "you will be officially banned from prom."

My stomach was a cinder block, plunging to the bottom of the Challenger Deep.

"WHAT?" said Wynonna.

"Nuh-uh," said Holden.

"Ooh, I hope I get Viola," Imogen whispered to herself.

"Yuh-huh," said Principal Durden. "I'll talk to security and make sure you never set foot in prom. *Unless* you attend each and every day of class, as well as the final production—which is *conveniently* the day before prom."

Holden's face was solemn. He sent a subtle, contemplative glance my way. I responded with the obvious look of someone whose stomach was resting on the bottom of the ocean. He returned his gaze to his mom.

"Fine," said Holden. "Ezra and I will do the Shakespeare thingy. Right, Ezra?"

Principal Durden looked at me expectantly. Meanwhile, I had temporarily forgotten how to breathe.

"*Right*, Ezra?" Holden repeated. There was nothing subtle about his look now. He was glaring at me.

He was doing this *for* me.

I pinched my mouth shut and nodded my head—because if I *opened* my mouth, I might start hyperventilating.

"Screw this," said Wynonna. She pushed her chair back, stood up indignantly, and started for the door. "Screw this Shakespeare bullshit. Screw prom. I'm out."

She opened the door, walked out, and slammed it behind her with a mighty *THWACK!*

The silence that filled Principal Durden's office was tense and slightly asphyxiating.

"Let . . . me talk to her," said Imogen. She stood up. "Oh, and I'm in. I mean . . . I accept the terms of my punishment. Um. Do I talk to you if I'm interested in the role of Viola?"

"You definitely don't talk to me," said Principal Durden. "I have no say in the matter whatsoever."

"Right. Yes. Of course."

Imogen hesitated awkwardly in the office for a moment, then rushed out the door after her friend. Miraculously, she managed to shut the door quietly behind her. There was a soft click, then a rapid clap of footsteps down the hall.

"So," said Principal Durden, "I suppose you two will be wanting a ride home?"

"Yes, please," I said.

"No thanks," said Holden. "Heroes don't accept favors from the totalitarian machine."

"Not even for Taco Bell?" she asked. "I'll buy, but it's out of your college fund."

Holden paused, mulling this over with grave consideration. Finally, he nodded. "Heroes can make an exception for Taco Bell."

• •

Piles Fork High School was famous for one thing: its theater program. It specialized in musical theater and was, in a word, phenomenal. The best in the state. Arguably, the nation. This was multi–award-winning shit we're talking about: the Dazzles, the Freddies, the Halos, the Teenies. It sounds like I'm using made-up words, but I swear to god, these were all real things! I knew this because Principal Durden gushed about them like they were her own greatest achievements. Every year, Principal Durden poured more and more of the school budget into the theater program. At this point, the theater budget outweighed all the core subjects combined.

If that sounds insane, that's because it is.

Theater was taught exclusively by Ms. Cicily Chaucer—rumored to be the great (times seventeen) granddaughter of Geoffrey Chaucer. Which I was pretty sure was bullshit. But she *had* been a cast member of the Broadway revival of the musical *Cats*. She claimed to have left because of "creative differences." No one really questioned her on that.

In fact, no one really questioned her on *anything*. When she claimed she needed a more "theatrical environment" for her classroom, Principal Durden allowed her to scout out off-campus locations. Ms. Chaucer finally settled on the Amityvale Theater, located in the very center of downtown. The Amityvale Theater was a historic venue for performing arts, though today was used more commonly for music, modern entertainment, community events, etc.

The school district rented out a time slot in a year-to-year contract.

As for Ms. Chaucer's handpicked students, they were the most snobbish, despotic group of theater kids ever to roam the stage. Imagine Sharpay and Ryan Evans from *High School Musical*, and multiply them by nine, and *that's* what we were dealing with here. They walked together, ate together, and, more often than not, made whoopee together. They were cliquish, bordering on cultish. Whenever graduation neared, they usually had their collective sights set on select individuals—a new generation of Sharpays and Ryans—whom they deemed worthy to enter their fold. All they needed was a proper blood initiation, maybe a pagan animal sacrifice for good measure, and they were no longer human. They were a superior species. They were the newest members of Ms. Chaucer's theater class.

At least, that was the case until a couple weeks ago.

That's when the drug bust happened.

You see, there was a *reason* why Piles Fork's theater program was the best. Why they were able to memorize lines like machines and kill it like the fucking Terminator. Why they sang and danced and performed like genetically advanced superhumans.

They were all on prescription drugs—namely medication for ADHD and narcolepsy.

In fact, Ms. Chaucer was *selling* them prescription drugs—Adderall, Ritalin, Moda, you name it. If *that* wasn't batshit crazy enough, there were even a couple Ryans sharing an eight ball of cocaine! Although Ms. Chaucer swore to god, she didn't sell them *that.*

Whatever the case, Ms. Chaucer was arrested. As for all the Sharpays and Ryans, they were pulled out of school and sent promptly to rehab.

It was all very low-key. No one actually *saw* it happen. However, when eighteen superhuman theater monsters suddenly fail to show up to school the next day—to say nothing of their supreme musical overlord—teenagers talk. And when necessary, they can even read the news.

Imogen didn't know about it because she was a decent human being who rejected the idea of gossip. I, on the other hand, knew *everything* because Holden told me. And he knew about it because he liked to sneak onto his mom's laptop and read her private school emails.

It later came out that Cicily Chaucer was kicked out of the *Cats* revival for attempting to sell cocaine to her costars. So, *that* didn't bode well for the impending coke charge. As for that generous budget Principal Durden had been pouring into the theater department, Ms. Chaucer had apparently been embezzling funds for her prescription (and maybe not-so-prescription) drug-dealing campaign.

This put a heavy and uncomfortable spotlight on Principal Durden. If she was ever going to live this down, she needed to fix this. And the first thing that needed fixing was a nationally renowned theater class that was currently—and very literally—nonexistent. It didn't need to be extraordinary. It only needed to *exist.* And hopefully be functioning to some degree. (And not as an upper-middle-class high school drug ring.)

Understandably, none of the existing faculty wanted to touch that position with a ten-foot stage prop.

There was, however, a young, aspiring staff member who had just barely earned his Bachelor of Arts at Southern Illinois University—a *theater* degree, if you can believe it—after nearly a decade of going to school part-time. Also, before his job at Piles Fork, he had a history of working in rehabs and said he could spot a teenager using from twenty yards away. He claimed he could tell what they were on just by looking at their pupils.

Principal Durden hired him on the spot as an adjunct teacher.

When she asked him his thoughts on filling the class two-thirds of the way through the school year, he said, "Do kids get detention around here?"

They did, obviously.

"Send those kids my way," he said.

• •

When the Durdens arrived at my cul-de-sac, everyone had already finished their chalupas, gorditas, and Doritos Locos Tacos. I offered to dispose of the garbage and ended up with our original to-go bag stuffed with every article of trash in the car—minus Holden's half-filled Baja Blast. He was still sipping on it when he rolled down his passenger-side window and offered his fist. I bumped it.

"Later, hero," I said.

"Later, gator," said Holden.

"Later, *gator*?" said Principal Durden. "Do kids still say that?"

"How dare you question what my generation says! I *am* my generation. And it rhymes. It's timeless!"

Holden rolled up his window, flashed a peace sign, and the Durdens rounded the cul-de-sac and sped off.

I turned around. It was now—and only now—that I chose to address the issue of the car in the driveway.

It was a modified, skeezy-looking Honda Civic with obnoxious yellow paint, a custom black hood with a gaudy scoop, a spoiler that belonged on a spaceship, and a NASCAR-level sticker treatment. It was covered in brands and decals that said things like ILLEST and LOWLIFE.

I recognized the car from the school parking lot. (What can I say? It stood out.) I *also* had no idea who it belonged to. Unfortunately, this was normal.

I took a deep breath and started for the front door. I was halfway up the driveway when I heard the screaming.

"Fuck you!"

"No, fuck you!"

"FUCK YOU."

The front door burst open and out came Jayden Hoxsie.

Jayden was a breed of male teenager in the *Douchimus maximus* family. He had spiky black hair, only worked his upper body at the gym, and typically wore his polo shirts so tight that his nipples were visible nubs in the fabric. He was also in the same grade as me—a junior—which made it all the more painfully awkward that he was in my house.

There was only one reason he would be there.

"Get the fuck out of my house!" said Willow.

Willow was my little sister. She was fourteen—a freshman. She was basically the human embodiment of Hot Topic—drawing a fine line between punk and nerdcore. She was 40 percent hair—long black emo hair, layered and styled for maximum volume—and wearing a Spider-Gwen tank top and black skinny jeans.

"Gladly," said Jayden. "Stuck-up whore."

Jayden took one look at me, then smirked like I was in on the joke. "'Sup, Ezra. Tell your sister to stop being such a bitch."

He clapped me on the shoulder as he walked past. I just stood there, dumbfounded.

"Fuck you!" said Willow. "Fuck you and your shitty car!"

"Ouch," said Jayden. "And here I thought you liked cars."

For whatever reason, that *really* set Willow off. As Jayden climbed into the driver's seat, she screamed and stormed out into the driveway, and started hitting and kicking the nose of the car. Jayden turned the key in the ignition with one hand and flipped her off with the other. He held it the entire time that he was backing out of the driveway. When he hit the gas, the modified exhaust let out a cracking roar that sliced across the neighborhood for blocks. A pair of burned rubber tracks followed him out of the cul-de-sac.

By the time he was gone, I heard our front door slam. I turned around.

Willow was gone, too.

"Willow?" I said.

I followed her inside.

Our house—like every house in the cul-de-sac—was a four-bedroom, three-bath, two-story exercise in upper-middle-class monotony. They only varied in their daring shades of gray. On the inside, our house was neat and clean and even a little "chic"—but in a boring, IKEA sort of way. Like my mom was replicating pages out of a catalog. It looked less like a home, and more like a display. If it had *any* sort of personality, it was an eerie *Stepford Wives* sorta vibe.

I crossed the cream-gray living room to the suede-gray stairs, and followed those up to a villa-gray hallway. Stopped in front of Willow's door, marked by a bright *Adventure Time* poster featuring nearly every character crammed together in a colorful tessellation. It was an act of open rebellion against the gray, and Willow knew it. Pure mutiny.

"Destroya" by My Chemical Romancc was blasting from her speakers, with the volume set to I Don't Want to Hear Anything Outside My Door.

I knocked anyway.

"Go away, Ezra!" she said.

I opened the door and walked inside.

Willow's bedroom was covered in pop-punk bands, Ryan Reynolds, and a wealth of nerd culture—anime, video game characters, obscure comic book superheroes who had yet to be milked by the Hollywood machine. Willow loved a lot of things, and she wore that love on her sleeves. She was rather shameless about it.

Willow herself was sprawled facedown on her bed, willing herself to disintegrate.

"Hey," I said.

She leaned up on her forearms and looked at me. Her eyes were red, swollen, and seeping with sadness.

"Whoa, are you . . . okay?" I said.

The word "okay" sounded feeble and useless coming out of my mouth. She clearly wasn't. Willow responded to it like she did to Jayden's "I thought you liked cars" comment. She bolted up from her bed, marched straight at me, and started shoving me out of her room.

"Get out," she said.

"What happened?" I said. "Why was Jayden here? Did he do something to you?"

"Why don't you ask Jayden, since you two are such great friends, and I'm such a bitch."

"What? No. Willow, we're not friends. I've never even talked to the guy."

"He knew your name."

"I mean . . . sometimes I let him cheat off my science homework."

Willow went back to shoving me out of her room. "Get out, get out, get out!"

"Hey, it's not like I *want* him to cheat off my homework. It's just easier than . . ."

I hesitated.

"Easier than *what*?" said Willow.

I had just stepped outside the confines of her room, but she stopped. Folded her arms. Waited patiently for a response.

My mouth gaped.

It's not that I had nothing to say. It's just that in every possible response I could think of—every possible *scenario*—I hated myself.

Willow shook her head, disappointed. "God, Ezra. You're such a pussy."

She took a step back and slammed the door in my face. My nose was half an inch from the poster on the door and the anthropomorphic purple blob character known in the *Adventure Time* canon as Lumpy Space Princess.

"It's easier than getting my ass kicked," I mumbled.

• •

I had a secret, and no one knew about it. Not even Holden.

You see, I lied when I said that my greatest strength was math. Math was merely my *least embarrassing* strength.

Yeah. I wasn't lying about accepting my inevitable life of celibacy.

If you were to go on YouTube, you would discover a channel under the username EzwardSlevinhands. This channel had upward of ten thousand subscribers and consisted entirely of Johnny Depp character impersonations (in full makeup, of course—the makeup was important). They were all performed by a single enigmatic teenage boy, and I'm obviously biased, but he was kind of good.

He was also me.

So here was the thing about Johnny Depp: as celebrity heroes go, he had kind of become a huge fucking disappointment. I had spent the greater part of my life idolizing the guy, and then his domestic abuse case hit the news. At some point, I just had to separate Johnny Depp the person from all the characters and roles I had grown to know and love.

I could do that.

His characters were amazing. They were also kind of terrible. But mostly, they were batshit gonzo insane. They ranked from pure, eccentric genius (Ed Wood, Sweeney Todd, Jack Sparrow) to bad, oh so bad (Tonto, Mortdecai, Jack Sparrow). Yes, the Pirates of the Caribbean film franchise had seen Johnny Depp all across the board. It was a blurry line that separated Johnny Depp's greatness from his not-so-greatness. But if I had to draw it somewhere, it would be between *The Curse of the Black Pearl* and *Dead Man's Chest.*

Nevertheless, I embraced *all* of Johnny Depp's roles, regardless of their critical reception: the Mad Hatter, Willy Wonka, Barnabas Collins, Sam from *Benny and Joon*, Raoul Duke from *Fear and Loathing in Las Vegas* (whom I bought the perfect bucket hat for, and then took it a step further and purchased a bald cap online, blending it perfectly into my scalp. It was my greatest makeup feat to date). Each video was essentially a highlight reel of my favorite quotes, edited into a phantasmagoria of Johnny-Depptitude.

SAM: "How sick is she? Because, you know, it seems to me that, I mean, except for being a little mentally ill, she's pretty normal."

RAOUL DUKE: "Let's get down to brass tacks. How much for the ape?"

WILLY WONKA: "Everything in this room is eatable. Even *I'm* eatable, but that is called cannibalism, my dear children, and is in fact frowned upon in most societies."

JACK SPARROW: "Me, I'm dishonest, and a dishonest man you can always trust to be dishonest. Honestly, it's the honest ones you want to watch out for."

SAM: (Stabs a pair of dinner rolls with a pair of forks.)
(Makes them dance.)
(Like, performs an entire fucking dance number.)

If this seemed out of character for me, that's because it was. I liked to draw attention to myself as much as I liked to draw dicks on my own face. This hobby started quite by accident. By the time I realized what I had gotten myself into—what I had *become* (a minor-league YouTube celebrity)—it had taken on a life of its own.

Maybe some lengthy, convenient exposition is necessary.

It all started on Halloween, my freshman year. I was Edward Scissorhands, and Willow (twelve years old at the time) was Lydia Deetz from *Beetlejuice*. With Mom and Dad's help, our costumes and makeup were on fucking point. I had ultra-realistic fake scars on my face, my longish hair was moussed up into a gravity-defying mess, and I had, like, honest-to-Gozer scissors for hands! (I'd tell you how expensive my costume was, but then I would have to kill you with my bare scissorhands, because it was a shameful, ridiculous amount.) We got the costumes for Mom and Dad's Halloween work party. The two of them were dressed as Morticia and Gomez Addams (*The Addams Family*), respectively, and they seemed as madly, *macabrely* in love with each other as their TV personas.

The Slevin family stole the show at the Memorial Hospital of Carbondale.

When we came home, Willow and I couldn't get out of costume. The costumes were just *too good* to be shed like snake skin, discarded ritualistically, never to be seen again.

So we went trick-or-treating.

For the record, Willow had vowed *not* to go trick-or-treating that year—or ever again, for that matter. And I hadn't gone since I was eleven, out of some skewed sense of maturity and/or masculine responsibility. It wasn't unwarranted. The last time I went, I was the victim of an insidious form of prejudice known as You're a Bit Old to Be Trick-or-Treating, Aren't You? It wasn't always spoken, but it was *always* conveyed. You could see the disappointment in the eyes of some old dude, expecting toddlers dressed as cupcakes, or princesses, or the Stay Puft Marshmallow Man, and instead getting this lanky impostor dressed as the purple ninja turtle. To be fair, I was a smidge tall for my age—at least a solid foot taller than my trick-or-treating companions, Holden (dressed as the red turtle, Raphael) and Willow (April O'Neil). Everyone thought *they* were fucking adorable. I mean, they *were*—but still!

The injustice of it was infuriating and humiliating and dehumanizing.

But the Edward Scissorhands year was different. That year, my costume filled me with power. Willow and I were high on the spirit of Halloween, and we talked each other into it.

It was amazing.

Even though we were starting late, catching the tail end of acceptable trick-or-treating hours, the people loved us. All of them. Every. Single. Door. Not only did I *not* get the stink eye—not once—but they praised me! Hailed me as some sort of All Hallows' Eve hero.

The costume didn't just make me *feel* powerful. The costume, itself, *was* power.

As we walked home, bags heavy with candy, my mind was reeling. Churning over the events of the evening. Processing what had just happened.

People thought I was cool.

People *liked* me.

When was the last time I was *liked*? I couldn't even remember. Maybe I was *never* liked. Not like this.

I had an idea.

"Do you want to make a video?" I asked Willow.

"A video?" she said. "What kind of video?"

I could tell by the way she asked, she was already in.

The idea was this: Edward Scissorhands Gives Lydia Deetz a Haircut. (That was *literally* the title of the video when I posted it to YouTube.) Here's how it went:

Lydia sits in a chair in the kitchen. Edward, meanwhile, fumbles to put a disposable hair-cutting cape (one of Mom's) around her neck with his scissorhands. By the time he finishes, the cape is mostly in shreds, but nevertheless, successfully wrapped around Lydia's neck.

Cut to Edward standing over the Gothic architecture that is Lydia's hair.

Edward proceeds to hack away like a poetic maniac. All we see is Edward—close up—and chunks of black hair spewing from the source like volcanic ash. (Mom sacrificed her Morticia wig for the cause.)

Edward finishes.

Cut to Edward standing over Lydia. She is wearing Willow's normal hairstyle, which is big and black and emo. Her hair is ironically twice the size it had previously been.

"I love it," says Lydia, flatly.

Edward and Lydia immediately start headbanging to the chorus of "I'm Not Okay (I Promise)" by My Chemical Romance, and the video ends.

I posted the video to YouTube but never told Willow about it. I don't know why. Maybe I was afraid she would make me take it down. Maybe I was being selfish. Like, I wanted this one special thing all to myself.

Either way, the video exploded. A thousand views in its first week. Ten thousand views its first month. Today, "Edward Scissorhands Gives Lydia Deetz a Haircut" had over a hundred thousand views.

There was a fire inside me, and I hadn't realized it until that moment. I had to make more videos. ESGLDaH was a spur-of-the-moment experiment, but I quickly fine-tuned a formula, consisting of things that I liked:

1. Johnny Depp characters.
2. Extravagant costumes.
3. Catchy lines.
4. Acting.

You'd think, at this point, I would have milked Johnny Depp for all he was worth. But that wasn't quite true.

Not just yet.

Johnny Depp was famous for collaborating with Tim Burton, who facilitated his need for weird roles. They were a match made in Weirdo Heaven. But my all-time favorite Burton/Depp collaboration—my favorite Johnny Depp role, period—was the criminally underrated *Ed Wood*.

God, I loved *Ed Wood*.

Ed Wood (1994) was the (mostly) absolutely true story of the eponymous cult filmmaker of the 1950s, often referred to as the "worst director of all time." Filmed in glorious black-and-white, it told the story of Ed Wood as he attempted to make several really bad films, leading up to his distasterpiece, the so-bad-it's-good *Plan 9 from Outer Space*. It was a tale of friendship (namely his friendship with iconic *Dracula* actor Bela Lugosi). It also explored Ed Wood's fondness for wearing women's clothing. He was straight as far as the history books were aware, but man oh man, the guy liked himself a nice angora sweater. Tim Burton was famous for humanizing marginalized characters, and *Ed Wood*—in all its quirk, kink, sincerity, and odd charm—was his magnum opus. On its surface, the film was about delusion and self-denial, but at its core—its beating, human heart—it was an ode to personal artistry in cinema, to being true to oneself, to being happy.

Despite its being my favorite Johnny Depp role, I had yet to deliver the inevitable Ed Wood video. Because if I was going to do Ed Wood, I *had* to do it dressed as a woman. I had to. It was not up for debate. This was a matter of necessity. And even though my YouTube channel was a secret, it was an *open* secret, with over ten thousand subscribers in on it. The pressure was real.

I think the fact that I *wanted* to do it so bad sort of scared me. It brought up years and years and years of me feeling like I was packaged improperly. Not "female trapped in a male body," per se. That was vastly oversimplifying the issue. Not even gender-fluid. (Trust me, I'd done my research.) That seemed to encapsulate something graceful—a sort of elegant transitioning between states—which sounded even further off from whatever *I* was. I was less a "fluid" and more a deformed solid. Like a half-eaten chocolate bar that had melted in the car and hardened into something vaguely horrific and probably inedible.

Honestly, all my research had probably only increased the confusion. There were just so many *words*, and *labels*, and *ways* that you could identify, the sheer volume was overwhelming. I was lost in it.

All I knew was that I felt . . . off. Misaligned. Sure, I didn't feel masculine. But I didn't feel like a fucking *human being* either! I was just this . . . thing. This thing that I fucking hated.

That was the one thing I could identify with, really.

The self-loathing.

• •

As a general rule, I never "went to bed." In fact, I avoided my bedroom entirely. It added a sense of claustrophobia to my need for sleep.

My brain just didn't work like that.

Instead, I would take my meds and then read web comics on the living room sofa, or watch movies, or seek out new (or old) music, or participate in some similar nonactivity. Or, if I was particularly wired, I would *deliberately* solve math puzzles. For fun. (I'm telling you, I have a problem.) If I was lucky, I fell asleep—at least for a little bit. It was like Russian roulette, except I was *hoping* for the bullet that made everything go away.

On bad nights—the nights where I experienced a flashback reel of every terrible thing that had ever happened to me, every stupid thing I had ever said or done, every regret that haunted me like a vengeful ghost—on those nights, I would listen to my favorite song, from my favorite album, from my favorite artist, on repeat.

That artist was Sufjan Stevens, and that album was *Illinois*, and that song was "Chicago"—also known as "Go! CHICAGO! Go! Yeah!"

It was kind of a masterpiece. Also, an antidepressant. Also, a transcendental experience.

The trick was to enter a sort of trancelike state. Basically, I would lie flat on my back in a pitch-black room with noise-canceling headphones. I would then will myself to disintegrate. To just... dissolve. I would float up and up and up, through the ceiling, through the roof, through the stratosphere, right into outer space. And I would no longer be myself. I would be part of something greater. I would be the universe, and the universe would accept me, because the universe and I were one. Our atoms were interwoven.

The goal was not to fall asleep. The goal was to stop hating myself.

It worked, mostly.

Tonight, however, was *not* one of those nights. Heck, tonight didn't even make the Billboard Hot 100.

Currently, I was watching *Inception*. I was kind of a Christopher Nolan junkie. (His movies were like puzzles, and like I said, I *loved* puzzles.) *Inception* was my favorite. The irony was not lost on me—an insomniac obsessed with a movie about dreams. There was just something soothing about taking something so vast and abstract and unknowable—dreams—and making them structured and rule-bound. Formatting the mechanics of dreams into a heist movie was a stroke of genius.

I was two hours in—halfway into the climax—when I heard it. The soft clicks of the lock. The gentle squeal of the front door opening and closing. Whoever it was, they were being awful quiet.

I glanced at the time on my phone. It was a quarter to midnight.

Leaning over the armrest, I caught my dad creeping quietly toward the stairs. He froze when our gazes connected. Blinked. Regained his composure in an instant.

"Hey, Ez," he said. "Whatcha watching?"

I'll just say it: My dad was cool. And not the sort of cool where it's obvious they are *trying* to be cool. He just *was*. Purely effortless.

It was all in his confidence. The way he carried himself, the way he spoke—casual but brimming with intelligence. And when he took the time to talk to you—which he did with a lot of people—he seemed to genuinely care, and he made you feel special because of it. In short, he was the ultimate people person.

He was the exact opposite of me.

"Inception," I said.

"Ah. The dream-within-a-dream one, right?"

"Within a dream within a dream within a dream," I said.

Dad chuckled. "Have you figured out if the top falls over or not?"

"I don't think you're *supposed* to figure that out. It's an open ending."

Dad nodded discerningly, like that totally made sense.

"I mean, I have a theory," I said.

"Of course you do!" Dad steered into the living room and sat on the adjacent armchair. "Let's hear it."

Dad was never home. But when he was, he at least tried to make up the difference.

"So, DiCaprio's wife kills herself because she thinks they're still in a dream and she's trying to escape, right?" I said.

"Right."

"But what if she's not dead?"

"Huh?"

"What if she was right all along? What if they *were* in a dream, and she escaped, but DiCaprio never does? The entire movie is just a layer of dream that DiCaprio never escaped. That's why the top keeps spinning."

Dad's eyes widened. He raised his fists to his head and exploded his hands open.

"Right?" I said. "Of course, Nolan covered his bases. There's a theory that his wedding ring is his *real* totem. The theory is that he wears the ring in the dreamworld and not in real life. And allegedly, according to Reddit, he's *not* wearing the ring at the end. Although I've watched the ending a dozen times, and it's damn near impossible to see."

"Huh."

"The moral of this story is that Christopher Nolan wants to fuck with our heads."

"Clearly," said Dad. He stood up and ruffled my hair—like he always had since I was a little kid. I can see why some boys might not like their dad ruffling their hair, but I liked it. In a disconnected world, it made me feel connected—if only for a moment. "I'm glad we had this talk. Is . . . uh . . . is your mom home?"

This was when things inevitably became awkward.

I hesitated. Then shook my head.

"Oh. Okay. Well, make sure you don't say the f-word around her, okay? Can't have her thinking I'm a bad dad, am I right?"

I nodded, but my reaction was somber. Sad, even.

I wanted to talk to him about Willow. I wanted to talk to him about a *lot* of things. But when all the things stacked up, I felt like a clogged drain.

I just choked.

Said nothing.

"Night, Ez," he said, and started down the hall to his empty bedroom.

The saddest thing was that you could *see* his relief.

"Night, Dad," I said.

It was all I *could* say.

• •

My parents were their work. Dad was a surgeon, and Mom was an internist (doctor of internal medicine). They often worked sixty-plus hours a week. Sometimes more. They both worked at the same hospital, Memorial Hospital of Carbondale—that's actually how they met—so you'd think they had a shot at a healthy marriage. However, Willow and I—through our own detective work—learned that they were cheating on each other.

This was back when Willow and I were close. When we still talked to each other.

It all started when Willow noticed a text on Dad's phone. It was from someone named Celia. It said:

I can't stop thinking about last night

Willow snapped a pic of it on her own phone and went directly to me. Barged into my bedroom and shoved it in my face. "Tell me this isn't what I think it is."

I took her phone and studied the picture. As the image sank in, I felt something die inside me—a slow death, full of pain and uncertainty.

"This is Dad's phone?"

Willow bit her lip. She nodded.

I spent another small forever studying it.

"It could be anything," I said.

"What else could it be?"

"Something . . . that happened at work," I said. "They work nights enough. Celia is another surgeon or a nurse—"

"I don't doubt that."

"—and something *happened*," I said, ignoring her. "Maybe something bad happened, a surgery went wrong or something, and she can't stop thinking about it."

"Or the thing that happened is Dad boned her," said Willow.

I took a deep breath. Exhaled. "Yeah. Or that."

For the next several days, Willow and I commenced an intensive stealth operation. We were determined to get to the bottom of this. Really, I think we hoped for proof that this adulterous scandal was just a product of our young, wild imaginations.

What we discovered instead were two boxes of condoms. One in the drawer between our parents' underwear drawers—unopened and close to expiring—and the other in Dad's gym duffel bag. Accompanying it was a nearly empty bottle of Neosize XL and a brand-new bottle of Sir Maximus.

As if that wasn't proof enough, one day while Dad was in the shower, we finally got ahold of his phone.

You couldn't unread the things that we read.

"Oh my god," said Willow. "How can someone as boring as Dad text like he's a character in an HBO show?"

That was actually a vast understatement, neighboring on praise. It indicated a hint of prime-time television class, which Dad did not have in these texts. He sounded more like a plumber in a cheap homemade porno.

Once we had eliminated any shadow of a doubt about Dad's faithfulness, we moved on to Mom's phone. We had to find out if she knew.

What we found instead were dick pics. Sooooo many dick pics. It was dicks as far as the eye could see. Most of them belonged to Derek—tattooed, shaved-and-trimmed, endowed-to-a-fault Derek—but these were occasionally interspersed with the dicks of Sean, or Milo, or Terrence.

Most of these only went as far as sexting. But occasionally they ended with a hotel address.

When Willow and I discovered our first video, we opted to put our detective work to rest.

We never confronted Mom and Dad about it.

We stopped talking about it.

And then we just stopped talking.

THREE

WHENEVER I WAS LUCKY enough to fall asleep, I never felt it happen. It just snuck up on me. I simply woke up—whether it was a half hour or eight hours later—and I would think to myself, *Well, that was lucky.*

I woke up.

My first thought was not, *Well, that was lucky.*

It was, *Where the hell am I?*

I was in a bedroom—which would have been weird enough on its own—but it wasn't even *my* bedroom. It wasn't even a bedroom I *recognized*. I was lying on my side, staring at a wall that was barely visible beneath everything plastered all over it. One half was covered in '80s band posters—the Clash, Talking Heads, Depeche Mode. The other half was a collage of blown-up photographs—photos of backwoods Illinois, of Carbondale, of Piles Fork High School.

I sat up in bed. Sheets of electric-blue hair cascaded down either side of my face.

Oh shit.

I reached up to touch my face. Neither my face nor my hands felt familiar.

I swallowed and glanced down.

I was wearing a loose-fitting Van Halen tank top. My gaze, however, shot straight down the valley of two soft mountains attached to my chest.

What the fuck, what the fuck, what the absolute fuck?

My head snapped upright. I rotated my gaze until I was looking at my reflection in a sliding-mirror-door closet.

I was Wynonna fucking Jones.

I didn't realize how far I was leaning over the edge of the bed until it was too late. There was a sharp chime beside me. I jumped and screamed—easily the girliest sound that ever came out of Wynonna's mouth—and lost my balance. My limbs flailed, but my legs were tangled in knotted-up sheets. I toppled over the edge of the bed, making a futile grab for the nightstand, which I *nearly* brought down with me. Instead, I merely knocked off the bedside table lamp. The lamp, however, had different plans. Gravity whipped the lamp cord taut, cleaning the surface of the nightstand in one fatal sweep. Bedside paraphernalia rained down like the biblical plagues of Egypt.

The good news was that I broke my fall with Wynonna's face. The bad news was that I was wearing it.

I heard it again—a sharp chime.

I opened my eyes.

There was a phone, like, three inches from my face—Wynonna's phone—and a text message from a number that the *phone* didn't recognize, but *I* did. It was *my* number.

I was still hanging halfway off the bed, legs knotted in sheets, like a mermaid on a clothesline hanging out to dry. My upper body, meanwhile, was spooled onto the floor like dog shit. I attempted to writhe my legs free, but mostly I just pulled the sheets down with me.

I sat upright, back wedged into the nook of the bed and the nightstand, and read the text:

Erza, pick up the ponhe, or I saewr to god, I'll kill you! I know yo'ure there!!

That was actually putting it generous because some of the letters were upside down. Some of the letters weren't even real letters! The longer I stared at it—tried to make sense of what I was looking at—the worse it became. The letters became fuzzy. Blurred out of focus.

I squeezed my eyes shut, holding the inevitable headache at bay. Opened them again.

Erza, pcik up the pnhoe, or I sewar to god, I'll klil you! I konw yr'uoe three!!

What the shit? Was Wynonna on drugs?

The screen went black. I swiped to open it.

It went directly to her lock screen.

Shitballs. How the cock was I supposed to know her—

Ding! Another text.

the cdoe is 1234.

Well, okay then. I typed the code and unlocked the phone. I discovered twenty-three missed calls and fourteen missed texts. Half of them appeared to be threats—although I didn't bother attempting to read them. Just *looking* at them was giving me a headache. The letters were scrambled, backward, upside down, imaginary.

The rest of the texts were the code.

I called her back. She answered before the first ring finished.

"WHAT THE HELL IS GOING ON, SLEVIN?" said my voice, but angrier than I had ever heard it. "WHY AM I YOU?"

I didn't even know where to begin processing the question. Just the thought of it made me dizzy.

"Uhhhhhhhh," I said, thought-provokingly.

"You're a witch, aren't you? This is some kind of *witchcraft*. ISN'T IT?"

"Wha—? No! Are you serious?"

"Don't play dumb with me, Slevin. You did this before. I know you did."

"What, back at the school?"

"No! I mean, yes, that, too. But I'm talking about back when we were kids."

Huh?

"My whole life, I thought I was crazy," said Wynonna/Ezra—Wynezra? "I saw a fucking *psychiatrist* because of that shit. You did it before, and now you're doing it again BECAUSE YOU'RE A WITCH!"

"What are you even *talking* about?"

"Don't you dare lie to— *Ohhhhhhh* my god."

I didn't know what was happening on the other line, but it sounded excruciating. Maybe even lethal. Mildly alarming, considering that she was me.

"Whoa, are you okay?" I said. "Am *I* okay?"

"What an excellent question!" said Wynezra. "One of us is *clearly* not okay because I'm currently rocking a GIANT. RAGING. BONER!"

Oh.

"Why?" said Wynonna. "Why do I have a boner? Is this some pervy Viagra thing?"

In a situation where I literally had *no clue* what was going on, it was kind of refreshing to be asked a question that I *did* know the answer to. I latched onto it for dear life, like Leo and Kate on that floating door amidst the wreckage of the *Titanic*. It had a disturbingly calming effect on me.

"It's called morning wood," I said, matter-of-factly. "And it's a normal male anatomical function."

"Oh my *godddddddd*," she whined. "I'm not sure what's worse, your gross morning wood, or the fact that you make me sound like a total dweeb."

"Where are you?"

"In a bathroom?" she said, like she wasn't sure. "I'm trying to figure out how to pee, but this thing won't go down!"

"Wait, what? Are you touching my—"

"Oh, don't flatter yourself, Slevin. I don't *want* to touch this thing, and I *won't* if I don't have to. But I have to pee so bad I'm gonna die. How do you make it go down?!"

"You're asking the great unanswered question of mankind," I said. "Be sure to tell us when you figure it out."

"What? Are you fucking kidding—"

I sighed. "Look, just . . . sit down."

"Sit . . . down?"

"Sit down and lean forward."

There was silence on the other end. Quiet shuffling.

"It's still aimed at my face," said Wynezra. "Now what?"

"Um. You kind of have to just wait."

"Wait?"

"And . . . *will* it down."

"*Will* it down?" said Wynezra.

"Like, willpower."

"What, with my mind? With my goddamn telekinesis?"

"Look, you just have to wait and concentrate, okay? That's all I can tell you."

"Oh god, I hate you. I hope my period comes early, you bastard."

"What?" I felt a sudden wave of alarm.

"You heard me!" Wynezra screamed. "I wish the blood curse upon you *and* your stolen va-jim-jam!"

"Can you stop screaming?" I hissed. "Is my sister still home?"

"You have a sister?"

"Yes!"

"Well, I don't think anyone else is here. In case you haven't noticed, we're late for school."

I pulled the phone away and glanced at the time display. She was right. School was starting in five minutes.

"I have to *peeeee-eeeeee-eeeeeeeeeee*!" Wynezra cried.

I sighed again. "Okay. I give you permission to touch it."

Wynezra stopped crying. "What?"

"You're gonna have to bend it down. *Muscle* it down."

"Are you kidding? This thing is pure bone! It'll break before it bends."

"I know it *seems* that way, but there's a little bit of wiggle room. You're not bending *it* so much as the axis."

"What does that even *mean*?"

"Just lean forward, push it down, and aim for the top of the bowl. You should be able to get everything inside."

"Oh boy, here we go."

Even over the phone, I could hear the stream of pee hitting the porcelain full force.

"Ahhhhhhh," said Wynezra, in a tone of low-key panic. And then it escalated. "AHHHHH."

And then, relief.

"Ohhhhhhh," said Wynezra. "Well, shit. *Now* it's down. What is that all about?"

"Anatomy," I said, like the punch line of a joke. "Am I right?"

I laughed uneasily. Wynonna did not reciprocate. The conversation plunged swiftly into a vacuum of silence. The impending anxiety attack I had so successfully been holding at bay was finally closing in, going straight for the jugular, choking me.

I took a deep breath.

"Aside from the *riveting* possibility that I'm a witch," I said, "any other ideas why this is happening to us?"

I didn't expect her to have an idea. Heck, I didn't even expect her to have a response! Perhaps *no one* could *ever* know why something like this was happening to us. It defied logic. It defied *science.* This was purely in the realm of speculative fiction—somewhere between sci-fi and magic.

"You really don't remember," she said, "do you?"

"Remember *what*?" I said, exasperated.

She paused. Seemed to mull it over. "Can you drive a stick?"

"What?"

"We should talk about this in person. My car's a stick. Can you drive it?"

"Uh . . ." I said.

It was kind of a funny story, actually. And I meant "funny" in the ironic, *unfunny* sense. My dad taught me to drive a stick—or *tried* to teach me, I should say—last summer. This was the result of the '63 Corvette Stingray he randomly decided to buy me for my sixteenth birthday. (Seriously, so random. I didn't even know what a Stingray *was* before he bought me one!) But alas, now I had one, and boy oh boy, how lucky was I? So now I *had* to learn how to drive a stick.

Little did Dad know, we were embarking on an impossible, absurdist quest in the vein of *Don Quixote*.

By August, our collective blood pressure was hypertensive at best. When it became obvious that I would learn to accept my own mortality and death before I learned to operate a manual transmission, he silently admitted defeat. Sold the Stingray and got me a Subaru instead.

I think, deep down, the Stingray was the car he always wanted—probably since *he* was sixteen years old—but he felt silly or vain buying and/or keeping it for himself. I think, by getting it for me, he thought he was fulfilling all my wildest dreams. And not sending me to an early grave in a cherry-red casket made by Chevrolet.

So, in answer to Wynonna's question: No. I could *not* drive a stick. It was a hard no. Harder than space diamond.

"Uh, well, I mean," I said, moronically. "It depends on your definition of 'drive.'"

"Oh god, never mind," said Wynezra. "Do *you* have a car?"

"I have a Subaru?" I said, like I wasn't sure if it was a car or not.

"In the driveway?"

"In the garage."

"Keys?"

"Uh, they're on my dresser upstairs. My bedroom is just past the door with the *Adventure Time* poster."

"Cool," she said. "Meet me outside." And then, as an afterthought, "Don't do anything weird with my body."

She hung up.

I pulled myself out of my bed/nightstand nook, kicked my legs out of the sheets, and staggered to my feet. The entire mechanics of my body felt off. For starters, the hips. They were very much . . . there. But the subtle differences in the way I moved were only a slight distraction from the fact that I wasn't wearing any pants.

Wynonna's *body* wasn't wearing any pants.

Just a pair of soft black panties that hardly felt like they were there. They hugged the bizarre curves of my body, emphasized the fact that my bulge had been hijacked, and were neatly tucked into my butt.

Now that I *knew* they were in my butt, it was hard for me to *not* notice it. In fact, it was horribly distracting. I considered the possibility of changing underwear—the type that left your butt crack alone—but that involved taking these ones off, and *that* sounded like a challenge for a different day. Instead, I scoured the bedroom for pants. Clothes were lying everywhere—cluttering the floor, draped over the bed frame, occupying every available flat surface. I searched for the least formfitting thing I could find, which was kind of a Where's Waldo? situation.

Just as my resolve was about to crumble, I stumbled upon a pair of baggy gray sweatpants. I pulled them on. I then slid barefoot into a pair of fat DC skater shoes. I returned to the closet door mirror and evaluated myself.

Oh god. My nipples.

They were like a pair of twin pistol barrels, locked and loaded and ready.

A bra. I needed a bra.

Once again, I faced the moral dilemma of *taking something off* in order to *put something on*.

I was way too virgin to handle this much responsibility. I slid the mirror door open and plundered the closet in search of an alternative.

The alternative presented itself to me almost immediately—a gigantic baby-blue puffer coat. Very reminiscent of what Adam Sandler wore in *Little Nicky*. Though it was stuffed in the very back of the closet, there was no hiding this puffy blue monstrosity. I pulled it on, zipped it up, and stepped in front of the mirror door.

I looked like an idiot. Or Wynonna did, I should say. But any trace of commando tits had been eliminated.

That was good enough for me.

I opened Wynonna's bedroom door and peered outside. The hallway was empty. No sound. I crept out, tiptoeing across the hardwood floor. The hallway walls were littered with picture frames.

As much as I wanted to get out of this unfamiliar house as soon as possible, my gaze drifted inevitably to the pictures. Most of them were old. I could tell because Wynonna looked under ten—even younger in some. In nearly every photo, her mom and dad were on either side of her, crouching to her level. And every time, Wynonna would reach her arms up to hang around their necks. This pose appeared in a variety of locations—the park, the swimming pool, Disney World.

Wynonna was an impeccable amalgamation of her parents.

Despite how old these photos were, Wynonna's face was unmistakable. Her strong jaw and cheekbones (her dad's), her regal nose (her mom's)—all of which Wynonna had now grown into. Most notable was the lopsided way her lips curled when she smiled. I was more used to seeing it as an antagonistic smirk, but still—it was 100 percent, trademark-brand Wynonna.

Her eyes, however, were different. Her eyes were full of something here. It was visible in every single picture. Something vivid and wondrous and infinite.

Something I had never seen in Wynonna's eyes before.

"And Sleeping Beauty arises," said an older, weathered female voice. "Off to the arctic tundra, I see."

I turned and discovered a woman in the hallway. She had the same prominent nose as Wynonna and her mom. But this woman was *not* her mom. She was too old—in her sixties, at least. That's not to say that she wasn't beautiful. She absolutely was. The woman held herself with a certain elegance, wearing a sweeping gray turtleneck poncho thingy (it looked much more sophisticated than it sounds), and her hair done in some sort of tousled pouf updo. All in all, very Meryl Streep.

I glanced down at myself and my less-than-elegant Adam Sandler cosplay. My mouth stammered until words came out. "I was . . . cold."

"Oh, I do hope you're not coming down with something," she said. She turned and started back out the hallway, into what appeared to be the kitchen. Her voice bellowed down the hall, "The last thing I need is to get sick before my presentation!"

Slowly, I followed her out into the kitchen. The place was small but classy—stainless steel countertops with matching barstools, dark—almost black—mahogany cabinets, and a wide, third-story window view, slanting outward, overlooking downtown Carbondale.

The woman grabbed her keys and thermos off the counter, took a sip, and started for the door.

"Do me a favor, Nona," said the woman. "If you are sick, please quarantine yourself. I have some NyQuil in my medicine cabinet. Knock yourself out—as literally as you please."

With that, she walked out the door. She even went so far as to lock it behind her.

Well, that was interesting. Wynonna's grandma, I assumed? If so, she was apparently one of those "classy grandmas"—the sort of grandma who used to be Grace Kelly or Audrey Hepburn.

I waited sixty seconds. Then exited behind her.

Wynonna's house was actually a condo called the Lakes. It was a fancy affair with designer wool carpeting, crystal wall sconces, and a matching chandelier in the lobby. And boy, what a lobby! I shuffled across the black marble floor—past the pillars and art installations and chic-but-uncomfortable-looking chairs—attempting not to gawk.

"Have a good day, miss," said the concierge.

I looked over my shoulder rather stupidly, then realized *I* was the "miss." I forced a smile, waved awkwardly, and shuffled even faster toward the glass front doors.

I waited on the curb for about five minutes before my Subaru screeched around the corner on the left. It came to a slow, dramatic halt in front of me—just enough time for the driver's-side window to roll down. I felt a little speechless as I watched my own face gape at me.

"What . . . the hell . . . are you wearing?" said Wynezra.

I glanced down at myself, lifted my arms uncertainly, and then flopped them at my sides.

"Your clothes?" I offered.

"I hid that coat in the back of my closet for a reason," said Wynezra. "You look like the Michelin Man mated with a Smurf."

"Why do you have it, then?"

"It was a Christmas present from my grandpa, dummy! When your grandpa gives you clothes for Christmas, you don't actually *wear* them. You hide them in your closet, and you lie through your teeth about what a great present it was. That's how it works. Get in the car."

I thought of offering to drive. Wynezra, however, was throttling the steering wheel in the ten-and-two position. She seemed fully ensconced in the driver's seat and all the powers it entailed, so I quietly climbed in the passenger seat and shut the door. Wynezra punched the gas, and we took off, with no spoken destination. That was okay. We were just here to talk. To figure things out.

It wasn't until now—seeing my own body from a third-person perspective, through Wynonna's eyes—that I realized how much bigger I was than her. Maybe only two or three inches taller, but my jaw was wide and angular, and my shoulders had a lanky broadness to them, and my limbs were long and ropy and powerful-looking—at least compared to the limbs I was currently operating.

Why didn't I feel that big when I was myself?

"Your grandpa?" I said. "Is this the grandpa who's married to your grandma? I mean . . . the woman you're living with?"

It occurred to me that I was making all sorts of assumptions. I didn't even know that that was *actually* her grandma.

Wynezra's eyes widened. "Oh god. You met Carol?"

"So she's *not* your grandma?"

"What? No, she . . . she is. Just . . . what did she say?"

"She thought I was . . . or you were . . . she thought *we* were sick. Or coming down with something."

Wynezra looked all sorts of confused. "What?"

"Because of the coat," I clarified. "I told her I was cold."

"Oh."

"So, she told us to go quarantine ourselves."

"She told us to *what*?"

"Yeah. She told us to lock ourselves in our room and . . . uh . . . 'knock ourselves out with NyQuil.' I think those were her exact words. So I guess we have a free pass from school today!"

I said this last part optimistically. Wynezra, however, did not share my enthusiasm. Her face—*my* face—was crumpled into a scowl. She slammed the steering wheel.

"God, who does she think she is?" said Wynezra. "Queen of the whole goddamn world, that's who. Ugh! I *hate* her."

"You *hate* your grandma?" I said.

In all honesty, I had never met anyone who hated their grandma. This was uncharted territory in my understanding of the universe.

"Dude, don't even," said Wynezra. "You don't even know."

"I mean, she didn't *seem* like she meant it in a mean way."

"You don't *know* her, Ezra. I *do*. Everything she says, everything she does . . . it's like a snide little insult. She pretends to be polite, but deep down, she's a condescending bitch who thinks she's better than everyone else—especially me. Or *you*, for that matter." Wynezra chuckled bitterly. "Get used to it, Wynonna Jones."

"So . . . where are your parents? Why not live with them?"

Wynezra grew silent. Every muscle in her face seemed to atrophy.

Oh shit? Were they . . .

Were they *what*? Divorced? Walked out?

Dead?

"Let's not talk about my parents," said Wynezra, calmly—calmer than I'd heard her all morning.

I nodded silently. We drove like that for a while—not saying a thing to each other.

"What do you remember about *Romeo and Juliet*?" she said finally.

"What? Like, in general?"

"No, not 'in general.' You were in the play, right? The one from fourth grade?"

I responded with a confused look. That just pissed her off.

"Why am I even asking you?" said Wynezra. "I *know* you were in it. You were the star of the fucking show! You and Imogen both. Just nod your head and show me that you *acknowledge* this was a thing that happened."

I nodded my head—slowly—like I was acknowledging my way into a trap.

"Okay," said Wynezra. "Good. Now tell me what you remember about the night of the performance."

It *was* a trap.

"Are you making fun of me?" I said.

"Can you just *not* be an insecure little bitch?" said Wynezra. "Just for *one moment*? Tell me, exactly, what do you remember?"

"I forgot all my lines!" I said, throwing my puffy blue arms in the air for emphasis. "I forgot *everything*, like a complete dipshit. There. Are you happy?"

Wynezra did not look happy. Her lips—*my* lips—were pursed skeptically.

"You *remember* forgetting your lines?" she said. "Like, you remember standing there, on the stage, not remembering them?"

That was a weirdly specific question. All things considered, however, it hardly ranked on the weird-o-meter.

"I mean, it was weird," I said. "Like, I *knew* my lines, but I felt disconnected from myself."

"Disconnected?" For once in her life, Wynonna seemed interested in what I had to say.

"Yeah! Like I was *seeing* myself forget my lines. Like an out-of-body experience. Like I was sitting in the . . ."

I stopped. Choked softly on my words.

Like I was sitting in the audience.

I turned. Looked at Wynezra. *Now* she looked happy. Or, at least, like I had validated her entire existence. She had contorted my face into a maniacal grin—eyes vast, lips coiled, all teeth exposed—like some sort of villain.

"Oh my god," I said. "What do *you* remember?"

"That was *me*!" said Wynezra. "You saw *me* forget all your lines."

"Are you saying we—"

"Swapped! Yes! That is *exactly* what I am saying!"

I stared at Wynezra, mouth ajar. She was glowing. Or possibly losing her mind. If there was a blurry gray area between happiness and insanity, that's where Wynonna was.

"I was *at* that show," said Wynezra. "I came to see Imogen, obviously. But next thing I knew, I was on the stage, and I was *you*, and Ms. Lopez was trying to shove a script in my face. Like, fuck that shit. I was outta there."

"Curled up in the parking lot," I said, mostly as a revelation to myself. "Crying."

Wynezra shot a dangerous glance at me.

"No, no, no, I'm not making fun of you," I said, raising my hands backtrackishly. "That's just what I remember. I didn't *remember* running out of school. What I remembered was waking up in the parking lot, curled up in a ball—"

Wynezra's eyes narrowed to life-threatening slits, daring me to say "crying" one more time.

"Anyway . . . yeah," I said.

"You do know what *else* happened that day," she said, "don't you?"

She looked at me, and I looked at her. Even though we were looking at our own eyes, they met with an unspoken understanding.

Like celestial spheres overlapping.

Eclipsing.

"The eclipse," I said, breathless.

Wynezra nodded. "The first one, from seven years ago."

What we were experiencing wasn't random. It was a *continuation* of something that happened seven years ago.

But why? What did that *mean*?

"So . . ." said Wynonna. "What do we do?"

"What do we *do*?"

"How do we fix this?"

Even though I was in a different body, the physical sensation of how I handled stress translated perfectly. My stomach was set to spin-dry. My chest was being vacuum-sealed against the scaffolding of my rib cage. My brain was an alarm, blaring: *Don't panic don't panic don't panic*, which was undoubtedly the worst form of panicking.

So naturally, I played it cool and shrugged.

"Wait it out?" I said.

Wynezra cinched her eyebrows (my eyebrows) together and glared at me incredulously. I was discovering a palette of facial expressions I didn't know I had.

"Wait it out?" she said. "That's your plan?"

"I mean, think about it," I said. "We only swapped once before. And it only lasted for . . . what? Ten, fifteen minutes?"

Wynezra bit her lip.

"We *did* only swap once," I said. "Didn't we?"

Wynezra jutted her newfound masculine jaw out. She appeared to be thinking, and not in the most reassuring way.

"*Didn't* we?" I said, more frantically.

"I don't know!" said Wynezra. "I've spent the past seven years convincing myself that it never really happened. I only remember the play so well because there were, like, two hundred witnesses. I think . . . I think we swapped maybe one more time?"

"One more time?"

"*Maybe?* Like I said, I went to a psychiatrist for this shit. My grasp of what did or didn't happen is kind of Jell-O salad."

"Okay . . ." I offered a hollow, lobotomized nod. "Well, whatever the case, whatever this is"—I made an ambiguous gesture between the two of us—"I don't think it's permanent."

Wynezra nodded in a way that was listening, and hopeful, and probably not believing a single word I said. Who could blame her? *I* hardly believed a word I said. This was some next-level Twilight Zone shit we were in. But if we were going to survive this ordeal, we needed to keep our cool.

"With that said," I continued, "I think the most important thing right now is staying on the same page with each other. We each have our own lives, and there's a balance that needs to be maintained. The last thing we need is to screw things up for each other."

"Okay . . ."

I took a deep breath. This was when things were going to get tricky.

"We need to go to school," I said.

"School?"

"More importantly, we need to go to that theater class."

Wynezra snorted. "Nope."

"We need to be in that play!"

"Wrong again."

"I need to go to prom!" I said. "I *can't* get banned from prom. I just can't."

"Why?" said Wynezra. "Give me one good reason why you just absolutely *need* to go to prom."

I bit my lip.

"So you can ask *Imogen* to prom?" Wynezra prodded. "So you can ask out a girl who has no idea that you're obsessed with her BECAUSE YOU NEVER TALK TO HER?"

"What?" I said. I immediately felt my body flush. My sweat glands were going the way of Chernobyl. "I am *not* obsessed—"

Wynezra snorted.

"Okay, okay. Maybe . . . it's possible . . . that I have a *small* crush—"

Wynezra snorted.

"Okay, a moderately sized, *normal* crush—"

Wynezra snorted.

"Fine! I have a big, fat crush on Imogen. I have since fourth grade. I'm obsessed with her, and I can't stop thinking about her. Are you happy?"

"Why would that make me happy?" said Wynezra. "That's just creepy."

"Oh, c'mon. Like you've never had a crush on anyone."

The sky went dark. I hadn't been paying attention to our surroundings—where we were even heading—until now. It was all concrete ramps, pillars, and rows of expensive cars. We had pulled into a parking garage.

"Where are you going?" I said.

"Home," said Wynezra.

She pulled into a convenient open spot by the silver doors of an elevator. Exited the car. Strolled leisurely off, leaving me behind.

"Wait!" I said. "Can we even park my car here?"

"Not my problem."

I became an immobilized fixture in the passenger seat, paralyzed with indecision, glancing between my illegally parked car and my body—possessed by the spirit of a teenage anarchist—storming off.

"Dammit," I muttered. I jumped out of the car and chased after her.

When I caught up to her, she had already pressed the up button on the elevator, causing it to light up. The door opened almost immediately.

She stepped inside and pressed the button for the third floor. I reluctantly followed. Slowly, the elevator door closed—like a solemn metaphor of any chance I ever had of asking Imogen to prom.

"Let's talk this over," I said.

"If you want to go to school as me, go without me," she said. "Go ahead. Ruin my reputation. But there is no way I'm going to school pretending to be you, and there is NO WAY I'm doing Shakespeare."

"You do realize that this is a half-assed production, right?" I said. "Principal Durden is filling it with detention kids! So if you're worried about not being any good, I can assure you that *no one* is going to be any—"

"*You* do realize that I don't give a fuck, right?"

The elevator door opened into the long, wool-carpeted hallway, lit by crystal sconces. Wynezra stormed out.

I followed.

"You're not even you," I said. "What's your grandma gonna think when she sees some random boy in her house?"

"Her name's Carol," said Wynezra. "Stop calling her my grandma. That makes her sound like a decent human being."

"What's *Carol* going to think?"

"She works at the university until shit-thirty in the fucking evening. So I don't have to worry about her for a while."

"Is she a teacher?"

"She's the head of the department of anthropology."

"What's anthropology?"

"It's, like, fancy social studies."

Wynezra marched directly into her room and threw herself on her bed. She lay there for only a brief moment—then tweaked her head up, glancing from side to side. She reached her arms out, spread-eagle, measuring the width of her mattress.

"Well, this sucks," she said. "I feel like my queen just turned into a full."

"Carol's going to come home eventually," I said. "What if we haven't changed by then?"

Wynezra sighed. "Then I suppose it'd be helpful if you were here, so you could tell her I'm your new boyfriend."

"What?" I shrieked. I *actually* shrieked—activating feminine vocal frequencies Wynonna had never dared to utilize.

"Or my gay friend. Although I'm probably not very convincing. I'm wearing day-old clothes, and I haven't showered. Your body smells like fermented heterosexual frustration. Hmm. On that note . . ."

Wynezra bounced off the bed and waltzed out of the room.

"Where are you going?" I said.

"Shower," said Wynezra.

"What? But . . ."

"Oh, c'mon. I've already seen your package in full throttle. I need to shower. I smell like actual balls."

"Yeah, but—"

"Would you rather we hop in the shower together, blindfolded, and scrub each other's bodies? Is that more appropriate?"

I felt a bonfire of embarrassment ignite inside my face.

Wynezra laughed. "Oh my god! Who'da thunk I could blush like that?"

Wynezra walked into the bathroom, stepped in front of the mirror, and then took off her (my) shirt. Then—to my horror—she flexed.

"Oh baby!" she said. "Look at those deltoids!"

I had no idea what a deltoid was, but she appeared to be putting an obscene amount of emphasis on the shoulder-y region.

Once Wynezra was satisfied, she grabbed the door. "Okay, peep show's over, pretty lady."

She closed the door in my face.

Well, this was a total disaster. What was I supposed to do now?

I retreated to Wynonna's room and sat on her bed. Then I fell back on the mattress, arms flailed out. In Wynonna's baby-blue puffer coat, I felt like I should be sweeping my arms up and down, making a snow angel.

Wynonna *knew* I had a crush on Imogen.

I'd question *how* she knew it, but who was I kidding? It was probably super obvious. How many people turned into speechless idiots when they were within the immediate vicinity of Imogen Klutz?

Then a thought occurred: Had Wynonna and Imogen ever *talked* about me?

Wynonna said that Imogen had no idea I had a crush on her. But how would she know that? Maybe Imogen never said anything about it—that could be evidence enough.

Or *maybe* Wynonna knew this because she *asked* Imogen about it. I could already see the hypothetical conversation in my head:

Wynonna: *I'm so cool. I'm so badass. PS: I think Ezra has a crush on you.*

Imogen: *Why ever would you say such a thing? Surely, he and I are merely friends who share a platonic bond that transcends the spoken word. By the way, did you notice his elegantly disheveled hair today? Very debonair.*

I suddenly couldn't stop thinking about the hypothetical conversation that took place.

I could *ask* Wynonna if said hypothetical question actually took place. But that would be embarrassing. Besides, I just so happened to be in her bedroom—the most sacred and private place of teenagekind—and Wynonna was currently distracted, showering my naked body.

Did she keep a diary?

I jumped off the bed and started snooping. I started with her bedside table, then moved to her cluttered desk, then to her dresser. With each place I looked, I made sure not to disrupt the intricate order of her chaos. Nothing, nothing, nothing. I took a step back and absorbed the bedroom in all its anarchy.

If I were Wynonna's diary, where would I be?

Hell, if I were Wynonna's diary, would I even *exist*? Wynonna didn't exactly seem like the diary-keeping type. Maybe *no one* was the diary-keeping type these days. Everything was digital.

Did she have a computer? A laptop?

The desk was empty, but my gaze continued to scan the room.

It stopped on Wynonna's backpack, dropped delicately to the right of the door. An electric cord was sticking out of the open zipper.

Bingo.

I plopped myself in front of her backpack, cross-legged, and rifled through the contents. The computer—a silver MacBook covered in stickers—was easy enough to locate. It was tucked in a fabric slot designed for laptops. I pulled it out carelessly—not realizing the electric cord was still plugged into it, and most of said cord was tangled beneath Wynonna's ultra-graffitied notebooks, several papers and assignments, and a small shoe box covered in some sort of scrapbooking treachery. So basically, when the laptop came out, so did all of Wynonna's shit—the shoe box, the notebooks, dozens of papers—spilling all over the floor.

"Crap!" I hissed.

I stopped pulling on the laptop. Gently slid it back into its pocket. I then gathered all the papers and assignments and notebooks and attempted to stack and arrange them how they probably—hopefully—had been organized. Carefully, I slid them back inside. Then I turned my attention to the shoe box. Every square inch was covered in a scrapbook-style arrangement of pictures.

All the pictures were of Holden Durden.

FOUR

WHAT IN THE HOLY name of fuck?

I hovered over the shoe box. Studied the pictures—just to make sure that my eyes weren't playing tricks on me. That this wasn't some water-in-the-desert optical illusion. Surely this was just someone who *looked* like Holden from a distance, but when you looked closer, you realized the guy was actually six feet tall with a giant mole on his face, and his name was Pierre because he was a foreign exchange student from France. Theoretically.

I leaned forward. Absorbed the images.

Nope. It was Holden.

If that wasn't already the damnedest thing, there was also the *nature* of the photos to consider. Holden was never looking at the camera. Never. These were paparazzi-type pictures, taken at school while he was going about his daily routine—in the halls, at his locker, eating in the cafeteria. This meant that I was in a majority of these pictures—at least, I *would* be, except that I had been mostly cut out, and when I wasn't, I was just a human-colored smudge in the background.

I lifted the lid off the shoe box. Inside was a portable cassette recorder/player—a super retro–looking one at that—and a series of colorful cassette tapes stacked to the side. No two tapes were the same color. A strip of cardboard acted as a divider, keeping everything wedged in place.

I pulled out a cassette tape—a yellow one—and examined it. I realized it had been spray-painted that color. There was no label.

I removed the cassette recorder. A pair of headphones was already plugged in and wrapped around it. I unwound the headphones and pressed the open button.

I inserted the yellow cassette tape, closed the deck, inserted the headphone earbuds in my ears, and pressed play.

"Hey, Holden," said Wynonna's voice. *"This is going to sound crazy, and my heart is beating in my throat just thinking the words, but I'm going to say it: I like you."*

Oh. My. God.

I kept listening.

"Do you ever have that feeling when you're around someone where the room grows brighter? Where the air is suddenly crisp and biting and fills your lungs with icy electricity? And your skin tingles, and your chest throbs, but in a good way, a really good way, and the world is alive with details you never would have noticed, all because of this one person?

"I hope you haven't—unless that person is me. Because that's literally what you do to me."

I stopped the player.

Ejected the tape. Set it aside.

Grabbed another tape from the box—a red one—inserted it, closed the deck, and pressed play.

"'Sup, Holden," said Wynonna. *"I'm just gonna say it: I like you. What you do with that information is up to you. I really couldn't care less.*

But, you know, if you wanna date, or... hook up, or... whatever... you know. Just lemme know. I'm down to clown."

It ended there.

I ejected it. Grabbed a black tape from the box. Inserted it and pressed play.

"Fuck you, Holden. Why can't you just get a hint? Do I have to spell it out for you? You know what? I'm not even gonna say it! You don't deserve that much. All I'm gonna say is, what kind of girl has to tackle a guy to the ground, just to get his attention? Huh? I swear, you wouldn't know a hint if it kneed you in the balls, dropped you to the floor, and started kicking you in the ribs! I'm not the one with a problem, Holden. You are! Fuck! Fuck, fuck, fuck, fuck—"

I stopped the tape. Switched it out for a bluish-gray one. Pressed play.

Wynonna was sobbing.

"I'm sorry," she said, sniffling. *"I'm sorry I can't just tell you how I feel. I'm sorry I'm the way that I am. I just... I wish you could see inside of me. I wish you could know that I'm not this horrible person you think I am. I... I..."*

She started sobbing again.

Stop. Eject. I switched the blue-gray out for a neon-orange tape.

This one began with the fierce, jagged strum of an acoustic guitar. The tune sounded familiar, but I couldn't put my finger on it.

"Come on, Holden!" Wynonna belted out.

That's when it clicked. It was "Come On Eileen" by Dexys Midnight Runners. Well... sort of. A raw, angsty, Joan Jett–style rewrite of "Come On Eileen."

Poor old Nona Jones
Sitting sad upon the patio
List'ning to sad songs from Edge and Bono

Wynonna cried
Sang along, who'd blame her
You're grown
So grown
Now I must say more than ever
Too ra loo ra too ra loo rye aye
We can sing this tune forever
Come on, Holden, oh I swear, gentleman
At this moment, you mean everythin'
You in that shirt
My thoughts are pure dirt
Oh, so dirty
Ah, come on, Holden

I liked to think of myself as a genuinely sympathetic human being. However, evil may have prevailed for a moment as a sinister smile crept across my face and I thought to myself:

I have the ultimate blackmail on Wynonna.

Then it happened—a flash.

Suddenly, hot water was pouring down on me, and my surroundings had altered entirely and so had the position of my body. I was standing, hands against the wall, head hanging down, letting the water hit the back of my neck and run down the planes of my body.

I was in the shower.

I was naked.

I was me.

That's when I heard the scream—Wynonna's scream—from the floor of her bedroom where I left her.

All of her secrets laid out in the open. Her own vulnerable words wailing in her ears.

I had expected a reenactment of the scene from *Psycho*. Silhouette appears outside the shower curtain, knife is raised overhead, slash, slash, slash. Ezra Slevin topples over the edge of the bathtub, ripping the shower curtain down with him. Camera fixes on his open, lifeless eye, slowly panning out to reveal his terrified face pressed against the tile of the bathroom floor.

Okay, so maybe my paranoia was a tad dramatic. Still, I expected *something*. I waited in the shower a long moment for that something, but it never came. I held my breath when I finally heard footsteps in the hall. They grew louder.

And then they grew quieter.

Then I heard the front door open and close.

"Wynonna?" I said.

I turned the shower off. Listened breathlessly for a sound. Wynonna was just faking me out, right? I would walk out of the shower with a towel around my waist, and *then* she would jump out of nowhere, cosplaying as her quite-possibly-dead mother, and stab me to death.

I dried myself with a towel, wrapped it around my waist, and stepped out of the bathroom.

"Wynonna?" I said again.

I peeked inside her bedroom. No Wynonna.

I did, however, notice that the baby-blue puffer coat—and the rest of the clothes Wynonna had been wearing—were unceremoniously shed into a pile on the floor.

Maybe she was hiding?

I wandered into the kitchen. Into the living area. I even dared to look inside Carol's bedroom—a dim, foreboding, sophisticated-looking chamber with a massive, wooden, antique canopy bed carved and polished like a throne, some sort of Persian-ass rug, and a hefty copy of *Anna Karenina* on the nightstand.

No Wynonna.

She seriously just left me here.

Maybe she went to school? Where else would she go?

I returned to the bathroom and got dressed. Pulling on day-old clothes that I had slept in—after a shower, no less—should have been the most unpleasant experience imaginable. However, I was kind of grateful to be putting on *my* clothes at all.

After double-checking to make sure I had car keys on me, I left Wynonna and Carol's condo. I navigated my way through the hallway, back to the elevator. Took it down to the parking garage. Power-walked to my Subaru, which—thank god—didn't have a ticket.

I hopped in, turned the key in the ignition, backed out, and stomped on the accelerator.

I floored it all the way to school.

• •

"Dude," said Holden. "Where the hell have you been?"

I closed my locker door, and there was Holden's face—where a masked serial killer would be if my life were a horror film.

Nope. Just a body-swap comedy—funny to everyone but me.

"Uh," I said. "I slept in."

"No shit," said Holden. "Just in time for lunch. Well, I guess if anyone has a right to sleep in, it's you."

The hallway was a riptide, pulling everyone and everything into the cafeteria. Holden and I stepped into the flow of bodies, submitting to the undertow.

Today, on the Piles Fork lunch menu, was "pizza." You'd think it would be impossible to ruin something as simple and perfect as pizza, but Piles Fork had it down pat. The trick was to make the crust too thick and crunchy, with too little sauce, too little cheese, and turkey pepperoni. Then they burned it.

"You know you live in a dystopian society when the pizza is consistently worse than the meat loaf," said Holden.

"Right?" I said. "I bet Katniss Everdeen wouldn't touch this shit. This is how you start the Hunger Games."

We made a straight line to the trash, dumped our pizza, and then veered to the vending machines. Funyuns it was!

By the time we sat in our usual corner of the cafeteria, Holden had a contemplative look on his face.

"So I did some research," said Holden.

"Oh no," I said.

"Twelfth Night," he continued. "Imogen is gunning for the main character, Viola, right? And knowing Imogen—being the drama nut and overachiever that she is—she's probably going to *get* the part. Right?"

"Probably."

"You, my friend, need to get the part of Duke Orsino."

"Who the hell is Duke Orsino?"

"He's the leading male role, and the guy Viola has a crush on the entire play."

Already, I felt the social anxiety and early-onset stage fright crushing my insides. "Oh man. I dunno. I don't think I can handle a role where I'm romancing it up with Imogen. I'll probably forget all my lines and stress-puke."

"No, see, that's the thing!" said Holden. "Duke Orsino *isn't* romancing it up with Viola. He's romancing it up with *Olivia*!"

"Who the hell is Olivia?"

"I dunno, some chick. It's, like, a love triangle. Viola is pretending to be a dude for some reason, and Olivia has a thing for Dude Viola."

"Okay, I'm confused."

"Have you ever seen *She's the Man* with Amanda Bynes?"

"No," I said. Which was a lie. I had watched *She's the Man* at least thirteen times with Willow, before she disowned me as a brother.

"Oh . . . well, me either," Holden lied.

I knew, for a fact, that Holden had a not-so-secret crush on Amanda Bynes. He inherited her entire filmography and every season of *All That* from his older brother, Nate—now graduated from college, working as a software engineer—who *also* had a crush on Amanda Bynes. It was a Durden family tradition.

"But allegedly," said Holden, breaking the awkward silence, "*Twelfth Night* and *She's the Man* are basically the same thing."

I nodded ambiguously, because I think I understood what he was saying now, but I was still trying to pretend I hadn't seen *She's the Man* at least thirteen times. Essentially, I was aiming for Channing Tatum's role as "muscular heartthrob and overall sexual male object." Great.

Flash.

Suddenly, Holden was Imogen—sitting directly across from me, her enigmatic eyebrows knit together with deep concern. We were in a different corner of the cafeteria, and—most shocking of all—I had a half-eaten pizza in front of me. Right next to an open bag of pork rinds.

Shit. There was pizza *in my mouth.*

Peter, Bjorn, and John! Was there *anything* Wynonna was incapable of eating?

I swallowed the wad of chewed pizza under the greatest duress.

"It's okay," said Imogen. She leaned forward, extending a long, slender hand. Grabbed my right hand—*Wynonna's* hand with the electric-blue nails—and covered it with her other hand. Squeezed it. I immediately felt my body temperature skyrocket. "You can tell me. Is it about Holden?"

I felt something move down my cheek.

I reached up with my free hand—the hand that wasn't currently sweating like a storm trooper at a shooting range in Imogen's grasp—and touched my face. I felt the lines of moisture.

I was crying.

Wynonna was crying.

There was a moment when the universe became perfectly synchronized. I obviously knew where Imogen sat at lunch, and Wynonna apparently knew where Holden sat. We didn't even need to turn our heads. My gaze drifted to my two o'clock, and there was Ezra "Wynezra" Slevin, looking right back at me. Our eyes were interlocked, silently screaming, bloating out of our faces.

"Bathroom," I blurted out. "I need to go to the bathroom."

"Oh," said Imogen. "Okay."

She pulled her purse onto her shoulder and stood up.

What the . . .

"No!" I said. I shook my head desperately for emphasis. "No, no, no, no, no."

"No?" Imogen looked confused.

I glanced at the half-eaten pizza in front of me.

"It's the pizza," I said. "Goes through me like a brick. Believe me, anyone and anything in the vicinity when this bomb drops—"

"Whoa," said Imogen, in a way that meant "Stop, please!" "Okay. Message received."

I stood up. And then I nearly tripped and biffed it. It was then that I noticed the shoes I was wearing—punk-style black heels with metal studs.

If there was a God, he clearly hated me. If not, I had the evolutionary luck of the dinosaurs.

"Are you okay?" said Imogen. She didn't even wait for an answer.

She jumped up, moved around the table, and grabbed me for stability—one hand on my arm, the other on my hip. Because hips were a thing I had now.

This was the part where I *would* have had a raging boner. However, since my equipment had been rearranged, I felt something very different happening downstairs, and it was kind of freaking me out.

"I'm okay," I said—or *tried* to say, but my voice cracked. I didn't even know girls' voices *could* crack. "I think my heel broke."

"Really?" said Imogen. She crouched down and examined my shoe—placing a hand on my thigh for balance. "It doesn't look like it—"

"Nope, definitely broke!" I exclaimed. I fumbled desperately to undo the straps on my shoes, then pulled them off. Beneath them, I was wearing fishnets. I slowly scanned my wardrobe upward—a ratty plaid skirt and a Pat Benatar T-shirt. Okay, the shirt was admittedly kind of cool.

Once the deathtraps were off my feet, I stood up—heels in hand—and rushed in slippery stocking feet to the cafeteria exit.

"Ezra!" Holden's voice sliced through the bog of chatter. "What the hell, man?"

Instinctively, I looked over my shoulder. Holden, however, was talking to the *other* Ezra, who also happened to be making a hasty exit.

Wynezra had mirrored my timing. We reached the hallway at the same moment, at which point I almost expected her to bolt in the opposite direction.

Instead, she grabbed my elbow and pulled me into the girls' bathroom.

"Ow, ow, ow!" I said. "Hey, I'm not allowed in here! Or . . . well, *one of us* isn't allowed in here."

Wynezra shoved me into the nearest stall and locked the door.

"I've had it up to here with you," she said. She raised her hand half a foot above her head, indicating where "here" was.

"You think I *want* this?" I shrieked. I raised her studded heels like a murder weapon. "I almost died in these things! Are you trying to kill me?"

"If it gets me my life back, then sure!"

Wynezra's arms became rigid at her sides. Taut ropes of fury. Looking at her—at the hatred seething out of her teeth and nostrils—I realized this wasn't even about the body-swapping.

It was about the notebook.

It was about her secret.

I bit my lip. "Look… I'm sorry about snooping—"

Wynezra gave a sharp bark of laughter. It sounded so totally like her, it was weird seeing and hearing it come out of my mouth. "Please. Why don't you just get it over with?"

"What? Get *what* over with?"

"We both know where this is going. You're either going to blackmail me or you're going to go straight for the jugular and ruin my life. Well, I'll help you make your decision." She leaned forward, hands braced against the stall walls, until her face—*my* face—was only inches away. "I don't bend to blackmail."

She straightened herself, turned, and exited the stall.

"Wait," I said.

Wynezra whipped around. "No! No waiting, Ezra! If you're gonna do something with this big fucking secret, then do it already. I'm not gonna sit on my hands, hoping it goes away. I'm not gonna get strung along by your twisted little scheme. Go ahead. Tell Holden. Go have a big fucking laugh over it. It's not like I was planning on going to prom with that asshole anyway. I'm banned, remember? I don't give a shit."

"I can help you," I said.

The words just sort of came out of their own accord. They had a collective mind, separate from my own.

"What the . . ." Wynezra reared back. "Did you listen to a word I said? I'm *not* getting strung along by whatever it is—"

"I'm not stringing you along," I said. "As far as I see it, I don't have any leverage over you. I don't *want* any leverage over you. What I want is your help. I think we can help each other."

Oh my god, why was I still talking?

My mouth had gone rogue. Mutiny was afoot.

Wynezra was silent for a long moment. The hard edges of her face did not soften. But the guard in her eyes *did* lower ever so slightly.

"What do you mean?"

"I like Imogen," I said. I took a deep breath to quell the swift-approaching anxiety attack, closing in like the shark from *Jaws* with ominous theme music and everything. "I want to go to *prom* with Imogen. You and I both know I can't pull that off on my own. I can barely talk to her—let alone ask her out. And then there's the issue of her actually saying yes. But you *know* her. You know how to *talk* to her."

"This sounds like blackmail," said Wynezra. "What's in it for me?"

"I know how to talk to Holden."

The cogs and the gears behind Wynezra's gaze were clicking into place. Rotating slowly to life.

"And *you* know how to talk to Imogen," I continued, leaving a super-obvious trail of bread crumbs to my point. "And prom is just around the corner. So . . ."

Wynonna stared at me.

"Whaddaya say, Wynonna Jones? Are you *down to clown*?"

Wynezra's mouth slithered into a great big devious smile. "I've been known to dabble in a little tomfoolery."

FIVE

THE PLAN WAS SIMPLE: Wynonna would help me get a date to prom with Imogen, and I would do the same for her and Holden. We would use this body-swapping curse to our advantage. When life gives you lemons, right?

Was it an act of blatant dishonesty toward our best friends? Yeah, sort of.

Could we live with that dishonesty on our consciences? Definitely.

There were so many flaws in the plan, however, it hardly functioned as a plan at all. For starters, if by some miracle we pulled this off, there was no guarantee that I would be me and Wynonna would be Wynonna when prom night arrived. For all we knew, we could get stuck going to prom with our best friends! And that was *if* we pulled this off. Which was unlikely. Especially with the first major disclaimer that came out of Wynezra's mouth.

"I'll help you all I can," she said. "But I should warn you, Imogen already has a crush on someone."

I had suspected as much. A girl like Imogen didn't just *not* have a crush on anyone.

I took in a deep breath. Exhaled. Nodded.

"Okay," I said, rather acceptingly. "Who is it?"

"I can't tell you that."

"What? You have to tell me!"

"Psh! No, I don't. I have to get you a date with Imogen to prom. And I will. At least, I'll do everything in my power to do that. And I'll tell you anything else you need to know. But I literally *cannot* tell you that. Imogen swore me to secrecy. She made me swear on my mom's—"

Her words came to a dangerous halt.

"Anyway," she said, "I can't tell you."

"Okay, well . . ." I said, "does she have a chance with him?"

"What makes you think it's a him?"

My jaw dropped. "Is it a girl?"

Wynezra pursed her lips. She was clearly having a moral dilemma, deliberating whether or not to impart even the slightest hint of information.

"The person Imogen has a crush on . . . is a guy," said Wynezra. "And no, nothing's ever going to happen between them. So you can stop worrying about it."

I let out a deep breath. Okay. Maybe this thing was doable after all.

"And, Ezra?" she said.

I glanced up from the infinitesimal hole in space I was drilling into with my mind.

"Don't try to pry any details from Imogen about who it is," she said. "Believe me, you'll be opening a can of worms you don't want to open."

I nodded dismissively. "Yeah, sure. So we're doing this Shakespeare thing, right?"

Wynezra sighed. "If I have to."

At that moment, the bathroom door opened. In walked a girl whom I didn't recognize. I gave a startled jump—then remembered that *I* was a girl. The girl who walked in, meanwhile, jumped at the sight of Ezra Slevin—especially the disgruntled I-hate-Shakespeare look on his face.

"Yeah, yeah, I'm leaving," said Wynezra, and she walked out.

• •

My first item of business as Wynonna Jones was to kiss some serious Allegra Durden ass.

"You're *what*?" said Principal Durden. Her elbows were propped up on her desk, fingers interlocked, eyes peering over the knot of fingers.

"Sorry," I repeated. "I'm *sorry*."

Principal Durden continued to stare at me like this was some *Invasion of the Body Snatchers* scenario. Which it kind of was.

"What do you want?" she said.

"I want to do the Shakespeare thing," I said. "I don't want to be banned from prom."

If Principal Durden's eyes narrowed any further, they'd be sealed shut.

"Please?" I said.

"So . . . what?" said Principal Durden. She unraveled her knot of fingers and leaned back in her swivel chair. "Did some hunky boy come along and change your mind?"

No, I thought, *but I might be taking your son to prom, so CAN IT, PRINCIPAL DURDEN!*

I smiled politely. "You'll just have to wait and see."

Principal Durden gave a perplexed sigh. Then she reached into her desk and pulled out the *Twelfth Night* pamphlet. Handed it to me.

"You'll be there?" said Principal Durden. "On time? For the whole thing? Your teacher will tell me if you're not. Don't think that because this class is off campus, the rules are more lax. If anything, they're stricter."

"You can trust me, Principal Durden," I said. I offered a winning smile as evidence. "I'm a new person today."

She didn't seem to believe that for a second—but she gave a stiff nod regardless. I stood up and started to walk out.

"Wynonna?" she said.

I turned around. "Yeah?"

She was looking directly at my blue toenails, visible through my fishnet leggings.

"Part of our shoe policy is . . . you have to wear them."

I sighed.

• •

The key to walking in heels was to walk slowly. Also, to pray silently to Every Deity Known to Mankind. (Or Womankind, as the case may have been.) I even made room in my prayers for the Flying Spaghetti Monster. As an "atheist schmuck," I was taking a leap of faith in the form of the shotgun effect.

Turned out, heels were the least of my problems.

Wynonna and I exchanged locker combinations. There, taped to her locker door, I discovered her printed-out schedule. Wynonna put it there the very first day of school, and it hadn't budged since, thank [insert Every Deity Known to Man and Womankind + Flying Spaghetti Monster].

That's where my real problems began. Because reading Wynonna's schedule was like cracking the Zodiac ciphers. Basically, it was the cell phone fiasco all over again.

Ditiagl Atrs & Pohotgarhpy
7:55–8:45 (Preiod 1)
Cialtin Kreiragn—Mdeia Lab

Aemrcian Sgin Lnagague
8:50–9:40 (Peirod 2)
Amnada Tomeoy—306

Boilogy
9:45–10:35 (Peroid 3)
Daune Anzazolne—207

Egnilsh
10:40–11:30 (Poired 4)
Cadncae Homles—215

Lucnh
11:35–12:20 (Preiod Lunch)

Gbolal Sduteis
12:25–1:15 (Peirod 5)
Annie Gruenwald—203

Preclauclus
1:20–2:10 (Pireod 6)
Jhon Mihceal—307

Seepch
2:15–3:05 (Peoird 7)
Aimn Lniedr—218

What.

The fuck.

Again, I was being real generous here, because some of these letters were backward, some were upside down, some were *not even real letters*. Either that, or we were borrowing from the Russian alphabet, with similar letters sprouting bizarre new appendages.

This was more than just drugs. Instead of speaking in tongues, she *saw* in tongues. The very words in front of her eyes were translated into the Adamic language or Alienese or whatever.

Fortunately, it was harder for Wynonna's gift of tongues to screw up room numbers. Although this was probably less to do with the numbers themselves, and more to do with the fact that they weren't strung together in long, hard-to-deal-with clumps.

First-period Media Lab was easy enough to figure out—Digital Arts & Photography. Fortunately, I didn't really have to *do* anything. It was mostly just sitting in front of a computer, listening to Ms. Kerrigan talk about Photoshop and the fine line between artful enhancement and shameless desecration. From there, it was smooth sailing from class to class. All lectures, all day long. Given the circumstances, I was totally okay with this.

When the end-of-school bell rang, I wandered out of seventh-period Speech in a daze. Shuffled to Wynonna's locker and packed Wynonna's backpack. Before I could pull it on—or even shut the locker door—I was assaulted from behind by a gangly bundle of limbs.

"You're doing Shakespeare!" Imogen squealed, approximately two inches from my left ear.

She hugged me from behind, pinning my limbs to my side. The physical touch alone would have been enough to paralyze me. But then there were her breasts, pressed precariously against the pressure points of my spine in the ancient Chinese art of *dim mak*—the touch of death.

"Why didn't you *tell* me?" she said.

She released me from her dim mak death hold—only to skip beside me and grab my hand.

Oh my god. Imogen was holding my hand.

Okay, I mean . . . it technically wasn't *my* hand . . . BUT STILL.

"I had to get told by Principal Durden," Imogen continued. "Even *she* was surprised you didn't tell me."

Deep breaths, Ezra. Deep breaths. In through your nose, out through your mouth.

"I . . . wanted to . . . *surprise* you," I said—unable to speak more than three-syllable spurts. "Surprise!"

"I'll say," said Imogen. She seemed to notice me tensing up. She let go of my hand. "So you're driving, right?"

"Yeah, sure," I said, mindlessly.

"Great. Where'd you park?"

We were walking out the front doors of Piles Fork and down the concrete steps. I was already starting toward the B-Lot, raising my hand to point, when I realized:

That's where *I* parked—not Wynonna.

I didn't *know* where she parked.

I didn't even know what her car *looked* like.

And if I did, it wouldn't matter because I COULDN'T DRIVE A STICK.

My brisk pace just sort of floundered to a confused halt. Imogen took a couple steps past me, then stopped and turned awkwardly.

"You okay?" said Imogen.

“Yeah!” I said, forcing an ungodly level of enthusiasm into Wynonna’s face. “Here’s an idea: What if we get a ride there with Ezra and Holden?”

Imogen looked at me like I had proposed we drive in a clown car filled with thirty-eight clowns.

“You’re serious,” said Imogen finally, after a silence that spanned the cosmos.

“Yeah!” I said. The longer I forced the smile on my face, the more I felt like the Joker—Jack Nicholson version. “We’re all in this together, right? Might as well make the most of it!”

Imogen’s eyelids narrowed to slits so thin you could have flossed them.

It appeared there was no way out of this without at least a *granule* of truth.

Now, whether it was *my* truth or not was a different matter entirely.

I dropped the smile like a veil of lies.

“Prom,” I said. “I want to ask Holden to prom.”

Slowly, Imogen’s eyes widened like a pair of flowers blooming in a fast-motion time lapse.

“Oh. My. God,” she said. “You’re doing it. You’re actually *doing* it!”

Once again, I was forced to smile like an idiot. Or a Batman villain. It occurred to me that smiling was maybe the *least* Wynonna-like thing I could do. However, the Smiley Train was already rolling, and there was really no stopping it at this point.

Once I dropped the P-bomb, Imogen became a Holden-seeking missile. Meanwhile I trailed behind desperately in my punk heels, trying—and failing—to keep up.

She found Holden in less than a minute. By himself.

He didn’t look happy.

Mostly, he looked irritated. And maybe a little bit mystified. He was standing aimlessly in the middle of the B-Lot, hand cupped over his eyes like a visor, scanning the after-school pandemonium. Between the two of us—Holden and me—there was a very *Where in the World Is Carmen Sandiego?* vibe going on.

Where the fuck was she? Wynonna, I mean. Not Carmen Sandiego.

"Hey, Holden!" Imogen exclaimed. "You're going to theater, right? At the Amityvale? Can we get a ride with you?"

Holden gave Imogen a look that was not unlike the "clown car" look she gave me.

"What?" he said.

"A ride," Imogen repeated. "To the theater. You guys are going, right?"

Holden glanced from Imogen (bubbly, ecstatic, teetering on the edge of hysteria), to me (distressed, confused, trying to take as few steps as possible in these deathtrap heels), and back to Imogen.

"Pretty please?" said Imogen.

Holden's gaze drifted suspiciously, wandering nowhere in particular. Maybe he was looking for the hidden camera filming this obvious TV-show prank.

"Where's Ezra?" I asked, mostly as a tension breaker.

"That's what *I'm* wondering!" said Holden. The response practically erupted out of him. "Every time I try to talk to him, he freaks out, makes up some weird, obviously fake excuse, and runs off."

His suspicious gaze locked onto me.

"You didn't say anything to him, did you?" said Holden. "Scare him off some—wait." He looked at Imogen. "*We?* Did you say, 'Can *we* get a ride with you?'"

"Uhhhhh . . ." said Imogen.

His gaze returned to me with a calm, murderous look.

"*You're* going now?" he said. "Jesus, no wonder Ezra's freaking out! So, what? You just changed your mind?"

The good news was that I had just diverted suspicion from Wynonna and her shit performance as Ezra Slevin. The bad news was that she was clearly cracking under the pressure of being me. Or maybe she was cracking under the pressure of being *Holden's best friend*. Either way, our disguises were looking awfully paper thin. If I wasn't convincing as Wynonna, this plan could very well blow up in our faces.

C'mon. Think, Ezra, think! What would Wynonna say? Think Wynonnish thoughts.

"Yeah, that's right," I said. "I changed my mind. You got a problem with that, shortstop?"

Imogen's mouth fell open.

Okay, maybe I overstepped. In the spectrum of douchey things you could say to another human being, jabs at Holden's height were off the douche-o-meter.

Holden's jaw clenched. A shadow of something flashed past the windows of his eyes—like a passing silhouette in a dark doorway.

Hate?

Whatever it was, it was gone in an instant.

"Fine," said Holden. He turned exclusively to Imogen. "But you have to find Ezra. Find him, and you can ride with us."

"Okay," said Imogen, nodding overenthusiastically. "You know what? I'm going to check the main office. Maybe Ezra's getting the deets about this Shakespeare thing from Principal Durden. But hey, you guys wait here in case he shows up, okay?"

Imogen started off before either of us could protest. But not before giving me the most obvious wink in the universe. It was the sort of excessive wink that was usually accompanied by a pair of thumbs-up.

But for the sake of being clandestine, she instead hooked her thumbs in her pockets and sauntered off like some hard-boiled private investigator. Very noir.

Flash.

Suddenly, I was lying on my side in the back seat of a car. I recognized the upholstery immediately. It was *my* car—the Subaru. The way my knees were curled to the side in a near-fetal position, it was obvious I was attempting to stay below the window level. I was *hiding.*

Wynonna was hiding. What the hell?

That was when I noticed the background music. And I say "background" generously, because it was blasting from my phone, which was lying directly beside my left ear on the back seat, the volume cranked up to Who Needs Eardrums, Anyway?

The song was "We Belong" by Pat Benatar. Wynonna had pulled up the music video on YouTube.

She was having a real Pat Benatar sort of day, wasn't she?

What happened next was pure ninja. I hopped over the center console, slid masterfully into the driver's seat, shoved the key into the ignition—it had been clutched tightly in my left hand the whole time, leaving a key-shaped imprint—and turned it. The Subaru engine gave a less-than-mighty roar.

As I peeled out of my spot, left hand gripping the twelve o'clock on my steering wheel, my right hand fumbled with the auxiliary cord. I started the song over and cranked the car stereo volume to I Want to Feel the Song in My Teeth.

If Wynonna needed Pat Benatar, then I would give her Pat fucking Benatar.

"Many times I tried to tell you . . . many times I cried alone," Pat sang softly. *"Always I'm surprised how well you cut my feelings to the bone."*

I squealed around the corner of the B-Lot, cutting off Imogen's path to the school. Lucky for me, Wynonna had already started chasing desperately after her. Even Holden was trailing behind at a slow and confused pace.

I rolled down the window, just as Pat reached the chorus.

"*WE BELONG TO THE LIGHT, WE BELONG TO THE THUNNNNDER,*" Pat wailed, with an untamed heartache that only the '80s knew. "*WE BELONG TO THE SOUND OF THE WORDS WE'VE BOTH FALLEN UNNNNNNDER.*"

Imogen seemed irked that her matchmaking moment had been foiled. Wynonna, meanwhile, shuffled to a halt in her punk-heel tracks—completely and utterly mortified that I was blasting the anthem of her bleeding heart.

"Dude!" Holden shouted. He was several yards away but rapidly closing the gap. "Where the hell have you been?"

"Where have *I* been?" I said. "Where have *you* been? I've been looking everywhere for you!"

"You've been . . . *what*?" Holden's left eye started twitching, like the harbinger of a stroke.

I took a deliberate moment to notice Imogen and Wynonna. "Oh, hey! Were you guys all planning on riding together? I can drive!"

While Wynonna and Imogen exchanged looks, I made sure to wink discreetly at Holden—like this was our plan all along. Holden gave an exasperated sigh, shook his head, and started for the passenger-side door.

"Oh, shotgun!" said Imogen. She beat him to the door. "I have dibs on shotgun!"

"What?" said Holden. "You can't call shotgun."

"Why not?"

"Because best friend always gets shotgun!"

"That's not a rule. The rule is: Whoever *calls* shotgun *gets* shotgun. The end. No epilogue, no addendum."

Wynonna shoved her way between the two of them. Opened the passenger-side door, slid inside, and shut the door behind her.

Holden and Imogen stared at her through the open window, slack-jawed.

Wynonna pressed the automatic window button. It rolled up with a long, intense *VUHRRRRRRR.*

Then she locked the door.

• •

It was one of those awkward car rides where nobody was talking, the tension was thicker than a bowl of Chunky Campbell's Soup, and only half of us knew why. The other half—Holden and Imogen—were silently puzzling over the highly unusual behavior of their respective best friends.

Wynonna was brooding like a vampire in the passenger seat.

All I could focus on was how *uncool* she was being. I'd never seen her with her shit so *not* together.

I really wanted a moment alone with her. Just to ask her what was going on. I mean, I *kinda* knew what was going on—but I felt like there was a whole layer beneath the surface that I was missing.

I turned my attention to the road.

Downtown Carbondale walked a fine line between quaint and sketchy with a chance of violent crime. The SIU Power Plant—yes, Southern Illinois University had its own *power plant*—pumped plumes of smoke into the air like the cove beneath the Piles Fork bleachers where all the skeezy kids vaped. We crossed some allegorical-looking train tracks, passing college apartment complexes that maybe *used* to be decent, but now they had an eerie Roman Polanski vibe. Past Polanskiville, it was all ancient houses, ancient businesses, with a faint undercurrent of *ancient evil.* Like a fictional Stephen King town with a dark secret—a sort of Midwest Derry or Castle Rock.

The Amityvale Theater itself was all used-skeleton-colored stone walls, an ominous dark brick tower, and a vertical, Toblerone-shaped sign that read AMITYVALE in a red vintage font—visible on two separate, slanted sides. It was probably impressive in the 1920s—back when flappers were the "cutting edge"—but now it was only impressive in the sense that it was most likely haunted.

I mean, Amity*vale*? C'mon. You're not fooling anyone.

"All this time, I thought Ms. Chaucer was spoiled," said Holden. "I'm kind of shocked she settled for this dump."

"Maybe she was into the occult?" I offered.

"Welcome to the seedy underbelly of the drug world," Imogen whispered.

"It was *Adderall*," said Wynonna, exasperated. "Adderall is not part of the seedy underbelly of *any* drug world. God, why did I even tell you about that?"

"I feel like I'm in *Breaking Bad*," Imogen squeaked.

Wynonna sighed, looking the Amityvale Theater up and down. "This place *does* look like it was baptized in unholy water. Or tetanus. You know what? Maybe prom's overrated."

Both Imogen and I reacted in various stages of panic, directed at no one in particular.

"What, are you afraid all the Shakespeare kids will be more thug than you?" said Holden.

He then proceeded to do voices.

Holden's "voices" were—as all "voices" are—terrible. One voice sounded like Jason Statham if he was deaf to his own voice. The other sounded like Rocky Balboa after Creed turned his face into a soufflé.

Holden Balboa: "Whaddaya in here for?"

Holden Statham: "I'm in here for armed robbery and murder and hate crimes against kittens."

Holden Balboa: "Whadda YOO in here for, Wynonna Jones?"

Holden's Wynonna-voice was basically Lisa Simpson. It's like he wasn't even trying.

Holdonna Jones: "I broke a window with MY BIG BUTT."

Wynonna's nostrils flared like a pair of kilts in a Scottish hurricane. She unceremoniously exited the Subaru, slammed the door behind her, and marched toward the serial-killer-corpse-storage theater.

The rest of us followed—very reluctantly. Holden's amused chuckle faded like a wisp of smoke.

The Amityvale Theater wasn't much better on the inside. It was all deteriorating motif-patterned carpet, splotchy black-painted concrete floors, less-than-sturdy-looking pillars, and walls that *used* to be red but now required a fresh coat of blood. Er, paint. (No, definitely blood.) If you craned your neck back, the ceiling was a spiderweb of wooden framework, and between those, *actual* spiderwebs. We passed a tomb of a box office, a moldy concession stand, and proceeded down a long, narrow—but surprisingly well-lit—corridor.

"Did they actually *use* this place?" asked Holden.

I shrugged. "All of their *actual performances* were either at the Varsity Center or the McLeod Theater at SIU."

Wynonna rolled her eyes. "You would know that, wouldn't you?"

Imogen walked with quiet steps, head lowered, like she was traversing the lawless jungle of the Darién Gap.

"This is where the drug deals transpired," she whispered.

We pushed through a pair of gloomy double doors into the actual theater room.

It was big. I'd give it that. The auditorium seating was steep—a waterfall of plush red chairs, crashing down into the basin of an empty orchestra pit. A pair of treacherous staircases ran along either side. The stage was vast and scratched and worn to a husk. Like it had been clogged to death—pulverized by malicious Riverdancers. In front of the stage were two push racks filled with tacky costumes; a large mobile whiteboard with the words *Welcome to Theater!* scrawled in purple dry-erase marker; and a folding table with a coffeemaker and biodegradable cups. The whole thing had a very Alcoholics Anonymous vibe.

There was a small handful of kids already seated, but I was putting forth great effort not to make eye contact.

"Welcome, welcome, young thespians!" said the last person in the world we expected to see. Although we didn't see him until he spoke. He was standing just inside the entrance, back flat against the wall, like an actual serial killer.

It was Ziggy—the Piles Fork High School groundskeeper.

Ziggy was a tall, lanky dude with a goatee, sleeve tattoos, Jesus-y hair, and a look on his face that was part stoner, part sagely and all-knowing. He walked a very precarious line.

"Ziggy?" I said.

"What?" said Imogen.

"No way," said Holden.

"Ziggy fucking Donovan?" said Wynonna fucking Jones.

Okay, so Ziggy was kind of a legend at Piles Fork. Not only was he cool, but he was disgustingly talented. He could outskate the skater kids. He could outplay the rocker kids on every instrument they threw at him. HE COULD OUT-SPIN THE FIDGET SPINNER...ERS. Really, he could outdo anyone at anything. If you thought you were good at something, chances were, Ziggy could do it better.

The weirdest thing about Ziggy Donovan, however, was how nice he was. And how he tried to be friends with everyone. Like, he had a *genuine interest* in each of our shitty lives. Hence how the four of us each knew who he was.

"What are you doing here?" said Imogen.

"What am I *not* doing here?" said Ziggy. "Am I right?"

The four of us exchanged confused glances.

Ziggy gave a clarifying cough. "I'm what modern society likes to call 'the Boss,'" he said, air-quoting. "But I prefer to think of myself as a 'Spiritual Guide' to the 'Sphere of the Bard.'" Again, air quotes and more air quotes.

"You're in charge?" said Holden.

"You like *Shakespeare*?" said Wynonna incredulously.

"What's *not* to like?" said Ziggy. "I'll have you know, Shakespeare changed my life."

"Shut up. No, he didn't."

"Cross my heart, hope to die," he said—tracing an actual X over his heart with his finger. "I could tell you quite the story, right here and now. But let's save that for introductions, yeah?"

It was only when Ziggy escorted us down into the gulch of the theater that I recognized some of the other kids present. I might have been surprised by some of them—notably Jayden Hoxsie, sitting in the front row—wearing a different-colored polo shirt, but one that was still two sizes too small, stretched across his chest like spandex.

Unfortunately, I was a little too preoccupied with the emo-haired freshman girl, awkwardly leaning forward, one skinny arm folded against her stomach, the other propped up on it, scratching her eyebrow in a feeble attempt to hide her face.

It was Willow.

Flash.

SIX

WYNEZRA AND I TURNED our heads slowly, eyes the size of jawbreakers, meeting each other's gaze with pained exasperation.

Willow seemed to notice that her alleged big brother was directing his jawbreaker stare elsewhere. Which made her visibly confused.

"Willow?" said Holden. "*You're* here?"

He looked at Wynezra for some sort of explanation. But as far as Wynezra knew, Holden was talking about a tree. Or Warwick Davis. She glanced desperately at me for clarification.

"Isn't that your little sister, Ezra?" I said. I nodded my head hintingly at Willow.

"Uh, I guess so," said Wynezra. Her momentary panic subsided into a smoke screen of cool indifference. "Like I give a shit."

She sat down.

Willow had been ignoring me for months. So I was just a little bit shocked that she seemed genuinely hurt.

Holden was baffled. He glanced from Willow to Wynezra. Since Wynezra had been acting weird all day, he returned his concern to

Willow, who was honestly kind of like a little sister to him. "Did you actually sign up, or is this a detention thing?"

Willow shrugged uncomfortably, indicating this was *definitely* a detention thing.

"Holy shit," said Holden. "What did you *do*?"

"Holden, *mi compadre*," said Ziggy. "We don't ask people what they *did* here. What they did is in the past. We only ask what they're *going* to do. Think forward, not backward."

Then he directed a sad glance at Wynezra.

"And you should *always* give a shit about your little sister."

Wynezra's arms were folded in a knot. She gave a shrug that only seemed to emphasize the lack of shits she gave.

Jayden Hoxsie—sitting on the exact opposite end of the circle from Willow—gave a douche-y snicker and winked at Willow.

"Bitch," he whispered.

"Yeah, fuck you, too, Hoxsie," said Wynezra.

Wynezra seemed to have forgotten that she was not Wynonna Jones, who took no shit from nobody, but rather Ezra Slevin, shit depository personified. Or, at least, quiet and submissive witness to any and all shit flung anywhere.

Jayden Hoxsie bolted up from his seat so fast, his theater chair thundered up and down.

"What did you say?" said Jayden.

Wynezra didn't back down.

"Well, what I *said* was 'fuck you, too,'" said Wynezra. "But what I *meant* was, go buy a shirt that fits, you irrelevant fucktrumpet. No one wants to see your knobby little nipples."

By the time Jayden started charging Wynezra, Ziggy intervened like a giant human rubber band, slingshot into the fray.

"Okay, okay, okay," said Ziggy, hands raised. "Let's cool our jets, yeah? Just simmer on down now. Yeah, that's it. Let's not get detention all over our detention."

Wynezra sat down, not giving a microscopic fuck more than she did fifteen seconds ago. Jayden, meanwhile, looked like an irritated cat—spine arched, face pulled back, every hair on his body an exclamation point. Finally, with great suppression of douchery, he managed to sit down without spouting a lame insult out of his douche nozzle.

Let me just say: I had never seen me act like such a badass in my entire life.

It was just a little bit discouraging to remind myself that it *wasn't* me.

Holden, looking like every truth he knew in the world was false, sat down quietly. I *started* to sit down—a seat away from Holden—but Imogen swiftly butted in front of me. Stole the seat. Winked and wobbled her head at the seat between her and Holden.

I sighed and sat down.

It was only now—after Willow's presence had fully settled—that I was able to absorb everyone else in attendance. There were fourteen other kids—eighteen of us total—most of whom were not terribly surprising. The ones I recognized included:

- Tucker Cook—local redneck and aspiring pyromaniac. He was a wiry, freckled, blond-haired menace who got in trouble last year for "having a Harry Potter fight" with his older brothers in the school parking lot. What they were *actually* doing was shooting one another with Roman candles. But, to be fair, Tucker kept yelling, *"Stupefy!"* and *"Avada Kedavra!"*

- Daisy Munk—she was huge. And I don't mean fat. She was Piles Fork's very own Brienne of Tarth. She was devastatingly huge, and even *more* quiet. So when the entire football team decided that slapping Daisy's ass was fun, she said nothing. When it became their new official side-sport, and they started keeping score, keeping tally on a whiteboard in the boys' locker room, she said nothing. When she finally reached a breaking point, grabbed running back Nick Swenson's arm, and broke it on the nearest doorframe, she said nothing. When rumors started spreading that the violence was the result of months of sexual harassment, and she was asked to testify at a school board meeting... Well, you get the idea. With no victim testimony, there was no way to hold the boys accountable, and only Daisy was punished.
- Sebastian O'Hara—an urban legend. Most of it was speculation and hearsay, but the "story" was that he was in a relationship with a boy named Oscar who went to Trinity Christian Academy. When it came out among Oscar's peers that he was dating a boy, he became the target of a vicious—sometimes even violent—bullying campaign. One incident left Oscar hospitalized with a broken wrist, fractured rib, and a concussion. The headmaster dismissed it as "falling down the stairs"—but thank *actual* God for the three boys who "witnessed the accident" and reported it immediately! What followed was something out of a slasher film. For the next several weeks, Sebastian stalked those three boys—reportedly wearing an antique rubber Captain Kirk mask that he ordered online. If you're familiar with the fun facts of the 1978 horror classic, *Halloween*, that's *exactly* what Michael Myers wore—only spray-painted white. Sebastian didn't bother spray-painting his; it was scary enough on its own. Sebastian cornered those boys

individually—in dark neighborhoods, hallways, isolated public restrooms, etc. Of course, these were only rumors, but in no variation of this story did those three boys walk out of the situation without serious psychological trauma.

- Patrick Durfee—Willow's ex-boyfriend. I actually liked Patrick. I mean, he was kind of a wiener—gawky, skinny to the point of resembling a fragile baby bird—but he was always nice and polite. *And* he was a freshman. He earned *major* points for being Willow's age. And for the fact that, ever since Willow broke up with him, I kept discovering unfamiliar cars in my driveway. God, why couldn't we revert to a matchmaking society where older brothers chose suitors for their littler sisters?

Ziggy hoisted himself onto the lip of the stage and sat facing us, suede Supra Stacks dangling. Meanwhile we, his theater class—allegedly all detention kids, here by coercion or threat—were scattered across the red theater seating like the last survivors of a grueling game of checkers. Ziggy had us go around the room—top to bottom, left to right—stating our name, what we wanted to be when we grew up, and our favorite Shakespeare play. (What a loaded question.) Some people took this very seriously. Imogen, for example, wanted to be an obstetrician—whatever the hell *that* was—and her favorite Shakespeare was *Much Ado about Nothing*. Then there were others, such as Tucker Cook, who wanted to be a wizard, and his favorite Shakespeare was *The Lord of the Rings*.

"*Lord of the Rings* isn't Shakespeare," said Ziggy.

"What?" said Tucker. "Yeah, it is."

Willow was the last person in the circle. She wanted to be "happy" when she grew up—how very emo of her—and her favorite Shakespeare was "*Romeo and Juliet*, the DiCaprio version."

"All right, my turn," said Ziggy. He clapped his hands together and ran a Keanu Reeves hand through his Keanu Reeves hair. "Well, not to toot my own horn, but I'm *doing* what I wanted to do when I grew up. That is, operating dangerous machinery at school, hanging out with all you cool kids, and making some Shakespeare magic. And, not to be clichéd or anything, but my favorite Shakespeare is *Hamlet*. Can anyone *quoth* me some *Hamlet*?"

"To be, or not to be?" half a dozen kids muttered in unenthusiastic chorus.

"To be, or not to be?" said Ziggy. "The ultimate existential question. What most people don't realize—people who only know that line out of context—is that Hamlet is contemplating suicide."

Sebastian had whispered something to Daisy that made her laugh—something I had never seen her do before. At the words "contemplating suicide," however, they both went silent.

"Now, a lot of people think Hamlet is just a whiny little tool," said Ziggy, "but you need to understand where he's coming from. His dad was murdered by his uncle. His mom has gotten remarried *to* that very same uncle! Who wouldn't be upset? If you ask me, he has every right to complain—even if it's just through the fourth wall to an unseen audience. At first, he's listing off the pros and cons of death, and honestly, it's mostly pros. He compares death to a 'little sleep,' which doesn't sound so bad. But then he wonders: Do we *dream* when we're dead? And if so, would they be bad dreams? Nightmares? The fact of the matter is that our existence after death is unknowable, and it's that sense of the unknown that truly scares him. The only thing greater than that unknown is the inevitability of death. So, if we all die, does it matter when? Does it matter how? Does it matter if our life is taken by another human being? Are we merely prolonging the inevitable? Hamlet is asking the big questions, and he's not just asking them for himself. If you ever get a chance to read his soliloquy, note that he never says 'I' or 'me.' Never. So, when he says 'to be, or not to be,' he's talking about life itself. He's asking whether or not people should exist."

Ziggy interlocked his fingers. Stared infinitely at the floor, through an invisible portal in time.

"When I first read that," he said, "I was going through some heavy stuff in my life. I asked myself, 'Should I exist? Do I have a *reason* for my existence?' And honestly, I couldn't think of one. Not one single reason. But somehow, that didn't make me want to end things the way I thought it would. Instead, it made me want to *find* a reason for my existence. That was the start of a quest for me. Just as I hope that this introduction to Shakespeare will be the start of a quest for you."

Ziggy hoisted his legs onto the ledge and stood up. Tucked his hands behind his back and paced, exploring the generous stage space.

"*Twelfth Night* may not be as heavy as *Hamlet*," he said, "but it tackles some themes: the thin line between love and suffering, the ambiguity of gender, the folly of ambition. Although this is mostly told in the form of a hilarious love triangle."

Ziggy went on to explain the nuts and bolts of *Twelfth Night*: a shipwreck separates Viola from her twin brother, Sebastian. (Yep, a fictional Sebastian. Three guesses who gets *his* part.) Viola thinks Sebastian is dead. She disguises herself as a man, takes on the name Cesario, and gets a job serving Duke Orsino, who she decides is a hunk, a hunk of burning love. Duke Orsino, however, has his sights set on the wealthy countess Olivia. The Duke asks Cesario—aka Viola—to woo Olivia for him. Olivia, however, has a thing for Cesario and confesses her love to "him."

This is the main story of *Twelfth Night*. But there's also a weird side story in which Olivia's steward, Malvolio—who is kind of a pompous dillweed—gets pranked by other characters in Olivia's social sphere into thinking that Olivia has a thing for him. The cast of characters in on this Elizabethan-era episode of *Punk'd* includes: Olivia's chaotic uncle, Sir Toby Belch; her rich would-be suiter, Sir Andrew Aguecheek; her servants, Maria and Fabian; and her melancholy jester, Feste.

Basically, everyone hates Malvolio, and you would, too, if you knew him, and he is about to get what was coming to him

"Now that we've got that out of the way," said Ziggy, "let's talk about auditions. They're happening right now."

The entire circle's reactions ranged from "Huh?" to "Shit" to "Sweet baby Jesus on a unicorn in outer space." That last one was unspoken, but I could see the essence of it in Imogen's eyes.

Okay, maybe I was projecting. That's what *I* was thinking. But to be fair, Imogen didn't seem like she *wasn't* thinking it. Her dilated pupils were like tiny screaming mouths.

Ziggy walked offstage, vanished behind a frumpy red curtain, and returned with a Proustian stack of typed pages. They were divided intermittently by sheets of construction paper, separating individual scripts.

"Here's how this is going to work," said Ziggy. "I'm gonna pass these scripts around. Then I'm going to give you five minutes to collect yourselves."

"Five minutes!" said Imogen, in a high-pitched, last-dying-words sort of way.

"Then you're going to tell me which character—or charact*errrssss*—you're interested in. If you're interested in any. And then you're going to read—or dare I say, *recite*—the lines of your choosing. Then I'll decide the role that I think you're best suited for. This will all be very fast-paced, and I'm sure many of you will think I'm an unfair, authoritarian douchemonger, but we're about a month behind schedule, so that's how we're gonna roll. Any questions?"

The entire theater was a mausoleum of silence. Ziggy hopped down from the stage and was already handing out scripts. If there *were* any questions, they were transmitted in the form of Morse code through our rapidly escalating heartbeats.

He handed the final script to Willow. She accepted it like a copy of her own obituary.

Imogen turned to me and gripped me rather insanely by the shoulders. Her eyes were canvases of painted madness.

"I need the next five minutes exclusively to myself," she said, all in one breath. "Is that okay?"

It was a Shakespearean miracle is what it was.

"Yeah, sure," I said, shrugging casually.

I hadn't even finished saying "sure" before Imogen hugged me, and then slid off her seat and plopped herself on the floor. Seeing as we were in the front row, she immediately set to spreading the pages across the cold, painted concrete, drilling her focus into every line underneath the name Viola.

The miracles didn't stop there. Holden raised a bored hand and asked, "Is there a bathroom? I have to take a massive number two."

"Good god," said Sebastian. "You wanna tell us the texture and consistency while you're at it?"

"I would if I was a fortune-teller," said Holden. "Rain check?"

He winked at Sebastian, who proceeded to make a visible retching motion with his face.

"Out the door, around the corner to the left," Ziggy said, pointing in an ambiguously leftish direction. "The toilet paper's running low, though, and I forgot to buy more, so wipe with trepidation."

Holden was already jogging to the bathroom, shouting, "YOU'RE FIRED, ZIGGY."

After Holden reached the door and slammed it behind him, Ziggy chuckled and said in a low voice, "There's a brand-new twenty-four-pack under the sink. I just wanted to make him sweat."

That comment seemed to push the imagery in Sebastian's visual register into meltdown mode. He gagged.

Meanwhile, I looked at Wynezra, and Wynezra looked at me, and the words our eyeballs said were "We should talk." We both stood up with our scripts and wandered nonchalantly up either aisle of stairs leading to the back of the theater. At this point, I was becoming quite skilled at not walking like an idiot in heels. We stopped several feet apart, backs facing the stage, staring vaguely at the same faded, blood-colored wall.

"I need you to get me the role of Duke Orsino," I said.

"Oh my god," said Wynezra. "Why, pray tell, do you *need* the role of Duke Arsenal?"

"Or-sin-o!"

"Whatever!"

"I *need* it," I said, "because it will get me close to Imogen."

"Oh *gaaawwwwd*," said Wynezra.

"Imogen is obsessed with this play. She's determined to be Viola, and I'm sure she'll get it. She'll put *everything* into this role. And that entire role revolves around her *fawning* over the Duke. We agreed to help each other, right? I need you to do this for me, Wynonna. Will you help me, or won't you?"

"No."

"No?" I said. I wondered if I was mixing up her meaning with a double negative. "No, you won't . . . *not* help me?"

"No, I *won't* help you, Ezra! Not with this. I'm sorry."

"You have to help me! We made a deal. I help you, you help me."

"It's not that I *won't* help you. It's that I *can't* help you."

"What do you mean?"

"Come on. You *have to* know what I mean by now. Don't make me say it."

"Say *what*?" I said. I was thoroughly perturbed at this point. "That you're selfish, dishonest—"

"I'M DYSLEXIC," Wynezra screamed quietly through her teeth. Or my teeth. Once again, I faced the bizarre sensation of a stranger doing things with my face that had never been done before. In this case, I was staring at a version of Ezra Slevin who looked like he could kill me.

And then the words sank in.

"Dyslexic?" I repeated. I couldn't hide the shock in my voice.

"Seriously?" said Wynezra. "You sat through an entire day of my classes. There's no way you didn't notice."

"I mean, they were mostly lectures . . ." I started to say. But I remembered all too clearly Wynonna's Kryptos-wannabe class schedule. The cipheric text messages.

"Shit," I said.

"Yeah," said Wynezra, nodding furiously. "Shit is right. That is what I've had to deal with every day of my entire fucking life. At least, until we started jumping bodies. It may be *your* consciousness, Ezra, but it's stuck inside *my* brain. And my brain was not built to read. Ever."

As I processed what she was saying, I became acutely aware of the stack of pages—filled with words—clutched in my now-sweaty grasp. My eyes wavered ever so slightly.

Wynezra noticed.

"Go ahead," she said. "Look at it. Soak it all in."

I lifted the stack of pages. Slowly, like a spacecraft on an alien planet, my gaze lowered onto the first page.

TLEWFT NHIGT

Atc 1, sence 1. Dkue Osrno'is Pcalea

Etenr DUEK ONISOR, CRIUO, adn oehtr Ldros; Msuicanis anettnidg

DEKU ONISRO

Fi misuc be hte food of lvoe, paly on;
Gvie em excsse oi ft, taht, srufienitg,

Duke Orsino's line—I'm sure it was his—went much further beyond that, but I had to look away, because the letters were moving. The entire page looked like it had been printed on the surface of a small ocean that I was gazing down at from a helicopter view. It was swaying and flowing in such a way that it left me dizzy trying to decipher it.

This was worse than the class schedule. There were too many words. Too many letters and indecipherable characters. They all blurred together into perfect nonsense.

That is what I've had to deal with every day of my entire fucking life.

Wynezra's words were gyrating inside my skull.

At least, until we started jumping bodies.

"Wait," I said. "That's it! We can both read when we're inside *my* body! Wynonna, we can still do this! *You* can still do this. You can read right now. You can get me this part—"

"Are you listening to a word I'm saying, shitwit?" said Wynezra. "Let me spell it out for you: I. Do. Not. Read. EVER. I'm not going to pick up some fucking hobby that's gonna disappear the moment we get this nightmare fixed. I'm *not* going to get this part for you. I'm going to get the most under-the-radar non-role that Ziggy can give me, and if you know what's good for you, you'll do the same because news flash: YOU CAN'T READ EITHER! Not right now. *Those* are the conditions of our agreement, okay?"

There was a part of me that was deeply sympathetic to her plight. Really, there was.

There was also another part of me that was sick and tired of her shit. That hated how she was basically a cooler, more badass version of me. That didn't like her out of pure principle. Had Wynonna ever been nice to me, *ever*? And now—now that I had the biggest blackmail on her since the Alexander Hamilton sex scandal of the 1790s—had anything changed?

If I were going to go to prom with Imogen—and I *would* go to prom with Imogen—I needed to cut Wynonna down to size.

I wouldn't blackmail her. But I had other—more *appropriate*—ways of making her suffer.

"If you don't get me that role," I said, "then I will. As you."

Wynezra laughed. "You'll *what*?"

My face was deadly serious. "I will get you—Wynonna Jones—the role of Duke Orsino."

She snorted. "Good luck with that. You can't read, remember?"

My face didn't budge an inch. I was well aware of what I was capable of.

We stayed like that for a long, intense moment—staring each other down, waiting for the other person to make the next move. Wynezra's eyes chiseled into my so-called poker face, digging for the hint of a bluff. But my face was a fortress, stone-cold and impenetrable.

The stakes had been set. Neither of us was budging.

Wynonna would not get me a meaningful role in this play. She might even get me cast as a mute peasant. Or maybe I'd get stuck backstage, moving props.

The fires of my revenge had been lit. My mercy was a dry field, waiting to be swallowed aflame.

"Uhhhhhhh . . ." said a familiar voice, coming from a sudden figure in our peripheral.

We both turned. There was Holden, mouth slightly ajar, looking at his best friend like a complete stranger. Who could blame him? The mild-mannered, sleepy-eyed, pushover Ezra Slevin of yesterday was gone. In his place was an Ezra Slevin whose cagey eyes were filled with nothing but hate.

He had no idea. He was looking at the wrong Ezra.

"Time's up!" Ziggy called out, hands cupped around his mouth like a megaphone.

Wynezra and I pried our death glares away like a pair of locked antlers—slowly, jaggedly, dubiously—ready to re-engage at a whiff of treachery. When we finally broke free and separated, I cast a sideways glance at Wynezra, hoping she'd make some effort to maintain appearances with Holden.

Nope. She left Holden in the dust. Marched straight to the front row and sat down. Holden trailed awkwardly behind—indecisively—like a lost hiker without a compass.

Goddamn you, Wynonna.

When I sat back down, reclaiming my seat beside Imogen, my irritation had not gone unnoticed.

"Whoa," she said. "What's with the poopy face?"

I took a cavernous breath. Shook my head—mostly as a means of shaking out the fury. Forced the most low-key, Wynonna-like smile I could muster. It was hard to gauge my success without a mirror. I probably looked like Tina Fey telling dad jokes.

"Nothing," I said. "I'm fine. Just about to do something really crazy."

"Crazy?" said Imogen, thoroughly intrigued. "Do tell."

"It's a surprise."

"Ugh. I hate surprises."

"You'll love this one."

Imogen rolled her eyes and smirked. "If you say so."

It wasn't until the theater quieted and Ziggy took to the stage that I realized: I just had a conversation with Imogen. Like, one that didn't involve me nearly hyperventilating, or having a panic attack, or a sexual meltdown.

"All right," said Ziggy. "Any volunteers to go first?"

Imogen's hand shot up in a perfectly straight line from her shoulder, fingers squirming.

"Imogen Klutz," said Ziggy. "And you're auditioning for . . ."

"Viola," said Imogen.

"Ah, the duality of Viola," said Ziggy, nodding approvingly. He stepped back, sweeping his arms across the stage. "The floor is yours."

Imogen stood with uncharacteristic grace—like even *that* was something she rehearsed. Glided softly up the stairs and took to the center of the stage. Pressed her fingertips together like a prayer.

"I left no ring with her," said Imogen. Her voice was an intense hush, her eyes suddenly big and wild with confusion. *"What means this lady? Fortune forbid my outside have not charm'd her!"*

Imogen delivered her lines with delicate fluster. Her gaze barely touched the page. This particular scene was when Viola suspected Olivia had a crush on Cesario—her male alter ego. It was also when she realized she was trapped in a love triangle. She liked Duke Orsino who liked Olivia who liked Cesario/Viola. What a fucking pickle. Imogen conveyed the essence of this pickle with a swooning sort of lamentation. It was funny, sad, and kind of perfect.

"O time! thou must untangle this, not I," Imogen concluded. *"It is too hard a knot for me to untie!"*

Imogen finished with a skirtless curtsy in her pink jeans and sequined cable-knit sweater. Those of us who had a decent respect for humanity and genuine theatrical talent—meaning pretty much everyone but Jayden Hoxsie—applauded and cheered. Imogen smiled bashfully and retreated to her seat.

She *tried* to retreat, at least. Unfortunately, her curtsy did not unfold properly. The toe of one tennis shoe caught behind the other, and she biffed it, face-first. Her hair softly fell over her face like a burial shroud.

"Jesus Christ!" said Wynezra. She was already out of her seat, on her knees, helping Imogen up before any of us could swear properly. "Are you okay?"

Unlike me at Imogen's last biffing, Wynezra was all hands aboard. Her hands found the right, appropriate places on Imogen's shoulder and abdomen, pulling her up while she steadied herself on her hands and knees. When Imogen knelt upright, Wynezra brushed the hair out of her face. Particularly the matted lumps sticking to the blood between her nose and split upper lip.

I studied the art of Ezra Slevin being a hero to Imogen like a prophetic vision.

"Oh god," said Wynezra. "We need to get you cleaned up. Here, let's—"

By then, it seemed to sink into her head who she *was* and who she *was not*—aesthetically speaking.

". . . let's . . ." Wynezra stammered, "let *Wynonna* clean you up." She sent me a "Get your ass over here" look, accompanied by a slight but demanding head gesture.

"Yeah, yeah, yeah," I said, nodding like a complete idiot.

I hurried over, then hesitated awkwardly, fumbling for the best way to help Imogen up. She made things easy for me—grabbing my shoulder, pulling me down, and draping herself over me like a mink scarf.

"Okay . . ." I said, hoisting her up. "Here we go. Easy. Watch your step."

We staggered to the restroom. Halfway there, I heard a choking gasp. I looked at Imogen, her face obscured by curtains of sandy hair.

A series of tears had accumulated at the bottom of her chin, then dropped to the floor.

When we made it into the restroom—a surprisingly clean, single-toilet deal—she braced herself on the sink. She turned on the faucet, cupping her hands beneath the steady stream. Splashed water in her face repeatedly, erasing the blood. Erasing the pain.

"Are you . . . okay?" I said.

Imogen gave a helpless shrug. "Are any of us ever *really* okay?"

"Uh . . ."

"It's like Hamlet said: To be alive is to be in a state of dying. That's just the human condition."

"Um . . ." I said.

C'mon, Ezra. Words!

"I'm pretty sure the human condition is more than just dying," I said. "Like, there's gotta be *at least* one whole section about living."

Imogen laughed—a short, on-the-edge-of-tears sort of laugh. Her lips pulled into a frail smile. "What do you know about the human condition?"

"I know that I'm here for you."

Imogen bit her lip.

"I know that if you're *carrying* something," I said, "you don't have to carry it alone."

Imogen let out a sharp, jagged breath, like a serrated blade. It seemed to take everything in her not to start crying again.

"It's just . . ." she said, "I feel bad for Viola."

"What? Viola? The *character*?"

I stared at her while she stared at her reflection in the mirror.

"She's trapped," said Imogen. "She loves someone, but that person loves someone else, and even if he *didn't*, she's trapped in a role that prevents them from ever being together."

"But they *do* end up together," I said. "I mean . . . don't they? They do in *She's the Man*, so I just assumed they do in *Twelfth Night*."

"I guess," said Imogen. "But Viola doesn't know that. Not yet."

What the . . . Did this have to do with the mystery guy Wynonna said Imogen had a crush on?

Who was I kidding? Of course it did! Man, who the hell was this guy? And why was Wynonna so convinced they'd never get together?

"You know," I said, "you don't have to be someone else around me."

Imogen pulled her gaze away from the mirror. Looked directly at me.

"I want to be best friends with the *real* Imogen Klutz," I said. "*Whoever* that is. Not the fake Cesario version."

Imogen sniffed. Dabbed her eyes with her sweater sleeve. Offered the first real smile I had seen all day.

"Thanks, Wynonna," she said. "That means a lot to me."

• •

When Imogen and I finally rejoined the circle, auditions were nearly finished. It was a fairly brief process because most of these kids didn't give a shit. There were exceptions, though. Sebastian auditioned for the role of Sebastian—surprise, surprise—and he nailed it. Tucker was shockingly literate and took his audition seriously—despite auditioning for the role of Gandalf. (He read the lines of Sir Toby Belch, the crazy uncle.) And then there was Daisy, who proceeded to recite more words than I had heard her speak in a lifetime.

The Shyamalan-level plot twist of them all, however, was Jayden. I wouldn't go so far as to call him "the best male performance"—honestly, that probably (bafflingly) went to Tucker—but he was good. Really good. And even weirder, he wasn't a total douche about it.

Holden was next—he volunteered to go before Wynezra—and performed his role with a sort of cultish fervor he usually reserved for worshipping the hacktivist group Anonymous. This was weird especially because he was auditioning for either Curio or Valentine, which were non-roles. However, they were also Duke Orsino's servants and basically his best bros. Holden was clearly trying to be in a role close to me.

Little did he know, Wynonna was going to fuck things up catastrophically.

"Very good, very good," said Ziggy, clapping. "All righty, Ezra. You're next."

Wynezra stood up, winked at me, and strutted up the stairs to the center of the stage. Then she extended her long, ropy arms like she was pinned to a clothesline. Her face became brazenly emotionless as she stared straight ahead.

And said nothing.

"Uh . . ." said Ziggy. He glanced precariously at an open folder in his hands, purportedly outlining the cast of characters. "And you're auditioning as . . ."

Wynezra leaned slightly toward Ziggy but otherwise remained stiff and lifeless.

"I'm a tree," she whispered.

The entire theater fell apart with laughter. Literally everyone joined in—even Jayden, who should have hated the bold, new Ezra Slevin at this point.

Everyone except Holden and me—two best friends who were sitting right next to each other, and yet light-years apart.

All because of this clown masquerading in my body.

Wynonna fucking Jones, you are going down.

"A tree?" said Ziggy.

"Or a billboard," said Wynezra. "Did they have billboards back then? Really, I'm flexible in the inanimate object department."

"Suit yourself, amigo," said Ziggy. He clucked his tongue with disappointment and checked something off in his folder. "Wynonna, you're up."

I took a deep breath. Stood up. Ascended the stairs and stepped onto the center of the stage.

I did not bring my script with me.

"What role are you auditioning for?" said Ziggy.

"Duke Orsino," I said flatly.

I noticed Imogen's mouth fall open. I noticed Wynezra drop her head in her hands. I *even* noticed Holden, wide-eyed, as he seemed to study the very fabric of reality around him. Surely, there was a tear in the multiverse that had sucked him into this alternate dimension.

Before I could notice another thing, I closed my eyes, cleared my throat, and said:

"But soft! what light through yonder window breaks?
It is the east, and Juliet is the sun.
Arise, fair sun, and kill the envious moon,
Who is already sick and pale with grief,
That thou her maid art far more fair than she . . ."

I barely had to think the words. They just . . . came out of me. Like they had always been there. A part of the bedrock of my very being. In the window of my mind, I saw nine-year-old Imogen standing on the balcony of a cardboard castle tower. (Technically, she was standing on a small ladder. The magic of the moment, however, made that cardboard castle real.) Meanwhile, I—nine-year-old Ezra Slevin—stood off to the side, hiding behind cardboard shrubbery, lost in a character who was lost in her eyes.

"She speaks yet she says nothing: what of that?
Her eye discourses; I will answer it."

Imogen had yet to hit her Jack Skellington–level growth spurt. She was still swimming in baby fat, and she was beautiful. Her face was a perfect, da Vincian circle—rounder than the puff sleeves of her princess dress—eyes wandering dreamily across the lights of the stage. She pretended to prop two chubby elbows on the cardboard balcony railing and rested a cherubic cheek in her palm.

"See! how she leans her cheek upon her hand
O! that I were a glove upon that hand,
That I might touch that cheek!"

That was it.

I was done.

I opened my eyes—only to discover that the world had become a still frame. Wordless, breathless, frozen.

Finally, the dilation in the space-time continuum seemed to catch up with itself. Everyone shot up like the earthy shock wave of a meteor impact, exploding with applause. Even Jayden Hoxsie applauded, which was a conundrum of sorts. The notable exception was Wynezra, whose jaw appeared to be flying south for the winter.

And then there was Imogen. She was clapping, but she was also staring at me with complete perplexity. Like I was an alien.

Like I was someone she didn't even know.

Ziggy didn't waste a moment announcing the official roles. He vanished behind the mobile whiteboard and scribbled furiously with his purple dry-erase marker. It was during this brief interval that—*flash*—Wynonna and I were back in our bodies.

Thank god. I wasn't too keen on going home to a place that wasn't my *actual* home.

"Oh man," said Ziggy. "Oh man, oh man. Are you guys excited? Because *I'm* excited."

The reactions were wide-ranging. Some groaned. Some laughed nervously. Others—like Imogen—took the phrase "edge of your seat" to a literal level. The amount of chair she actually sat on was molecular. Her arms and legs, meanwhile, were wound together like cinnamon twists.

Ziggy grabbed the whiteboard by one side and turned it. At the very top, like the foreshadowing of a Shakespearean tragedy, were two words:

Viola: Wynonna.

SEVEN

IT TOOK ME A long moment to pull my gaze away from those two names, and the colon that separated them. That *joined* them. I scraped my eyes downward, and the sound they made in my head was a fingernails-on-chalkboard sort of sensation.

Duke Orsino: Holden

Olivia: Imogen

Sebastian: Sebastian

Malvolio: Willow

Maria: Daisy

Sir Toby Belch: Jayden

Sir Andrew Aguecheek: Patrick

Feste: Tucker

Fabian: Thad

There were eighteen roles total, and I had to drag my gaze down all eighteen of them—like I was dragging my face across a grocery aisle strewn with broken glass—until I came across my name at the very bottom.

Servant: Ezra

I was a nameless role.

Considering Wynonna auditioned for the role of a *tree*, I should have counted myself blessed. Or—agnostically speaking—lucky. Or—scientifically speaking—the axiomatic mathematical outcome of probability theory. Who was I to say? All I knew was that the Flying Spaghetti Monster hadn't done shit for me lately.

I glanced at Wynonna, expecting her to protest. Surely, now that she was herself, she would drop out of the role. And if Ziggy wouldn't let her, then she would drop out of theater.

But she didn't. Instead, she was looking at Imogen.

Imogen looked shattered.

If vengeance was measured in how deeply you damage a person—regardless of collateral damage—then I had succeeded. It was the revenge of hurting the ones you love. It was the worst kind.

Wynonna could drop out of theater, sure. But nothing could undo the damage I had done.

• •

We weren't the only ones upset about the casting. Willow cornered Ziggy after things wrapped up.

"Malvolio?" said Willow, like it was an STD. "Isn't he, like, the worst role?"

"What does that mean: 'the worst role'?" said Ziggy. "Malvolio's the fifth *largest* role, and you've got some killer acting chops. Not everyone can pull off a role like Malvolio, Willow, but I think you can."

"But doesn't everyone hate him? Doesn't the *audience* hate him?"

"Malvolio's a complex character. Yeah, he's not very likable. But that doesn't mean he isn't important. I think we can learn a lot from Malvolio's behavior and how the other characters treat him."

Willow seemed deeply unsatisfied with that answer, but she gave up trying to fight for a different role.

I waited outside the entrance of the warehouse—arms folded, leaning against the tin wall—in a mild, friendly ambush.

"Hey!" I said as Willow walked out.

Willow jumped, placed a hand over her heart, and successfully failed to have a heart attack.

"Jesus!" said Willow. "What is with you today? You're acting really"—she hesitated, rummaging for the right word—"different."

"Oh, you know . . ." I said, and shrugged. As if that *meant* something and wasn't a total evasion of her question. "Hey, do you need a ride?"

"Oh. No, I'm good."

"You're *good*?"

"I already have a ride."

"With who?"

"Thad Magnino."

Here's what I knew about Thad: It was short for Thaddeus. He was Jayden Hoxsie's best friend, he was a junior, and he was here—an honorary member of theater, god knows why. Sexual harassment, maybe? He had moppy blond surfer hair, a tan, too many wristbands, and a reputation for being a total player. In the *Douchimus maximus* family, Thad was an apex predator.

"Thad?" I said. "You're kidding, right?"

The thick black lines of Willow's eyes narrowed. She shook her head. "I've gotta go."

She walked past me.

"Wait!" I said. "What are you doing here? Did you get in trouble? Do Mom and Dad know about it?"

Willow snapped rigid. She whipped around.

"Do Mom and Dad know about *anything*?" she said. "Do they know *you're* here?"

I didn't know what to say to that.

"Fuck you, Ezra," she said, and she stormed off.

• •

The drive home was awkward and silent.

Holden asked if he could be dropped off first. That's when I knew things were bad.

After I dropped Holden off, Imogen asked if she could be next.

"Actually," said Wynonna, "I was wondering if you wanted to hang out!"

This was the first thing Wynonna said to Imogen the entire drive. Really, it was the first thing anyone said to anyone.

"I can't," said Imogen, standoffishly. "I have . . . a thing."

"A thing?" said Wynonna.

Imogen nodded, not even making eye contact with Wynonna.

"Oh," said Wynonna. "Okay."

By the time we dropped Imogen off, the tension in the car had amplified tenfold. As I drove Wynonna back to the Lakes, I opened my mouth. My hope was that words would come out—miraculously, of their own volition—and somehow mend the state of things.

"Don't," said Wynonna.

"But—" I said.

"No."

When we arrived at the Lakes, Wynonna stepped out of the car. But she didn't shut the door. Not right away. Instead, she seethed, allowing her fury to intensify.

"You won this round," she said. "But this isn't over yet."

“Wynonna, wait,” I said. “I’m not trying to *win* any—”

Wynonna slammed the car door, marched up to the entryway of the Lakes, and vanished behind the glass, reflecting the bleeding colors of the falling sun.

EIGHT

I WOKE UP. THAT ALONE was a bad sign.

But then there was the crushing migraine, like my head was pinned beneath the tire of a Ford Super Duty, the churning feeling of everything on my inside wanting to be on my outside, and a half-drained bottle of pinot noir on Wynonna's nightstand. Sweaty clumps of blue hair were matted across my face, and my breath—if I had to brand it and give it a name—smelled like Eviscerated Decomposing Corpse®.

I groaned and rolled onto my side. There was Wynonna fucking Jones, staring bleary-eyed back at me through the reflection in her mirror-paneled sliding closet door. Vomit was crusted on my chin, and all over the Echo & the Bunnymen T-shirt I was wearing.

Great.

Only twenty-four hours into this nightmare, and I was *sooooooo* past feeling embarrassed in a girl's body. I crawled out of bed with all the maneuverability of a tank, marched straight to the bathroom, and stripped naked. I shed Wynonna's vomit-y clothes like a snake sheds its skin—with purpose, a natural evolution, no looking back. I immediately stepped into the shower and cranked the heat and water pressure to I Don't Want to Have Skin Anymore. Hot jets rained down on me, washing away the sick and the sweat and the self-destruction of yesterday.

Finally, after several minutes of physical and spiritual cleansing, I was drawn against my better judgment to glance down.

Now, I'm no virgin when it comes to nudity. (Only when it comes to sex.) I've seen all of *Game of Thrones*. And after *Game of Thrones*, what is there possibly left to see?

The answer is: a lot.

Wynonna's body was weird. And I don't mean that as "unattractive." More like *unexpected*. Her tits had a bizarre shape (not as round as I expected), and her nipples had a strange color (brown, very brown), and then there was the so-called va-jim-jam. Except it was kind of hard to get a good look at it because it was covered in hair.

Again, nothing unattractive about it. It was just . . . weird. Like I was an astronaut exploring the surface of an alien planet. Unexpected and intriguing.

Getting dressed was a different experience today. Maybe it was just the cataclysmically rough start to my morning, or the shitstain-of-a-day that was yesterday, but I really felt like *not* looking like shit.

I pulled on some plain blue panties that fit comfortably. There was maybe a part of me that thought I had to match Wynonna's hair and nails. Then I rummaged through Wynonna's jeans until I found what *I* thought were the nicest pair. They were the only pair that were solid charcoal, with no fake rips or tears. They were skinny and formfitting, but not thick and stiff—unlike nearly every pair of jeans I had ever owned. The material was flexible and fit like a glove around my ass—an assglove—which *sounds* horribly invasive, but god, they felt so right!

Next up: the bra.

I settled on a blue one that matched my underwear—not that

anyone would know, but *I* would, and matching seemed important to my mental health right now. There seemed to be a lot of straps involved, however, and it took me a solid thirty seconds to figure out which end was the top. It then took me *five whole minutes* to realize that the only way to clip it together was around my waist. When I solved *that* mystery, it slid up smoothly, and sliding my arms into the shoulder straps was easy-peasy.

Picking out a shirt was kind of fun. Wynonna had *tons* of them, and plenty of cool ones at that. I don't think I truly appreciated her '80s obsession until this moment, looking at her shirts. They extended far beyond '80s bands, although the bands she had were stellar—the Smiths, New Order, Depeche Mode, Siouxsie and the Banshees, Joy Division.

She had an *Akira* shirt.

She had a FRANKIE SAYS RELAX shirt.

She had a *They Live* shirt with alien newscasters and a teleprompter that said WATCH TV.

Most of the T-shirts were boxy, however, and fit me weird. I assumed they were probably designed for men. (Fucking sexist corporate agenda, as Holden would say.) So I settled for an off-white Rainbow Brite tank top that was, not gonna lie, *totally* badass in a way that only Wynonna could pull off, and—because I felt a little weird about my bra straps—a cropped red faux-leather biker jacket. It ended in daring red corners at my rib cage—exposing Rainbow Brite atop her trusty, rainbow-maned steed, Starlite, dashing across an actual fucking rainbow, boo-yah.

I slipped on ankle socks, a pair of checkered Vans, and stepped in front of the mirror.

Overall, everything checked out—maybe even checked out *nicely*! Except for the hair. The hair was a great blue disaster.

Shit. How did Wynonna do her hair?

Wynonna's hair ended mostly at her chin, but it was hardly straight. Nothing ended at the same length. Everything about her style felt organic. It swerved off to one side—her right side; left, if you were looking at her—and it just sort of . . . splayed. She *did* often wear beanies, but it was hardly like she just showered and threw a hat on her head. She did *something* with it. But what? Did she use a product?

I returned to the bathroom and opened the medicine cabinets.

It was like opening the door to a meth lab.

There were balms, and clays, and matte texturizers. Root-boosting powder, and dry powder shampoo, and volume paste. Sugar spritz, and sea-salt spray, and light molding cream.

Okay. Fuck the hair.

I grabbed a comb, parted my hair on the left, and shoved a beanie on my head.

• •

It wasn't that I didn't know *how* to drive a stick. It's just that—in the spectrum of things I was good at—operating a stick ranked only slightly higher than my ability to do Wynonna's hair.

But that was before I was a girl, trapped in a fancy condo, with no means of escape except either a ride from Wynezra . . . or a stick shift. And since today was all about learning to put on bras and contemplating the possibility of feminine hair product, then what the hell—I'd take my chances with the stick.

I grabbed Wynonna's keys, lying atop her dresser, and ventured into the parking garage. I still had no idea what her car looked like, but my beacon of hope was the clicker on her key chain. I mashed the unlock button like I was playing *Mortal Kombat*. The distant honking echo led me to a green '93 Saturn.

Okay, Wynonna Jones. Let's see what you can do.

• •

In normal circumstances, I was only vaguely aware of the vehicles around me. Aware enough to not merge into them. To travel safely from Point A to Point B. But I didn't, like, take special note of the make, model, and specific shade of color of the vehicles to be compiled in my top secret "morning traffic" dossier.

I was *acutely* aware of a Chevy Malibu trailing lazily behind me—a clandestine shade of Government Espionage Black. It never attempted to pass me. On the contrary, it seemed eager to see how many full stops I could screw up. I was sure I wasn't disappointing.

I stalled at three stop signs and two lights—at one of which I stalled *multiple* times in a row. I *almost* stalled all the way through a green light. Everyone behind me moved to the other lane, passing me indignantly, until there was no one left behind me. It was only at the very end, when it started to turn yellow, that I finally made it through. Getting going again after a complete stop was always the hardest part for me—that balance between letting off the clutch and putting on the gas. But that incident successfully got me flipped off by three separate people. The last middle finger came from a truck with two college-age guys. The driver slowed, and the guy in the passenger seat rolled his window down.

"Fucking bitches," said the guy in the passenger seat. "I told you. Fucking bitches never know how to drive."

He then offered me the finger, and the driver punched the gas.

I wondered what Wynonna would have said or done in that situation. Even though I knew Wynonna would never stall like that, the potential scenarios made me smile.

Then I thought: What would *Sebastian* have done in that situation?

Probably follow them home from an inconspicuous distance, go to a costume shop, dress up like Freddy Krueger, and let his imagination run wild from there.

That scenario made me laugh—even if it was just to myself in a car I could barely drive.

I laughed until I glanced in my rearview mirror.

The black Malibu was still behind me.

Every hair follicle on my body spiked in an upward wave—from my toes to the nape of my neck.

How could he *still* be behind me? He should have passed me at the last light. *Everyone* passed me at that light. Was he following me?

He.

It *was* a he—a man in a ball cap, aviators, and rocking a full beard like it was part of the disguise.

Of course, the moment he seemed to notice me noticing *him*, he turned. Vanished down an empty neighborhood street.

I blinked several times, wondering if I had imagined the whole thing.

I spent the rest of the drive glancing at my rearview mirror, neurotically. The Malibu never reappeared.

• •

Now that I *knew* I was dyslexic—or rather, that the body and mind I *inhabited* was dyslexic—I saw the signs everywhere. (Aside from the letters of the English alphabet being alive, and moving, and not entirely English anymore.) Several of Wynonna's classes were smaller than average. They seemed designed to meet the needs of certain students in a low-profile manner. It was difficult to pin down exactly what those needs *were*, but it was clear they existed. I noticed teachers wander and check in on particular students. Sometimes repeatedly. If something didn't seem to be working, it wasn't uncommon for the teacher to squash the lesson like Play-Doh, and then reshape it into something else entirely.

In the case of Wynonna—who had the social niceties of barbed wire—the attention to her needs was in the structure. Her teachers kept their notes as verbal as possible—hence the lecture-y nature of yesterday. Today, however, was more discussion-oriented. Some teachers also incorporated an abundance of imagery. The one teacher who *did* lecture used a PowerPoint, and—now that I was paying attention—I couldn't help but notice each slide was low on words and high on visual stimulation.

They were the sorts of classes where you didn't recognize the effort until you looked for it. Suddenly, it was all you could see.

I sort of became lost in my observations. Before I knew it, the fourth-period bell rang, and I was staring down the barrel of the existential shotgun known as lunch period. Where the high school hierarchy separated like oil and water—the losers from the cool kids, the riffraff from the gods and goddesses, the Weirdos Who Are Not Okay from the People Who Wear Masks of Normalcy and Okayness.

Considering that I was Wynonna, I figured I ought to wear a particular mask of normalcy and okayness and sit with Imogen.

Except I couldn't find her.

Not at her normal table, not in the lunch line, not anywhere.

Amidst the rush of warm bodies, the roar of blurring conversations, and the clatter of trays and silverware, Imogen's absence was loud. Blaring.

As if I wasn't expecting this.

It was a throbbing scar in my memory. I could still see the shattered look on her face. She lost the role she longed for, and to who? Her best friend who didn't want it. And yet, here was some facade of Wynonna, auditioning for Duke Orsino out of nowhere, quoting Romeo like it was *The Princess Bride.*

Shit! Like, in *what* universe would Wynonna have memorized lines from *Romeo and Juliet*? God, what was I thinking?

I wondered which was worse for Imogen: The betrayal? Or the creeping uncertainty that her best friend was not actually her best friend?

Imogen's dizzying absence left me reeling, desperate for stability. It was under those circumstances that I saw *my* best friend—Holden Durden—sitting alone, and confused, and kind of helpless.

Of course, Ezra wasn't there. Wynonna probably woke up in my body, was upset that she didn't have a crippling hangover, and set out in search of other mind-altering substances to slosh her consciousness into oblivion.

I sat down beside Holden.

"Hey," I said.

Holden looked at me like I was wearing a neon-pink '80s-themed straitjacket with shoulder pads and matching leg warmers.

"Can I sit here?" I said.

Holden continued to stare a moment longer. Then he returned his focus to his uneaten meat loaf and shrugged. "You can do whatever you want."

He poked his meat loaf with his fork. It didn't move or screech or anything, so I guess that was good. Finally, he set the fork down and took a swig of chocolate milk.

"Whoever thought that meat should be cooked in a 'loaf,'" I said, air-quoting, "should have their procreation privileges revoked."

Holden nearly spewed his chocolate milk. He only barely managed to choke it down, and even then, some of it seeped out of the corner of his mouth and dribbled down his chin.

"I mean, people say the word 'loaf,'" I continued, "and I can only hear my dad saying 'pinch a loaf.' And then I can't do it. I just can't do it anymore."

Apparently, Holden didn't choke *all* of it down. Because the moment I said that, we had an Old Faithful situation. Chocolate milk on his meat loaf, chocolate milk on *my* meat loaf, and splatters of chocolate milk in between. It was like a really gross Rorschach test.

"Easy there, buddy," I said. "You need a napkin?"

Holden was still laughing, wiping his mouth with his bare hands. "Oh god. I need a towel. Or a shower." He glanced at my meat loaf with its freshly spewed chocolate milk glaze. "Sorry about that."

"Psh! Please. I'd rather eat my own liposuction."

"Oh my GOD," said Holden. He was on the verge of tears. "Stop it. You're going to make me gag on my own tongue."

"I'd like to see that."

Holden shook his head as he pulled napkins one by one out of a napkin dispenser. "Whatever. It's not like you'd ever need liposuction anyway."

Holden's entire countenance seemed to change. At first, I thought he was becoming standoffish. It took me a second to remember that I wasn't myself, I was Wynonna Jones, and—holy shit—was Holden blushing?

It was less like *actual* blushing, and more like everything that came *with* the act of blushing: the timid smiling, the fidgety eye contact, the fact that he was *still* pulling napkins out of the napkin dispenser. Like, Jesus, how many napkins did he need? His mind was *totally* not connected to his body at the moment.

Holy shit, holy shit, holy shit.

On the one hand, this was super weird. My best friend was crushing on me. Even if I wasn't—strictly speaking—*me*. The sexual tension was there, and it was thick.

On the other hand . . . I felt powerful.

It's not like I was *hungry* for power. I wasn't aspiring to be some railroad tycoon-ing, newspaper magnate-ing, Donald Trump–ing orange megalomaniac. Or a Dark Lord. But the power was there. It was real. It was a gravitational pull around my very being, and Holden had been sucked into my orbit.

It felt good.

Whoa, whoa, whoa. Okay, Sméagol. Put your Precious away for half a goddamn second. We had a job to do. At least, we did if we wanted Wynonna's help. And I *needed* her help if I wanted to go to prom with Imogen. What better way to make amends with her—to get back on track with the Plan—than to get her a foot in the door with Holden?

"Do you wanna hang out?" I asked.

Holden looked at me like I had asked him what the universe was made out of.

"After school," I said. "You know, since . . ."

The implication was: You're a best friend short, and I'm a best friend short, so . . .

"What's going on?" said Holden.

"Uh," I said.

"Why is Ezra acting so strange? In fact, why are *you* acting so strange? You both started acting strange at the same time—the *exact* same time—and I refuse to believe that it isn't connected."

Holden leaned forward until he was uncomfortably close to my face. Studied me like a Sudoku puzzle.

"Did you two have sex?" he asked.

"WHAT?"

"It's fine if you did," said Holden. He leaned back, folding his arms. "I'm not judging. I just want to know what the hell's going on."

It was such an outrageous accusation, I could barely form a response.

"N-n-n-no," I stuttered finally. I had to mentally remind myself who I was. "*Ezra* and I . . . did NOT . . . have s—"

"How did you quote Romeo?"

The question caught me off guard. "What?"

"Yesterday," said Holden. "You recited *Romeo and Juliet* during your audition. You were quoting Romeo *specifically.* I only know that because my best friend in the whole world has those *same fucking lines* memorized. He played Romeo in elementary school, and it was, like, the pinnacle of his entire existence. So how do *you* have those lines memorized?"

My mouth opened and closed like a goldfish.

"And while we're at it," said Holden, "Duke Orsino?! That was the *one* role Ezra was dead set on getting. And suddenly, he's a psychopath who wants to be a tree, and you're fluent in Shakespeare and are gunning for the role instead. And don't even get me *started* on that vengeful look on your face. You were auditioning for that role like you were getting back at someone. And that someone was Ezra. Am I right? Tell me that I'm wrong. I *dare* you to tell me that I'm wrong."

I had to hand it to Holden: He was observant. His penchant for conspiracy theories probably only helped the situation.

"Here's what I think happened," said Holden. "I think you were picking on Ezra like you always do. And I think you always pick on him because *maybe* you have a thing for him. And I'll just say it: Ezra is a pretty sexually frustrated guy."

Wow. Thanks, buddy.

"Anyway," he continued, "one thing leads to another. Suddenly, the sexual tension pops, and you guys just do it. Like, in the janitor's closet, maybe."

I raised a dubious eyebrow.

"Okay, maybe not the janitor's closet. It's not important *where* you guys did it. The important thing is that you *did*. You did *it*. You banged. Maybe Ezra lured you in quoting Romeo or something. Yeah, that's where you learned it! Ezra's smooth Romeo lines. You swooned over those words, and you memorized them in your heart, and then you banged."

My god. Did Holden live in a daytime soap opera?

"But then it was weird," said Holden. His eyes drifted as he thought. "And maybe Ezra realized he didn't have a thing for you. That maybe he made a big mistake. And that turned him into an angsty psycho. And you—heartbroken—decided to exact revenge upon him, using the very same Romeo lines with which he swooned you."

Holden ended his rant sort of breathless. He returned his focus to me.

"Am I close?" he said—suddenly not so sure of himself.

Okay, here was the thing: Wynonna and I had a lot of explaining to do. We had inadvertently burned bridges for each other—perhaps the most important bridges of all: our friendships—and with those bridges burned, we couldn't very well help each other out.

But maybe Holden was onto something with this "sex" scenario. It could explain my and Wynonna's irrational behavior. It could explain why we had inexplicably distanced ourselves from our best friends.

And, in all honesty, it was nothing for Holden and Imogen to get upset over. If anything, Holden and Imogen would be sympathetic! They knew about our *real* crushes. They would know that this was a mistake on our parts—a lapse in good judgment, driven by our tortured hearts.

It could draw the four of us closer together. Which could make my and Wynonna's jobs *sooooo* much easier.

I gave a great sigh, like the proverbial jig was finally up.

"I can explain," I said.

• •

I basically fed Holden's story right back to him. Because he had hypothesized the whole thing on his own, I didn't even have to convince him of anything.

"I knew it!" he said. "Goddammit, I knew it!"

He looked rather proud of himself—which was good. Feeling proud meant he wasn't angry.

"Ezra and I screwed up," I said, in conclusion. "He and I both know that. We want to make things normal again. But it might take a while for things to adjust. Some days, Ezra might not be himself. I might not be *myself*. We need your and Imogen's help in that department. Ezra needs *your* help."

"Yeah, yeah, of course," said Holden, nodding.

"I know about his crush on Imogen."

"Holy shit! He *told* you?"

"We had sex. Is that *really* more surprising than us having sex?"

Holden had to think about that for a second. Shook his head slowly. "No. I guess not."

"Okay, so . . . look. It's probably best if I talk to Ezra first. Let him know that I talked to you. In the meantime, can I ask a favor?"

"Uh . . . sure?"

"Can you talk to Imogen?"

"What? You want *me* to talk to her?"

"I don't know where she is. And even if I *did*, I don't know if she'd talk to me. She really wanted to be Viola, and . . . well, you were there."

Holden bit his lip. Nodded thoughtfully.

"If you talk to her," I said, "maybe she won't be mad at me anymore. Then I can help you matchmake Ezra and Imogen."

Holden received that last bit like a baseball to the head. He sort of wobbled back in his seat for balance. "Wait. You'll *help* us?"

"Dude," I said. "The sooner they're together, the sooner all this awkwardness will be behind us. Why *wouldn't* I help you?"

Holden looked me dead in the eyes—dead as a redshirt in *Star Trek*.

Then he cracked a grin. He extended his hand to shake on it.

"Wynonna," he said, Humphrey Bogart–esquely, "I think this is the beginning of a beautiful friendship."

• •

I was still Wynonna by the end of school, so I hightailed it to my house. *Ezra's* house. I only stalled once, but it was at a stop sign in my neighborhood with no witnesses. So it was *almost* like it never happened.

All the while, I kept my eyes peeled for that shady-as-fuck Malibu with its matching driver.

No Malibu. No skeezy bearded dude, dressed for a stakeout. The drive home was completely sketch-free.

When I finally pulled into my cul-de-sac, I came to a *verrrrry* slow stop in front of my house.

There was another strange vehicle in the driveway. The good news was that it wasn't the Malibu. The bad news was that it was a douchey-looking short-bed Escalade. It was the sort of flashy identity-crisis-of-a-vehicle you drove when you wanted the *reputation* of a truck but none of the responsibility. The best compliment I could give it was that it wasn't Jayden's pimped-out Honda Civic.

I put the Saturn in neutral, pulled up the parking brake, turned off the engine, and stalked up the driveway. I passed the Escalade and went straight to the garage door. Raised myself on my tiptoes and peeked through the small garage window.

My Subaru was still inside.

I marched to the front door with my arms straight, fists pinned to my hips. My hand reached for the doorknob like I was going to strangle it. It was only with the greatest self-control that I stopped myself.

I knocked instead.

I heard silent whispering from inside. Then silence.

The door opened. On the other side was Thad Magnino.

Thad looked me up and down like I was a piece of meat—the exotic sort that wasn't exactly his type but that he was willing to try at least once. His snacky eyes made me feel like I was wearing Saran wrap for clothes. Like I was somebody's fucking leftovers in the fridge, up for grabs.

"Can I help you?" said Thad. He paused before adding, sort of hopefully, "Are you one of Willow's friends?"

"I need to talk to Ezra," I said flatly.

"Oh." There was disappointment in his expression, but also something else. Like he was silently evaluating a challenge. "Well, Ezra's not home right now—"

"Ezra!" I yelled.

"Whoa, what the— I just told you, he's not home!"

"EZRA SLEVIN, I KNOW YOU'RE HERE."

"What the hell?" This came from Willow. She approached the doorway, every inch of her crawling with irritation. And then the recognition clicked. "You're that girl from theater." And then, back to irritation. "What do you want?"

I *wanted* her to explain what the fuck this guy from *my grade* was doing answering the door to *my house*, hanging out with *my little sister*, who was a freshman, for god's sake! But I couldn't very well say that because I wasn't me.

Fortunately, Wynezra appeared at the top of the stairs, wearing a sleepy but curious expression. The floor creaked beneath her feet, and that made both Willow and Thad jump and spin.

"Ezra?" said Willow, slightly traumatized. "How long have you been here?"

Wynezra glanced lazily at a watch that wasn't on her wrist, then chuckled and shrugged. "Since . . . all day?"

Willow's eyes became distant, like a small universe inside her head was imploding and disintegrating into stardust.

"Well, it's been a pleasure," I said to no one in particular, marched upstairs, grabbed Wynezra by the arm, and pulled her into my bedroom.

I closed the door and threw my back against it, as if that might magically make it soundproof.

"What the fuck?" I said, as if that adequately encapsulated all the questions I was trying to ask.

"Dude, I just wasn't feeling like school today—" said Wynezra.

"No, no, no, no, no," I said. "Not you. What the fuck are *they* doing?"

"What? Your sister and Player McGee?"

"Yes!"

Wynezra's eyes wandered and her lips puckered into a small, secretive hole. "I'm not sure you want to know."

I grabbed Wynezra by the biceps, wide-eyed and vaguely psychopathic. "Tell me."

"Okay, well . . ." said Wynezra. "It starts with a *B*."

"Uh-huh," I said, nodding, and racking my brain over every sinister thing I could think of that started with the letter *B*.

"And ends with 'lowjob.' "

I stopped nodding. The axis of my neck seized up.

"Look, I just didn't want to say the word," said Wynezra, hands raised in a cease-fire. "But yeah, your sister gave Dick Tracy the ol' mouth-to-south. I saw them when I snuck downstairs to forage for food."

My jaw had lost the ability to close. It was hanging by the sinews.

"Sorry," said Wynezra, as an afterthought.

"WHY WOULD SHE DO THAT?" I said in a soft, calm, falsetto scream.

"Dude, I don't know," said Wynezra. She flopped on my bed, clearly losing interest in the conversation. "Sometimes girls do things. For reasons."

"What reason could there *possibly* be?"

"Okay, you are *clearly* new at the girl thing. I'll spell it out for you in easy-to-understand words: She obviously likes him. I mean, aside from the fact that he's a total tool bag, he's got a sexy California surfer thing going on."

"No." I shook my head. "Something's wrong."

"She's your little sister. I get it. No one likes to see their little sister with anyone."

"No!" I insisted. "I mean . . . just two days ago, Jayden Hoxsie was here."

"Jayden? As in *Thad's best friend*."

"Yeah, same one who's in *Twelfth Night* with us. Except when *he* was here, Willow was really mad at him for something. Screaming 'fuck you' and stuff. And I've seen other random cars here, too—all guys from school. I've seen her mad at at least half of them, but she won't tell me anything. I'm telling you, something's wrong."

"Huh," said Wynezra. "That *is* weird."

I ran my tongue along my teeth inside my lips, deliberating. It was the first time I had done it as Wynonna. The sensation of feeling someone else's teeth inside your mouth was possibly the weirdest thing of all. Even weirder than the no-dick situation, which was Alejandro Jodorowsky–weird.

"Can you talk to her?" I said.

"Me?" said Wynezra—propping herself up on the bed with her elbows. She *almost* looked amused. Almost.

"You're better at talking to people than me."

"I don't know about that."

"Please?"

"Dude," said Wynezra. "Don't take it personally. Imogen has an older brother, and she loves him to death, but she would *never* confide in him about . . . you know . . . stuff like *that*."

"Stuff like *that*?" I repeated.

"Sex stuff."

I immediately wanted to ask Wynonna what sort of "sex stuff" Imogen *had* to confide. It was a screw turning slowly, drilling twist by twist into the center of my curiosity. But I refrained.

"Can you ask her when you're . . . *you*?" I said.

Wynezra actually started laughing. "Seriously?"

"Maybe she just needs a female role model she can confide in," I said. "She doesn't have any sisters, and my mom's always gone, and even if she wasn't . . . well . . . there's some trust issues. But you're cool! You're *hip*!"

"You did not just call me hip," said Wynezra. She covered her face with her hands, barely suppressing the laughter. “What are you, seventy years old?”

“Please, Wynonna. She’s my little sister. I’m worried.”

“If you’re so *worried*,” said Wynezra, “why don’t you go talk to her? You’re the *female* right now. You’re cool, hip Wynonna, *and* you know your sister better than me. Go break the ice.”

“How?” I said, hysterically. “How does one *break ice*?”

“Just shoot the shit.”

“What does that even *mean*?”

Wynezra sighed. “Fine. When I’m *me*, if I *happen* to sit next to her in theater, or if I see her in the hall at school or whatever . . . I’ll talk to her.”

I was so ecstatic, I could have hugged her. But she was lying on my bed, and we were in each other’s body, and that probably would have been the *weirdest* possible thing I could do. So I didn’t.

I had ridden the Tangent Train far enough. It was time to get back to business.

“I talked to Holden,” I said.

That might have been the most inconsequential thing anyone had ever said in the history of inconsequence. Except that I was Wynonna.

Suddenly, the context was revolutionary.

Wynezra’s expression seemed to make that deductive leap as her face seemed to say “Who gives a fuck?” but then connected the dots and held that “fuck” like Christine Daaé from *Phantom of the Opera*. FuuuuuuuUUUUUUUUUUCCCKKKKK!

She sat upright, crawled to the foot of my bed, and perched on the edge like a gargoyle.

“What did you say?”

“Well,” I said, “I may have told him some untruths.”

I told Wynezra everything—from Holden “blushing,” to my

attempted flirtation, to Holden's accusation—all of which led up to the Great Untruth. That she and I had sex, and that's why we were acting weird.

I told her that Holden agreed to talk to Imogen.

I told her that Holden said this was "the beginning of a beautiful friendship."

All the while, Wynezra's face was a panorama of overacted expressions—from bliss, to outrage, to horror—all the way to Holden's "beautiful friendship" comment, which seemed to defuse the nerve endings in her face.

"Casablanca?" she said. "He quoted *Casablanca*?"

I was kind of impressed she even knew what *Casablanca* was.

"Yeah?" I said. "I guess? Is that bad?"

"Well, it wouldn't be bad if he said, 'Here's looking at you, kid.' But he said, 'This is the beginning of a beautiful friendship.' That's what Humphrey Bogart says to the cop. I don't wanna be the cop! I wanna be Ingrid Bergman!"

"I think you're reading too much into Holden's pop culture references. Honestly, I don't think he's even seen *Casablanca*. He probably saw it referenced in an episode of *Family Guy*."

"Oh," said Wynezra. She nodded hopefully. Enthusiastically. "Yeah. Okay."

"So are we on the same page with this story?"

Wynezra nodded. Again, enthusiastically.

"Are you going to freak out on Holden and run off like a crazy person the next time he tries to talk to you?"

Wynezra blushed. I'd never seen her blush before, but she wasn't *her* anymore, she was *me*. The pasty complexion of Ezra Slevin was the perfect palette for my cardiovascular system to turn my face into a fucking billboard for my embarrassment. It was bizarre witnessing it in the third person.

"*Are* you?" I persisted.

"I had a boner," she blurted out.

"What?"

"Multiple boners. Like, every single time he tried to talk to me—*boing!* There it was, pitching a tent in my pants. I had no choice. I had to run."

I felt it in my gut. Pulling at the corners of my face. It took every fiber of willpower in my entire being not to . . .

. . . not to . . .

Nope. The willpower was gone.

I started giggling.

"Hey!" said Wynezra. "It's not funny!"

I started full-on laughing. And apparently, a facet of Wynonna's laughter was snorting. I snorted.

"You suck," said Wynezra. "I hate you."

I started crying.

• •

I didn't leave Wynezra completely high and dry. The dick-owning gender had had millennia to adapt to the great wonders and inconveniences of the dick. And as a dick-owner—well, time-share-owner these days—I had picked up a few tricks.

"You tuck it under your waistband," I said.

"You *what*?" said Wynezra. "How?"

"Very sneakily. Like a ninja. You just slip your hand in, grab the rod, and slide it under your belt."

Wynezra looked astronomically skeptical. "That sounds complicated."

"Not as complicated as explaining to your crush why you have the Tower of Pisa in your pants."

Wynezra considered this. Nodded thoughtfully. "Duly noted."

"But there are also preventative measures."

"*Preventative* measures? Why didn't you start with that?"

"Well, these measures are often frowned upon."

"Jesus Christ. Frowned upon by *who*?"

"Uh . . ." I said. I had to pause and think. "For starters, probably Jesus Christ."

When Wynezra looked confused, I proceeded to slide my hand up and down an imaginary cock in front of me.

"Oh my god," said Wynezra. She shook her head. "No way. I am not choking your chicken."

"Hey, currently it's *your* chicken," I said, raising my hands defensively. "I will get no pleasure out of it. Only you. I'm just trying to help."

"And how exactly is masturbating supposed to *help*?"

"It defuses all the sexual tension in your body," I said. "Duh. I mean, you *might* still get a boner, but after you've masturbated, it'll be *much* easier to look at Holden as a person and not five feet nothing of sexual desire."

Wynezra glared at me.

"I'm just saying," I said.

"Okay," said Wynezra, relenting. "Fine. *How* do I masturbate?"

"Ummmmmm . . ." I said, uncomfortably. "The age-old tools seem to be lotion, tissues, and your porn of preference. But . . . I would just say, *you do you*. I'm sure you'll figure out what feels good."

Wynezra gave me a prying look.

"What?" I said.

"Are you sure you're okay with this?" she said. "Me . . . you know . . ."

She mimicked my hand-sliding-on-imaginary-cock gesture.

"If you get Imogen to *like* me," I said, "you can choke that chicken seventeen times a day. You can choke it until I get penis cancer. Or dick-related superpowers."

Wynezra gave a feeble smile. It was the smile of someone who was grateful but in a broken sort of way.

The smile of someone with a secret.

• •

Wynonna and I were back in our own bodies by evening. I had driven to the Lakes and was just pulling into the parking garage when—*flash*—I was lying stomach-down on *my* bed, with *my* Xbox controller in my hand, playing *Forza Horizon 5*. The Lamborghini I was apparently racing smashed into a tree while I was winding around a tight bend.

The imagery in front of me—coupled with what I had been doing just seconds earlier—caused me to drop the controller.

Shit.

I rolled around on the bed and fumbled for my phone. Felt it brush my leg from inside my pocket.

I whipped it out, fumbled for Wynonna's number in the recent calls, and pressed the call button. As the tone rang, I made a mental note to add her to my contacts—shit, add her as one of my *favorites*—for emergencies' sake.

The call went to her voice mail:

"Heeeeeeeeeyyyy, I'm not here right now. So . . . better luck next time."

Beep!

Oh my god.

I hung up and tried again.

This time, Wynonna picked up on the second ring. We both screamed simultaneously into our phones. I said, "OH, THANK GOD," and she said, "AHHHHHHHHHHHH."

"Are you okay?" I asked.

"Yeah, yeah," she said. "Good thing you were only going twenty miles per hour and your foot was on the brake. I almost went right into a concrete pillar."

"Shit. But you're okay?"

"Just got my heart racing a bit. But yeah, I'm okay. Prolly didn't help I was playing that fucking video game."

I nodded breathlessly, even though she couldn't see me.

"Well . . ." she said awkwardly. "I should go."

"Wynonna?" I said.

"Yeah?"

"I'm glad you're okay."

She was silent for a moment.

"Thanks, Ezra," she said finally, and hung up.

I spent the rest of the night memorizing Viola's lines. I memorized them until 3:14 a.m. when I was suddenly—magically—fast asleep in someone else's body.

NINE

FOR THE THIRD MORNING in a row, I woke up as Wynonna Jones. Even if *everything else* about our body-swapping situation was random as fuck, at least *that* was consistent.

I had just showered and was halfway through getting dressed—a routine I was definitely starting to enjoy—when Wynezra called.

"Can I pick you up?" she said. "We need to talk."

"Uh, sure," I said. "Is everything o—"

She hung up.

As I finished getting dressed, I racked my brain over every possible thing Wynonna had potential to be mad about. On a normal day, this would have been a very long list. Today, however, I honestly couldn't think of a single thing.

Resigning myself to whatever fate lay ahead, I took a chance on some ripped jeans (now that I was wearing them, they looked really good on Wynonna; maybe even *classy*), a pair of high leather boots that reached mid-calf, and a tank top that said WHAT'S YOUR DAMAGE, HEATHER? God, I loved her shirts.

No jacket. The bra straps and I didn't give a fuck today. We were feeling good. Confident.

I was outside and on the curb for about ten minutes before Wynezra arrived. She was driving slower than usual. When she pulled up alongside me, she barely even looked at me.

Her face—*my* face—looked tired.

Oh.

I suddenly had an idea what this might be about.

I climbed into the passenger's-side door, closed it, and we drove, basking in a void of tension.

"For the past three nights in a row," said Wynezra, still not looking at me, "I've woken up at three fourteen a.m. In your body. And *then*, I lie awake until the sun comes up and your alarm goes off."

I nodded quietly, weighing the pros and cons of telling her that *I* felt refreshed and great. Surely, the moral reward of self-sacrifice for her fellow man—or woman, currently—would quell her suffering.

"WHAT IS WRONG WITH YOUR BODY?" she said loudly, like she was deaf to her own voice. "Why can't I sleep?"

"I have a sleeping disorder?" I offered questioningly.

"So, what? You just lie awake every night until three fourteen a.m., and then *bam*! You're nice and cozy and asleep in my body?"

I hadn't really thought about it until now. But yeah, that's exactly what was happening. No wonder I felt so good.

"You *do* know what three fourteen is, right?" she said, after I failed to respond.

"Uh . . ." I said. "Pi?"

"What?" Wynezra looked at me like I was the *actual* disease dumb people were afflicted with that made them stupid. "No! It's the witching hour, dumbass."

"The . . . witching hour?"

"Between three and four a.m.," said Wynezra. "It's believed to be the hour when supernatural phenomena are most likely to happen. The hour when black magic is most powerful. I read all about it on Wikipedia."

"Huh."

"When did you say your sleeping disorder started again?"

I was pretty sure I *didn't* say—quite frankly, I didn't like to talk about it—but since she was suffering *with* me, I figured she was entitled to the information.

"It started in fourth grade," I said. "I was nine years old."

I thought about mentioning the car accident. But then I thought: Why do I need to tell her about every freaking facet of my life? So I withheld that tidbit. It's not like there was anything to *tell.* I didn't remember anything!

Regardless, Wynezra seemed to process what I had given her with great interest.

"In other words," she said, "after *Romeo and Juliet.*"

I sighed.

"After the *eclipse,*" she pressed. "After we *swapped* for the first time!"

"Can we not psychoanalyze me today, Dr. Jones? I'm really not in the mood."

"But I'm right, though, aren't I?"

I shrugged. "Maybe? I don't know. It was a long time ago. My doctor says my insomnia is trauma-related."

"Maybe. Or *maybe* it's supernatural-phenomena-related."

I rolled my eyed. "I don't have chronic insomnia because I body-swapped once when I was nine."

"No, of course not. You have chronic insomnia because you body-swapped once when you were nine, and it fucked up the one fictional scenario where you and Imogen end up together, not to mention your adorable little acting career."

My entire body was sent into premature rigor mortis.

Oh my god. Did she find out about my YouTube channel?

Did I leave a costume piece out?

No. I was too thorough. Every time I finished a video, I boxed the costume. Stowed it away in the darkest reaches of my closet. I would never be so negligent.

Deep breaths, Ezra. She doesn't know. She's just referring to Shakespeare. That's all. Play it cool. Play it cool like Donnie Brasco.

"Your YouTube channel is cute," said Wynezra, cracking a smile that sealed my fate. "*Reeeeal* cute."

Jesus Christ Superstar. Take me now.

In that moment, I was actively contemplating the best way to throw myself from the vehicle so that it would kill me instantly. We weren't going fast enough, but perhaps if I just slid out, I would roll under the tires. But that was only sufficient if it crushed my head or maybe several vital organs. If it only ran over an arm or a leg, that would mostly just suck.

Wynezra laughed. "Relax, man! I liked it. It was really good."

Headfirst. I had to go headfirst. Basically, grab the bottom lip and swing myself beneath the car. It was the only way if I was going for maximum chance of fatality—

Wait, what?

I looked at Wynezra. Her expression was one of deep amusement, but there was also something else. Sympathy, maybe? Was Wynonna even *capable* of sympathy?

"Look, I'm sorry," said Wynezra. "You left a window open on your computer, and I was bored, and obviously I couldn't sleep, and… Okay, I'll just say it: I watched your entire channel."

This seemed like an appropriate moment to die. And yet…

"You *liked* it?" I said.

"I'll be honest," said Wynezra. "I think Johnny Depp has lost his fucking mind. I think we're watching his midlife crisis on the big screen. But with that said… you *nailed* him, man. I mean, your Sweeney Todd? Jesus, it gave me chills! Where did you learn to sing like that?"

Okay, so if you're a cultured human being, or perhaps just a disturbed one, you know that *Sweeney Todd: The Demon Barber of Fleet Street* is a musical. A gory, *horrifying* musical about a serial killer barber who murders his victims with a straight razor and then processes their corpses into meat pies that he sells to the public. But a musical nonetheless. So naturally, I had to sing for his video.

I didn't "learn to sing" so much as I just watched *Sweeney Todd* on an endless repeat until his voice was an echo, a rhythm in my head. From there, it was pure mimicry.

I shrugged. It was all I could do. I was still stuck at: "You *liked* it?"

"Man, I can't *wait* to show this to Imogen," said Wynezra. "She's gonna freak."

"Whoa, whoa, whoa, whoa, whoa, whoa, whoa," I said. "You can't show this to Imogen."

"What? Why not?"

"Because *you can't*!"

"Dude. You already have, like, a million subscribers."

"Ten thousand," I corrected nervously.

"Exactly! Ten *thousand* subscribers! What does it matter if one more person sees it?"

"It matters because I *know* that person."

"You know *me*, and *I* saw it."

"Yeah, well, I didn't exactly have a choice in the matter. Besides, I listened to your Holden tapes, so . . ." I glanced at the word "karma" tattooed on my inner forearm. Raised it for Wynezra to see. That made her chuckle.

"Damn straight," she said, shoving me playfully. "Karma, bitch."

I rolled with the shove, attempted to smile, but the smile was strained.

"Please don't show Imogen my videos," I said. "I'm not ready for her to see them. Not yet. No one knows about them. Not my family, not even Holden."

"What? Seriously?"

"Seriously."

Wynezra sighed. "Okay. I'm just saying, they're impressive. And if you want to *impress* Imogen, well . . . But hey, whatever, it's your life. I won't show Imogen the videos."

"Thanks, Wynonna."

Wynezra shifted uncomfortably in the wake of my gratitude. She shrugged it off like an unwanted hand on her shoulder.

"There's nothing to thank," she said. "Don't thank me. It's so not necessary."

We drove in silence for a long moment.

"Are you *sure* you don't remember anything else about fourth grade?" she said. "Anything about . . . us?"

"Us?" I said, confused. "Like, me *and* you?"

The way she had said it, it almost sounded like *she* remembered something. *I* certainly remembered nothing. Wynonna was nothing but a fear-filled blur in my fourth-grade memory banks.

"Do *you* remember anything about us?" I asked.

Wynezra hesitated. Then shook her head. "It's nothing."

Maybe I was overanalyzing. But it didn't *sound* like nothing.

I relaxed in my seat, as if giving myself permission to disintegrate peacefully. My eyes drifted to my passenger-side mirror.

A black Chevy Malibu trailed behind us, maintaining a distance—biding its time—like a patient predator.

I reeled forward in my seat. "Oh shit."

"What?" said Wynezra.

"I think I'm being followed."

"WHAT?" Wynezra leaned forward, squinting into the rearview mirror.

"The black Malibu," I said. "He was following me yesterday morning."

"Oh. My. God." There was dangerous recognition in her eyes. "That bastard."

"You know him?"

Wynezra leaned back and throttled the steering wheel. "Yeah. I know him."

I leaned forward and studied the vehicle in my side mirror. It was the same driver: bearded, ball-capped, aviator-ed. The perfect lazy man's disguise. The moment he realized he had been spotted, he went rigid with panic. Changed course.

Well, he *tried*. This time, however, there was a Volvo in his blind spot. He started to merge hastily into the right lane, the Volvo whaled on its horn, and he swerved erratically back into his own lane.

"Oh no, you don't, motherfucker," said Wynezra.

She spun the steering wheel like Ahab aboard the *Pequod*, with an utter disregard for human life. Flipped a U-ey. The Subaru tires screamed bloody murder. Suddenly, we were punching it in the opposite direction. The Malibu finally merged and turned right into an empty neighborhood street. Wynezra speared left, hot on his tail.

Er, wait.

Past his tail.

We accelerated past him entirely. Merged in front of him.

Then Wynezra slammed on the brakes.

The Malibu braked, too—but he also attempted to swerve around us. Wynezra swerved wider. We came to a dead halt diagonally across both lanes, blocking him off.

Wynezra jumped out of the car. Stormed toward the Malibu in a great and terrible Oz-like fury.

The man exited the vehicle, too. He even went so far as to remove his sunglasses. He was big. Real big. Also, he had a Chinese-style dragon snaking across his forearm, disappearing beneath his rolled-up flannel sleeve. The guy could easily kick Wynezra's ass.

He also looked scared. But maybe not so scared of Wynezra.

He looked scared of *me.*

Several times, I caught him glancing my way, then to Wynezra, then back to me. All the while, his face was flushing with shame.

He looked so familiar, but for the life of me, I couldn't figure out why.

"Who are you?" said the man.

"You got a lotta fucking nerve," said Wynezra.

"I asked, 'Who are you?'"

"Who am I? I'm the guy your daughter told to come out here and tell you to get fucking lost! That's who! You don't *get* to know who I am!"

Holy shit. *Daughter?* This was Wynonna's *dad*?

Already, Wynonna's dad seemed to know he had lost this fight before it even started. He looked lost, flustered, wholly ashamed of himself.

"Look, I'm sorry," he said. "You're right. I shouldn't be here. Let me just . . . let me apologize to her."

Wynezra was shaking her head before he even finished. "Five. That's how many seconds you have before I call nine-one-one."

"Hey. There's nothing to stop me from seeing my own daughter. I have a legal *right*—"

"Explain that to the police when we tell them you've been following her to school. I'm sure that'll look real great next to your *criminal record*, douchebag."

The man opened his mouth, but nothing came out. He was defeated.

"Four," said Wynezra. "Three. Two—"

"I'm going, I'm going," said the man, hands in the air.

He climbed into his Malibu.

Started the engine.

Drove off.

When Wynezra returned to the car, she was cold, flat, emotionless. She was the Great Wall of China of pent-up feelings. Her barriers were probably visible from outer space.

"Daughter?" I said.

"I don't talk to Imogen about your videos," said Wynezra. "You don't talk to me about my dad. That's the new deal. Deal?"

"But . . . I should know this, shouldn't I? For appearances' sake?"

Wynezra slammed both fists on the steering wheel, causing it to wail. "THIS IS NOT A FUCKING REQUEST."

I bit my lip. Nodded.

I must have looked scared out of my tits because Wynezra immediately looked apologetic.

"Sorry," she said. "I'm just . . . I'm not ready to talk about him. Not yet."

We drove the rest of the way to school in silence.

• •

"Hey, Wynonna."

I just closed my locker, and there was Imogen—coming straight toward me, like a careening vehicle, with no sign of stopping.

She wasn't smiling.

Likewise, my reception was very deer-in-the-headlights.

Oh my god. Was she going to fight me?

Not that I would ever "fight back" against Imogen. However, I immediately found myself statistically analyzing who would win in a fight between Wynonna and Imogen. Wynonna was the safer bet—she had a sturdier build, like Lagertha on *Vikings*—but Imogen was taller, with a longer, more wiry armspan.

Imogen plowed into me, coiling herself around me in a fierce hug.

"I'm sorry," she said, her voice muffled in my hair. "I'm sorry about everything."

My arms floundered awkwardly at my side until—finally—they returned Imogen's hug. And then I patted her on the back, like an idiot.

Imogen pulled away, smiling, and extended a gentlemanly elbow. "May I escort the lady to her next class?"

I blushed and took her arm. Just the touch of my palm against her small bicep kind of knocked the wind out of me.

"I only have one question," said Imogen. "*Do* you like Ezra?"

Boy, what a question. I had to keep the end game in mind here: Wynonna/Holden and Imogen/me. I had to keep the Wynonna Directive clear. But I *also* had to make myself look good.

"Ezra's great," I said. "Maybe if I wasn't totally into Holden? But no. It was a rebound. Or a *psychological* rebound, I guess."

Imogen gave a relieved sigh, like the world suddenly made sense. "Okay. That's what I figured."

"But Ezra's great."

"I'm sure he is!"

"If I get a date with Holden to prom, you should . . . you know . . . for *convenience's* sake . . ."

"Go to prom with *Ezra*?" said Imogen. She laughed, like that was the funniest thing she'd heard all week. Then, in a low, deliberately stupid voice, she said, *"Oh, okay."*

I cringed internally. Time to change the subject.

"I'm going to talk to Ziggy," I said. "Tell him I don't want to be Viola."

Imogen jerked away from me. "No! I want you to be Viola!"

"But—"

"No buts." She shook her head furiously. "I *hate* myself for being upset that you got the role. I think it's *fantastic* that you got it. You deserve it."

"But I don't want it."

"Yeah, and I'm sure that has nothing to do with me being a selfish, lousy, no-good friend about it."

"What? No. I didn't even audition for the role."

"Wynonna." Imogen grabbed me by the shoulders and looked at me intensely. "I *want* you to be Viola."

"You do know I'm dyslexic," I said, "don't you?"

It wasn't exactly a rhetorical question. I was genuinely curious if she knew.

"Don't be stupid, dummy," said Imogen. "You're a smart, capable, courageous girl who can do anything she sets her mind to. I mean, those Romeo lines, my god! You had those puppies *memorized*."

"But, Imogen—"

"Please!" said Imogen. It was at that moment that her face flushed red. Her lips were mashed awkwardly together, quivering. "If you don't do it for you, do it for me."

Tears welled in the corners of her eyes.

Whoa, what the hell? That escalated quickly.

"*Please* be Viola," she said. "I'll never forgive myself if you don't."

"Fine." I surrendered. "Okay. I'll do it."

What else could I say?

• •

Today's lunch was a cheesy potato casserole dish, listed on the lunch schedule as "funeral potatoes." They actually weren't terrible—per Piles Fork tradition—but they were clearly an omen.

A decision had been reached by the Powers That Be (meaning Holden and Imogen) that the four of us would dine together. We sat at the same table like four characters in the remote setting of an Agatha Christie novel—forcing smiles, pretending we wanted to be here, not really trusting anyone.

"So," said Imogen, forcing the biggest smile of all. "This is nice."

Holden, Wynezra, and I all nodded—although it probably looked more like we were bobbing our heads at an experimental-jazz bar, pretending we were cool enough to appreciate the diddley bow or the vibraphone.

Wynezra's gaze strayed to the vending machine. She gave me a look that said, "Would it be suspicious if I bought a bag of pork rinds?"

I gave Wynezra a look that said, "Yes. Get Funyuns instead." But apparently, it didn't translate.

“I’m gonna get me some pork rinds,” said Wynezra, and then she was off before anyone could object.

Imogen and Holden were in a race to see whose jaw could hit the floor first. They slowly looked at me like I was somehow responsible.

“What did you do to him?” said Holden.

Keep it cool, Ezra. Be funny. Tell a joke.

“Apparently liking pork rinds is a sexually transmitted disease,” I said.

Imogen’s eyes became so wide, they threatened to engulf her entire face. Holden raised a hand to his mouth, discreetly suppressing his actual gag reflex.

Wynezra was back with her pork rinds—bag open, already popping them in her mouth, faster than you could say, “AHHHHHHHH.”

“Whad I mish,” said Wynezra through a full mouth.

Imogen pulled herself together quickly. Interlocked her fingers and directed a meaningful look at Wynezra. “So, you’re too cool for Shakespeare these days?”

Wynezra swallowed. “Not *too cool for Shakespeare.* I just . . . *really* like trees.”

• •

Because lunch was *such* a smashing success, the four of us decided to ride together to the Amityvale again. And once again, Ezra Slevin drove. Only this time, the role of Ezra Slevin was played by our budding young actress, Wynonna Jones. And she was gunning for the Oscar in the vein of Heath Ledger’s Joker.

“Speed limit,” said Imogen, gripping her armrest. “There is definitely a speed limit.”

"Speed *limits* are for speed *dimwits*," said Wynezra.

Holden and I exchanged glances in the back seat. It was the sort of thing that would have been extremely normal for us to do in the presence of Wynonna doing her usual crazy shit. Except this time, I was Wynonna. I had to remind myself of this. Had to remind myself that—*because* I was Wynonna—the look could mean something else entirely.

I couldn't shake the feeling that, somehow, Holden could see through my disguise.

That, somehow, he could see I was actually me.

• •

Ziggy didn't waste a moment with this Shakespeare business. At two-oh-five sharp, he set us on a crash-course performance of the five scenes that—in their entirety—composed all of Act 1 of *Twelfth Night*.

Script in hand, of course. He wasn't insane.

Scene 1 began with Duke Orsino and his servants/best bros, Curio and Valentine. Curio suggested they go hunting for hart (male deer), and boy did that set Duke Orsino off.

"Why, so I do," said Holden. Shockingly, he didn't stumble over a single line. *"The noblest that I have. Oh! when mine eyes did see Olivia first, methought she purged the air of pestilence. That instant was I turned into a hart, and my desires, like fell and cruel hounds, e'er since pursue me."*

Wynezra, sitting beside me, made a face like a little kid being force-fed cough syrup.

"It's a play on words," I whispered into her ear. "Hart—h-a-r-t—is a deer, but it sounds like *heart*, and Duke Orsino is saying *his* heart is the thing being hunted, metaphorically, by his desire for Olivia—"

"I know what it *means*, assclown," said Wynezra. "I just didn't realize I was signing up to watch Holden swoon over *Imogen* every day."

We didn't have to worry about Imogen eavesdropping. Olivia wasn't in this scene. Imogen had relocated to the farthest corner of the warehouse to read her lines in some semblance of quiet. She wasn't up until scene 5, and she was determined to have *something* memorized.

"Duke Orsino ends up with *you*, remember," I said.

"Maybe," said Wynezra. "Or *maybe* he ends up with *you*."

"Does it matter?"

"It matters if there's any *kissing* in this play." She looked at me, expectantly. "Is there?"

Oh shit. *Was* there?

I frantically flipped to act 5 of my script, scouring for any sign of "romantic" stage directions.

"If Holden kisses you first," said Wynezra, "I will be so pissed."

• •

The scenes progressed. Rather haphazardly, but they progressed nonetheless.

A shipwreck left Viola stranded and believing that her twin brother, Sebastian, was drowned. Then, for reasons, she persuaded the ship captain to dress her as a man and present her as a servant to Orsino.

Then there was disorder in Olivia's household. Olivia was mourning the recent deaths of her father and brother. Her uncle, Sir Toby Belch, was drunk and exercising his inebriated sense of humor. (Jayden made for a fine alcoholic uncle.) The maid, Maria (Daisy), scolded Sir Toby for upsetting the peace—but, like, in a friendly, sexually charged sort of way. Sir Andrew Aguecheek (Patrick) was a doofus knight whom Sir Toby had brought along to woo Olivia. But really, Sir Toby was just manipulating Sir Andrew for shits and giggles, and also spending all his money. Feste (Tucker)—Olivia's melancholy, philosophical, and oddly hilarious jester—also stumbled in completely sloshed, and got shit from Maria as well, because apparently she was the only vaguely responsible person on the premises. Lastly, Malvolio (Willow), Olivia's steward, entered and proceeded to shit on everyone's party.

Everyone—even Maria—hated that motherfucker Malvolio.

Everyone's acting was messy and kind of terrible, but today was our first *real* day of acting, and we were basically here by school mandate and/or coercion, so it was kind of forgivable.

In the next scene, Viola was dressed as a man—going by the name Cesario—and had become employed by Orsino. Her first job, given by the Duke himself, was to send a message of love from him to Olivia.

"Prosper well in this," said Holden. *"And thou shalt live as freely as thy lord, to call his fortunes thine."*

"I'll do my best to woo your lady," I said, and then, softly, through the fourth wall, *"yet, a barful strife! Whoe'er I woo, myself would be his wife."*

Thus, we learned that Viola had a case of the hots for the Duke. But this was only a *preface* to the Moment We'd All Been Waiting For. (And by "we," I mean "I.")

In scene 5, Olivia was about to meet Viola (dressed as a dude, of course).

"The honorable lady of the house, which is she?" I said.

"Speak to me," said Imogen. *"I shall answer for her. Your will?"*

Olivia knew better than to confess her identity. She was quite apt at handling the trolls Duke Orsino sent her way, professing his unrequited love. She'd been dodging his not-so-subtle advances for a while now, and he still hadn't gotten the hint. Duke Orsino had a very if-at-first-you-don't-succeed-try-again attitude. Applied to modern-day dating ethics, it was superbly creepy and annoying.

"Most radiant, exquisite and unmatchable beauty," I said. *"I pray you tell me if this be the lady of the house, for I never saw her."*

Unfortunately, Duke Orsino's messenger monkey or not, Olivia was no match for Viola's boyish charm. With young Cesario saying suave things like "*good gentle one, give me modest assurance*" and "*by the very fangs of malice I swear,*" who could blame her? Olivia crumbled and confessed her identity. She then inquired:

"What is your parentage?"

"Above my fortunes, yet my state is well," I replied. *"I am a gentleman."*

"Get you to your lord. I cannot love him. Let him send no more—unless perchance YOU come to me again... to tell me how he takes it. Fare you well."

And then—after I exited the stage—Olivia confessed a bit more.

"I am a gentleman," said Imogen, repeating the words with fervent adoration. *"I'll be sworn thou art: Thy tongue, thy face, thy limbs, actions, and spirit, do give thee fivefold blazon."*

She raised a tight fist to her chest.

"*Not too fast!*" she instructed her racing heart. *"Soft, soft!"*

Oh. My. God. Was there a thing in this world hotter than Imogen performing Shakespeare?

I *wanted* to feel like progress was happening. That I was making some real strides forward with Imogen. She and I had some serious chemistry onstage.

Problem was: I wasn't me! I was Wynonna. And as far as Imogen was concerned, this was the BFF chemistry she and Wynonna had had since the dawn of time.

I let out a deep, sexually frustrated breath, pulled out my phone, and glanced at the time—five minutes till.

Thank god. I was falling way too hard for Imogen right now. I was falling like a meteor—like the one that killed the dinosaurs—trailing fire and stardust and annihilation behind me.

Nothing falling this hard could end well for anybody.

• •

The second Shakespeare practice ended, Willow made a straight line to Wynezra. No hesitation. There was almost a sense of urgency in every step.

"Hey, Ezra," she said.

I probably reacted just a bit too much—considering that I *wasn't* Ezra, and I was standing thirty feet away. And it took Wynezra just a little too long to realize that Willow was talking to her.

"Oh, hey," said Wynezra, finally. "What do you want?"

Willow shifted uncomfortably. "Can I get a ride home?"

Wynezra glanced indiscreetly at me. I nodded my head furiously.

"Yeah, okay," said Wynezra. She glanced over Willow's Black Veil Brides–level emo hair. "Just don't shed on the upholstery."

Willow's eyes were so wide, they were eclipsing her eyeliner. She was clearly offended. "Excuse me? Fuck you."

"Hey, I'm kidding!" said Wynezra. "The hair's badass."

She clapped Willow on the shoulder—but probably just a little too hard. Willow hadn't braced herself for the impact and nearly tipped over.

"Whoa, sorry, don't know my own strength," said Wynezra, which was probably true. "You're a scrappy little runt, aren't you?"

Willow gaped at this stranger in her big brother's body.

"Imogen has permanent dibs on shotgun," said Wynezra, "so you're stuck in the back seat with Holden and Wynonna. Wynonna's cool, FYI. You two should be friends."

Wynezra winked at me. Willow watched with confusion, then looked directly at me.

In a moment of panic, I dropped my gaze and scoured the vicinity for a convenient place to redirect my attention. The first thing I saw was Holden's butt—he was turned the other way, talking to Imogen—so I did the unthinkable and smacked it.

I—as Wynonna Jones—smacked Holden's ass.

There was so much adrenaline coursing through my body, however, that I smacked it just a little too hard. It probably hurt. Holden, meanwhile, yelped and whipped around.

Imogen's jaw plunged.

Wynezra stared at me with unparalleled horror.

"RACE YOU TO THE CAR," I screamed in a mentally deranged sort of way, and bolted to the car like I meant it.

Against all the odds in the universe, Holden actually chased after me.

• •

The drive home was quiet. This had everything to do with the ass-smacking. Holden and I grew awkward after racing to the car. (Holden won, by the way.) I was a little distracted by the aftermath. Like, what was the winner supposed to get anyway? Another smack on the ass? Meanwhile, Imogen was stunned silly by my brazenness, and Wynonna was flushing—practically *slow-roasting*—with embarrassment in the driver's seat.

Willow sat between me and Holden, observing our silence like some sort of bizarre performance art piece.

Finally, she turned to me.

"I like your hair," she said.

I couldn't remember the last time Willow had complimented me. Maybe she had *never* complimented me. And I guess, if you wanted to get technical, she wasn't complimenting me now either; she was complimenting Wynonna. Wynonna's hair had nothing to do with me.

But I'd be lying if I said I wasn't flattered.

"Thanks," I said. "I like yours, too."

I glanced at the driver's seat and the back of Wynezra's head. She was casually observing us in the rearview mirror.

"Don't listen to Ezra," I said as an afterthought. "He has shit taste in hair."

"Hey!" Wynezra protested. "I said it's badass, didn't I?"

Holden chuckled. "I agree, Willow. It's very badass."

"Would it be weird if I said I want to touch it?" said Imogen.

That comment earned laughs from just about everyone.

"I'm serious!" said Imogen. "There's just so much *texture* and... and *girth*! I just want to stick all of my fingers in it and wiggle them around."

We were dying. We were already dead.

Everyone was dropped off in the same order as last time. First Holden, then Imogen. Once we dropped Imogen off, Willow offered me shotgun—which I took, gratefully. Mostly, I hoped that it would give me some sort of communicative advantage with Wynezra.

It didn't.

Wynonna and I hadn't swapped back yet, and things were probably about to get weird.

Once we pulled up to the front curb of the Lakes, I fidgeted in the passenger seat.

"Welp," said Wynezra. "Don't tell Carol I said hi."

"It was nice meeting you," Willow chimed in from the back seat.

“Oh. Yeah.” I said, flustered. “You too.”

“We should hang out sometime,” said Willow.

She seemed to immediately regret saying that.

“I mean, if you’re ever not busy doing . . . you know . . . whatever—”

“I’d love to hang out,” I said.

Willow lit up. “Oh! Great! Here, lemme get your number.”

“You two are too cute,” said Wynezra, and pretended to gag.

I flipped Wynezra off with one hand and pulled out Wynonna’s phone with the other. Willow and I exchanged numbers. Finally, I was forced to unceremoniously exit the vehicle and go home to a place that was basically an alien planet to me.

I crossed the lobby, took the elevator, and treaded lightly down the hall with a special sort of dread—like I expected to round the corner and discover a pair of dead ghost twins in matching blue dresses blocking my path, offering to play with me forever and ever and ever.

The good news was that I reached Wynonna’s condo door with nary an ectoplasmic trace of dead ghost twins.

The bad news was that, just as I was reaching for the doorknob, the door opened and Carol exited.

She had her purse on her shoulder, a scarf around her neck, and a pair of sunglasses that—at this late hour—would have made Corey Hart proud.

“Well, well, well,” said Carol. “Look what the cat dragged in. Coming in a little late now, aren’t we?”

My mouth stammered for words. Finally, I uttered a feeble “Sorry.”

“Dare I ask where you’ve been? Off gallivanting with Ponyboy and Sodapop and the rest of your poor, misunderstood street urchin friends from the wrong side of the tracks?”

“I was at Shakespeare practice.”

"Ha! Of course, you were! Let me guess: Beatrice of *Much Ado*? The great battler of wits and words? No, no—Lady Macbeth. Yes. That's it. You two seem to have similar temperaments."

Wow. I think I was starting to understand Wynonna's dislike for Carol.

"Actually," I said, "we're doing *Twelfth Night*. And I'm Viola."

"Oh, of course, of course!" said Carol. She clearly didn't believe a word coming out of my mouth. "The great *cross-dresser*. Oh, I should have guessed Viola from the start—"

"Make me a willow cabin at your gate," I said, *"and call upon my soul within the house. Write loyal cantons of contemned love and sing them loud even in the dead of night; halloo your name to the reverberate hills and make the babbling gossip of the air cry out 'Olivia!' O! you should not rest between the elements of air and earth, but you should pity me."*

Carol's mouth had slipped open in increments until she was completely slack-jawed.

"But how did you—" she said. "I thought you couldn't—"

How did Wynonna *memorize the lines*? You thought she couldn't *read*? Fair questions. However, Carol had made one extremely flawed assumption about Shakespeare.

"Shakespeare's plays weren't meant to be read," I said. "They were meant to be *seen*." I then did an awkward, made-up gang sign with both hands and said, "YouTube, muthafuckas."

Carol was speechless. Finally, she removed her sunglasses and looked at me—looked at *Wynonna*—like she was seeing her for the first time.

Eventually, she blinked, and her mind seemed to settle into this new reality.

"I was just off to visit your mother," she said. "Care to join me?"

Ohhhhhhh boy. Okay. This was happening. Let's think this one through. Weigh out the pros and cons.

The pros:

- This was a valuable opportunity to build Wynonna's relationship with her grandmother. (Which, I was sure, was in direct violation of Wynonna's wishes. But c'mon, it was her *grandma*!)
- After meeting Wynonna's dad—stalker and possessor of criminal records—I was *insanely* curious to meet her mom.
- The curiosity was literally killing me.
- Okay, not *literally*, but you know what I mean. I *had* to know.

The cons:

- Wynonna would *literally* kill me if she found out.
- Literally.

"I understand if you don't want to—" Carol started to say.

"I'll go," I said. "I'd like to go."

• •

We drove to a cemetery.

It was at that moment—as we pulled off the main road and onto a gravel one weaving between the plots—that I realized the horrible extent to which I was violating Wynonna's privacy.

I don't know what I expected. Her dad had a criminal record. I guess I figured *whatever* her mom's deal was, it couldn't *possibly* be worse than that.

Oh boy, was I wrong.

Speaking of wrong, let me tell you about this cemetery. The perimeter fence was falling apart. The trees were knotted and haggard. The grass was choppy at best. (At worst, dead.) The tombstones themselves looked like ancient relics from a forgotten era. I was pretty sure people stopped burying their dead here after the North defeated the South.

Carol pulled over. There were no parking spaces. Only a soft fade between the gravel and grass.

"She bought her own plot here, you know," said Carol. "She did it just to spite me."

"To . . . spite you?" I said. I was trying hard to pretend I didn't know this cemetery was absolute shit. At *best*. At worst, the tombstones probably formed an inverted pentagram and secretly opened up a gateway to hell.

"She bought it before she graduated high school."

"WHAT?"

"Oh yes," said Carol, nodding earnestly. "She was seventeen. Your age."

"Why?!"

"She obviously thought she was being real clever. I swear, the girl went to *one* Marilyn Manson concert, and she was never the same."

"Aren't plots expensive?"

Carol extended her arms, gesturing elaborately. "She obviously got a good deal! I'm surprised she didn't bargain for a Buy One, Get One Free. I could've *filled* one, I nearly died when I found out about this shithole."

"And you still buried her here?"

Carol sighed. Pulled out a lighter and a pack of cigarettes. Popped one out and inserted it into the tight slit of her mouth.

"People don't make good decisions when they're mourning," she said, and exited the car.

I exited after her.

We walked slowly as Carol lit up. Released stressful drags like sighs into the overcast air. Mostly, I was trying to follow her without *looking* like I was trying to follow her.

"Are you *trying* to inhale my secondhand smoke?" she asked. "Is that what the kids are doing these days?"

"Uh," I said.

Think, Ezra, think. Ask a question.

"What did you think of my dad?" I said.

"Oh, well," said Carol, rearing her head back slightly. "We're having *this* conversation now, are we?"

"I mean, you don't have to answer if you don't—"

"No, no, it's fine. Roscoe Jones is the sort of man I'd call an ignorant cur. He was rugged, and masculine, and adventurous, and stupid, and he swept your mother away like a monsoon. I *loathed* him. Still do."

We arrived at the tombstone. It was a simple affair—small, monument-style, galaxy-black granite. The words were carved and pale: JOSEPHINE "JOSIE" JONES.

The years were surprising.

Namely, the second year. I did the math in my head—just to make sure it was as suspicious as I thought it was.

Seven years ago.

She died *seven years ago.*

The year of the first eclipse.

"How did it happen?" I blurted out, tactlessly.

Carol looked at me curiously. "You *know* how it happened."

"I'd like to hear it from you."

Carol gave a beleaguered sigh. Dropped her cigarette and stomped it out. Pulled out another one.

"It's simple, really," she said, lighting up. "Your father was driving drunk. Both you and Josie were in the car. He blew past a stop sign and got T-boned by another vehicle. It hit the passenger side."

She took a long drag.

"By the time the ambulance arrived, Josie was dead."

I felt the puzzle pieces snapping into place in my head.

"And Roscoe was arrested," I said softly.

I realized my mistake—saying *Roscoe* instead of *Dad*—and nearly cringed myself to death. But Carol didn't even blink.

"Arrested and charged with reckless homicide," she said. Every word was sharp and embroiled in justice. "Sentenced to five years in prison. No parole."

God. *Damn.* It was all starting to make a devastating sort of sense. Why he was following Wynonna. Why she wanted nothing to do with Roscoe.

Because Wynonna was all that he had.

Because Roscoe killed her mom.

That was when the thought returned, stronger than ever: *I shouldn't be here.*

"How long has it been?" I said nervously. "Since we did this last, I mean."

Carol looked astronomically confused. "Did *what*?" A pause. *"Visit your mother's grave?"*

I nodded timidly. Judging from Carol's bewilderment, I could already tell I wouldn't like the answer.

"You've *never* taken me up on my offer. Not that *I* can remember. Unless dementia is finally rearing its ugly head." Carol studied me like a riddle. "In fact, I was under the impression that you hadn't been here since the funeral."

I *really* shouldn't be here.

"What makes you say that?" I asked. As if I needed further proof.

"As I recall," said Carol, "that's what you *told* me. Right before you threw my *coffee mug* at my *fine china*. I'm still not sure which I'm more upset about. That mug was a *Deviehl*."

Oh my god. We needed to leave here now. Before Wynonna and I—

Flash.

• •

I called Wynonna twelve times in a row. No answer. I called again—nearly an hour later—and she *finally* picked up on lucky number thirteen.

"What the fuck?" she said. Her voice was a choking sob. "What the *fuck*, Ezra?"

"I'm sorry," I said. "Carol asked if I wanted to visit your mom, and I didn't know what to say, and I obviously didn't know about the situation, and—"

"You could have said no! You could have said, 'Fuck you, Carol!' You could have said *anything*! But no, you had to go stick your big fat nose in my . . . in my . . ."

Wynonna screamed. I could almost feel the impact of her phone as it was thrown across the room. Then, from a muffled distance, I heard several more objects being thrown, kicked, slammed, destroyed. At one point, I was pretty sure she ran her hands across the tops of her desk and dresser, flinging everything off in a mighty sweep.

Then I heard her collapse on the floor.

I heard her cry.

TEN

THERE WAS ONLY ONE rule in the entire universe that governed my and Wynonna's body-swapping. That was that the first swap of the day happened exactly at 3:14 a.m. every night.

Now that Wynonna had shed light on this mysterious detail, I paid special attention to it. I set my phone alarm for 3:10 in case I fell asleep—which I did, whoop-de-doo—and stared at the large, noisy analog clock in my living room. When it was 3:13, I was on the very literal edge of my La-Z-Boy reclining seat. It took a small eternity for that needle-like second hand to reach the fifties. And when it did, I couldn't help but hold my breath.

Fifty-seven . . . fifty-eight . . . fifty-nine . . .

The minute hand shifted a notch.

I held my breath for several infinitesimal seconds. Then I glanced down at myself—which was still, notably, myself.

What the hell?

All this time (all twenty-ish hours of it), I had been taking Wynonna's word for it—that the swapping happened exactly at 3:14 a.m. I guess she was off. That actually wasn't terribly surprising, considering that she was recording these times *after* she was waking up in my sleep-inept, insomniac body.

And then I had an absurd, seemingly irrelevant thought: Pi wasn't 3.14. It wasn't even 3.14159265359, although that was a little bit closer. Pi *couldn't* be perfectly defined by a written number because pi was *infinite.*

3.1415 . . .

I glanced at the second hand on the clock.

Thirteen . . . fourteen . . . fif—

Flash.

• •

"It's pi," I said.

This was the very first thing I said to Wynezra when she picked me up. I know what you're saying: "Why was she picking you up? I thought she *hated you*?" Well, I thought so, too. But for reasons beyond my understanding, she was in an inconceivably better mood now. She had called this morning, apologized for last night, and said she had good news on the prom-plan front, which—she admitted—she hadn't done shit with so far, and she apologized for that, too. Also, she had an addendum to our agreement. That was actually the main thing she wanted to talk about. I appreciated her honesty. I told her she could offer all the addendums she wanted, but only after I told her about a very important discovery I had made. Then she picked me up, and I told her, "It's pi."

"Please tell me you're talking about dessert," she said, "and not fucking math."

"Why would I be talking about dessert?"

Wynezra dropped her head on the steering wheel and sighed.

"I was watching the clock," I said, "counting down the seconds, and we swapped at *exactly* three-fourteen and fifteen seconds. Wynonna, the next two digits in pi are *one* and *five*! I bet if I timed it with a clock that counted in measurements smaller than seconds—milliseconds and nanoseconds and . . . and . . . and yoctoseconds—"

"*Yocto*seconds?"

"—I'm willing to bet it would measure the digits of pi right down to the nearest planck!"

"What the hell is a planck? Actually, scratch that. I don't want to know. What makes you think your clock is even that accurate?"

"I check and adjust all the clocks in our house weekly to an online world clock. It's one of my hobbies when everyone's asleep. You're just going to have to trust me when I say that I'm very anal about the time."

"Oh, I don't doubt that."

"Anyway," I said, "that's the gist of my hypothesis. Although I don't really know where to go with it from there. The sci-fi nerd in me wants to say it has something to do with the fourth dimension—time added to space—but that actually makes no sense. Our measurement of time is a human construct, and even then, there are time zones to account for. Why Central Time? I would hardly say that the space-time continuum is somehow bending to a construct that allows states like Texas to know when the Dallas Cowboys are gonna get their asses kicked."

Wynezra looked at me like I was the dumbest thing on YouTube.

"God," she said. "You make me sound like such a geek. You have a total hard-on for pi, don't you?"

She wasn't wrong. There was something just a little *provocative* about pi. By definition, pi was the ratio of a circle's circumference to its diameter. This was significant because, no matter how big or small that circle was, the ratio remained the same. This was what you would call a mathematical constant. It indicated a certain infinitude to the nature of the circle. Pi was—in mathematical terms, no less—a transcendental number. It was non-algebraic. It wasn't the root of *any* polynomial integer. Pi was an irrational number with an infinite number of digits in its decimal representation, never settling into a repeating pattern. Which was fascinating, and awesome, and—yes—even a little sexy.

But I refused to admit that out loud.

"Whatever," I said. "You have a hard-on for the eighties. I bet you jerk off to John Hughes films."

That caused Wynezra to snort and laugh in a hysterical sort of way. When she finally regained control of herself, she said, "I like that you can say I jerk off to *anything*, and it isn't even anatomically incorrect. And, for the record, John Hughes films are the *sexiest*. Anyway, that's not important. What's important is the addendum."

"Which is?"

"Carol visits my mom once a week. If you're in my body when she does, I want you to go with her."

I blinked. "Wait. You *want* me to visit your mother's grave?"

"Carol was nice to me all evening. Like, I was a *total bitch* to her, and she was nice to me. I think she thought I was having a mental breakdown or something. I mean, I probably was, but... Anyway, you two seem to get along well, and I feel bad about everything, and, like... it's not like I *don't* want to visit my mom. It's just... it's *hard,* you know? It makes me feel terrible about myself and my life."

Wynezra was fidgeting uncomfortably in the driver's seat. This was clearly the last thing in the world that she wanted to talk about. It unearthed layers of herself that she would rather stay buried. But she pushed through it like a civic duty.

"Anyway, promise to do that," she said, "and I'll promise to help you fix your relationship with Willow—*in addition* to us getting each other our prom dates with Holden and Imogen. Is it a deal?"

"What makes you think my relationship with Willow needs to be fixed?" I said. This was sarcasm, of course, because Willow hated me as much as the Republican Party hated the environment.

Wynezra narrowed her eyes at me.

"Okay, deal," I said.

"Great," she said. "Because Holden started texting me last night."

My eyes inflated inside their sockets. "Seriously?"

Wynezra smiled in such a way that exposed all of her—my—teeth. In retrospect, it was less a smile, and more a facial spasm. It teetered between ecstatic and terrified, but was mostly on the verge of another nervous breakdown.

"Holy shit," I said. "How'd it go?"

"Awful. I have the flirting skills of a lonely crazy person stranded on a desert island. I went back over everything I texted him and immediately wanted to cheese-grate my brain."

"Oh."

"But he *likes* me!" she exclaimed. "I'm almost *positive* he likes me. And I think that has everything to do with you. Like, slapping his ass? Oh my god, what were you *thinking*?"

I definitely wasn't "thinking" during that part. And I almost admitted this; however, I quickly became distracted by an erroneous detail.

"Wait," I said. "You *texted* him?"

The implication was simple: She was dyslexic. How was she able to *text* him, let alone *read* his texts?

Wynezra met my confusion with judge-y eyes. With one hand on the steering wheel, she reached into my purse. (Yes, I was using Wynonna's one and only purse—a turquoise, acid-washed punk bag with metal studs—because the pockets of girl pants were basically impossible to use unless you were looking to store a very large coin, like a doubloon.) She pulled out her phone, unlocked it, and raised it to her mouth.

"Okay, Siri," she said. There was a soft chime. "Show me my messages."

"You've got several text messages," said the female robot living inside Wynonna's phone. *"Here are the five most recent. The first one is from Holden 'Hottie Bugatti' Durden. Do you want to hear it or skip it?"*

"Hear it," said Wynezra.

"It says, 'Hahahahahahahahahahaha.'" The robot inside Wynonna's phone made sure to enunciate every "ha" like the rivets in a rumble strip on the side of the interstate. *"'Ur funny wynonna.' Do you want to reply, repeat it, or go on to the next one?"*

"Reply," said Wynezra.

"What's the message?"

"I want to bone you with Ezra's dick."

My jaw dropped as the words scrolled across Wynonna's phone.

"Got it," said the robot inside Wynonna's phone. *"Do you want to send this?"*

"FUCK NO," said Wynezra. "Jesus, Siri. Delete that shit."

Wynezra closed the screen on the phone, raised it high over the purse in my lap, and mic-dropped it like a rock star.

• •

When Wynonna actually *tried*, the results were shocking. She pulled out all the stops at lunch.

"Hey, Imogen, I like your sweater," said Wynezra. "Did you get that at Marshalls?"

"Uh, T.J.Maxx, actually," said Imogen. Still, she seemed impressed. "Good guess, though."

"T.J.Maxx! Dammit, I knew it. T.J.Maxx was my next guess. Anyway, the sweater looks great. It really makes your eyes pop."

The sweater was solid cerulean blue on top and solid beige on the bottom, including the bottom halves of the sleeves. If her arms hung straight down, it was like someone drew a straight line across her arms and torso, separating the colors.

And yes, it made her eyes pop. Made them blossom, even.

"Thanks," said Imogen. Her smile showed she was clearly flattered—*if* unsure how to process the compliment.

Holden glanced covertly at me, not about to be outdone in the compliment game by his formerly socially inept best friend. I was wearing an army-green parka over a black top that ended just below my belly button—featuring the face of this three-eyed sphynx cat thingy—a pair of cutoff shorts, and burgundy-red combat boots.

"I like your . . ." he started to say. Then he did a double take at my shirt. "Is that a cat?"

I glanced down at my shirt and shrugged. "I have no idea *what* it is. But it's badass, right?"

"*Very* badass," said Wynezra, before Holden could formulate a response.

Holden just nodded stupidly.

• •

Imogen ambushed me the moment I stepped outside of class. Almost predatorily. God, how did she do it? Did all of her classes end two minutes early?

"What do you think of Ezra?" said Imogen. "I want your honest, extremely biased opinion."

My mouth temporarily lost motor function.

"You had sex, obviously," she said, filling in the silence. "And that seems to have popped his social cherry—or opened the floodgates, sheesh! And I know you joked about me going to prom with him. But what do you *really* think?"

Holy shit. Holy *shit*. Holy shit floating in holy water in the holy porcelain throne of God.

"What do *you* think?" I said, for lack of brain capacitating.

"I think I need to move on," said Imogen. "And I don't know how that's going to happen if I don't *do* something. And maybe I just need a friend, and Ezra . . . I mean, if he's *anything*, he's *friendly*. And most importantly, I want to go to prom with you without being a third wheel. Because from the looks of it, you and Holden are . . . well, you know. Things are looking good."

For whatever reason, she didn't *sound* like things were "looking good." She sounded sad. Dejected, even. However, I was a tad preoccupied with the fact that she was talking about GOING TO PROM WITH ME.

Okay, so the "friend" part was less than stellar. But this was *huge* progress. It was almost *too much* progress. The sheer scale of the progress was so tremendous, it didn't make any sense. I dropped a hint, and Wynonna complimented her sweater, and suddenly she was talking about prom?

But I already knew why. She needed to "move on."

She needed to get over Mystery Guy X.

How long could she talk in riddles about being "trapped in a role" and needing to "move on" without saying this guy's name?

As much as I was dying to know his identity, however, part of me knew that the knowledge could be crippling. The last thing I needed was to discover that this guy she liked was absolutely nothing like me. What I *needed* was to prove myself. And, according to the history of my and Wynonna's predicament, I was usually myself by evening.

"Tomorrow's Saturday," I said. "Let's do something."

"*Do* something?" said Imogen.

"A date. A *double* date. We can eat at Fat Patties and go see a movie after. Don't ask *me* about Ezra. Get to know him yourself!"

"Oh, I dunno," she said. "I don't really see the point."

"The point?" I said. I couldn't help but sound a little offended. "The *point* is having fun! Don't you believe in fun?"

"Fun, for me, is reading a book, or having a girls' night with you, or bingeing *Downton Abbey*."

"Think of it as a girls' night with me!" I said. "Only there's two boys invited. And I have dibs on Holden."

Mentioning Holden did the trick. "Holden" was the code word that activated Imogen's preprogrammed BFF directive, and all the selflessness and sacrifice that entailed.

"You're right," she said, nodding. She almost sounded sure of herself, too. "It *will* be fun. Let's do it. What movies are best for dates? Romantic comedies?"

A sinister smile slithered across my face. "Horror movies."

• •

And that was how we ended up buying four tickets to *Splatter IV: The Reckoning*.

Imogen actually insisted that I let her set everything up. I think she felt bad about being resistant to the double date idea. She called

Wynezra directly, asked "him" on the date, and then told "him" to pass the word on to Holden. She informed them that we would be picking them up at seven p.m. sharp.

Dress was semiformal.

You see, Imogen only agreed to all this under one stipulation: that we do makeovers and she dress me up like a Barbie doll.

Imogen didn't strike me as the makeover type. How bad could it be? If she wore makeup, it was so low-key that you didn't *know* she was wearing makeup. And her wardrobe was very un-*Vogue*, to say the least.

When I first mentioned the stipulation to Wynezra—between sixth and seventh period—she laughed.

"She's only the makeover type for *special occasions*," said Wynezra. "And when a special occasion *does* arise, it's like all that pent-up feminine instinct explodes out over her. You're gonna look like a Disney princess."

• •

Everything was perfect. We had a double date. Holden and Imogen were *excited* about said date. Imogen was even talking about prom! All of this was, like, pinnacle-of-my-life great. Things had never been better.

So why couldn't I stop thinking about Wynonna?

She was obviously damaged. And I didn't mean that as an insult. I meant it in a way that I could totally relate to. The longer I was in her body, the more I felt like there was a blur between Who She Is and Who I Am, and her sadness felt like my sadness, and I just . . . I wanted to help her. I barely even *knew* her—and half the time, I couldn't even *stand* her—but I wanted to help her. Whatever that meant.

Maybe that's why I felt emboldened. Maybe it was because my last attempt at "meddling with Wynonna's life" had been met with reward.

I stayed up until 3:14 a.m. googling "Roscoe Jones."

This wasn't about curiosity. It was about gathering intel. It was about taking action.

It was about making right an irrevocable wrong.

Of course, I stopped a few minutes before 3:14 a.m. Closed my browser windows. Deleted my search history. Stripped down to my boxers, climbed into bed, and pulled the covers up to my chin to maintain some semblance of "trying to sleep."

I swear to god, I just wanted to help.

ELEVEN

ON ANY OTHER SATURDAY morning—stranded in Wynonna's house, in Wynonna's bedroom, in Wynonna's body, with nowhere to go—I might have had no idea what to do with myself. I wasn't scheduled to play Barbie with Imogen until one thirty. Meanwhile, at Slevin Manor, Wynezra was going to attempt the impossible and "sleep in."

(Good luck with that.)

But actually, this was great. You see, I *did*, in fact, have somewhere to go. And most importantly, I needed Wynezra distracted if I was going to pull off the nefarious shit I had planned.

At eleven o'clock sharp, I arrived at Newell House. (I only stalled once.)

Newell House was a restaurant. Arguably *the* restaurant—by Carbondale standards anyway. A three-story cube of a building with sandy stucco walls, narrow arched windows, and black-and-white-striped awnings. It was classy in the quaint, rural sort of way you might expect from a town whose only tourist attraction came from outer space. It used to be a hotel, but the hotel burned down in the early 1860s. It was rebuilt but burned down *again* in 1901. (The place was *definitely* haunted as fuck.) It was rebuilt again, underwent several aesthetic changes, and in 2003 became a restaurant.

Two years ago, they hired award-winning chef Roscoe Jones—recipient of the Jean Blanchet Chef of the Year, and the James Beard Regional Chef Award (Great Lakes). In other words, he was kind of a big deal. However, his hiring was very hush-hush because he was also an ex-convict.

I nervously adjusted my outfit. I was wearing a long black-and-white-striped punk sweater over leggings and laceless oxfords. I definitely wasn't *trying* to match the restaurant, but here we were. I sighed despairingly.

Took a deep breath.

Walked inside.

The walls were lime green—except in random redbrick patches—decorated in 1920s French poster art. The tile floor was speckled and patterned in whites and browns and salmon pinks. Caged chandelier lights hung low over each booth.

This was it. This was as fancy as Carbondale got. Like Kate Middleton dodging paparazzi, incognito.

The place was empty. But only because they opened at eleven. The guy who unlocked the door—a manager-looking sort with a mustache and an overall midlife crisis vibe going on—opened it and held it for me.

"Good morning, miss," he said, smiling against the weight of his own existence. "Will anyone be joining you?"

"Nope, just me."

"Nothing wrong with that. Right this way."

I followed Midlife Crisis to a nearby booth. He handed me a menu and asked me what I'd like to drink. I said coffee. Not that I *needed* coffee. I was so awake, I was practically enlightened.

Midlife Crisis left. Returned quickly with my coffee. Still smiling. "Here you go, miss. Do you need more time with your menu?"

I looked him up and down. He was wearing a purple crosshatch-patterned dress shirt and a plain yellow tie. The hair on his head was thinning like the Indo-Burma forest. Total manager material.

"Are you the manager?" I asked.

Midlife Crisis chuckled in an unfortunate sort of way. "Yeah. We're running a tad scarce on servers today. Everyone likes to get sick on the weekend. So, if you're looking for a job . . ."

He kept laughing in a way that sounded like he was crying inside.

I looked at the menu. Back at Midlife Crisis. "Can you ask the chef what he recommends? Is that weird?"

"No . . . of course not . . ." said Midlife Crisis, shaking his head politely, although this was clearly the weirdest thing he'd been asked all week. "Lemme go ask."

"Thanks. I'm his daughter."

Midlife Crisis had already begun to walk away, but my departing comment stopped him in his polished loafers. He turned around.

"*Luis's* daughter?" he asked, like he already knew that was impossible.

"*Roscoe's* daughter," I said. "I'm Wynonna."

Every ounce of existential dread vanished from Midlife Crisis's countenance. His eyes were pure "holy shit." Apparently, Wynonna was a hot topic of conversation at Newell House.

He nodded stupidly and wandered off. I watched him, following his path across the restaurant, through a pair of silver doors leading into a well-lit kitchen.

Seconds later, the silver doors cracked open again, and a full-grown man peeked through them, hunched over like a little kid. Though only a sliver of him was visible, it was a giant, unmistakable sliver.

It was Roscoe.

I smiled and waved.

His eyes went wide, and he disappeared into the kitchen.

It was at least a solid minute later before he finally reappeared.

He was wearing a black double-breasted chef jacket with matching slacks. He filled them like a hurricane in the Gulf of Mexico. The guy was ginormous—at least six feet tall and built like the body double for Jason Momoa.

Every muscle was stiff. His face was an effigy. The guy was petrified.

When he finally reached my table, I thought he might vomit.

He opened his mouth.

I was *sure* he was going to vomit.

Words spilled out. They spewed everywhere—violent, chunky, relentless.

"I can explain," he said. "I was only following you because I recognized your car one day, and I noticed you were having trouble with your manual transmission, so I just wanted to make sure everything was okay. Plus, the crime rate's not great around here. Like, there's this serial groper who keeps making the rounds on the local news—total psycho creep—and he seems to be targeting college girls around campus, which is right by where you and Carol live, and anyway, I promise I wasn't following you. I mean, I obviously was, but not in a weird way. Um. How's Carol?"

Wow. I felt so bad for this guy. My heart was breaking just listening to him *try* to talk.

"Would you like to sit?" I said. I gestured to the seat across from me—in case he tried to sit on the floor. He seemed to be in that sort of mental state.

He fumbled with the chair but managed to insert himself into it.

Now that he didn't have a ball cap to hide anything, his hair was unfurled—longish, dark, silvery around the ears, although it fell awkwardly. Constrained. Like it had been in a man-bun only moments ago. (I was sure there were health code rules about that.) His chin, meanwhile, was a mystery beneath his beard.

He had Wynonna's cheekbones. Or, I guess, it was the other way around.

"Is this okay?" I said. "I'm not going to get you fired, am I?"

"Huh? Oh, no. Theo's filling in for me while we talk. He said to take as much time as I need."

"The manager?"

"Uh. Yeah? He's actually a really good chef. He worked in the kitchen before he became manager."

"He seems like he's having a bad day."

Roscoe chuckled sadly. "His husband left him."

"Oh damn," I said.

"They have two kids. A boy and girl. Four and six years old. He left all of them."

"Oh *shit*," I said. "That's awful."

Roscoe nodded in a light-headed sort of way. "Yeah. It is. Plus, the servers here are a bunch of unprofessional shits. Theo gives them a little slack, and they walk all over him."

We were quiet for a moment. Roscoe looked like he was either waiting for permission to talk, or he was wondering if this was all just a lucid dream he might be waking up from soon.

"Can we talk about the accident?" I said.

Roscoe's breath stopped short. He ran out of breath like a vehicle running out of road at a dead end.

Still, he managed a stiff nod.

"Okay," I said. "You start."

I was determined to make Roscoe put forth all the effort here. First, I needed to know *for sure* this guy wasn't a total piece of shit.

Already, Roscoe looked like he was about to cry. His eyes were glossy, and red, and weary from existence. But every ounce of testosterone in his Spartanic vessel forbid him from shedding tears. So he blinked, and kept blinking, until his tear ducts slurped the moisture back in and redistributed it to manlier locations, like his pits.

"Okay," he said, nodding. "Yeah. Well, it happened. And it was bad. Every bit as bad as it sounds. And there's nothing I can do to take back what I've done. My time in prison doesn't even *begin* to make up the difference. Your mother was irreplaceable, and I'm a pathetic substitute for the parent you *should* have had. And I'm sorry. Even though I know *sorry* doesn't even begin to cover it. Also, um, I know it doesn't change anything, but I've been sober for seven years now."

"Seven years?" I said, trying hard not to sound impressed.

Roscoe nodded, a little more hopefully. "Yeah. I go to AA meetings when I can, but . . . it's a little tricky in the restaurant business. I work nights, mostly. But I, uh . . . I just got my seven-year bronze medallion. Actually . . ." He reached into the pocket of his slacks, rummaging. "Here, I've got it on me."

He pulled a bronze coin out of his pocket and set it on the table in front of me. It sounded heavy, landing with a thick *clunk*. Around the outer edge, it read, *To thine own self be true*, and featured a triangle at the center with a word at each side—*unity* and *service* and *recovery*. Inside the triangle was the Roman numeral VII.

I didn't know shit about AA medallions, but this looked pretty legit to me.

I nodded sternly, trying hard not to *look* impressed.

"Anyway," he said, grabbing the coin, pocketing it, "I know these are all just words, and words are nothing without the actions to back them up. I don't expect you to let me back into your life. I don't expect *anything* from you. But I'm honored that you would even think to come here and have this conversation with me. I know... I know it wasn't easy. It's probably not easy to even *look* at me. But I'm grateful. Thank you, Wynonna."

Okay. I knew it was a little premature to make judgments, but I already kind of liked this Roscoe guy. At least, for the time being, I had determined he wasn't a "total piece of shit."

On to Phase Two.

"Look," I said. "I obviously have a lot of anger about what happened. And I'll tell you right now: You're catching me on a good day. Tomorrow might not be a good day. Tomorrow, I might want to punch you in the face."

Roscoe nodded rather acceptingly at this revelation.

"The truth is," I said, "I feel like there are two people inside of me. One of those people wants this to work out. Wants to give you a chance. Maybe even have a real father-daughter relationship with you."

Roscoe's entire countenance flickered, lighting up.

"The other person inside me wants to murder you in your sleep," I said.

Roscoe's "lighting up" process pulled back hard on the reins. Reeled it back in to a reasonable dim glow.

He went back to nodding, accepting the terms of his fate.

"I'm not sure if I'll be able to have that relationship with you," I said, finally. "But I'd like to try. Maybe we can take it slow? One day at a time?"

Roscoe was a dog, and I had just thrown him the greatest fucking stick of his life. He would have chased that stick off a cliff. He perked up, and he was trying so hard not to lose his shit with joy, and he was so totally failing.

"In the meantime," I said, "just . . . be aware of that other person inside of me. This may not make any sense, but she's the one who needs you the most. She's the one who's hurting. She needs someone who understands that she hasn't healed properly. Really, she's just a bunch of broken pieces duct-taped together. But *I* think she needs you. Does that make sense?"

"Absolutely," he said. "Yes. Of course. Whatever you want. You are in charge."

The confused look on Roscoe's face, however, indicated that it made zero sense. Maybe even negative sense. But he wasn't about to admit it. Right now, he was the King of Understanding Metaphors. He nodded with so much raw determination, he could've skipped astronaut training and gone straight to the part where we launched him into outer space. If that's where Wynonna was, he was so fucking there.

Oh well. He didn't need to understand right now. He'd understand the moment he crossed paths with the wrong Wynonna.

"So . . ." I said. "You went to culinary school in Switzerland? That's cool."

"Yeah," he said. "It *was* cool. It was also hell."

"Hell?"

"Oh yeah. It sucked hard."

I offered a prodding look.

"Imagine Gordon Ramsay cloning himself and running his own cooking school."

"Yikes."

"Yikes is right. The Swiss method is generally: Kick them when they're down. Wear steel-toe boots while you're at it. Then gently insert the knowledge into their submissive, catatonic brains."

"Wow. Sounds great."

"It was a learning experience. And it wasn't *all* bad. The training programs at most Swiss academies combine traditions of European culinary schools, including the French and Italian ones. Essentially, you're getting the *full* culinary experience. And even though the courses are taught in English, they also offer German, French, and Italian to expand your employment possibilities."

"No shit," I said, genuinely impressed. "Can *you* speak any of those languages?"

"Ein bisschen," said Roscoe, in a guttural, phlegmy accent.

"Whoa. What was that?"

"C'était allemand," he said—this time in a *completely* different accent. Relaxed. Delicate.

"Okay, *that* was French. Was that first one German?"

"Sei molto bravo a capire gli accenti," he said, in a *third* accent. Suave. Flowing. Probably Italian.

"Now you're just showing off."

Roscoe chuckled. "You're good at picking up those accents."

"You're good at picking up *three different languages*!" I exclaimed. "There *are* just three of them, right? Please tell me there are only three of them."

"Just three. And to be fair, I learned French in high school. And I'm not *good* at any of them. At my best, most of my instructors would've told you that I sounded like three different *kinds* of bumbling village idiot."

"Friendly lot."

"I'm actually pen pals with some of them now."

"Pen pals?" It came out of me in a stifled burst of laughter.

"Hey, pen pals are the shit! That's how we roll in prison."

It felt so inappropriate to laugh, but I couldn't help it. I laughed.

"Guess I just never really warmed up to the whole 'social media' thing," he said. "I don't like the idea of putting my whole life up on display. It's not exactly something I'm proud of. Besides, letters have just always felt more genuine. But I'm all about phone calls! In fact, I was just on the phone with one of my teachers the other day—Leif Lindberg. He just started a restaurant in Bern—that's the Swiss capital—and it's already opening to rave reviews. It's called Waldeinsamkeit, and get this: He offered to fly me out there and basically offered me a—"

He stopped himself.

"A what?" I said. Even though the "what" was painfully obvious. "A *job*?"

Roscoe shifted uncomfortably.

"But you're not taking it, right?" I said.

"No." He shook his head sadly. "I'm not taking it."

He didn't need to tell me why. We *both* knew why he wasn't taking it. There was only one thing tying him down to Carbondale.

A thing who wanted nothing to do with him.

"Anyway," I said, desperate to change the subject, "we need a way to keep in contact. A secret way so, uh . . . *Carol* doesn't know I'm meeting with you. Because *Carol* will definitely kill me if she finds out."

By Carol, I of course meant Wynonna. If *anyone* was going to get murdered in their sleep, it would be me. I had to handle this situation with tact.

Roscoe stopped nodding. Something seemed to click. "Uh. I have a burner phone."

"A *burner* phone?" I said.

What I wanted to say was "What possible reason does a *non-criminal* have for owning a burner phone?" But that seemed insensitive, given the circumstances. So instead, I merely accosted him with my leeriest stare.

Roscoe seemed to overcome an intense internal battle, and whether he won or lost, the battle ended with a resolute sigh.

"It's for online dating," he confessed.

My confusion seemed to produce visible question marks floating around my person like a magical aura. So, he expounded.

"I'm not seeing anyone," he clarified, "if that's what you're thinking. It's just easier not to use your real phone number when you're dealing with people you've never met before. I haven't even used the thing yet. It's just . . . *I'm* just . . . you know . . ." He hesitated.

He said "you know" in a way that indicated that *I knew*. Which I didn't.

"I know *what*?" I said.

"I'm just trying to move on," said Roscoe.

He immediately seemed to regret it. Shrank beneath his own words.

"Okay," I said, nodding. "Yeah. That makes sense."

Roscoe stared at me. Stunned. Speechless. His eyes said, "Who are you, and what have you done with my daughter?" The irony was not lost on me.

Finally, he snapped out of his daze. Cleared his throat. "The . . . uh . . . the burner phone's in my car. Still in the package. I'll go get it."

I followed him out to his car. He rummaged through the passenger side of his car—an embarrassing disaster area littered with energy drink cans, candy bar wrappers, and Burger King paraphernalia. Like, Jesus, how was this dude so cut?

Sure enough, he emerged with a no-contract smartphone, still in its unopened packaging, still in the Walmart bag he purchased it in.

He removed the receipt, crumpled and shoved it in his pocket, and handed me the bag.

"Thanks," I said. I shifted uncomfortably. "I should be going now."

"Oh. Okay."

The tension was thick. The tension of a father who wanted to hug his daughter but knew he had no right. Besides, I *wasn't* his daughter. I wasn't about to delude the man. I wasn't doing this for him.

I was doing it for Wynonna.

TWELVE

IMOGEN ARRIVED AT THE Lakes a half hour early to pick me up. Her excuse was that she had been sitting by the door, checking her phone every couple minutes for the past hour, *literally* losing her mind. She emphasized the *literal* part. Claimed that she was seconds away from a psychosis situation. Real *Black Swan* stuff.

Imogen was *literally* too adorable to argue with.

First, we went "semiformal dress shopping." Naturally, we went to T.J.Maxx, and when that failed us, we went to Marshalls. Basically, I followed Imogen around the store while she said "Oooh" and "Ahhh" and draped dresses in my arms until my biceps ached. Then I tried them on.

I thought I was becoming an expert in wearing girls' clothes, but it turned out there was a whole dark underbelly of girls' fashion that I had yet to meet: semiformal wear. Some of these dresses were complicated. Some were like puzzles made out of fabric, and the puzzle wasn't solved until it was on your body, and you didn't look like a complete idiot. One particular dress—this embarrassingly short, denim-blue thing—had an overabundance of straps and sashes that needed to be untied and retied to fit it to your shape, and after ten minutes of trying to figure it out, I had to do the unthinkable.

"Imogen?" I mumbled.

"Yeah?" said Imogen's voice from the other side of the dressing room door. "Is everything okay?"

I let out a ragged breath. "I can't figure this thing out."

"Oh. Would you like some help?"

"If that's okay?" I said. Except my voice totally cracked on the word "okay."

I unlocked the door, Imogen came in, and locked it behind her. Then she looked me up and down with great amusement, like a circus attraction.

"Wow," she said, suppressing a giggle. "You look like a Christmas present that my baby brother wrapped."

"Help me," I said.

"Here, let's take this thing off and start over. I think you have all the wrong things tied in the wrong places. Arms up."

Before I could even think to object, she grabbed the bottom and lifted it up to my tits. My arms flew up, but it was mostly a reaction to my panic. The dress came over my head, and Imogen immediately set to work unraveling the puzzle.

There I was, in a tiny four-by-five room, with Imogen, in Wynonna's bra and panties. I was so embarrassed and sexually overwhelmed, I was unraveling faster than the dress.

"Okay, let's try this again," she said.

This time, she lowered the dress and had me step into it. She pulled it up the curves of my body until it seemed to slink into place. Then she moved behind me, adjusting and tying the straps and sashes.

"You seem different," she said.

My entire body tensed up, like I had been caught in a lie.

"What do you mean?" I said, finally. My voice—even if it wasn't *mine*—had never sounded so incriminating.

"It's not bad," she said. "You're just quieter. More . . . vulnerable. And I mean that in a good way. I miss this. I miss being this close. I feel like there's been a . . . not a *wall* between us, but a *layer*. And not even a *bad* layer. More like a *protective* layer. And it's weird. Ever since you and Ezra, I feel like that layer just disintegrated."

I nodded because words eluded me.

"Anyway," she said, "thank you for being you."

I know she meant that as the most genuine of compliments. Given the circumstances, however, it made me feel dirty, and ugly, and treacherous. Imogen had so much trust in Wynonna. And I *wasn't* Wynonna. I was a liar in the perfect disguise.

"Okay, done," she said. "Turn around."

I turned around. Imogen's eyes lit up.

"Oh. My. Gosh," she said. "This is it. This is the one."

Then, inexplicably, she gathered up all Wynonna's clothes into a bundle in her arms—minus the burgundy combat boots I was still wearing—and left the dressing room with them.

"Come on!" she said. "I'm buying."

"What?" I said in mild terror. "I can't go to the register wearing this!"

"Sure you can! I'm a regular, and Phoebe's at the register. Phoebe lets me do this all the time."

Sure enough, Phoebe did.

"Mm-mm, girl," said Phoebe. "Rockin' that dress. Here, turn around, lemme scan you."

Next up: nails.

Imogen ordered French mani-pedis for both of us. I wasn't going to lie, it was probably the most relaxing thing I had ever done in my entire life. I closed my eyes and nearly fell asleep, I was so in my Zen. It was only when we were finished that I discovered my fingernails had gained a centimeter or two. I tried to open Imogen's car door, and they clicked uncomfortably against the exterior.

"Is it supposed to be this impossible to use my hands?" I asked.

"I know, right?!" Imogen exclaimed, like she had been holding her cynicism in. "Isn't it maddening?"

"Then why did we—"

Imogen balled her hands as much as her nails would allow, smooshed them into her cheeks, and squealed, "BECAUSE WE LOOK SO DARN FREAKING CUTE."

We drove straight to Imogen's house and burrowed ourselves in her bedroom. Her bedroom was pink and frilly—like she hadn't attempted to redecorate since fifth grade—and featured bookshelves filled with old box sets like Anne of Green Gables and Little House on the Prairie. There was also an assortment of posters, ranging from *The Sound of Music* to *Pride and Prejudice* to Josh Groban. Imogen pulled out her desk chair, faced it away from her armoire mirror, and made me sit. I was instructed that I wasn't allowed to look until she was finished.

"I've been watching a ton of makeup tutorials lately for therapeutic reasons," she said. "Here's hoping I learned a thing or two in the process!"

Imogen went to town on my face. I closed and opened my eyes when she told me to, puckered my lips, and was instructed on a second-to-second basis to be very, very, *very* still. I mostly succeeded.

Finally, Imogen took a step back. Her eyes grew large and soft, and her mouth opened, on the fringe of breathless.

"What?" I said. "Is everything okay?"

"Huh?" said Imogen. She snapped out of her daze. "No, it's...

you're just *perfect* is all." She nodded at the mirror. "Go. Look at yourself."

I stood up and turned around. What I saw reached into my lungs and stole the air right out of me.

The true mastery of Imogen's art was that it only served to draw attention to Wynonna's natural features. The eyeliner was laid in thin, perfect lines, the mascara turning her already full lashes into an obsidian picture frame. Her eye shadow was a natural color, but there were possibly three or four different shades blended together in different parts, giving a surreal dimension to the shape of Wynonna's already uniquely proportioned eyes.

The contouring beneath her cheekbones drew attention to their broadness and strength.

The lipstick was the one truly bold thing: the most intense red I had ever seen. Red like the fire that gave birth to the universe. Red like the lifeblood of everything. It was the sort of red that burrowed into your soul, never to be forgotten.

Wynonna looked beautiful.

I looked beautiful.

That was the strangest thing—that it became very difficult to separate the beauty I was looking at from the beauty I felt. And I *felt* exquisite.

"Okay, now that *you* look like an angel princess, maybe I should make *myself* look not like a hobo," said Imogen. She leaned into the armoire mirror beside me and examined herself, making odd faces. "I'm thinking of plucking my eyebrows."

A spike of panic impaled me from top to bottom.

"NO," I sort of screamed.

Imogen jumped back from the mirror, startled.

"You just have really nice eyebrows," I said. "Please don't pluck them. Please. I can't say 'please' enough. I'll get on my knees and beg if I have to."

"Okay!" said Imogen, thoroughly amused. "I'll keep the eyebrows. Although I'd be lying if I said I wasn't totally tempted to let you beg anyway."

I dropped down to my knees, clapped my hands together, and interlocked my fingers. "Please, please, please, please, pleasepleaseplease."

Imogen rolled her head back and sighed. "You are way too adorable for your own good."

• •

Imogen enlisted the help of Mrs. Klutz to do her makeup. Mrs. Klutz was basically a shorter, more diva version of Imogen. Imogen got her height from her dad, who was one nightmare short of the Slender Man. (He worked for the IRS. I had no idea what he did, but I imagined him as an agent/collector of sorts, visiting the tax-delinquent with a briefcase in one hand and a scythe in the other.)

Mrs. Klutz asked what my shoe size was. It was seven. (Thank god I was curious and had looked inside Wynonna's burgundy boots this morning.) Mrs. Klutz squealed with delight, told me we were the same size, and said I could borrow a pair of her heels.

Mrs. Klutz's shoe closet was the Willy Wonka's Chocolate Factory of shoe closets.

Under any other circumstance, I might have been reluctant to try on another pair of heels. But right here, right now, I was a kid in a candy store. Shit, I was Charlie Bucket!

For the longest time, I just looked. There were a lot of shoes, and the concept of "making a decision" was just a little bit overwhelming.

And then I saw them.

They were blue. Probably the exact same denim blue as my dress—which might have seemed like an incredible coincidence, except that Mrs. Klutz had damn near a billion shoes, so statistically speaking, it made sense. The meat of the shoe was a thick, lacy design, like the pattern of butterfly wings, slowly engulfing the foot. The heel, itself, was daunting—long, powerful, and deadly, jutting downward like the Sword of Damocles.

I put them on.

I felt long, powerful, and deadly. I also felt a bit like Cinderella. Like, if Cinderella had magical powers, conquered Disneytopia, and ruled with an iron fist as the Mistress of All Evil.

I spent the next half hour practicing walking in them—back and forth, back and forth—in the Klutzes' master bedroom until I wasn't a complete idiot in them. I only stopped when I heard Imogen calling.

"Wynonna! Wynonna, where are you?"

I exited the master bedroom, smooth and calculated, as Mistresses of All Evil should. Our paths met in the hallway.

"Ooh, nice kicks," said Imogen.

I was too busy plunging down the seemingly infinite abyss where people fall when they fall in love.

Imogen was wearing a long white floral-patterned summer dress that tied around the neck and draped down her like a flowery waterfall, all the way to her ankles. Taking her height into consideration, it was a *very* long dress. Her hair was straightened into elegant sandy curtains, her makeup was subtle and stunning, and her perfume was disorienting in the best way possible.

"Wow," I finally managed to say. "You look . . ."

Brilliant. Gorgeous. Sensational. Ravishing. Devastating.

"... good," I said.

No amount of makeup could hide the fact that she was blushing. Hard-core.

"Semiformal my ass," I said, when I could finally do words. "You look like Cate Blanchett."

Imogen wrung her hands bashfully. "Thanks, Wynonna."

• •

The plan was to pick up Wynezra and Holden at Holden's house. We arrived at the Durden residence at *exactly* seven p.m., just as Imogen had foretold. The "boys" answered the door together, which was kind of cute, if not a little weird.

Wynezra and Holden didn't clean up too bad themselves. Wynezra was wearing a dark blazer, sleeves rolled halfway up the forearms, over a plain white V-neck, and probably the nicest pair of jeans I owned. My out-of-control mop of hair was even combed into something vaguely Jonas Brothers. Holden had a fresh haircut, was wearing a checkered dress shirt tucked into a pair of formfitting khakis, and smelled like way too much cologne, but at least he was trying. It was probably the nicest either of us had ever looked, which was kind of sad.

Wynezra definitely noticed when it came to Holden. She was incredibly stiff and kept stealing glances at him.

Holden, meanwhile, was too busy noticing *me* to notice.

"You look pretty," said Holden. And then, as if realizing how awkward that sounded, followed it up with, "Uh, pretty *good*," which was definitely worse.

"Aw, thanks," I said. And then, realizing I should probably compliment him too, said, "Your cologne is very... musky."

Wynezra was staring at Holden's ass in those khakis—then

snapped upright when the prevailing silence started to ring like a red flag.

"Damn, girl," she said to Imogen. "You look *fine*."

My eyeballs practically popped out of my head. I shot Wynezra a "Tone it the fuck down" look.

"D'aww, shucks," said Imogen. She punched Wynezra playfully in the shoulder and said, "You look pretty spiffy yourself."

Welp. Now that the awkwardness had reached critical, we all moseyed silently out to Imogen's car.

"You four have fun!" said Principal Durden, who until this point had been silently spying on us around the corner of the kitchen. She followed us out to the doorway and perched there like an excited, anxious, helicopter-parenting vulture. "I love you, Holden. Remember to take your indigestion medicine."

"Oh my god," said Holden, between his teeth.

"I'll make sure he takes it, Mrs. D!" said Wynezra, cheerfully.

Holden opened the back door of Imogen's car. And then he stood there. It took me a second to realize he was opening it *for* me.

"Oh," I said. "Thank you."

I climbed in, he shut the door, and started walking around to the other side. Wynezra apparently hadn't coordinated the chivalrous door-opening scheme with Holden, though, because she was already in the passenger seat, and Imogen was walking around to the driver's side.

Wynezra, not even turning around to look at me, said, "If we haven't swapped by the time the movie starts, should I make a move on Imogen? Yes or no?"

You have to understand that Wynezra asked this in a window of mere seconds. Maybe a mere *second*. I had no time to ask what "make a move" meant. I had no time to consider the consequences. I only had time to utter one single-syllable word.

All I could think of was Imogen getting "a move" from some semblance of Ezra, and that sounded amazing.

"Yes," I said.

Imogen and Holden entered their doors at exactly the same time.

"Let's get this girl some Fat Patties!" I screamed, to divert attention from the fact that I was having a mental breakdown.

But in that moment, it was a *good* mental breakdown. Probably the *best* sort of mental breakdown. Like that moment on a roller coaster when the nose tips downward, and you plunge, and the momentum flings your heart into your esophagus, and you throw your arms into the air and think, *I am going to die*, but it's okay because this is also probably the greatest moment of your life.

THIRTEEN

"YOU OKAY?" SAID HOLDEN. "You haven't touched your Big Fat Patty."

I loved Fat Patties. Let me start there. With that said, there were two things I hadn't taken into consideration: 1) Wynonna's stomach was significantly smaller than mine, and 2) I was sick with anticipation over Wynezra "making a move" on Imogen.

So, in my state of disintegration, I ordered my usual: the Big Fat Patty.

The Big Fat Patty was a force to be reckoned with. It was a pure monster of a burger—truly insurmountable unless you were a teenage boy with a metabolism like the Indy 500 and an affinity for masochistic behavior.

"I think my eyes were bigger than my stomach," I said.

"I'll say," said Imogen. "You *always* order the Lasso Patty."

"Yeah, weird," said Wynezra, who was munching on the fries that came with *her* Lasso Patty.

Once it became painfully clear that I wasn't going to conquer even a fraction of this Burgerzilla, I asked for a to-go box.

We picked up, and it was off to the AMC 8.

At the concessions, we somehow agreed on ordering two large drinks with four straws (even though I felt extremely germy about the inevitable backwash situation) and also two large popcorns and two M&M'S. We then dumped the M&M'S into the popcorn. We may have been teenagers, but we were wise beyond our years and knew the ways of the world.

As we claimed our seats in the theater, Imogen sat next to Wynezra, who sat next to Holden, who sat next to me. We sat quietly—perhaps a little *too* quietly—through the previews, and then the theater went just a little bit darker and quieter.

The first thing to appear on-screen was the cut, bloody, and bruised face of Jane Jenkins—the "final girl" of the past three Splatter films. She had a red security blanket wrapped around her shoulders and was being escorted by a pair of medics. In the background was the burning wreckage of the Terrorland theme park—the setting of *Splatter III: Land of Terror*. Police were attempting to fend off the hordes of reporters arriving on the scene, holding out microphones, shouting out a blur of questions.

One reporter—a determined young woman with curly red hair—found a gap in the police barrier and broke through.

"Is it true that Buddy Borden is dead?" she asked.

Buddy Borden was the mutant killer of the past three Splatter films. He wore a splatter mask—a real thing worn by British tank operators in World War I—in which the top half was leather, with a series of shutter-like slits over the eyeholes, and the bottom half was chain mail. Buddy also happened to be Jane's biological father, although we didn't learn that until *Splatter II: Buddy's Back*.

"He better be dead," said Jane. "I decapitated him with a fucking roller coaster."

The screen went black, and screeching string instruments filled the silence, and the title—*Splatter IV: The Reckoning*—literally splattered across the screen.

"God, these movies are so terrible," I said. "I love it."

"Whoever picked this movie out," said Wynezra, "I hate you."

"I thought you loved these movies," said Holden.

Wynezra gave a manic, uneasy laugh. "Yeah. Right. Just kidding, guys. I'm so stoked."

"Shhh," said a person sitting behind us.

The screen opened to a beautiful college campus—"one year later"—where Jane had made a cast of all-new friends (again), the lot of whom would undoubtedly die (again): the Super Sweet New Boyfriend, the Plucky New Best Friend, the Dude Bro Tool Bag whom the Plucky New Best Friend totally wanted to shag (at least one of whom would die during said shagging), and the Nerdy Comic Relief with Superior Knowledge of Horror Movie Tropes who—in a weird, meta sort of way—had become the tropey-est trope of all.

Seeing as it was the anniversary of Buddy Borden's death, the five friends decided to revisit the cabin at Camp Skudakumooch—setting of the original *Splatter*—where the evil known as Buddy Borden was born. Surely this was not a terribly fatal idea.

Jane Jenkins and Plucky New Best Friend were in their dorm room, packing up for the weekend getaway, when Plucky New Best Friend said:

"You know, Jane, when you and Liam got together so fast after... you know... Terrorland... I was a little worried. But I feel like you two are really good for each other."

"I feel like he's helped me heal," said Jane. "His mom's in a psychiatric hospital for murdering his dad, and my biological dad was a radiation-mutated psycho killer who murdered my mom, my dad who I thought was my real dad, three of my best friends in the whole world, two boyfriends, one guy I was *really* into, and . . . *so* many others, I can't even handle counting."

"You're doing a good job so far," I said.

"Shhhhhhhhhhhhhh!" said the eponymous Shusher behind us.

"Do you think he's going to . . . you know?" Plucky New Best Friend made a circle with her thumb and index finger, and then pushed her ring finger in and out of it. "Put a ring on it?"

"What? No!" said Jane, in a way that indicated she totally wanted a ring on it. "I mean, maybe. We've, you know, *talked*."

"Interesting. Because *I* heard that just yesterday, he and Chuck went to . . ." Plucky New Best Friend leaned forward. "*Jared*."

"I sure hope Jared paid for that advertisement," I said.

"Shhhhhhhhhhhhhhhhhhhhhhhhhhhhhhh!" said Shusher.

Wynezra whipped around. "Do you mind? Your shushing is easily the loudest thing in this whole theater."

"Shh," said Shusher.

Wynezra's head rotated, like she was scanning the theater. "There's two open seats in the very back, Imogen. Do you wanna sit there instead?"

She then gave a subtle sideways nod in my and Holden's direction, and winked at Imogen.

"Um," said Imogen, seeming to pick up on the hint. "Yeah?" And then she started nodding. "Yeah, sure."

"See you guys after the movie," said Wynezra, and she gave another wink, and it was definitely meant for both Holden and me.

"Shh—" Shusher started.

"SHHHHHHHHHHHHHHHHHH!!!" said Wynezra, throwing her entire body—my body—into it. She then straightened, adjusted her blazer with a sharp tug, and she and Imogen weaved out of the aisle and moved to the back of the theater.

It was just me and Holden and the armrest between us. Thank god for the Dr Pepper in the cup holder.

Holden took a long sip of the Dr Pepper, then—very sneakily—swapped hands and set it in the opposite cup holder.

Okay. Well. This was happening.

"Can I have a drink?" I said—even though I really wanted nothing to do with the Dr Pepper. All I could think of was the accumulated backwash over the past fifteen minutes.

Holden nodded, slightly embarrassed, and handed over the drink. I took the smallest sip I could get away with, then set it back in the cup holder between us.

Your move, Durden. Wynonna "Hard-to-Get" Jones is in the house.

Holden resolved to set his entire arm on the armrest, regardless. His hand was wrapped around the Dr Pepper as some sort of excuse. Then his grip lessened, ever so slightly. Then he sat completely upright in his seat, and his arm rotated just enough to allow his hand to fall open, palm facing the ceiling. His fingers gaped upward, like the teeth of a Venus flytrap.

I sighed inwardly. I knew what I had to do. Wynonna was making "a move" with Imogen. I could only assume she expected as much effort on my end.

I grabbed Holden's hand.

There was nothing soft or subtle about it. I grabbed it like a TV remote—simultaneously purposeful and lazy and just a little bit exasperated. Holden immediately tensed. Then his fingers interlocked with mine.

Then his palm started sweating.

Wow. Holding hands really was the worst. Was this a universal thing? Or was it just something girls had to suffer through?

"Do you really think Liam's going to propose?" said Jane.

"If he does, Jane, he'll be dead in the morning," I said.

In my peripheral, I saw Holden lean in my direction and look at me. I honestly thought he was going to whisper something to me, so I looked at him.

Then he kissed me.

Whoa.

Whoa, whoa, whoa, whoa, whoa.

Full disclosure: This was my first kiss. (Thanks a ton, bro.) So I literally had no context in which to evaluate what was going on here. To his credit, Holden's lips were surprisingly soft, and his breath even smelled vaguely minty. After the initial impact of our lips, however, he started moving his mouth an awful lot, like he was trying to eat something that wasn't dispensing properly out of my mouth.

He pulled away when he realized I wasn't kissing back. I must have looked a little bit terrified, because he reared back like he had made a fatal miscalculation, and even let go of my hand.

"Are you okay?" he said. "Did you not want . . ."

He couldn't even finish the sentence, he was so mortified.

"No, it was great," I lied. Then, to fill in the awkward silence, I said, "Thank you."

"Oh," he said. "You're welcome."

I was about to turn back to the movie, but he leaned in to kiss me again. He didn't hold anything back this time. I quietly submitted to my fate and attempted to kiss him back. His hand touched my cheek, and it actually felt pretty good. And then his hand massaged into my hair, and wow, that felt even better!

Then his free hand grabbed my very bare—very exposed—leg, and I felt a twinge of panic.

His hand drifted onto my inner thigh, and glided up—very, very *up*.

Holy fuck.

I bolted up from my seat.

"I'm sorry," I said. "I have to . . . I have to use the . . ."

I was searching for the word "bathroom," but it wasn't coming to me. So I squeezed through the aisle as fast as I could, and power-walked frantically for the exit.

It was only as I was passing the last row of seats that I saw them—Imogen and Ezra. Except Ezra was sucking on Imogen's neck, and Imogen's head was rolled back, and her mouth was open, and her eyes were wild with euphoria.

And then her eyes dropped, and she saw me.

I ran out of the theater.

I veered into the alcove that led into the restrooms, and there I stared Robert Frost–esquely at two paths, one leading to the men's restroom, and one leading to the women's, and that's when I started crying.

I barreled into the women's restroom, passed a woman who shot me a concerned glance, locked myself in the far-back-corner stall, and collapsed on the toilet seat.

I wasn't even sure what I was specifically crying about. It could have easily been the way Holden was touching me, but it also could have been the way I felt this body reacting—churning in a very sexual way that was both familiar and alien—or it could have been that I had my first kiss with my best friend whom I had nothing but platonic feelings for, or it could have been that Wynezra was "making a move" on Imogen, and deep down, I didn't want that. Because even though she was wearing my body, it was still her inside, and it would be her experience, not mine.

I completely fell apart at that point—choking, sobbing, dying.

Someone knocked on the door.

"O-o-o-occupied," I said between choking sobs.

"It's me, Imogen."

Oh god. Oh Christ. Oh literal Jesus of Nazareth.

I wiped away at my face, sniffed back the sadness, and took several strangled breaths.

"I'm fine," I said.

"Can I come in?" said Imogen.

"I'm fine, really."

"Oh, I know. I just need to use the bathroom."

It was the most perfect, ill-timed joke. I burst out laughing, and then my laughter turned into sobbing all over again.

"I want to talk to the real Wynonna," said Imogen. "Not the fake Cesario version."

"I'm not the real Wynonna," I said. "I've been lying to you this whole time."

"Okay. Well, can I talk to whoever is in this stall?"

Who was I to object to that? I leaned forward and unlocked the stall. Imogen entered, then locked the stall behind her.

"I'd offer you a seat, but . . ." I gestured elaborately at the lack of additional toilet seats in the stall.

"Is this seat taken?" She pointed at my lap.

I cracked a smile that indicated it was not.

Imogen sat in my lap. For someone as skinny as she was, she was surprisingly heavy. I guess all that extra length and height had to go *somewhere*.

"I saw you kissing Holden," she said.

Of course she did. She and Wynezra were sitting in the very back—very top—of the theater. I was sure they saw everything.

"Was it not what you were expecting?" said Imogen.

"It's not that," I said. And then I thought of Holden reaching up my leg, and I felt sick. "Not *just* that. It's . . ."

God, how to word this?

"I don't feel like myself is all," I said.

"Oh, right," said Imogen. "Because you're not the real Wynonna."

I chuckled. "Exactly."

"So, who are you?"

"I guess I'm the fake Cesario version."

"Hmm. That sounds like a pickle."

"Yes! It's a fucking pickle is what it is. Thank you!"

"You know," said Imogen, "Olivia isn't in love with Viola."

Wait, what?

"She's in love with *Cesario*," said Imogen. "That love was never fake to her."

I looked at Imogen. Only now, Imogen's face was close—dangerously close—and her breath was shallow, and her eyes were large and intense and filled with so much compassion that I didn't deserve.

It was like someone lit a fuse, except that fuse separated in two, and reached both Imogen and me at the same time, igniting us like carefully timed fireworks.

We kissed.

Our lips met like waves crashing on a rocky shore—jagged, and rough, and alive. My hands were in her hair, ruining the freshly straightened curtains, and hers were on my face, cradling it like something precious. Imogen raised a leg, tucked it in, and slid it past me with impossible, balletic grace, until she was straddling me. She bit my lip. My frustratingly long fingernails scraped down the length of her back. Her hands ran down my neck, my bare shoulders, sliding down the curves of my chest. And then she grabbed my breasts, firmly, and squeezed them like she meant it.

Oh. My. God.

Something surged inside of me—an ecstasy I had never known. I lost all scope of the situation—who I was and what I was doing. My eyes became level with the rapidly forming hickey that Wynezra had left on Imogen's neck. My mouth latched onto it like a bull's-eye.

"Ohhhhhhhh," said Imogen, and her eyes rolled into the back of her skull. And then she laughed. "Oh my god. Did you tell Ezra that was my spot?"

Huh?

"What am I saying?" said Imogen. "Of course you did. You're the only person who knows my body like that. Thanks a lot, traitor."

My mouth let go—growing slack with realization.

Imogen wrapped her arms around me, squeezing me like she never intended to let me go. The sexual intensity defused, and there was nothing left but the deepest, purest, most heartbreaking affection.

"I feel like I've been holding my breath," said Imogen. Her voice was like an open wound. "Ever since last summer. And now . . . now I can finally breathe."

I felt the truth slip around my neck like a noose, pulling tighter with each passing second. Wynonna lied to me. Or, at least, she smudged the truth significantly.

Imogen was in love with someone, but it wasn't a boy.

Imogen was in love with Wynonna.

FOURTEEN

MY WORLD HAD EXPLODED, and all sound had been absorbed in the blast. The only thing left was this ringing sensation that was everywhere and nowhere all at once. Imogen's mouth was moving, but there were no words.

"What's wrong?" said Imogen. Her voice punctured a hole in the silence—muffled, but coming rapidly into focus. "Why are you looking at me like that?"

"I've made a terrible mistake," I said.

Imogen took this like a slap to the face. She stood up from my lap. Backed against the wall of the bathroom stall. Shook her head.

"No," she said. "Don't do this to me again."

"It's not what you think," I said.

"Well, what is it?"

Her lip was quivering. I wanted to tell her that this was as hard for me as it was for her, but I wasn't even sure *that* was true. It was *heartbreaking* to me. The chances of my one and only crush over the past seven years ever liking me—*me*, Ezra Slevin—had just dropped astronomically. But Imogen—who'd apparently already received this rejection once before—looked like I had removed her heart *Temple of Doom*–style and was lowering her slowly into a ceremonial fire pit, sacrificing her to a twisted Spielbergian interpretation of the goddess Kali.

"I'm not who you think I am," I said.

"Stop *saying* that!" said Imogen. "Cut the metaphorical bullcrap. You're not Viola *or* Cesario, okay? You're Wynonna freaking Jones! And I know I'm not insane when I say that I *know* you have feelings for me. I can feel it. I've been feeling it all week! I thought I was crazy—that I was just seeing what I wanted to see—but this is real. Look me in the eyes and tell me this isn't real. Tell me you don't have those sorts of feelings for me."

"That's not the problem."

"No, the problem is you refuse to *accept* that you have feelings for me."

"That's not the problem either."

I was crying now. God, why could I not stop crying? I had this aching, strangled feeling, like my body had been filled with cement, and it had all settled and hardened in my lower abdomen, putting pressure on everything, and this was all too difficult, too *much*, and for the life of me, I could NOT. STOP. CRYING.

"Then what's the problem?" Imogen demanded.

I couldn't do this. I jumped off the toilet, fumbled with the lock, and rushed out of the bathroom.

Wynezra and Holden were standing just outside. They appeared to be having a heated discussion of their own.

"No, your advice was bullshit," said Holden. "I did *exactly* what you said, and she freaked—"

"You did *not* do what I said, I was *watching*," said Wynezra. "She was not into—"

"She said it was *great*! She said *thank you*!"

"Who the fuck says 'thank you' after you kiss them? She was being *polite*, and that was *exactly* what I told you to look out for—"

"Wynonna, wait!" said Imogen.

Wynezra and Holden had been completely oblivious to my presence until Imogen barged through the bathroom door. I turned around, ready for a continuation of the fight I had not signed up for, when she grabbed my face and kissed me.

It was so hard for me to not kiss her back. Everything about it felt so right. The only thing wrong was that it wasn't meant for me—a detail so pervasive, it tainted the whole thing.

When she pulled her lips away, she was crying, too.

Holden's jaw dropped.

Wynezra lost the color in her—my—face.

"I'm done hiding," she said. "I'm done pretending I'm not who I am. I love you, Wynonna. And if you can't accept that—"

"I'm not Wynonna," I said.

"Stop saying—"

"I'm Ezra!"

That halted the conversation like an emergency brake. There was only the sound of my heart pumping blood into my head, thrumming in my ears.

"What?" said Imogen. She shot a ridiculing glance at Wynezra. "Then who's—"

"That's Wynonna," I said. "We've been body-swapping ever since the eclipse. *That's* why we've been acting weird. We didn't have sex. That was a lie."

Imogen shook her head. "If you think this is funny—"

"It's true," said Wynezra.

Imogen stared at Wynezra, then glanced incredulously between the two of us. Fury was wafting over her like steam. "You two have sex *one time*, and suddenly you're a couple of coconspirators? You've got each other's back over a joke this . . . this . . . *stupid*?"

"If you're Ezra," said Holden, looking directly—scathingly—at me, "then why did you go on a date with me?"

"Because Wynonna likes you," I said. "And I like Imogen. And we decided to help each other get dates with the two of you to prom."

I turned to Wynezra, who shrank under my glare.

"Now I realize we were only helping ourselves," I said.

"This is stupid," said Imogen. "This is so dumb. If you expect me to believe this *Freaky Friday* bull—"

"How do you think I knew how to kiss you?" said Wynezra. "No one could have told me how to do that."

Imogen bit her lip.

"There's only one way you two are going to know who we are," I said. I marched over to Holden. "Ask me anything. Something *only* I would know."

"Yeah!" Wynezra's eyes ignited with excitement. She turned to Imogen. "There's a *shit-ton* of stuff that only I would know. C'mon, hit me with anything. Something that I would never tell Ezra."

Imogen's face was turning red. Her face slowly crumpled—a synthesis of emotions, all of them bad.

"That's the thing," said Imogen. "I don't think there's anything you two wouldn't tell each other."

She looked at Holden. "Are you ready to go, Holden? I don't want to be here anymore."

Holden nodded silently. His gaze was lodged firmly in the fabric of space, refusing to make eye contact with either of us.

"Wait, what about us?" said Wynezra.

"Call your parents," said Imogen. "Get an Uber. I really don't care *what* you two do. As long as it doesn't involve me."

With that, Imogen and Holden left us at the AMC 8. They abandoned us with purpose. I had never seen a pair of people want to get away from another pair of people so fast.

There was no way this could possibly get worse. My best friend hated me, the girl I was in love with hated me, and I felt sick, and bloated, and the pressure in my lower abdomen was becoming unbearable, and my vagina felt itchy and sticky and—

"Oh my god," said Wynezra.

I looked at Wynezra, then realized that she was staring at my crotch. I glanced down.

A trickle of blood was seeping out of the bottom of my dress, all the way down my leg.

I couldn't help it. I started crying again.

• •

While I was an inconsolable mess, Wynezra told me to go to the women's bathroom and lock myself in a stall until otherwise instructed. I did as I was told. Now that I knew I was having a period, the contents of my lower abdomen felt like they had been liquefied with an electric mixer. I pulled my underwear down, sat on the toilet, and felt my insides spill outside. I glanced down with a sort of terror usually reserved for the scared little kid who watches a horror film through their fingers.

Blood.

Ribbons of blood unspooled in the water into thick, soupy clouds, like something out of *Jaws*.

Was this really what a period was supposed to feel like? Because this seemed worse. This seemed apocalyptic in nature. A biblical End of Times situation, like the Book of Revelation was fulfilling prophecy, except inside my vagina. And that was to say nothing of the nausea, or the crushing headache, or my boobs hurting, or the feeling that someone was stabbing me in the stomach with a fork and twisting up my insides like a spool of spaghetti. This period was special. This period must have known I was a guy, and I was intruding on the Sacred Rite of Menstruation, and it had resolved to kill me with its own secret ways.

I heard the bathroom door open, and then Wynezra's voice. "Ezra?"

I sobbed in response.

Wynezra knocked on the stall door, and I unlocked it. She entered holding this orange-wrapped thing that looked like candy at first, but then I remembered the context of the situation, and I immediately wanted to die.

"It's a tampon," said Wynezra.

"Where the hell did you find a *tampon*?" I said. "Concessions?"

"The girl at concessions. I told her we had an unprecedented emergency, and she has to clean up the bathroom, so . . ." Wynezra shook the tampon like a maraca. "One of us needs to stick this puppy in the doghouse. Since you're the one bleeding, I'll let you make that decision."

I evaluated my hands and the added length of my French-manicured fingernails. I would have started crying again, but my tear ducts had been milked dry, so mostly, I just made the ugliest face imaginable.

"Right," said Wynezra. "I'll do it."

It actually wasn't as bad as I thought it would be. I was expecting pain, and horrible invasiveness, and maybe something vaguely pagan and ritualistic. But I hardly felt a thing. When Wynezra told me it was over and to pull my panties up, I glanced down and there was nothing but a string dangling down there. I was basically a human party popper, but that was the weirdest part of it, and it was purely aesthetic.

"I was expecting to feel more," I admitted.

"It might be *your* first rodeo," said Wynezra, "but it's not this vagina's."

After that ordeal, we argued over which of our parents/guardians was the worst option to call for a ride.

"You can call Carol if you *want*," said Wynezra. "I'm just saying, she'll make our lives a living hell every second of the drive."

"But she'll pick up?" I said.

"Reluctantly."

"Okay. Well. I don't think my parents will pick up."

So, we created an order to our call list that ranked the pleasantness of the pickup over the likelihood that they would actually pick up the phone. I had Wynezra call Dad. No answer. I had her call Mom. Again, no answer.

"Are they really that busy?" said Wynezra. "I mean, the hospital knows they have *kids*, right?"

"They might not be—strictly speaking—busy with *work*," I said.

"Oh?" she said. And then her eyes widened. "Oh! You think they're doing it with other people?"

"I *know* they're doing it with other people."

I went on to explain—in NC-17–rated detail—how I knew that.

"Damn," said Wynezra. "Derek's dick sounds like a national treasure."

"Can we please not talk about Derek's dick?"

"Hey, you were the one going into graphic detail. I'm just expressing my admiration. But, um, that sucks about your parents. Do you think they know about . . . you know . . . each other?"

"I don't know how they *couldn't* know. They work at the same hospital."

"Damn," Wynezra said again. "Your parents need to sell the TV rights of their lives. This would make for a *highly watchable* hospital drama. And hey, you and Willow could be the side story that rakes in the younger audience demographic!"

"I'm going to call Carol now," I said.

I called Carol.

"Let me guess" was the first thing Carol said when she picked up. "You got arrested for a DUI, and I'm your phone call."

"What? No! I'm at a movie."

"Fascinating. Is it starring Dame Judi Dench?"

"Uh, no?"

"Then you felt so terribly impressed to call me because . . ."

"I was on a double date, and our ride left without us."

"Us? Who's us? Is us a boy?"

"Us is a boy, yes."

"And I suppose this boy needs a ride home?"

"Yes, Carol," said Wynezra, who was standing close enough to overhear the conversation. "In an ideal world, that would be how this plays out."

"If that's not too much trouble," I said.

"You tell me if it'll be trouble. Are you two going to be all over each other in the back seat? Will I have to pry your young, sexually charged bodies apart with a crowbar?"

"Christ, no," I said. "He's not even my date."

"What?"

I sighed. "Our dates left together."

"Your date left with another *girl*? Or boy? Sorry, I guess I don't know what the dynamic is here. Probably not important."

It was more important than she knew, but definitely not in the way she was thinking.

"It's not what it sounds like," I said. "It's . . . complicated."

"I'll say," said Carol. "Text me the address. I'll get there as soon as I can."

"Thank you, Carol," I said.

There was a long pause on the other end. Finally, "You're welcome, Wynonna."

I was about to hang up, but Carol's voice chimed back in, slightly louder—in a naked, vulnerable sort of way.

"Wynonna?"

"Yeah?" I said.

"You can call me Grandma," she said. Then, rather hastily, "If you *want*, that is. What I'm saying is, I'm not opposed to the title."

Wynezra overheard that, too. Her eyes were bugging out of her skull.

I nodded reflexively. "Okay. Yeah. Thanks . . . Grandma."

There was another prolonged pause. Finally, she hung up.

"Dude," said Wynezra. "Did you just call Carol *Grandma*?"

"She *is* your grandma," I said. "Isn't she?"

"Biologically speaking. But she's also a bitch. And I like to think that the latter title is the one that resonates loudest with her whole thing."

"Can I tell you what I think?"

"Christ. Do I have a choice?"

"I'm not saying that Carol *isn't* rude. She obviously is. But I think you're probably *just as rude*, right back at her."

"Duh," said Wynezra. She leaned forward and flicked my right forearm—hard—where the word "karma" was embedded in my skin. "Karma, bitch. She gets what she deserves."

"Ow!" I said, cradling my arm to my chest. "That hurt!"

Wynezra chuckled. "Sorry. I forgot you're on your period."

I glanced at the word "dharma" on my left forearm. "What does this one mean?" I raised the tattooed arm in question.

"Dharma?" said Wynezra. "That's the name of the evil corporation on the TV show *Lost*."

I stared at Wynezra until her straight face splintered into a smirk.

"It's a principle in Buddhism," she said. "And Hinduism. And a bunch of other Isms. It's basically a way of living that keeps you in sync with the cosmic order of things. It's perfect alignment."

"So, like, being a good person?"

Wynezra rolled her eyes. "Sure. Being a good person. Let's go with that. But I know where you're going with this, and let me just stop you right there because who the hell is anyone to say what 'being a good person' even means?"

"I'm not saying Carol *deserves* kindness. But that's the point of kindness—giving it when it's *not* deserved. You and Carol both lost someone you love, and even though it was seven years ago, I know it still hurts. I'm just saying. I think people are more than what they do and don't deserve."

"You think you're so much better than me, don't you?" said Wynezra. Her eyes narrowed into dangerously thin lines. "Don't you ever talk to me about my mom again."

Wynezra turned and stormed out the glass exit doors into the fluorescence-stained darkness.

• •

I found Wynezra sitting on the curb, hugging her knees—my knees—in a tight, furious ball. I sat down next to her.

"Jayden told me to tell my sister to stop being a bitch," I said. "He did it right in front of both of us. And he patted me on the shoulder when he said it. Like I was his buddy, and I was in on the joke. And I just let it happen."

Wynezra said nothing.

"I don't know how it is in real life," I said, "but in the movies, big brothers always protect their little sisters. And I'm like the exact opposite of that. I just let things happen because I'm such a fucking coward. You can only claim to care for someone so much when your lack of doing anything about it speaks so much louder. I'm so desperate for Willow's validation, but really, I don't deserve it. I'll be honest: I'm jealous of you when you're in my body. You're such a *cooler* version of me. Like, in theater, when Jayden was being an asshole to Willow, and you called him a . . . a *fucktrumpet*? And you made fun of his shirt and his 'knobby little nipples'?" I air-quoted. "And the most painful part was how much Willow seemed to instantly *respect* you."

Wynezra was finally looking at me.

"Truth is, I'm pathetic," I said. "I'm pretty sure 'being a good person' is impossible when you're as pathetic as I am. When you're too much of a coward to stand up for the people you care about."

That was all I had to say. I stopped talking. I glanced down at a tiny—almost invisible—magenta spot that had managed to bleed through my dress. But no matter how small it was, now that I had noticed it, there was no un-noticing it.

Wynezra cleared her throat.

"Holden touching your leg like that wasn't *entirely* his fault," she said. "I kind of . . . gave him *tips*."

My head snapped up. "What?"

"But they were tips meant for *me*, not you. It was in case we swapped back—which I was almost *sure* we would have by now—and I guess it was kind of a filter, too, in case we *hadn't* swapped."

I was so confused, and my face probably said as much.

"There were *tiers*," said Wynezra. "Tier one: hold hands. I didn't think you'd actually *let* him hold your hand, but I knew you were trying to get me a date to prom, too, so I had a second tier: kiss. Like, make out for a little bit. And I thought *for sure* he wouldn't get that far with you, and that's when I told him Wynonna would want him to start . . . you know . . . getting a little handsy on the inner thigh."

I stared at Wynezra.

"Look, girls get horny, too!" she said defensively. "I watched Holden change into seven different outfits. I was in his bedroom, and he was changing right in front of me, and he wanted my opinion on how he looked, and I just really wanted him to touch me. So, sorry for getting a little preemptive."

I laughed.

"What?" she said.

"Nothing," I said, not very nothing-ly.

"What's so funny?"

"You're just kind of adorable as me."

That actually made Wynezra smile. "You're a pretty smokin' Wynonna yourself."

Again, we sat, marinating in the silence and the brisk bite of evening in April. This tiny dress was rapidly becoming "not enough." I pulled my legs up to my chest and squeezed them for warmth. I clenched my teeth, but even that couldn't stop the inevitable rattling. A deep shiver dug its way into my core.

I didn't notice the blazer until Wynezra had already put it on my shoulders. I looked at her, just a little bit mind-blown.

"Thanks," I said, which barely scratched the surface of my gratitude.

"Hey, I'm doing it for me, not you," she said. "I know how cold I get. Don't want myself to catch something. And it's your coat."

I smiled. "Well, thanks anyway."

Wynezra didn't respond for a long time. Meanwhile, I slipped my arms into the sleeves of the blazer and attempted to wrap them around my legs. Tucking Wynonna into the smallest ball imaginable, I was just barely successful.

"Sorry about the Imogen thing," said Wynezra. "I should have told you the truth."

She should have. But I kept that comment to myself.

"To my credit, I'm almost positive she's not *one hundred percent* into girls," said Wynezra. "I mean, you wouldn't believe the crush she has on Colin Firth. And Hugh Grant. And the immortal spirit of Alan Rickman. She has a real soft spot for British men over fifty. She just has a really big crush on me, too."

"What happened?" I asked. "Imogen said something about last summer?"

"We were experimenting. For me, I think it was purely an outlet to release all the pent-up feelings I had for Holden. It was fun at first, but then things got a little intense between us, so I tried to back away, but Imogen didn't want to back away, and... well... we kind of had a falling-out. It wasn't until the end of the summer that we finally made up again. When school started, it was like nothing had changed. Except it was probably only like that for me. Because... well, you know."

Wynezra looked at me. The sort of look that was trying so hard to be meaningful, even though it was frail and breaking.

"I really wanted her to like you," she said. "The plan was real to me. I hope you know that."

I nodded thoughtfully. I was trying not to feel bad for myself, but it was hard to not be just a little bit jealous of her. Not only was Wynonna a better Ezra than me, but Imogen was in love with her, too.

God, how could I be inside Wynonna's body, and I was still jealous of everything she was, and everything I wasn't?

• •

By the time Carol arrived, Wynezra and I still had not swapped. I politely introduced Carol to "Ezra Slevin" and Carol politely introduced herself. Carol and I made idle chitchat—about movies (mostly those starring Dame Judi Dench), about *Twelfth Night,* about—in a very abridged version of the truth—how tonight had gone terribly, terribly wrong.

Wynezra observed our friendly banter from the back seat, openmouthed.

When we reached my house, Wynezra and I still had not swapped, so we dropped Wynezra off, and I drove home with Carol.

By the time Wynonna's wonderful brain had started releasing melatonin into my bloodstream, circulating to all parts of my body, I changed sleepily out of my bloody clothes and into shorts and a tank top, and crawled into bed.

I fell asleep.

Wynezra and I didn't swap back.

FIFTEEN

WE DIDN'T SWAP BACK the next day either.

Or the day after that.

Or the day after that.

ONE MONTH LATER

SIXTEEN

IT WAS FINE AT first. I needed to learn Viola's role, and Wynezra was very committed to her three lines as Servant, and being in a single body without having to worry about the late-afternoon swap made things significantly less stressful for both of us.

But then we *kept* not swapping.

It wasn't the swap itself that was bad. It was not knowing if our lives had changed permanently—if we had each become a different person entirely—and the thing that every human being takes for granted, "being yourself," was suddenly not an option for us anymore.

It was the possibility of forever that scared us.

Before this mess, I "never saw" my parents. But that was hyperbole because of course I saw them *sometimes*. They had to buy fucking groceries occasionally and stock the refrigerator and pantry to ward off Child Protective Services. But now it had been a month—one whole month—and I had not seen my parents, and it made me want to cry.

The crying part was probably also due to the fact that I was on my period again. (It was that time of the month!) I was cramping like a motherfucker, my boobs were more sensitive than my feelings, and Jesus, my feelings were out of control.

On the plus side, after last month, I liked to think I had become a minor-league expert at tampons. (No, Wynonna didn't help me after the first time.) I resolved to figure this shit out on my own. I read dozens of online articles. I practiced. I even examined the Port of Entry with a handheld mirror.

And I bought lots and lots and lots of tampons.

I had them in my purse, in my locker, and the motherlode stashed in Wynonna's bathroom at home. I bought some pads, too, but I quickly decided that I didn't like those. Yeah, they were "noninvasive," but they also made me feel like I was wearing a tiny diaper. And if you put the tampon in right—and, I had learned, the wrong size tampon gave plenty of opportunity to put it in *not right*—it hardly felt like it was there.

Imogen still wasn't talking to us.

Holden still wasn't talking to *me*.

Holden and Wynezra, however, had made a truce. Holden obviously didn't believe that we had swapped bodies, but he wasn't the type to hold a grudge either, so they made up shortly after the double date.

He didn't ask who Wynezra thought she really was. And Wynezra never told him.

Wynezra *did* ask, however, if I could sit with them at lunch. Holden said he wasn't ready for that. So she asked if she could take turns every other day, sitting with him, then sitting with me. He said that was fine.

Wynezra asked me if that seating arrangement was okay.

It was the last day of my first period, so naturally, I was on the brink of tears.

"W-w-w-why are you asking me?" I said. "Do what you w-w-w-want. I don't care."

That was another thing: Wynezra had become surprisingly considerate of me. I'd say we became friends, but it honestly felt like something different.

Something *more.*

Nothing romantic, of course. Christ, no. I still tended to think she was loud, obnoxious, and stupid, and she thought I was an annoying little chickenshit. But we were intertwined in each other. It was almost as if we had been melted, molded together, and then separated and hardened into two entirely different beings.

"How are you today?" Wynezra asked me at lunch.

"Bleeding," I said.

"I'm sorry. Do you need some chocolate?"

She wasn't even being sarcastic. I could see in her eyes that she totally meant it. And that made me want to cry, so I thought of things that made me happy, that made me laugh, like cat videos, and cheesecake, and Chris Farley, but that only seemed to make it worse, and then I remembered that Chris Farley was dead, and I completely lost it.

Wynezra pulled her wallet out of her back pocket, removed a dollar, and ventured off to the vending machines. A minute later, she came back and set an Almond Joy in front of me.

I stared at it like a log of dog shit sealed in a candy wrapper, which it basically was.

"Almond Joy?" I said. "Of all the amazing candy bars in the whole wide world, you get me a fucking *Almond Joy*?"

"Almond Joys are great," said Wynezra.

"I hate coconut," I said. "I hate *almonds*! They taste like *actual* balls."

"They have antioxidants."

"Then antioxidants taste like balls!"

"Try it. Call it a social experiment."

"A *social* experiment?" I said. I was so mad, I could barely even decipher what she meant. So, out of pure rage, I ripped open the Almond Joy and took a big bite. I hoped it was so disgusting that it made me sick, and I puked all over Wynezra's shirt, which had a picture of a velociraptor and said VELOCIRAPTOR = DISTANCERAPTOR/TIMERAPTOR, and it was my favorite shirt! *That's* how mad I was.

I chewed.

I chewed some more.

I swallowed.

"This actually isn't terrible," I said, and I took another bite.

"I tried an Almond Joy the other day," said Wynezra. "I hated it."

"Whad? Sherioushly?"

"You wanna hear something even crazier?"

I swallowed, took another bite, and nodded. This candy bar was fucking delicious.

"I don't like pork rinds anymore," said Wynezra.

I choked on the candy bar in my mouth, gagged, and then spewed it across the table. Wynezra leaned left, just barely dodging the largest, saliva-lubed chunk.

"Are you *serious*?" I said, totally moved on from my near-death experience.

Wynezra nodded, gravely serious. "Would I joke about pork rinds?"

She most definitely would not.

"I'm willing to bet," said Wynezra, "that you like pork rinds now."

There was a long silence as she allowed me to process this startling hypothesis. In order to cope with the implications, I inserted the last of the candy bar in my mouth, chewed, and swallowed.

"So, what you're saying," I said, "is that you didn't buy me a candy bar because you care about my feelings."

Wynezra rolled her head back and slapped a hand flat across her face. "I'm *saying* that I think our tastes have completely swapped."

"Buy me a bag of pork rinds, and we can prove it," I said.

I wasn't gonna lie, after that Almond Joy, I was totally craving something salty.

"I can't. That was my last dollar."

I scowled.

"Can you buy it?" she said. "For science?"

I grumbled as I pulled my purse onto my shoulder, hefted myself out of my seat like a sentient sack of potatoes, and dragged my feet every step of the way to the vending machine.

It was then that I realized: I really wanted those pork rinds. And I hadn't even *tried* them yet!

I walked faster until I was standing directly in front of the vending machine. It towered over me—foreshadowingly—like a vision of my own future mausoleum. I inserted my dollar, pressed the necessary buttons, and the metal twirly-whirl rotated until the pork rinds were released and dropped into the bottom hatch dispenser. I grabbed the pork rinds, ripped them open, and shoved one in my mouth.

Oh my god. I liked pork rinds.

I had practically emptied the entire bag by the time I returned to the table with Wynezra—chewing with a look of dead-eyed panic. Wynezra seemed grim but hardly surprised. She already knew what the outcome would be.

"Okay, confession time," said Wynezra. "I didn't come here to talk about food. I wanted to tell you about . . . something else."

I nodded as I therapeutically popped the last pork rind into my mouth.

"I don't think I'm sexually attracted to Holden anymore," she said.

I chewed that final pork rind intensely.

"But I was looking at Imogen the other day and . . . well . . . it's hard to say what I was *feeling*, but the boinger in your pants got particularly boingy."

I swallowed the pork rind like a metaphorical revelation of the devastating truth. It went down my digestive pipe like a rock.

"Ezra," she said, "I think we're turning into each other."

• •

I couldn't process my conversation with Wynezra. I *refused* to. I mean, neither Holden nor Imogen wanted anything to do with me, so what difference did it make?

I spent the rest of school compiling a list of the reasons why Wynezra was wrong—why we were still ourselves and not Animorph transformations into each other. It wasn't a terribly long list, but it was something. I cornered Wynezra after school.

"I'm way too emotional to be you," I said, by way of greeting. "Like, I feel like I want to cry every day, and I usually succeed."

"Okay . . ." said Wynezra.

I waited for her to tell me I was right, but she just stood there uncomfortably, saying nothing.

"When you were Wynonna, I never saw you cry," I said, as if my point wasn't clear. "You were always too busy acting tough and being a badass."

"You never *saw* me cry," she said. "That doesn't mean I *didn't* cry."

I stared at her in gaping astonishment. "Are you saying *this*"—I gestured to myself—"is normal?"

"I mean, sure, you don't act like I *acted*. But that's all it was—an act. You act how I *felt*. Most days, I *wanted* to cry. Shit, most days I succeeded—but alone, in my bedroom, with no witnesses. The whole badass, tough-girl routine was usually a smoke screen to hide the fact that I was so fucking sad and miserable."

"Are you sad and miserable now?"

"I'm human. What human *isn't* sad and miserable?"

A little Nietzschean, but okay. I moved on to my next point.

"I miss my parents," I said. "And I still care about Willow. If I was turning into you, my feelings for them should be disappearing, right? But if anything, being *you*—being away from my family—has just made those feelings more intense."

"Okay," said Wynezra. "I don't have an argument for that. I'm not trying to argue with you. I still have the same feelings for my mom. I was just sharing an observation, that's all."

God, arguing with Wynezra was the worst. She had become logical to a fault, arguing with such objectivity, it felt like she was emotionally removed from the conversation, which made me want to punch her in the face. I'd like to see her emotionally remove herself from *that*! It was like arguing with . . . with . . .

I felt the air vacuum softly out of my lungs.

It was like arguing with Ezra Slevin.

• •

The hardest thing about Wynonna being so nice to me was that the *one nice thing* I was attempting to do for her had inadvertently turned into a humongous, backstabbing sort of secret.

After school, I met up with Roscoe.

At Sonic.

For slushies.

Sonic and slushies had kind of become our thing. So much so that Roscoe stopped asking me what I wanted. I always ordered the same thing, and he always beat me there anyway. He'd usually call to confirm I was on my way, and by the time I arrived, my Strawberry Real Fruit Slush was waiting for me.

For himself, he ordered the Green Apple Slush with rainbow candy. The man was a child.

On weekdays, Roscoe usually worked evenings. He was a chef, after all, and a damn good one. Too good to be wasted on the lunch menu. So, this tiny hour between school and work was an ideal time to work on Operation: Reunite Roscoe with Wynonna.

Except Wynonna and I weren't swapping back.

And maybe we were turning into each other.

I pulled up beside Roscoe's Malibu in the adjacent drive-in stall. Abandoned the Saturn and hopped into his passenger seat. My Strawberry Slush was waiting for me in the cup holder.

"Philosophical discussion," I announced, casually. "You swap bodies with someone, *Freaky Friday*–style. You want to swap back. Screw waiting it out. You want to expedite the process. Tackle this shit with strategy and perspective. So: Does this have something to do with unfinished business or what?"

This wasn't the first time we'd had a "philosophical discussion" about the Freaky Friday Effect. It was actually the third. The first time, we discussed how something like this could happen from a scientific or mythological perspective. This turned into a meandering conversation about astral projection. Easily the most useless conversation of my life. The second time, we discussed *why* something like this would happen.

It usually had to do with moral life lessons. A little more effective. But it still wasn't helping me swap back.

Now I was in manic brainstorming mode. I needed to figure this shit out.

Roscoe just assumed I really liked *Freaky Friday*. And he was always down for critical analysis of absurd theories.

"Unfinished . . . business?" Roscoe repeated. The gears were churning.

"Like, Jamie Lee Curtis and I failed to do something as ourselves? So now we need to do it as each other before the universe will let us swap back?"

Roscoe inhaled a long, contemplative slurp as he processed this. Swallowed.

"Isn't that more of a ghost thing?" he said.

"Well, yeah, but . . ." I started to say, and then faded off.

He was right. It was *totally* a ghost thing.

"Yeah, it's like the movie *Ghost* with Patrick Swayze," said Roscoe.

I groaned.

"Swayze is murdered," he continued, undeterred, "but he can't pass on until he learns that his friend betrayed him, and he saves the love of his life, Demi Moore. Or something. Unfinished business."

I had seen *Ghost* once with the Durdens. Principal Durden had somehow convinced Holden and me that it was a "horror movie." And that's how we ended up sitting through two hours of Patrick Swayze taking his shirt off, Demi Moore spinning clay pottery as some sort of sexual metaphor, and slow dances.

Principal Durden was in tears by the end, practically disemboweling a box of tissues. Horror movie, my ass.

"You can keep your mouth shut," said Roscoe. "*Ghost* is a classic."

"Whoa, hey! I didn't even say anything!"

"You were *gonna*. I can see it in your eyes. Those judge-y little eyes of yours. I don't wanna hear it. *Ghost* is a masterpiece."

I laughed. Rolled my "judge-y little eyes." Slurped my slushie.

Finally, I could contain myself no longer.

"Okay, come on," I said. "A *masterpiece*?"

Roscoe shook his head and chuckled. "Don't go there. Don't even go there."

"Did the nineties have a different standard for measuring good movies? I mean, this was the decade of Furbies, so something was obviously going terribly wrong."

"Really, it all comes down to the possession scene," said Roscoe, ignoring me. "It's maybe the best scene in any movie, ever."

"Oh boy. Here we go."

Calling it "the possession scene" was misleading. That made it sound like a cool movie, which it wasn't. It was more accurate to call it the "dance scene." I mean, it was a Patrick Swayze movie, c'mon.

"Swayze just wants to touch Demi Moore one last time. Demi *believes* he's there, in the room, with her. Whoopi Goldberg lets Swayze possess her—*wear* her body—as a means of touching Demi. And when they do, Demi can f—"

"Fill the mandatory dance scene quota in a Patrick Swayze movie?"

"—*feel* him! She can *see* him! Even with her eyes closed, even while she's dancing with this woman she barely even knows, she *knows his touch*. She *knows it's him*. She can *see him with her heart*. And even though death has torn them apart, they can share this moment together."

Roscoe was rapidly disintegrating.

"All because Demi can . . . she can *see him*," he said. "She can see him with her *hh* . . . with her *hhh* . . ."

With her heart.

Roscoe cleared his throat. Hastily wiped his eyes with his sleeve.

"Anyway," he said, "Whoopi Goldberg was fucking fantastic, and don't you dare tell me otherwise."

I forced a feeble smile. "She was good."

I knew I shouldn't ask the question I wanted to ask.

But I asked it anyway.

"How did it happen?" I said. "The accident, I mean."

Roscoe bit his lip. His whole face became fragile all over again.

"Unless you don't want to—"

"No, it's fine," he said. Cleared his throat. "Um. We were at a party at a friend's house. Low-key, family-style stuff. I mean, everyone was bringing their kids, so . . . But there was alcohol. And I was drinking, and Josie was drinking, and—"

"Josie was drinking?"

"Well, yeah. Otherwise she would've driven."

I was kind of shocked. This was the first I'd heard of it.

"But it's not like we *planned* it that way," he said. "I was in one part of the house with my friends, and she was in another part with her friends, and when we were finally wrapping up and getting ready to go, well . . . Josie was sloshed. And I'm kind of a heavyweight when it comes to drinking. I thought I was fine, and we only lived a couple minutes away. If Josie was sober—if she had a clear mind—she would have told me no. She would have *stopped* me. We would've gotten a ride, or taken an Uber, or literally done *anything* else. But she wasn't. So, I drove."

Silence filled the delicate space between us.

"I hope you know," he said, finally, "that prison was never punishment for me. Losing *your mom* was my punishment. Losing *you* was my punishment. Nothing could ever measure up to losing the two of you. Prison was just time to think about what I'd already lost."

It was moments like this when I knew I had waded too far into Wynonna's personal life. Now I was neck-deep in it, and the current was pulling me in farther and farther. What could I do?

What could I say?

"I'm here now," I said.

I smiled to mask the lie.

SEVENTEEN

THE WEEKEND PASSED in a hazy blur—mostly due to the Two Very Big Things that would be happening the following weekend. This coming Friday, we would finally be presenting our legendary delinquent production of *Twelfth Night*, performing in the Piles Fork High School auditorium. (We were having it at school and not the Amityvale because—in Ziggy's actual words to Principal Durden—Amityvale was an "irreparable shithole.") Afterward, the PFHS Activities Committee would be spending the next twenty-four hours setting up for an even *bigger* event happening the very next evening.

Prom.

Not that I gave a shit about prom. It was mostly a haunting, surreal reminder. A cautionary tale of how an ambitious goal to ask out the girl of your dreams can lead to abandonment, isolation, and a crippling identity crisis.

That was maybe an oversimplification, but you get what I mean. Fuck prom.

Our *Twelfth Night* production, however, I was totally stoked for. Viola was my one and only escape from reality, and we had reached the stage of dress rehearsals. It was both daunting and exhilarating. Scripts were a thing of the past. We were reciting everything from memory, in full costume and makeup, and performing the whole thing in one fell, uninterrupted swoop.

Speaking of costume and makeup, Willow's Malvolio was easily the best. She had been made to look like a crabby old butler with fake wrinkles, a monocle, and white powder worked into her big emo hair, resulting in something very Ludwig van Beethoven. The only thing more convincing than her disguise was her performance. She was delightfully awful.

Even as the conspiring members of Olivia's household forged a love letter to Malvolio in Olivia's handwriting, convincing him that she was in love with him.

Even as Malvolio followed a list of silly, humiliating instructions outlined in the letter to "prove his love" to her.

Even as he was locked in a dungeon because he was clearly either mad or possessed.

I shit you not. This shit actually happened.

There were three stories being told: the love triangle, the prank on Malvolio, and a third that was small but crucial to *Twelfth Night*'s conclusion—the story of Viola's twin brother, Sebastian. After the shipwreck, Sebastian was rescued by a man named Antonio. Antonio nursed him to health, cared for him, and even agreed to accompany him to Illyria (despite being the sworn enemy of Duke Orsino), paying for all Sebastian's expenses. He cared for Sebastian so damn much, it was almost *certainly* romantic in nature—although it was never explicitly stated in the play. During this trip, Sebastian accidentally met Olivia, who was convinced he was Cesario. Sebastian was like "Ooh, pretty girl!" and Olivia was like "Cesario loves me!" and they immediately got married before the wisdom of time could allow them to question their poor decision-making skills. Meanwhile, Antonio got arrested by Duke Orsino's men. Poor bastard.

I was only in makeup in the beginning shipwreck scene. From then on—in the employment of Duke Orsino—Viola wore a bright blue waistcoat with big gold buttons, a white shirt with parachutes for sleeves, a cravat (which—speaking of identity crises—was something between a tie and a scarf, but clearly not either), breeches, stockings, and brass-buckle shoes. I was just the cutest little gent you ever did see.

Actually, I take that back. Holden was wearing a similar outfit, but with a darker waistcoat and cravat, and standing at five foot nothing, *he* was the cutest little gent you ever did see. Especially when Duke Orsino was angry.

In act 5, shit hit the fan. Duke Orsino arrived at Olivia's estate, learning of her marriage to a man she believed to be Cesario. Surely, his best bro had betrayed him hard-core. Meanwhile, Viola (the "real" Cesario) was caught in the cross fire.

"O thou dissembling cub!" said Holden in furious lamentation. *"What wilt thou be when time hath sow'd a grizzle on thy case? Or will not else thy craft so quickly grow that thine own trip shall be thine overthrow? Farewell, and take her; but direct thy feet where thou and I henceforth may never meet."*

"My lord, I do protest—" I said.

"O! do not swear!" said Imogen, touching my shoulder. *"Hold little faith, though thou hast too much fear."*

Imogen was wearing a froofy white dress, both elegant and kind of ridiculous. When she touched me, I didn't freeze up or shudder like I might have a month ago. I was very much in my role: a girl, dressed as a boy, secretly in love with a really stupid duke.

It was an odd thing, the way that Holden, Imogen, and I had such chemistry on the stage, and yet, the moment we were outside our roles, the walls were up, and we were back to not being friends. Back to not even *talking* to each other.

Eventually Sebastian appeared, and the cast of characters swore to god they were looking at a pair of doppelgängers. But Viola, who thought her twin brother was dead, knew who he was.

From there, things got awfully deus ex machinish. Olivia didn't seem to mind that she was married to someone who merely *looked* like Cesario, and Orsino got over the marriage pretty fast, too, because, hey, his best bud was a girl! He told Viola to go put on some girl clothes and preemptively declared that they would get married.

"Cesario, come," said Holden. He extended his hand, and I took it. *"For so you shall be, while you are a man. But when in other habits you are seen, Orsino's mistress and his fancy's queen."*

The first thing I noticed was how soft and nice his hand was.

The second thing I noticed was that my palm was sweating into his.

I immediately tore my hand away as everyone exited the stage. Holden shot me a glance that was confused and—dare I say—hurt? But I refused to notice, instead forcing myself to be psychokinesis-focused on Feste the Fool (Tucker) as he took center stage and sang a song about wind and rain and marriage.

• •

"I love performing Shakespeare," I said. "Really, I do. But the more I sit on this play, the more I realize it's kind of fucked up."

Willow laughed. "Right? I mean, I get that Malvolio's an asshole, but locking him up in a makeshift dungeon? That's a bit extreme."

Of all the shitty things that had followed my and Wynonna's body swap, one definitively good thing had come from it: my friendship with Willow. It started slowly, but she began texting me a lot. Most of it was small talk—*hey* or *you ready for dress rehearsals?* or *do you watch* The Magicians*?*—and evolved to heavier questions like *how do you know if a boy likes you?* or *how do you know if you're a good person?* To which I responded—via Siri—with things like, *He probably acts stupid whenever he's around you* or *I don't know. But I think you're pretty good.*

At first, I figured she thought of me as some sort of "female role model"—which was kind of funny, given the circumstances. But slowly, over the course of that month, I realized the truth.

She didn't have any friends.

I was *literally* her only friend—which was mind-blowing to me! I mean, she was smart, she was funny, and she was beautiful. What else, exactly, did a freshman girl need to have friends?

Though class was over, a lot of us had begun lingering well afterward. Not to mention, Ziggy had set up a foldout table with drinks and cookies. He clearly wanted us to take our time leaving. It was working.

"Why does everyone have to get married?" I said. "I mean, *everyone*! Even Sir Toby and Maria!"

"Everyone except Antonio," said Willow, shaking her head sadly. "Poor Antonio."

"I know. I secretly hope Fabian is gay, and they hook up in the after-credits scene."

"It would be kind of tragic to have a name like Fabian and *not* be gay."

"Everything about this play is kind of tragic. Duke Orsino's been stalking Olivia forever, even after she's said no a hundred times, and suddenly, she's married, and he's like, 'That's it. Put on your girl clothes, Cesario. We're getting hitched.'"

"Yeah, because he's *definitely* not rebounding."

"Absolutely not." I chuckled and gave a sad sigh. "I literally question everyone's judgment in this play."

"Do you want to have a sleepover tonight?" said Willow.

She blurted it out so fast—so sudden—I blinked and did a double take, just to make sure I hadn't hallucinated the question.

"Sorry," she said. "That was random. Just . . . between this play and prom, I'm a bundle of nerves, and my parents are never home, and I thought it would be nice to . . . but I understand if you can't. Sorry. You know what? Forget I—"

"I'd love to," I said.

"Oh!" said Willow. Her entire crabby-old-butler face lit up. "Okay! Yeah! Great!"

It had become impossible for her to speak in anything but one-word exclamations.

"Lemme just tell Ezra," Willow said finally when all the glowing seemed to be making her face hurt. She turned, and then jumped with a start.

Wynezra was standing right behind us.

"Whoa, hey!" said Willow, clutching her chest. "Didn't see you there. Is it okay if Wynonna—"

"Yeah, yeah, yeah," said Wynezra dismissively. And somewhat urgently. "Can I have a word with Wynonna?"

Willow looked at me, as if to confirm that that was okay. I gave her a subtle nod.

Wynezra put a hand in the center of my back and directed me to the far, far, far corner of the theater—well out of earshot of anyone.

"What's going on?" I said.

"I'm going to show you something," said Wynezra, "only because you would have already seen it if you were *you*, and I want you to know that it's real, and it's serious."

"Okay?"

Wynezra handed me her—my—phone, opened to a picture.

It was a nude of Willow.

A very private—very intimate—nude. One that was clearly never meant to see the light of day.

"JESUS FUCK," I said, pushing the phone away. "What the fuck? *Why* the fuck?"

"There's more."

Before I could object, she swiped her finger across the screen and shoved the phone in my face. It was the top of Willow's head. You could sort of see her face, but it was pressed against the pelvis of some dude. A long, surfer-tan arm with wristbands was gripping her hair, holding her in place.

But this wasn't just a picture. There was a play button in the very center.

I didn't dare press it.

"Remember that blowjob I told you she gave Thad? Well, apparently he made a home movie. And since I *know* you're wondering—no, she didn't know she was being filmed. I don't think she even knows this film exists."

I felt sick. I felt furious. I felt sick *and* furious, and it was a deadly combination. Like I could kill Thad and simultaneously puke on his corpse.

"Jayden texted both the pic and the video to me just a couple minutes ago. But it was a group message. It went out to, like, a dozen people."

I snapped. My head swiveled like a heat-seeking turret locking onto a target. Thad, Jayden, and a couple other guys had already changed out of their costumes. They were now crowded around something, laughing. Even Patrick was hovering on the outskirts of their group.

I stormed toward them.

"Ezra, wait!" Wynezra hissed.

It wasn't until I drew near that I realized Thad was holding up his phone, playing a video for them, and *that's* what they were crowded around. *That's* what they were laughing at.

My blood was boiling. My blood was molten magma, bubbling and spewing from the depths of the earth. My blood was a volcano.

The boys noticed my swift approach and parted awkwardly. Thad smoothly pocketed his phone. He was unfazed, playing it completely cool. And then he had the gall to check me up and down like a slab of meat.

I punched him in the throat.

Thad's mouth flailed open—gasping, wheezing, choking on his own windpipe. He dropped to his knees, hands cradled gently around his trachea.

"Fucking bitch!" said Jayden—although this seemed more an exclamation of shock than anything else. The whites of his eyes were more visible than his nipples in that tight-ass polo shirt.

I grabbed his nipples like a pair of volume knobs and cranked them until he was screaming in falsetto.

A tan, wristband-laden arm attacked me from behind, wrapping me in a chokehold. Thad's arm. I released Jayden's collar, scraping desperately at the crook of his arm, gasping for air. Nothing was coming through.

"I'll kill you..." said Thad, wheezing into my ear, "...you fucking cu—"

There was a delicious smack of flesh to flesh and bone to bone, and suddenly, I could breathe.

Wynezra had decked Thad clean in the face, and now she was on top of him, her fist moving in straight lines, up and down, up and down, like a vertical battering ram, pummeling his skull into the crust of the earth, to be excavated by archaeologists in the distant future and preserved in the Museum of Natural Douchery.

Something grabbed me by the hair and jerked my head back.

"I'll cut your fucking tits off, you fucking whore!" Jayden screamed.

I glanced down and spotted the tip of his shoe next to mine. I stomped on it. Jayden howled and let go of my hair. I spun one hundred and eighty degrees, swung my leg back, and then kicked like a cheerleader, aiming for the sky but connecting with his testicles, punting them into the top of his skull. Jayden's pupils shrank to mere specks in his irises. He crumpled to the floor, but that wasn't good enough for me because I was immediately on top of him. Unlike Wynezra, I took the two-handed approach, beating his face with both fists, whipping his head left, right, left, right, left, right—

It took the biggest person in the vicinity—Daisy—to pull me off Jayden's would-be corpse. Her big arms wrapped around my waist, hoisting me off, while my arms flailed, and my legs kicked, and I screamed.

I screamed words.

"SHE'S MY SISTER, YOU FUCKING PIECE OF SHIT, MY SISTER, I'LL FUCKING KILL YOU IF YOU EVEN LOOK AT HER AGAIN, I SWEAR TO GOD, I'LL CUT OFF YOUR COCK AND MURDER YOU IN YOUR FUCKING SLEEP—"

Ziggy attempted to pull Wynezra off Thad. She swatted him away—like a human-sized fly—but stood up and backed away with her hands in the air like this was a routine.

She was cool. She was done.

EIGHTEEN

WILLOW POSTPONED our sleepover. She was suddenly feeling very sick.

NINETEEN

THAD, JAYDEN, WYNEZRA, and I had separate meetings with Principal Durden that evening. She seemed to find it incredibly ironic that we were getting into trouble at the *very place* where we were being punished for getting in trouble *last time*.

Though Principal Durden was the one asking questions, I had more than enough questions of my own. Slowly, we got to the bottom of the truth.

It all started with a picture. And a breakup. And a very disgruntled ex-boyfriend.

It all started with Patrick Durfee.

The nude pic Wynezra showed me—the one Jayden sent to her and a dozen other people—had actually gone around school *last* month. It was the reason Thad, Jayden, Patrick, and Willow (yes, even Willow) had been punished and enrolled in theater.

You see, while Willow and Patrick were dating, Patrick asked for a nude. She sent it to him. Then, months later, she broke up with him.

Patrick was not happy about the breakup. As revenge, he turned the picture into a meme. But instead of a joke, it had an address—my and Willow's *home* address—and he sent it to several boys at school, including Jayden and Thad. From there, a rumor was born, spreading around school about how easy Willow Slevin was. That you could just show up at her house, and she'd give you a blowjob or whatever.

That's why there were so many random cars showing up at my house.

Some, like Jayden, seemed nice at first, and she let them inside. Then she learned what they really wanted, and she chased them off.

Some, like Thad, she had really liked.

Jayden was actually jealous of Thad's blowjob. He told Willow that Thad filmed her, and he had a copy of the video, and he would spread it around school if she didn't give him one, too.

Willow told him to go fuck himself. That's how Wynezra and a dozen other people ended up with the video and the original nude.

"So wait," I said. "What was Willow being punished for?"

"She sent the picture to Patrick," said Principal Durden.

My jaw about fell through the floor.

"They were dating!" I said. "The little fucking weasel pestered her for a picture, and she gave it to him! *He's* the one who spread the picture. Willow's the *victim* here!"

"She still shouldn't have sent that picture. That's unacceptable behavior at Piles Fork High School and is not tolerated. Also, do not swear in my office—"

"FUCKING BULLSHIT," I screamed. "She didn't take the picture at school. You're punishing a teenager for having an intimate life, and then being taken advantage of by her little fuckwit ex-boyfriend. Do my—do Ezra's parents know about this?"

"I called and left voice mails on both of their cell phones. I took their silence as agreement on the conditions of her disciplinary action."

My stomach plunged into a deep, dark abyss.

I stood up.

I walked out of the office.

"Where do you think you're going, young lady?" said Principal Durden. "You assaulted two classmates. We're not done discussing—"

"I am," I said. "I'm *so* done. Willow isn't going to be punished because she has a couple of shitty no-show parents who don't check their voice mail."

Wynezra was sitting in one of the chairs outside of Principal Durden's office, kitty-corner from Jayden and Thad, exchanging eyeball daggers with her. At least, Jayden and Thad were *trying* to do the dagger-glaring thing. But mostly, their faces looked like blueberry strudel. If they were glaring *anything*, it was razor-sharp pieces of strudel.

I grabbed Wynezra's hand, pulled her out of her chair, and dragged her behind me.

"Whoa, uh, where are we going?" she said.

"Where do you think *you're* going?" Principal Durden echoed.

"To the hospital!" I shouted.

• •

"Are you okay?" said Wynezra. "You look . . . distracted."

We had just entered Memorial Hospital of Carbondale from the parking garage elevator. The walls were utopia white, the tile floor was speckled in colorful geometric shapes, and—in regard to Wynezra's observation—I was eyeing everyone in scrubs or a lab coat like they were raging nymphos.

It was stupid. I *knew* it was stupid. What did I think Memorial Hospital of Carbondale was? A porno? Where every flat surface was fair game, reflex hammers and stethoscopes were bondage toys, and the climax happened inside a giant X-ray machine? My parents obviously weren't *doing* it here. But they *did* have sixty-plus-hour workweeks, and they were meeting their lovers *somewhere*. The way I figured, it was either here or Tinder. They didn't have time to meet anyone anywhere else.

Just the thought of it seized up my insides.

But then I thought of Willow.

Blood raged through my veins.

Nothing else mattered.

Finding my parents was easier than I thought it would be. All I had to do was go to the well-lit front desk of the well-lit lobby of Memorial Hospital of Carbondale—where lighting was more important than sex-in-the-workplace regulations—and say, very politely and very urgently, "Excuse me, we're having a family emergency, and we need to speak to our parents, Mark and Janet Slevin, they're doctors here, and they're our parents and this is a very urgent *family emergency*."

I was only half-lying about the "our parents" bit. It was half-true for both of us. The important part was repeating and emphasizing "family emergency." It was a well-known buzzword that few people questioned and possessed an almost magical ability to Make Shit Happen.

The woman at the front desk—a tired old lady with hair like cobweb-flavored cotton candy—gave us an alarmed look and quickly picked up the phone and started muttering urgently and Making Shit Happen. She nodded a couple times and then lowered the phone to her chest.

"Doctor . . . er . . . *Mark* Slevin is currently in surgery," she said. "But *Janet* is on her way over."

Wynezra and I stepped awkwardly to the side of the front desk, allowing the man behind us to complain about his pain medication, and no he didn't have an appointment, why should he need a damn appointment if that crock of a doctor of his prescribed him damn placebos, damn sugar pills, he'd sure like to see that doctor's doctor license, where'd he get it, Chuck E. Cheese's?

And then Mom appeared.

Mom was lean and healthy-looking, with a round—but certainly not soft—face. She gave the impression of being all hard edges, but maybe it was just her *presence* that was intense. Her teeth seemed to be in a perpetual state of clenching, and her eyes were constantly skeptical, and her brow was furrowed to the point of creating a labyrinth of forehead. In short, she seemed stressed. Maybe even *angry* that she was so stressed, which, in turn, only amplified the preexisting stress. It was a vicious cycle.

When she saw us—saw me, particularly—her brow furrowed so tight, she could have cracked a pistachio.

"Sorry," said Mom, returning her gaze to Wynezra. "I thought Willow was here. Is she okay?"

"Hi, I'm Wynonna, Willow's best friend," I said, kind of proud of myself that I wasn't even bending the truth—about being Willow's best friend, that is. I obviously wasn't Wynonna. "And no, Willow's not okay. This was just sent around school. For the *second* time."

Wynezra and I didn't even look at each other. I extended my hand palm-up, she slapped her phone into it, and I shoved it in my mom's face. It was the sort of thing that looked like we had rehearsed it, but I can assure you, we didn't. We were simply that cool.

"Oh my god," said Mom. Her skeptical eyes became huge, swelling with sickness. And then she blinked. "I'm sorry, did you say *second* time?"

Now that I had her undivided attention, I started from the beginning—that little shitbag Patrick Durfee—and proceeded through the whole harrowing story. The emphasis points were that Willow was being *punished* for this, that Principal Durden left her and Dad *voice mails* about this, and now we had a blowjob video on our hands—which I showed her. The good news was that "Ezra" and I might have assaulted and/or battered Jayden and Thad to the point of a felony—which was also, arguably, bad news.

Mom was trembling.

Mom was furious.

Not at Willow (although she certainly wasn't happy with Willow's life choices), and not at Ezra (although she had extremely mixed feelings about her son's sudden career in juvenile delinquency). She was mad at the little fuckers who did this to her daughter. She was mad at Principal Durden—her son's best friend's *mother*!

But—most importantly—she was clearly the most angry with herself.

By the time we finished, Dad showed up in his turquoise surgeon scrubs. Although the moment he saw Mom, his pace dropped rapidly, and he seemed to immediately reconsider whether participating in this family emergency was in his best interest. God, if this was what marriage was like, sign me up.

Mom noticed him, but not with her usual disdain. Instead, she returned her gaze to us.

"Thank you," she said. She looked at me specifically. "Thank you *both*. I'm glad Willow has such a good friend."

My smile faltered, if only slightly.

"Could I borrow your phone, Ezra?" she said. "I'll handle your father."

• •

What happens when two high-paid, overworked doctors leave their jobs early to address a family emergency and work together—despite their infinite differences—to be parents for once?

For starters, they threatened to press charges—against every boy involved, against the school, against Principal Durden herself—unless this shit was fixed. Like, miracle-from-Jesus fixed. Basically, someone had better walk on some fucking water. Otherwise, the Slevins would burn this school and its reputation to the ground. They would take this story to the *Chicago* fucking *Tribune* and the *Sun-Times* if they had to. And boy, did they have a headline for her: "Teenage Girl Sexually Harassed by Male Classmates, Is Punished for It by Principal."

With one parent, Principal Durden *might* have stood her ground. *Maybe*. But with two parents who had simultaneously left work early—still in their lab coat/surgeon scrubs—demanding blood and retribution, Principal Durden caved and admitted that maybe the punishment was "a tad hasty" and perhaps she "misjudged the situation." She promised to have the incident erased from Willow's records, and that she was free to drop out of theater.

Except that Willow didn't want to drop out.

"Are you kidding me?" said Willow. "The play is in four days! If I drop out two days before the performance, they're screwed. Then *Wynonna* is screwed, and she's the star of the play! Then *Ezra's* screwed, even though he only has three lines, and he auditioned to be a tree. Besides, I *want* to be in the play! Do you know how long I've practiced for this role?"

"Wait, Ezra's in the play?" said Dad. "I thought this was a detention sort of thing?"

"He and his friends, like, broke into school on a holiday."

"They did *what*? Why?"

Willow shrugged. "Your son's a menace to society. Anarchy is why."

"You know what?" said Mom. "I don't want to know why. That's not the issue right now. The issue is that you're in this play with *at least* three boys that have been sexually harassing you—God knows if there's more—so if you're not dropping out, I want *them* to drop out."

"What? No! They all have important roles!"

"You're kidding. You're telling me *all three* of those little bastards have important roles?"

"Jayden is Sir Toby Belch, and Patrick is Sir Andrew Aguecheek, and Thad is Fabian," said Willow, like this was all self-explanatory.

"So, what? You expect us to just let this play go on, as is? Then it's like you were never un-punished? Where's your *justice*, Willow? *You* may not care about your justice, but I, for one, want justice for you!"

"Wynonna and Ezra *did* beat the shit out of them," said Willow. "Well, two out of three. Wynonna kicked Jayden in the balls so hard, I'm pretty sure he's never going to have kids, and if he does, they'll probably look like Play-Doh people. Like, Wallace and Gromit. Besides, I'm pretty sure Jayden and Thad's parents might press charges against Ezra and Wynonna. If we can, like, nullify the charge-pressing on both sides, that sounds like justice to me."

By the way, this conversation was happening inside Principal Durden's tiny, undersized office. Mom, Dad, Willow, me, Wynezra, Principal Durden—we were all crammed inside it like outraged, argument-prone sardines. Wynezra and I, however, had resolved to sit quietly in the corner and not say a single word. Partly because things were resolving themselves well enough on their own, and partly because you couldn't buy drama this good on premium cable.

Mom looked at Principal Durden. "Are those boys' parents pressing charges?"

Principal Durden shrugged. "It's possible."

It was *very* possible. Both Thad and Jayden looked like we had beaten them with the ugliest stick from the ugliest tree of the ugliest forest. Their faces made me not want to eat blueberry strudel ever again.

"However," said Principal Durden, "given the circumstances, I'm sure we can come to an understanding. No doubt the Hoxsie and Magnino families don't want their boys on the front page of the"—she whipped out her index and middle fingers—"'*Chicago* fucking *Tribune.*'"

Mom smiled. "An understanding sounds good. I think we can do an understanding."

TWENTY

WILLOW AND I HAD our sleepover after all.

Technically, the Slevins invited me over for dinner, at which point, Willow piped up, "Can she sleep over, too?" It was a Monday, mind you. But today had been a crisis. Willow *seemed* okay, but I think everyone was still worried about her. I know I was. As for Mark and Janet Slevin—high on the victory of Being Good Parents—they couldn't very well refuse. Instead, they sort of adopted me.

"As far as I'm concerned," said Mom, "Wynonna is welcome to sleep over anytime she wants."

"I guess you're family now," said Dad, winking. "Just say the word, and we'll bust out the bunk beds in Willow's room."

"Yesssssss," said Willow. And then, in her best Arnold Schwarzenegger impression: *"Dooo eeet! Do eeet naaooooughwwww!"*

I'm not gonna lie. That felt fucking amazing.

Wynezra just grinned, knowing full well this was the most gratifying moment of my life.

• •

It was surreal—being in my own house again for the first time in a month.

It was one of those things you took for granted until it was taken from you. I found myself stalled in the entryway, just trying to breathe it all in. I lingered at the pictures on the wall: Mom, Dad, Willow, me. My small, dysfunctional, perfect family.

I stopped in front of the living room clock like an itch. It hadn't been adjusted in a whole month. Who knew how far off it had drifted. It was probably off by dozens of seconds. Maybe even a full minute!

"You okay?" said Willow.

I blinked. Remembered that I was supposed to be a stranger in this house. Smiled.

A great big genuine smile that kind of hurt my face.

"Yeah," I said. "Definitely."

• •

Dinner was Pizza Hut—greasy, cardiac-arrest-inducing, glorious Pizza Hut. What it lacked in the home-cooked-meal department, it more than made up for in family participation points.

I couldn't remember the last time my whole family sat down together for a meal. It was a rare, cosmic event—probably in the same league as the eclipse. Maybe rarer, because at least scientists could predict that shit.

After dinner, Willow and I changed into our pj's. But this was a mere superficiality. Neither of us planned to sleep. We were too worked up to sleep—wired, and restless, and alive.

Willow belly-flopped on her bed—gracelessly—then rolled onto her back so that her hair cascaded over the edge in an emo waterfall. She pointed at me. "Truth or dare."

"No," I said, shaking my head, giggling. "No way."

"Come on!" She slapped the empty mattress beside her. "I'll go easy on you."

I sighed and sat on the bed. "Truth."

Willow sat upright, but she didn't hesitate—not even for a second. "When Ziggy pulled you off Jayden, and you were screaming at him, you said, 'She's my sister.' Why did you say that?"

Well, shit.

I set myself up for this one. I only screamed that line loud enough for anyone in a five-mile radius to hear. I should've seen this question coming light-years away.

"Uh . . . you're like a sister to me," I said. "I don't have a sister, so . . . Sorry if that was weird."

"No." Willow shook her head hastily. "Don't be sorry. That's what I figured you meant. I was just flattered is all."

But even as she said this, she looked at me in a prying sort of way. Like she could see through my disguise.

"Truth or dare," I said, sort of frantically.

"Truth."

"Do you hate Ezra?"

Watch out, kids. Captain Buzzkill was in the house.

Willow reared back slightly. "What? No. Why would you ask that?"

"Uh."

"Does Ezra think that?"

Fuck, fuck, fuck. Fix this, Ezra, fix this.

"I think . . . that maybe he thinks that," I mumbled, like a total dipshit.

"Well, I don't," said Willow. "I love Ezra. He's my brother. I mean, he's frustrating sometimes, and kind of oblivious, but he's a boy, so I try not to hold that against him."

I bit my lip, and nodded, and was trying so very, very hard not to get emotional. I mostly succeeded.

"Sorry, that was a stupid question," I said.

"No, it's fine," said Willow. "Truth or dare. Pick truth."

"Uh, truth?"

She leaned toward me, fingers interlocked. "What is the nature of your and Ezra's relationship?"

"We're friends."

"You seem like you're more than friends."

"We're just really good, *really weird* friends. I promise. It doesn't make any sense, I know."

Willow nodded thoughtfully. She seemed awful accepting of this half-baked explanation.

"Truth or dare," said Willow. "Pick dare."

"Hey, it's my turn!"

"Pick dare. I dare you to pick dare."

"Oh my god," I said, laughing. "Fine! Dare."

Willow rolled off the bed clumsily, staggered for balance, and veered to her honest-to-god hope chest. It was an ugly, beat-up heirloom that she inherited from our grandma Slevin. Willow opened it and rummaged through the contents. It appeared to be filled with an odd assortment of sentimental items—old stuffed animals, art from middle school, ancient iPods probably filled with pop music she no longer felt comfortable associating with.

She pulled out a DVD and shoved it in my face—*She's the Man*.

"I dare you to watch the best movie in the world with me."

• •

Illyria and Cornwall were at war!

Except "Illyia" and "Cornwall" were boarding schools, and the "war," so to speak, was a soccer game. Still, shit was lit, and it was about to get lit-*er*.

AMANDA BYNES (disguised as a boy): Okay, you know what? I can't do this anymore. Everybody, I have something to tell you. I'm not Sebastian. I'm Viola.

CHANNING TATUM: Wait, wait. You're not Viola.

AMANDA BYNES: Yes . . . I *am*.

CHANNING TATUM: No, I *know* Viola. I *kissed* Viola.

AMANDA BYNES: You kissed *me*.

CHANNING TATUM: W-w-w-w-what are you . . . t-talking about, I didn't . . . I didn't kiss you.

Willow made a fake sobbing sound and pressed her hand to her chest. "Oh, my heart."

"Channing Tatum is so precious when he's flustered," I said.

Amanda (Boy)nes proceeded to pull off her fake sideburns, all the while explaining that the girls' team at Cornwall got cut, and the guys wouldn't let her go out for their team; therefore, she'd been pretending to be her brother for the past two weeks while he was in London. That way, she could make Illyria's team and beat Cornwall, because seriously, fuck Cornwall.

Then Amanda (Boy)nes pulled off her entire wig, and yep, "he" was a she.

Channing Tatum, however (flustered af), was in serious denial that his best bro was also the girl of his dreams. He politely informed her that just because she was wearing a wig, that d-d-d-d-didn't prove she was a girl.

Amanda Bynes thought that was amusing. That's when she lifted her shirt, and let the tits do the talking.

Cut to Viola and Sebastian's parents—awkwardly averting their gazes in the bleachers.

VIOLA/SEBASTIAN'S DAD: Is it just me, or does this soccer game have more nudity than most?

Willow cracked up at this part. We both did. The laughter was terminal. We would surely die.

"Dude," said Willow, wiping away a legitimate tear. "Do you remember when we were watching this, and Dad was in the room on his laptop?"

"Oh my god, yes!" I said. "All he hears is 'nudity,' and he's like, 'Whoa, what the hell?' "

Just thinking about it made me lose my shit all over again. I laughed.

Until I realized I was the only one laughing.

Until I realized what I had done.

"Truth or dare," said Willow, suddenly very serious. "Pick truth."

"Uhhh . . ."

"Are you Ezra?"

I didn't need to look in the mirror to know that I was wearing my confession on my face.

Last second, I decided to play it stupid.

"Ezra?" I said. "What are you talking about? How can I be Ezra?"

I was playing it *soooooo* stupid.

"Holden talked to me," she said. "He said that you told him that you and Wynonna were swapping bodies. That it's been happening ever since the eclipse."

"Holden said that?" My guard had been blindsided. I dropped it shamelessly. "When?"

"Yesterday. After you attacked Thad and Jayden. He wanted to know if I'd noticed anything . . . *different* . . . about you."

She didn't even bother specifying who she meant by "you." We both knew who she meant.

Holy shit. *Holy shit!* Did this mean Holden believed me?

"You're Ezra," she said. "Aren't you."

It wasn't a question. Not even remotely.

So I told Willow everything.

I tried to start at the beginning—although pinning down "the beginning" was trickier than it should have been. I settled with the most recent eclipse, and from there, worked my way forward, and backward, and upside down. I explained what Wynonna and I had pieced together from seven years ago, although so much of that was still a mystery to me.

Willow didn't speak a word the entire time. I spoke over the ambience of *She's the Man* and finished as the credits rolled all the way to the logos at the end, and the DVD returned to its obnoxious DVD menu.

I was kind of breathless by the end of it all.

I looked to Willow for some sort of feedback. A sign that everything had been received and registered properly.

"A *month*?" said Willow, finally. "You haven't changed back in a whole *month*?"

I bit my lip. Shook my head.

Willow threw herself at me. Hugged me. Crushed me in her embrace.

"I've missed you, Ez," she said. Only her voice was broken. She was sobbing. "I've missed you so much."

But this wasn't just about missing me. I could tell from the way she was suddenly trembling. Gasping for air.

It was the nude. The blowjob video. Months of sexual harassment *literally* knocking on her front door. It was all crashing down on her now, and she was sobbing, and she was drowning in it, and there was nothing for her to hold on to.

Nothing but me.

I held her. And I cried a little bit, too.

"I'm here," I said. "I've always been here."

"I know," said Willow—sniffling, smiling in spite of everything. "I know you have."

TWENTY-ONE

THE NEXT DAY, ROSCOE texted me: *Hey, wanna hang?* Which was great because I needed to gush about yesterday to someone, and Wynonna was already sick of me talking about it.

"It's great," said Wynezra. "Really, it is. BUT CHILL YOUR LITERAL PANTIES, BRO, IT WAS JUST A SLEEPOVER."

"How can you say that?" I asked. "Someone *believes* us!"

"Which is *great*. Unfortunately, it doesn't change the fact that we're still *stuck like this*."

Okay, so, she had a point.

I couldn't tell Roscoe the full story anyway, but I *could* tell him a version of it. That was good enough for me. Mostly, I was just excited and needed to spew words. Lots of them. And Roscoe would listen to me talk about anything, no matter how boring—algae, the keto diet, maybe even *Atlas Shrugged*.

I texted *yes*, and called him. He picked up on the first ring.

"Hey," he said. He sounded flustered, which was weird since he had texted me.

"Hey, yourself," I said. "Sonic run?"

"Actually, I'm feeling fancy. How about dinner at my place?"

"Dinner?"

"Yeah, dinner. I'm a regionally renowned chef, you know. It's a cardinal sin I haven't cooked dinner for you yet."

Again, I felt it. That creeping guilt that I was wading too far into this role. That maybe I wasn't even doing this for Wynonna at all.

That maybe I was doing it for me.

Naturally, I pushed that thought away—out of sight, out of mind.

"I like food," I said.

• •

I'd been to Roscoe's apartment once—two Saturdays ago—for breakfast. The place was nice. Simple. Clean. Which seemed suspicious for a single dude. (I had no doubt he cleaned the place like a serial killer at a crime scene before I got there.) His walls were decorated in minimalist art—lots of lines and squares, occasionally going crazy with an unruly trapezoid. He had several potted plants, including an adorable little bonsai tree on his coffee table. He even had a vinyl player with records like Damien Rice's *O* and Bat for Lashes's *Two Suns*. His whole thing seemed to be: hard on the outside, sweet and gooey on the inside.

Like Gushers, basically. Roscoe was a giant Gushers fruit candy.

It was that first day in his apartment, while perusing his vinyls, that I noticed he had Sufjan Stevens's *Illinois*. I held it dearly to my chest, turned and faced him, and said, "You do realize this is the greatest album of all time, right?"

Roscoe chuckled. "Are you just saying that because it's called *Illinois* and you live in Illinois?"

It was a fair enough question. But it was also pure coincidence. *Illinois* was a vision of pure genius. A transcendental work of art. It was lush and strange, jaunty and whimsical, epic and challenging. In their review for *Illinois, NME* magazine called Sufjan "a brainy little fucker." He literally immersed himself in the "Prairie State." Studied its lore like a sacred text. The entire album was teeming with bizarre facts and fascinating history. Sufjan was a genius, to be sure, and blisteringly clever, but, above all else, the album was brimming with heart.

It was a fucking symphony—a *triumph*—of the human condition.

I could have said all of this. But for the sake of not sounding like the nerd that I *obviously* was, I said, "Screw you. This album is the shit."

"Okay, okay!" said Roscoe, hands raised in playful defense. "Just trying to gauge how hipster you are."

"I prefer 'cultured,'" I said, air-quoting. "Sounds less douchey."

Long story short, Roscoe and I were a couple of cool cats.

But today was different.

When Roscoe answered the door, he was wearing a maroon dress shirt, dark slacks, and a tie. Even his hair was combed—slicked back and to the side, unleashing mild anarchy at the nape of his neck.

Not once in the history of ever had I seen Roscoe's hair combed.

I glanced down at myself—above-the-knee jean shorts, flip-flops, and an off-the-shoulder, oversized hot-pink sweatshirt that said RAD.

"I feel underdressed," I said.

"What?" said Roscoe. "No, you're fine! Come in."

He gestured me in just a little *too* enthusiastically. I reluctantly followed. The first thing I saw was that his normal dining table—a small disk on a single leg—had been transformed into something majestic. White tablecloth, candlelight, china, and the sort of silverware setup that involved multiple forks. A soft and swoony song with a hint of banjo was playing in the background for ambience—Sufjan, of course. "For the Widows in Paradise, for the Fatherless in Ypsilanti."

Something was up. So very, very *up*.

Something also smelled freaking delicious. Suddenly, it was all I could think about.

"Whoa," I said. I sniffed the air like a bloodhound. "What *is* that?"

Roscoe grinned. "That is Berner platte. Here. Sit."

He graciously pulled my seat out for me. I sat—suddenly entranced with the spectacle of everything. There were *so many forks*!

"What do you do with three forks?" I asked.

Roscoe chuckled. "The basic rule is you start with the outside cutlery and move inward."

"How many things are we eating?"

"Oh, a few."

It was a surprise five-course meal. Which *sounds* daunting, but the courses came in small, exciting spurts. The first course, for example, was a one-bite appetizer: Swiss chard tartlets with Gruyère. Gruyère was a cheese, apparently. They were basically special mini tarts, filled with an intense riot of sweet and savory: sautéed onion and fennel, sweet dried currants, egg, crème fraîche, pine nuts, Parmesan, and—of course—Swiss chard and Gruyère.

I only knew this because Roscoe carefully explained the composition to me, like a science. I just sat there and nodded thoughtfully, pretending I had enough culinary chic to know what the hell he was talking about, and that I wasn't some McDonald's-eating American dipshit, which I was.

Next was the soup: Bündner Gerstensuppe—a barley soup consisting of various, more traditional vegetables and Bündnerfleisch, a Swiss air-dried meat. Then a fish course, which Roscoe was quick to point out was *not* the main course: brook trout over a ratatouille crepe.

Finally, the entrée: Berner platte—aka the "Bernese platter."

It was essentially a wide range of meats served over juniper-flavored sauerkraut, potatoes, and dried beans. The original recipe called for more exotic meats, but seeing as this was Illinois, Roscoe settled for pork chops, knockwurst sausage, and Polish kielbasa, and slow-cooked the whole thing in AmberBock beer.

As a recovering alcoholic, Roscoe felt the need to explain to me that the alcohol cooks off. (Which I knew, obviously. I wasn't *that much* of a McDonald's-eating dipshit.) Still, I appreciated the dedication to his recovery.

I took one bite. Chewed. Swallowed.

"Oh . . . *my god*," I said. I took another bite. Involuntarily made the most obnoxious dish-savoring sound imaginable: *"Mmmmm-nnnngggghh!"*

It was impossible not to.

"Good?" said Roscoe.

I conveyed the word "good" with my eyeballs, then rolled them into the back of my skull.

"It was invented in the late seventeen hundreds," he said, "after the Bernese defeated the French at Neuenegg. To celebrate, the people of Bern held a victory feast, everyone bringing whatever they had on hand—hence the smorgasbord of meats."

I swallowed. "You sure know a lot about that country."

"Well, Bern is just a *city* in Switzerland. But, yeah. I like to think of it as my other home. In fact, in a lot of ways, Switzerland is my *real* home. Actually, that's what I wanted to talk to you about."

Suddenly, his fingers were interlocked on the table, and he was leaning forward slightly, and his full and undivided attention skewered me—every layer of me—like a kebab.

"How would you feel about moving to Switzerland with me?" he said.

I slowly leaned back as I processed this invitation. Or maybe I was just tipping over. Either way, I felt light-headed.

Roscoe cleared his throat awkwardly, like he'd never done it before.

"I'm sure you remember me talking about that job offer," he continued, filling the silence. "Well, it's a standing offer. And I want to take it. I want *us* to take it. I've already talked to Carol, and she said that she consents . . . as long as that's what *you* want. The plan would be to leave as soon as your junior year ends. That's about how long it'll take to get your passport anyway. My friend Leif is already making accommodations for our arrival. Just temporary stuff until we get on our feet. But . . . this is it. This is my life plan. Because let's be honest: I don't have a future here. But *there* . . . there, I *have* one! But I need you there with me. I can't do it without you. I can't *leave here* without you."

My gaze just sort of drifted through Roscoe. I had lost the ability to focus.

"So?" he said, nervously. "What do you think?"

Remember what I said about wading neck-deep into Wynonna's personal life? Well, I had suddenly—inexplicably—found myself at the bottom of the lake, and I was wearing cement shoes, and I had put those fuckers on myself. This was my fault.

What happened next was pure, primal panic.

"I can't go to Switzerland with you," I blurted out, "but not for the reason you think, just hear me out."

Roscoe looked like I had just punched him in the gut but then told him I had a good reason for it. He didn't respond. He just looked hurt.

"I'm not Wynonna," I said.

If that was supposed to give Roscoe something to work with, it was a breathtaking failure. He kept not responding. His silence stole the air out of the room.

I took a deep breath. It was probably best to rip this Band-Aid off. Peeling slowly would only make it hurt more.

"My name is Ezra," I said. "Wynonna and I have been swapping bodies ever since the total solar eclipse last month. It's the Freaky Friday Theory—the one I keep talking about. Only it's happening for real. In fact, we haven't swapped back for the past month. We've just been stranded in each other's body. Every time you think you've been meeting with Wynonna, you've actually been meeting with me—Ezra."

"Why are you doing this?" said Roscoe. His voice was frail. Breaking. Maybe already broken.

"Because it's the truth," I said. "The absolutely insane truth. Look, I know it's weird, but I care about Wynonna. I want what's best for her. She's been hurting for so long, and I want to help her, and I think the only way to help her is through you. Remember when I told you about there being two people inside me? THIS IS WHAT I WAS TALKING ABOUT. There's Wynonna and then there's me! Ezra Slevin!"

Roscoe's hurt and confusion were morphing rapidly into resentment. Maybe even anger.

"Remember that boy in the car with me? When you were following us, and he got out, and yelled at you? That was Wynonna. That was her inside my body. And yes, she still hates you, but you've got to believe me when I say this: All I ever wanted was to help. I just wanted her to have a family again, Roscoe. That's all."

That was all.

The Band-Aid was off. The wound was exposed. I had nothing left to say.

All I could do was wait, and hope, and listen. "Slevin?" he said. "Ezra *Slevin*?"

"Uh." I was caught off guard. "Yeah?"

His eyes became distant. A pair of orbs drifting off into outer space.

"That little boy," he said. "You're pretending to be that little boy."

"Little boy?" I was only slightly offended. "What are you talking about? What little boy?"

But Roscoe didn't answer. Instead, he started shaking his head. His eyes became glassy, his face shattered.

"This is cruel," he said. "I don't think you even realize how cruel you're being."

"What little boy?" I repeated.

Roscoe stood up from the table. Veered into the kitchen, opened the refrigerator door, rummaged through the contents.

Closed it with a six-pack of Michelob AmberBock in hand.

Well, five-pack technically. It was one bottle short, thanks to marinating the Berner platte. And then he just stood there—probably for the longest couple seconds of either of our lives.

When he eventually moved, it was with finality. Straight line to the trash can, stepped on the pedal that pops the lid, and dropped the beer in.

He veered for the front door.

"Whoa, where are you going?" I said.

"I'M GOING FOR A WALK," said Roscoe loudly.

As he stormed out the front door, I caught the faintest glint of it—just before the door slammed behind him.

Tears.

TWENTY-TWO

THIS WAS MORE THAN just digging a hole so deep, I couldn't get out. I had dug a hole so deep, I had successfully tunneled through the center of the planet and popped out the other side—only to wind up at the bottom of the Indian Ocean, crushed under roughly four hundred atmospheres of raw barometric pressure (5,878 pound-force per square inch). Metaphorically speaking.

There was no tunneling my way out of this one.

I needed to tell Wynonna the truth.

I spent most of lunch prodding my food with a fork. I wasn't even sure what it was. This was partly because I had the focus of a gnat who had discovered the human curse of self-awareness, and partly because it really was an indecipherable mass of slop. I think it was a casserole.

"Why so glum?" said Wynezra.

"Huh?" I said, snapping out of myself. "I'm not glum."

I forced a fake smile as proof. Mostly, it just looked like I was showing her all of my teeth, even the molars, which was probably frightening.

"You are not a good liar," said Wynezra. "Pro tip: Don't be a lawyer when you grow up. Literally, be anything *but* a lawyer. Or a professional poker player."

Now I just felt sick to my stomach. I crumpled in on myself, just to make the pain go away.

It wasn't working.

"Man, what happened?" said Wynezra. "Yesterday, you couldn't shut up about that sleepover. Now I actually *miss* you talking! Have I *ever* missed you talking? God, I must be having a crisis."

"I've secretly been meeting with your dad, and now he wants you to move with him to Switzerland," I sort of blurted out. And then my eyes went wide, and I slapped my hand over my mouth. Crap.

Wynezra had casually been shoveling Mystery Casserole X into her face. She halted mid-shovel, inches from her mouth.

Her hand—with the fork, with the casserole slop in its tines—wavered midair, like a reed in the wetlands.

"Sorry," I offered as an afterthought.

Wynezra's fork fell out of her limp fingers. Metal clanged, and slop splattered in a swift, chunky line across the table, like entrails.

Then she shot up from her seat. Her balled-up fists slammed down hard and fast and furious.

"What the fuck are you telling me, Ezra?" said Wynezra.

"Sorry," I said again. I probably couldn't say that enough, but it couldn't hurt to emphasize. "I was just trying to help."

"Help? How the *fuck* is this helping?"

"I was just trying to . . . to fix . . ."

"Fix?"

". . . fix your *relationship* with . . ."

"My *relationship*?"

"I mean, he's your dad!" I exclaimed, sort of helplessly.

"Who the hell do you think you are? There's nothing to *fix*. There is no *relationship*. That's the man who *murdered my mom*. He almost *murdered me*! And you think there's a relationship to fix there?"

"Oh, c'mon, he didn't *murder*—"

"RECKLESS. HOMICIDE," Wynezra screamed. "That's what he was charged with. According to the law, THAT IS MURDER."

I bit my lip. I really wasn't in a position to defend myself.

"How fucking dare you?" said Wynezra. She was shaking her head and pinching her mouth into something small and ugly. I mean, it was *my head* and *my mouth*, but it was *her pain*, and she owned it like it was her only possession. "You don't get to make my decisions. You don't get to *fix anything*. Stay the fuck out of my life."

Wynezra stormed off. Thunderous. Pluming with rage.

"Wynonna, wait—"

I tried to grab her shoulder.

She reacted like a spasm. Swung at my arm like a baseball batter, knocking my hand out of the park. Then both of her palms shoved me square in the chest.

For the briefest moment, I was airborne. No part of me was touching the ground. I was a leaf in the wind.

Then I was flat on my back. Stunned. Disoriented. Staring at the speckled ceiling like a galaxy. Leaf in the wind, my ass.

At first, I felt nothing.

Then I felt fire—in my chest, in my arm, in my spine, the back of my skull, everywhere.

It took me a second to relearn how to breathe. When I did, I blinked, craning my neck in manageable directions. There were heads and eyes everywhere, and they were all looking at me.

Well, half of them were looking at me. The other half were looking at Ezra Slevin, who, in turn, was glancing between her powerful hands and me—the girl she had knocked over like I was made of cards.

She looked horrified.

She looked devastated.

She rushed off as quickly as she could—disappeared from my rather limited field of vision—while I tried to not-die.

Honestly, not-dying was the least of my concerns.

• •

I looked everywhere for Wynezra.

But she was nowhere.

• •

By fifth period, I hated myself.

By sixth period, I was thinking suicidal thoughts. Nothing concrete or calculated or planned. It was chaotic. Desperate. A relentless thought spiral that went something like this:

I hate myself, I want to die.

I hate myself, I want to die.

I hate myself, I want to die.

I knew I wouldn't actually harm myself. But if I did happen to just . . . *cease to exist* . . . it would have felt like a mercy.

By seventh period, my life was a building on fire, and I needed to escape it, or I was going to die. I could barely even breathe.

I skipped seventh period.

I found a dark, unused classroom. I wasn't even sure whose classroom it was, or why it was empty, or where I even was. I only knew that I *needed* it.

I closed the door, immersing myself in pitch-blackness.

With the light of my phone, I pulled out a pair of Wynonna's headphones. They weren't noise-canceling, but they would have to do.

I plugged them into Wynonna's phone, pulled up Sufjan Stevens's "Chicago," and pressed play.

I lay flat on my back as bells chimed, strings swooned, and a menagerie of instruments thundered hopefully.

I was disintegrating. Dissolving.

Floating through the ceiling, through the roof, through the atmosphere, into outer space.

My atoms interwove with the universe. I *was* the universe.

The universe accepted me.

I felt myself breathe. My chest moving, my lungs graciously accepting and releasing air, oxygen feeding into my bloodstream.

I could breathe.

• •

By the end of seventh period, I slithered out of the dark, unused classroom. I timed it with the bell so I could exit stealthily into the stream of students flooding out into the hallway.

It was already a bad day. It seemed like the sort of day where anything could happen. And by "anything," I'm only referring to *bad* anythings—like contracting leprosy, or hitting all red lights on the drive home, or giving birth to the Antichrist. (I mean, I had the anatomy.) So, it was a bit surprising—as I collected my things from my locker, and I was on my way out the main entrance—that I was cornered by Holden.

Given the circumstances, I sort of reacted like I was being mugged.

"I have a birthmark," said Holden. "Where is it?"

"Aauhhhhhhgh!" I said.

Holden froze. "Wait, which Wynonna is this? Wynonna-Wynonna or Ezra-Wynonna? Are you currently switched?"

I had my hand over my heart and felt it slowly recede into a rhythm that *wasn't* on the verge of acute myocardial infarction.

"Ezra-Wynonna?" I said, like I wasn't sure, myself. "Wait, you believe me?"

Holden took a deep, meditative breath.

"I don't know what happened at lunch," he said, "but my best friend would *never* have attacked Wynonna like that. Plus, everything he was yelling sounded off. Plus, you said 'sister' when you freaked out at theater. *Plus*"—Holden had to take an even *deeper* breath for this next part—practically cosmic in scope—like he was inhaling the energy of the universe—"Willow believes you."

"Willow?" I said.

"Yeah. We got to talking late last night, and—"

"You got to talking *late last night*?"

"Yeah?"

"And where exactly did this conversation take place?"

"The dark web."

"WHAT?"

"Oh my god, *this*!" said Holden, gesturing at me like a flashing billboard. "*This* is what I am talking about. This is so Ezra, it's not even funny! Either this is the most elaborately staged hoax since the Voynich Manuscript, or . . ."

He fizzled out with a perplexed shrug.

"You believe me!" I kind of shrieked.

"I have a birthmark," Holden repeated, not entirely convinced. "Where is it?"

"It's on the underside of your penis, and it's shaped like Idaho.

You showed me it once when we were thirteen because you thought it might be cancerous."

"Who's my celebrity crush?"

"Amanda Bynes, duh."

"I've told one major lie in my life that haunts me to this day—"

"You lied at the DMV when you got your driver's license. You told them you were five feet when you're actually four foot eleven and a half."

Holden's eyes widened to the size of hard-boiled eggs. "Oh my god, it's you."

"It's me!"

"You're a girl!"

"I'm a girl!"

"I'd hug you," said Holden, "but..." He glanced trepidatiously at my tits.

I hugged him anyway. I squeezed him like I was stranded in the middle of the ocean, and he was the only thing for miles that floated.

And then I felt something nudge my thigh.

Something that was level with Holden's pelvis.

Holden and I yelped and broke apart simultaneously.

"I told you!" said Holden. "I *told* you. I'm the same height as your tits. You can't hug me if I'm the same height as your tits. Not to mention you're Wynonna, and I *like* Wynonna, and... Oh my god."

"What?" I said, while simultaneously trying to incinerate the memory of Holden's nudging penis etched in my mental archives of traumatizing experiences.

"I didn't start liking Wynonna until the week after the eclipse—while *you* were Wynonna."

Oh.

"So which Wynonna do I like? Wynonna-Wynonna or *You*-Wynonna?"

I sighed. "Look, it was a fucked-up thing Wynonna and I were doing. I was helping her get you to like her, and she was helping me get Imogen to like me. It was manipulative and wrong."

"So Wynonna *likes* me?"

I thought about my conversation with Wynezra the other day. How she thought we were turning into each other. I mean, maybe she was right to a degree, but...

But I was *definitely* not into Holden's inadvertent penis nudge. Maybe Wynonna wouldn't have been into it either. But I *knew* I wasn't.

"It's complicated," I said. "We've been stuck in each other's body for a whole month now. No swapping. We've actually been stuck ever since the double date."

"Holy shit."

"And I think being in each other's body for so long is affecting... what we *like*."

Holden stared at me for a devastating moment. "What do you mean?"

I related to Holden my entire conversation with Wynonna—the Almond Joy, the pork rinds, the uncertainty over her feelings for Holden, and her literal boner for Imogen.

"No!" said Holden softly, in faraway, detached horror. "You like pork rinds?"

I laughed.

"Just kidding," he said. "I don't care about the pork rinds. I'm just really sad that Wynonna doesn't like me anymore."

"She didn't say she *doesn't* like you. She's just... uncertain."

"But all this time, I've been eating lunch with Wynonna?"

I nodded solemnly.

Holden's eyes inflated, suddenly engorged with horror. "Oh no."

"What?"

"I've been picking my nose in front of her."

I felt the laughter in my gut, and it exploded out of me, releasing Wynonna's trademark snort. I snorted.

"Shit! And I keep forgetting to wear deodorant!"

I rolled my eyes, finally suppressing the laughter. "Don't take this the wrong way, but you're a little slow on the puberty bus. I don't think your sweat glands have evolved yet. I wouldn't worry—"

"Oh no," said Holden. His pupils shrank, and something seemed to die inside of him. "I farted in front of her."

Okay. I could see how this had become a matter of National Holden Security.

Holden grabbed me by the shoulders. "I didn't just *fart* in front of her! I farted and then *grabbed* the fart and threw it in her face!"

"Dude," I said. "Seriously?"

"I thought it was you! And I was still mad about the double date! I thought you deserved a good fart to the face."

"That is disgusting! And slightly horrifying."

"I know! What if Wynonna doesn't like me anymore—not because she's in your body—but because I was throwing farts in her face?"

I opened my mouth. Closed it.

He was right. What *if* that was all that it was? Maybe it didn't help Holden's chances with Wynonna, but then again, he *did* deserve to know who he was dealing with. You don't make your crush fall in love with you by being yourself. You do it by pretending to be someone a hundred times *cooler* than yourself and hide the true you, who is a total fucking disaster, behind a curtain of enticing white lies.

Just kidding. But there *is* such a thing as tact.

"You're right," I said, breathless and detached, as the gears were spinning out of control in my head. "Maybe that *is* why."

Holden groaned. "You're not supposed to *agree* with me!"

"No, no, no! This is *good*."

"It is?"

"You just need to put on the ol' Holden suave."

"Suave?" said Holden, confused. "What, like the shampoo?"

I sighed. "Remember when you were getting ready for the double date? And you were trying so hard to impress her?"

"Yeah?"

"Look, maybe this is a breach of confidentiality, but bro-to-bro, she was *super* turned on."

"What? Really?"

"Remember all that stuff *Ezra* told you to do with *Wynonna*? Except it backfired because Wynonna was me?"

Holden's eyes expanded with realization.

"That was *Wynonna* telling you to do that. Because she wanted you to do that to *her*."

Holden's mouth opened to roughly the size of a groundhog hole. Punxsutawney Phil could have fit through that thing.

"What should I do?" said Holden. "*When* should I do? I mean, you guys haven't switched back in a month. What if you never switch back?"

The moment he said it, he seemed to immediately regret it.

"I mean, of course you'll switch back *eventually*," he said. "I'm just saying . . ."

And then he kind of trailed off.

"No, you're right," I said sullenly. Resigned to my fate. "Maybe we'll never swap back."

Holden bit his lip.

"But maybe we *will*," I said. "And if you win Wynonna over while she's a guy? I'd say you've won her over pretty goo—"

Flash.

I was behind the steering wheel of my car.

My car—the Subaru.

My hands were on the steering wheel.

In the mere yoctoseconds that I was processing this startling turn of events, I noticed the bleeding neon of the elevated brake lights in front of me, coming in at *literal* breakneck force.

I collided with the mountain of a vehicle in front of me, and the hood of the Subaru crumbled like paper beneath the metal beast, and my head smashed into the steering wheel, and—

Black.

SEVEN YEARS AGO

TWENTY-THREE

IT HAPPENED SO FAST, I couldn't even process it. One second we were driving. The next, I was hanging forward, dangling against the shoulder harness of my seat belt, probably dead. At the very least, my soul felt like it had been jarred from my body.

"Ezra?" said Mom's voice. She was sitting in the passenger seat, slowly waking up from her own post-impact daze, a pair of airbags slowly deflating. The panic in her tone escalated. "Ezra, honey, are you okay?"

"Uh . . ." I said, dispelling the theory that I was probably dead.

"Does anything hurt?"

I slowly gave myself a once-over—as if seeing my individual body parts would help me decipher whether or not they were hurting. Mostly, I was shell-shocked, and discombobulated, and didn't know what was going on.

My forehead hurt a little bit—I was pretty sure it hit the back of Dad's seat—but my seat belt absorbed the brunt of the impact. And anyway, I didn't want to worry Mom. She looked worried enough.

I shook my head.

That was enough for her. She promptly moved down the line in priority order. Turned to Dad in the driver's seat.

"Mark?" she said.

Dad seemed awake. And aware. And acutely focused on the car in front of us.

Slowly, Mom turned her head.

The vehicle in front of us—a small white thing—was folded around the nose of our SUV. It looked like an aluminum can that had been stepped on sideways.

The passenger-side window was covered in blood.

It was a shattered spiderweb of cracks, nothing visible on the inside.

Nothing but blood. I had never *seen* so much blood. Not even in movies.

Suddenly, Mom was turning back around, smiling wide and slightly manic, blocking my view. "Hey, Ezzie! I'm going to go outside and help these nice people. Your father's going to come back there and make a phone call, okay? He's going to call nine-one-one."

Dad nodded, dazed. He seemed immensely glad that someone else was taking charge here.

"But I need you to do something for me, okay?" she said. "I need you to close your eyes. I need you to close them until I come back there and tell you that you can open them. No peeking. Can you do that for me, Ezzie? Nod your head if you can do that for me."

I nodded my head.

"Okay, close your eyes now, baby."

I closed my eyes. Closed them until there was nothing but black.

I heard both car doors open and close. The back door opened, I felt Dad heave himself beside me, and it closed again. I heard the faint whir of a dial tone.

"Yeah, I'd like to report an accident," said Dad. "We hit a car, I think they ran a stop sign. The woman in the passenger seat, I think she's . . . uh . . . Look, my kid's in the car with me, but it's *bad*. Uh. Lynbriar. Lynbriar *Lane* and . . . um . . . Bellchase *Drive*. Yes, Carbondale. Yes. *Yes*. Okay. My wife's a doctor actually, she's already checking on them. Yeah. Well, I *realize* that, but this woman really looks . . . Okay. Okay, thank you. Okay, bye."

Silence. I felt Dad's hand, ruffling my hair, pulling my head into his chest.

"How ya hangin' in there, bud?"

"I'm hangin'," I said.

"Eyes still closed?"

I nodded my head against his chest.

"Good. Keep 'em closed. We'll get you ice cream."

"Birthday-cake ice cream?" I asked.

"You bet."

"With sour gummy worms on top?"

Dad chuckled. "That sounds awful, but sure. Whatever you want."

We stayed that way for a long time. Not talking. Not really needing to. I knew something bad had happened, but beyond that, I hadn't a clue. Dad's presence told me that everything was going to be all right, and I guess that was all I needed to know.

I may have fallen asleep at some point. It was hard to tell. All I knew was that the whole blurry ordeal felt like hours, but the hours seemed to melt together into something smaller, more fluid, manageable.

Finally, the back door opened again. A new body filled the empty space beside me. Pulled me away from Dad and squeezed me. Held me desperately. I didn't need to open my eyes to know it was Mom.

I could feel her crying into my hair.

"Mom?" I said, sleepily. "Are you okay?"

Mom sniffed. "I'm okay, honey. I just love you so much. You and Willow both. You two are everything to me."

"Can I open my eyes now?"

Mom seemed to hesitate. "Okay. But before you do . . . there's an ambulance and some police cars here. But don't worry. They're all here to help, so don't be scared, baby. Okay?"

"Okay."

"Okay. You can open your eyes."

I opened them.

She wasn't kidding. I was immersed in a world of flashing lights, reds and blues, strobing relentlessly. I counted a total of four police cars, three tow trucks, two ambulances, and a fire truck.

One ambulance in particular stole my attention. This was because the back door was open, facing us, and two girls I very much recognized were sitting in the back.

The first girl was Imogen Klutz—aka the Most Beautiful Girl in the World. She was kind of the highlight: squeaky-clean, wearing crisp Hello Kitty pajamas, her hair completely wet, flattened in sheets down either side of her perfectly round head. It looked like she had jumped straight out of the shower for this.

Imogen's chubby arms were wrapped fiercely around the girl beside her, head resting on the girl's shoulder.

The second girl was Wynonna Jones—aka the Best Friend of Imogen Klutz. Her presence was kind of alarming. For starters, she appeared to be spattered in blood. Her brown hair was matted to her forehead, and everything else was drenched in sweat. Her clothes stuck to her like tape. Her face was empty. Numb. A sort of "dead inside" look oozed out of her. She had a red blanket wrapped around her shoulders, and have I mentioned that Imogen was holding her like she was the most important thing in the world?

Suddenly, I had completely forgotten about the blood situation. All that I could focus on was my overwhelming jealousy of Wynonna.

In some distant cubicle of my mind, I became aware of several things.

I was aware of the time—3:13 a.m.

I was aware of Imogen's mom and dad standing off to the side, talking to a police officer. I heard the words, even though they failed to register.

"Her grandmother is willing to assume guardianship, but she's currently out of town. She's trying to get here as soon as she can, but until then, well . . . the girl is obviously in a fragile state."

"It's no problem," said Mrs. Klutz, shaking her head. "No problem at all. Christ, I wish we could do more."

I was aware of Wynonna—looking directly at me.

At first, I was startled. She was looking so intently at me, it almost seemed resentful. Maybe it was. But the more I studied her, the more I realized it was *longing*. Like she wished she *was* me.

I failed to realize Mom was still holding me.

I failed to realize what that *meant* to Wynonna.

Tick—3:14 a.m.

Pi.

It was kind of a magical number for me—in the same way that 7:11 was a magical number for everyone else. "Seven-eleven, make a wish!" they would say. Well, I liked to make wishes on 3:14—although I usually made my wishes in the afternoon. Tonight was a rare occurrence. I had never stayed up late enough to make a wish at 3:14 a.m.

I didn't care that Wynonna was sweaty, dirty, possibly covered in blood. I didn't care that she looked like she was having the worst day of her life. All I cared about was that—right here, right now—she was the most important thing to Imogen Klutz.

In that moment, I wished I was Wynonna Jones.

• •

"You excited for the eclipse tomorrow?" said Mom, on the drive home.

I pretended to mull the question over. Shrugged. It was easier than telling Mom I didn't give one single crap.

"You *should* be excited," she said. "Did you know that Carbondale will experience the longest duration of totality in the entire United States?"

I did, in fact, know this. Everyone in town talked about it like it was the Apollo 11 moon landing—which it definitely wasn't.

"It's cool, I guess," I said.

Mom rolled her eyes.

"How about *Romeo and Juliet*?" said Dad. "You got those lines memorized?"

Now *that* was something I could get excited about. I gave a toothy smile. Nodded elatedly.

• •

I never fell asleep that night—the first blip in a pattern that would grow to haunt me.

I couldn't even begin to fathom the scar that accident left on my brain. The memory faded like a dream, but the scar remained. A scar filled with crumpled metal, and shattered glass, and blood. So much blood.

The next day, Mom, Dad, Willow, and I joined fourteen thousand people who crammed into Saluki Stadium for the biggest eclipse-viewing event in town.

At 1:20 p.m., the moon completely eclipsed the sun.

For a split second, I became someone else. Someone who was *also* at Saluki Stadium, watching the exact same eclipse, accompanied by a family—just not hers.

Someone who was doing everything she could to ignore the fact that her life had been ruined forever.

But it was a fleeting instant. A flicker.

The moment I sensed something was off, I looked away from the eclipse, looked around me, looked at my own hands.

I was myself. Nothing was out of the ordinary.

But not for long.

THE PRESENT

TWENTY-FOUR

I WOKE UP.

Reality sucker-punched me in the face. This wasn't a drill. It wasn't a dream, or a memory, or some pensive in-between either. I was *here*, and I was *now*. It was a very physical sensation.

Or maybe it was just the lingering impact of the steering wheel. My face seriously hurt.

I glanced down at myself. I was wearing a hospital gown, and there were wires everywhere—in my nose, in my arm, spooling around me like the entrails of a gutted cassette tape.

And I was me. I was Ezra Slevin.

"Hello?" I said, but my voice came out as a breathless croak. I tried harder. "Helloooo? Is anyone there?"

I was so focused on myself, I failed to notice that I wasn't the only person in the room. Three heads snapped upright in my peripheral: Willow, and Holden, and . . .

. . . and Wynonna.

Of the three, Wynonna looked the shittiest. Her eyes were

bloodshot and raw with devastation. Her mouth was a brittle line, ready to break.

At least, she looked like that for a fraction of a second. The moment our gazes interlocked, her eyes swelled. She bolted out of her chair and threw herself on top of me, sobbing into my chest.

"I thought you died!" she cried. "You're not allowed to die on me! You can't fucking do that!"

"Mom!" Willow shouted. "Dad! He's awake! Somebody, he's awake!"

Wynonna took a shuddering breath. "I only have so many people," she said softly. "I can't lose you, too."

• •

The world outside my hospital room window had long faded into darkness. Willow finally went home with Dad. Mom said she'd be right behind them. She told me that if I was feeling well enough in the morning, I'd be released. Currently, there was no sign of a concussion. No broken bones. No back or leg or knee injury, as was common with these types of accidents. As far as a neck injury, I had only the mildest of whiplash. The worst part was my face. The entire area around both eyes and the bridge of my nose was bruised, like I was wearing a bandit mask. But aside from looking like the Hamburglar, I was perfectly healthy. It was just a matter of waiting out the night and making sure I didn't spontaneously combust or anything.

When Mom left, it was just me and Wynonna and Holden. Wynonna appeared to want to talk to me *alone*, but Holden just seemed eager to talk.

"You're *you*!" he exclaimed. "I mean, you're Ezra-Ezra, right? Not Wynonna-Ezra?"

I glanced at Wynonna.

"Oh, I already told her and Willow that I believe you guys," he said. "She started freaking out mid-sentence, and I just *knew* you guys had swapped. So, I guess that was a stupid—"

Wynonna cleared her throat loudly. "Holden?"

Holden snapped rigid. He may have been a chatterbox, but Wynonna possessed the power to turn his words to sludge. Not to mention, he farted in front of her AND THREW HIS FART IN HER FACE. This was not the sort of embarrassment you live down.

"Yeah?" said Holden.

"Can Ezra and I have a word?" she said. "Alone?"

"Oh," said Holden. "Okay. Should I just wait outside the door?"

"It's probably going to be a while," said Wynonna. "And it's late. You look tired. You should go home."

Holden looked like he didn't know if he should be offended or grateful that she was so considerate of his REM cycle.

Wynonna let out a quiet sigh. "And if Ezra gets out tomorrow morning, we can all sit together at lunch."

Holden lit up. "Oh! Okay! Yeah!" He nodded incessantly to indicate how pumped he was.

Wynonna nodded to let him know that he could go now.

Holden left.

Wynonna walked slowly—inconspicuously—to the hospital room door, glanced outside to make sure that Holden was thoroughly gone, and closed the door. She flattened her back against the surface, every muscle a knot of tension.

Looked at me.

"I'm still mad at you," she said. "Don't go thinking you're off the hook just yet."

I deflated in my hospital bed.

"What were you *thinking*?" she said. "I mean, I *know* what you were thinking, unfortunately, but still, what were you THINKING? How did you expect this to work?"

I shrugged helplessly. "I mean . . . he's sorry. You have no idea how sorry he is."

"Not half as sorry as he should be."

"He hates himself for what he did."

"Good! He should hate himself!"

"He's been sober for the past seven years."

That one hit her a little bit. Not hard. Just enough for her to not have a comeback.

"I know what he did was unforgivable," I said. "But he loves you. He'd do anything for you. Aren't those the sort of people worth fighting for? Isn't that worth giving a chance?"

Wynonna didn't say anything. Her eyes were hard, and her mouth was pinched shut fiercely, but she said nothing. If anything, it meant she was listening. "I told him who I was," I said.

Wynonna reared back slightly. "You what?"

"I told him we were swapping bodies. That my name was Ezra Slevin."

"You told him you were Ezra *Slevin*?" she repeated incredulously.

It was the way she emphasized my last name that triggered it.

Roscoe's voice became an echo in my skull.

That little boy. You're pretending to be that little boy.

Wait.

This is cruel. I don't think you even realize how cruel you're being.

Oh my god.

Seven years ago, during that accident . . . Roscoe *saw* me. He saw a little boy sitting in the back seat of the other vehicle. And he must have known our last name. After being charged, convicted, and serving a five-year sentence for a Class 3 felony, he *had* to know the name of the people in the other car.

That's why he was so upset.

That's why he stormed off.

"Ezra?" said Wynonna. She waved her hand in front of my face. "You still in there?"

I blinked. Refocused on Wynonna.

"The accident," I said slowly, "the one from seven years ago . . . you know who was in the other car, don't you?"

Wynonna didn't react. She had already gone through the entire spectrum of emotions today. There probably wasn't much left to feel anymore.

She nodded her head. It was an empty—but definitive—nod.

"Why didn't you tell me?" I said.

"I thought you already knew. I mean, you were *there*."

"But I *didn't* know. I mean . . . I guess I did, sort of, but . . . I didn't *remember*."

"Yeah. I know."

I stared at Wynonna, beyond perplexed.

Wynonna shrugged. "I thought you were lying to me. Which . . . look, I was fine with it. I figured you didn't wanna talk about it, and I didn't wanna talk about it either. It wasn't until later that I realized you didn't have a fucking clue."

She paused. Bit her lip.

"So . . . you remember now?"

"I do *now*. It's like rear-ending that truck knocked it back into my head."

"Huh. Weird."

She didn't even know the half of it.

I told her everything—the forgotten memories I could suddenly recall in vivid detail. Making eye contact with Wynonna at the accident. Wishing I *was* her. And feeling somehow—inexplicably—that she was wishing for a similar thing.

I told her I made this wish at 3:14 a.m.

I told her about the sensation I felt at Saluki Stadium. That we might have swapped—ever so briefly—at the moment of the eclipse.

Wynonna's eyes grew progressively larger with every detail. I was apparently hitting some notes that resonated with her.

By the time I finished talking, I looked at her. Fishing for some verbal confirmation that I was on the right track.

"Yes!" said Wynonna. The word broke from her lips in a ragged breath. She was smiling and shaking simultaneously. "Fuck. Yes. I remember all of that."

• •

We talked all night—about the accident, about our memories, about our *feelings*. We even talked about Roscoe. Mostly *I* talked about Roscoe, and Wynonna listened. Still, that was a special sort of progress.

Then, at 3:14 a.m., we unceremoniously swapped.

Things were back to normal.

Well, a *form* of normal. But it was good enough for us.

"Damn," said Wynezra. "It feels like someone drove a spike in between my eyeballs, right into my brain."

I nodded empathetically.

"It also feels like I'm swimming naked in rose petals like that girl in *American Beauty*," she said. "Jesus, how much morphine do they have you on?"

"Enough to alleviate a spike driven in between your eyeballs, right into your brain?" I suggested.

"I'll say. Like, I feel the spike, but I also feel like I'm made of magic. Dude. I feel like a unicorn!"

I giggled helplessly. Wynezra on morphine was my new favorite thing.

"I realize I'm on drugs right now," said Wynezra, "but I'll do it."

I blinked. "Do what?"

"Talk to my dad."

I nearly fell over in my chair. "What? You *will*?"

"I'm not agreeing to go to fucking Switzerland with him," she said, hastily. "I'm not agreeing to *anything*. But I'll talk to him."

"That's great!" I said, trying—and failing—not to scream.

"Under one condition."

"Condition?"

"You have to be there with me. You started this mess, you have to see it through to the end."

I considered the offer. But not for *too* long. I was in, obviously. I was so totally in.

I nodded my head like an idiot.

TWENTY-FIVE

"EZRA" WAS RELEASED FROM the hospital later that morning. Mom saw to that. I waited outside while Wynezra underwent a routine checkup and some quick tests—performed by Mom herself—to make sure nothing was ruptured or hemorrhaging or concussed. Fortunately, Humpty-Dumpty appeared to be in tip-top shape.

Just in time for school.

Wynezra and I rode together. She drove, while I attempted to call Roscoe. After my third missed call, I left a desperate voice mail.

"Hey, it's me. Um, Ezra. I know you don't believe me, and you probably don't want to talk to me right now, but . . . look, Wynonna is willing to talk to you. The *real* Wynonna. So . . . yeah. Call me back. Please. Thank you. Um, bye."

I hung up.

Wynezra just shook her head in the driver's seat. "This is gonna be so much fun."

She was being sarcastic.

"It's a good thing I like you, Ez," she added—dare I say *coyly*?

I thought she was being sarcastic again. But then she smiled. It was a *super*-suspicious smile.

"What?" I said.

"What do you mean, 'What?' "

"What are you smiling about?"

"I'm not smiling," she said, which only made her smile even more.

"Are you kidding me? You're not even *trying* to lie properly!"

Wynezra sighed. Still smiling. In fact, her smile had reached a critical breaking point. "Okay. Fine. I have a secret, too."

I stared at her. "Which is . . . ?"

"Well, I can't *tell* you. Otherwise it wouldn't be a secret."

"Are you *kidding me*? You have to tell me!"

"Relax, Ezzie. You'll find out soon enough."

"What's that supposed to mean? And since *when* do you call me Ez or Ezzie?"

Wynonna just smiled—that knowing, tantalizing smile.

• •

She was right. I *did* find out soon enough.

When the lunch bell rang, I barely took a step outside of class when I saw Imogen, leaning against the opposite wall, a gigantic Union Jack purse slung over her thin shoulder. Her legs were locked straight, her hands were tucked behind her back, and her lips were pursed, small and impenetrable.

Her eyes were reddish and puffy, like she had been crying.

I halted barely a step outside the doorway, forcing the rest of the class to squeeze around me on either side. Remarkably, no one told me to move. Wynonna had *that* sort of reputation.

"Can we talk?" said Imogen.

Recently, I had spent a great deal of time *not* obsessing over Imogen, on the grounds that she wanted nothing to do with me. So it came as sort of a surprise when my stomach filled with butterflies. Or maybe just one giant, *kaiju*-sized monster butterfly, like Mothra. The butterfly situation threatened to explode me from the inside.

"Sure?" I said.

"Is outside okay?"

I gave a wobbly affirmative nod.

We followed the human traffic to the nearest exit. All the while not speaking a word. Not even looking at each other, really. We broke away from the teenage current and exited through a pair of side doors.

It wasn't the most scenic side of Piles Fork High School. It was a shady alcove, and the grass was dying in the shade. Ziggy had recently replaced the grass with new sod, but even that was dying.

But it was as good a place as any for Imogen to say what she had to say.

"I talked to . . ." she said, then hesitated. "I talked to *Wynonna*."

I blinked.

"The Wynonna who is currently Ezra," she clarified, so that there was no room for misinterpretation. "I talked to Holden, too. And Willow. And . . . I believe you. I believe all of you."

"Oh," I said. I wasn't sure what else to say. My stomach felt dense, and my lungs were collapsing, and Mothra was flapping her mighty wings.

"I think what you two did was messed up," she continued. "But . . . I think what *I* did wasn't right either."

"What *you* did?"

"I knew Wynonna didn't like me like that. We had a whole summer to hash that out, and I had a whole year to get over her. And I *did* get over her. But then . . . well, Wynonna really felt like a different person. And she *was* a different person. But literally. Because she was you. And . . . I think I kind of fell for that person. Just a little bit."

My jaw dropped.

"Look," said Imogen, "I knew better than to jump back into something with Wynonna. She's the best friend I've ever had, Ezra. And for the past month, I . . . I *haven't* been that friend to her. But you *have.* And if you know Wynonna, you know that friends are all she has. Ezra, you've literally been *all that she has*. And . . . and . . ."

Imogen's voice broke.

"I can never repay you for that." She sniffed, wiping her eyes with her sleeve. "But since it's what you and Wynonna were trying to do from the very beginning, and since I genuinely *adore you* as a human being, well . . . it's nothing really, but I figure this is the least I can do."

Imogen fumbled with her Union Jack purse, dropped to her knee, and pulled out both a corsage and a boutonnière—both pearly-white roses laced in ribbon—still inside their plastic cases.

My jaw was already extended to maximum gape. It could drop no farther.

"Ezra," she said, "whether you're you *or* Wynonna on prom night . . . will you go to prom with me?"

I just stood there.

Gaping.

Like an idiot.

"I should mention that Wynonna is asking Holden to prom as we speak," said Imogen, mostly to fill the silence. "It's supposed to be a double-date sort of thing. Just FYI, in case you're thinking of saying no—"

But I was already nodding my head like a dashboard bobblehead, and I was crying, and I was smiling so hard, it was undoubtedly ugly.

"Yes," I said. "Yes, please. I'd like that very much."

"Awww," said Imogen, and she stood up and hugged me. "You're a really sensitive guy, Ezra. I like that."

"I'm on my period," I said, sniffling.

Imogen laughed and squeezed me harder. "The fact that you know how that feels makes me adore you even more."

• •

Holden and I immediately texted each other, and then sprinted in each other's general direction. When we met in the hall, our eyes swelled like balloons, and we squealed.

"I just got asked to prom!" Holden screamed, waving his boxed boutonnière.

"Me too!" I said, shaking both my boutonnière *and* my corsage at him.

We kept screaming, hugged each other, and not five seconds later, I felt something nudge my thigh. Our scream transitioned into an "oh god, no" sort of wail, and we broke away. Holden threw his hands in the air, like he was under arrest.

"Sorry," he said. "I'm just excited, and you look like my prom date."

"You do realize," I said, "that you might be going to prom with Wynonna in *my* body."

"Oh, I know. That's actually a *good* thing. Otherwise, I might have a boner all night!"

I laughed.

"I'm serious!" he said. "And I still have to redeem myself for throwing my farts in her face. I'm pretty sure rocking a woody all night would be a step in the *opposite* direction."

I was laughing so hard, I couldn't breathe.

"You're a real pal, you know that?" said Holden, unamused. "Laughing at my misfortune. My life is being *ruined* by boners and farts, you know. This is not a laughing matter. This is serious."

"Stop it!" I wheezed hysterically. "I can't breathe! I can't . . . I can't *breeeathe*!"

• •

Rekindling our tradition of old, Wynezra, Imogen, Holden, and I carpooled to theater for our final dress rehearsal. Imogen and Holden let me ride shotgun in the Subaru while Wynezra drove.

We arrived at the Amityvale, got in costume and makeup, and performed our parts like we were born for this purpose.

Even Wynezra, with her three lines as Servant, delivered them with the greatest of . . . uh . . . servitude? In act 3, scene 4, she entered "Olivia's garden" while Malvolio (Willow) was wearing cross-gartered yellow stockings—per the instructions in the prank love letter—and Olivia (Imogen) was declaring, *"Why, this is very midsummer madness."*

Enter WYNEZRA.

"Madam, the young gentleman of the Count Orsino's is returned: I could hardly entreat him back: he attends your ladyship's pleasure."

Imogen's lips curled with delight. *"I'll come to him."*

The dress rehearsal was a flawless success. Even Jayden and Thad—with their tenderized slabs of meat for faces—were professional, and courteous, and performed their parts with minimum douchebaggery. Except for when the parts called for it. Sir Toby and Fabian were kind of horrible people.

When we finished, Ziggy applauded us and commanded us to applaud ourselves—which we did because we were fucking awesome.

Ziggy then broke down the details for tomorrow's big performance. It would be held in the school gymnasium (because Amityvale was an irreparable shithole) at three p.m. sharp. The reason it was starting so early was that prom was the following day, in the exact same gymnasium.

As Ziggy dismissed us, we dispersed in a mostly unified drove for the exit. Wynezra and Imogen were talking about prom dresses, and they dragged me into the discussion, because I might be wearing one of them. Wynezra and I resolved to split our combined tux and dress expenses. Holden must have felt a little left out of the prom-dress conversation, because he kept chipping in with his own thoughts and suggestions, so we decided, what the hell, we'd all go shopping together ASAP.

That's when we heard a wave of chatter from the front of the line. As we spilled outside into the late-afternoon sunlight, we witnessed our car—*my* car, technically—the Subaru, covered in hearts made of construction paper, and rose petals, and balloons tied to the side mirrors and door handles, and white words scrawled across the front windshield in window paint. They read:

You drive me wild.
Go to prom with me, Willow?
– Patrick

Patrick was standing awkwardly off to the side, receiving fist bumps and shoulder claps from the "dudes" and "bros" who composed the majority of Jayden and Thad's posse. But his attention was trained on Willow, who was standing in front of the car, motionless. She finally turned and made eye contact with him.

Walked right up to him.

"I should hate you, Patrick," she said. "But mostly, I'm just sad and disgusted. I don't know why you would think you have the right to ask me to prom. You *had* my trust and respect—and you just gave it away. You're worse than Thad and Jayden."

She marched directly to the car, leaving Patrick to marinate in the rejection.

She walked with fierceness.

She walked with pride.

Willow Slevin had cashed in the last fuck she had to give. Thad and Jayden and Patrick could rot in hell, and she wouldn't even blink.

• •

Prom had a theme—Winter Wonderland—and Wynezra and Imogen had the brilliant idea of dressing us all in accordance. Apparently, Holden and I were not so much *participants* in prom shopping as we were Barbie/Ken dolls they could dress up.

"But isn't this tacky?" said Holden.

"You know what's tacky?" said Imogen. "Your *attitude*. You look great."

"I feel like Colonel Sanders."

Yes, Holden was wearing a white suit. But it was *far* from Colonel Sanders. Maybe if a Hollywood biopic version of Colonel Sanders were on the cover of *GQ* magazine, played by Dave Franco. His suit coat had sharp black lapels and a matching black bow tie. His shoes were so shiny, they could have been sculpted out of obsidian.

"You look *great*," said Wynezra.

Holden blushed. He opened his mouth, as if to say, "You look great, too," but then seemed unsure whether he should say that to her *in my body* or to me *in her body*.

"You look finger-lickin' good," I said.

"Dammit!" said Holden. "I *do* look like Colonel Sanders, don't I?"

"Ezra!" Imogen growled through her teeth. She smacked me with her purse. "Stop provoking him."

"Do *I* look like Colonel Sanders?" said Wynezra, challengingly. "Because I think *I* look finger-lickin' good."

She was wearing a slightly off-white suit coat—like vanilla ice cream—with a black bow tie identical to Holden's and black slacks. She strutted seductively toward him, like a practiced male stripper. Holden was paralyzed in place. Even as she grabbed his hand, lifted it gracefully to her mouth, and inserted the very tippy-tip of his index finger between her lips, and proceeded to suck gently.

"Ooooookay," said Holden, but his voice cracked. He cleared his throat and tried again. "Okay. You've made your point. We can check you out now. I mean . . . we can *check out* now. We can check out your stuff . . . as well as my stuff. We can check out everyone's . . . stuff."

I made a slicing gesture across my throat at him.

Wynezra released Holden's finger from her lips, winked, and smacked him on the butt. "There's more where that came from, Colonel."

Holden—in a state of sexual crisis—discreetly adjusted his slacks.

Imogen sighed dreamily. "This is *so hot.*"

TWENTY-SIX

AFTER WE DROPPED Holden and Imogen off, Wynezra looked at me expectantly. I looked at my phone.

Still nothing from Roscoe.

"I could call him again?" I offered, hopefully.

Wynezra shook her head.

My heart sank. That was it. Without the magic of morphine, her willingness to talk to Roscoe had passed. Like an unpleasant kidney stone.

"Let's just go over there," she said.

My heart bounced back, trampoline-propelled, practically lodging itself in my throat. I nearly choked on it.

"Really?" I said. It came out as a sort of gasping wheeze.

"We'll go over there," said Wynezra. "If he still hasn't responded by the time we swap back, then we just knock the fuck on his door, Mormon-style."

Wynezra's face hardened ever so slightly. In that moment, I began to question the "friendly nature" of this drop-in visit.

"I want to talk to him as *me*."

• •

Roscoe's apartment was in a gated community. The key code I had was an individual number that dialed Roscoe, at which point he would push a number on his phone, and *that* would open the gate.

But Roscoe wasn't answering. Wynezra parked temporarily in front of the office. The moment a tenant drove through, she veered out and sped in behind them.

We waited about five minutes in the Subaru, parked directly in front of Roscoe's building, listening intensely and very uncoolly to the smooth jams of Alt Nation on Sirius XM when—*flash*—we swapped.

Just like that, Wynonna was out the door, marching up to his building. She looked about as ready to talk as a contract killer.

"Wait," I said—fumbling out of the driver's-side door, shuffling after her. "Wait, wait, wait. Maybe we should talk this over first?"

Wynonna shook her head. "No. I already know everything I'm going to say."

I followed Wynonna helplessly to Roscoe's door. She knocked... um... *fervently*. It was less a "We'd like to share a message about the Book of Mormon" knock and more a "POLICE, OPEN UP" knock.

Roscoe opened up. He didn't look happy.

Then he saw who it was.

He looked even *less* happy.

He smelled like hangover and self-loathing. His longish hair was stuck to one side of his face. He was wearing a Hawaiian shirt, khaki cargo shorts, and argyle socks with—god help us all—bright blue Crocs. All of this begged one's undivided attention and horror. But the thing that ultimately grabbed my attention was the inside of his apartment—the split second I saw of it—before he slipped outside and closed the door behind him.

Boxes.

Lots of boxes. Most of them looked like they were filled, taped shut, and stacked in cardboard pillars.

"Whoa, wait," I said. "Are you moving *already*?"

Roscoe turned his head. Looked at me like I was a complete stranger. I realized this was the first time he had seen me as myself.

"Um, I'm Ezra," I said. And then, as if I needed to clarify further, "The *real* Ezra."

Roscoe absorbed this slowly—about a thousand times slower than normal human information absorption. Nodded even slower.

"Are you moving?" I repeated.

Roscoe didn't even respond. Didn't even *acknowledge* that I had asked a question.

Looked at Wynonna.

"This isn't a great time," he said. "Sorry."

He sounded genuinely apologetic, too. Like he had finally come to terms with the reality of his situation. Like he was apologizing for *everything.*

But Wynonna was having *none* of that.

"Like fuck it isn't," she said. "Give me one good reason why I should go to Switzerland with you. Just one."

Roscoe's eyes were distant. Like the only way he knew how to handle the situation was to remove himself from it. To go to some faraway place where death was just a phase, hate didn't exist, and he wasn't responsible for losing everything precious to him in a single instant.

He said nothing. What could he say?

"Give me one reason why I should *forgive* you," said Wynonna. "Just one. Fucking. Reason."

Roscoe shrugged his shoulders, looking too broken for words.

"No." Wynonna shook her head fiercely. "Don't you dare shrug your shoulders at me. I asked you a *question*—"

"I don't have a reason for you," he said, finally. "I wish I did. But I don't."

Wynonna exploded. "Then what the fuck do you want from me? What *exactly* were you expecting to get out of this? That I have some biological obligation to accept you as my dad? Because I don't. As far as I'm concerned, I don't have a dad. You're *nothing* to me. You're just the motherfucker who *killed my mom*. You want my forgiveness? Then give me my mom back, you drunk piece of shit."

Roscoe's eyes were wet, glossed over with sadness. But he didn't blink. He took every word like it was a punch he deserved.

By the end of it all, he nodded. Accepting.

"You're right," he said. "I don't deserve your forgiveness. I don't deserve *my own* forgiveness, let alone yours. All I can tell you is that I'm sorry. That there isn't a day that goes by that I don't hate myself for what happened. I wish I could somehow make it up to you. But truth is, I can't. I can't *ever* give back what I took from you. Or Carol. Your mother was irreplaceable. She was too good for this world, and she was *certainly* too good for me."

A tear trickled down his cheek. Disappeared into the foliage of his beard.

"I never expected you to forgive me," he said. "I just thought I got lucky."

I had been so lost in Roscoe's apology, I hadn't even thought to look at Wynonna.

Her face was red. Her eyes were slits, compressed with emotion. She was shaking.

"Yeah?" she said, finally. "Well, you thought wrong."

She stormed off. Across the building hallway, down the stairwell, out of sight.

I glanced hopelessly between the two of them. For the briefest moment, Roscoe and I made forlorn eye contact. There was even a flicker there—somewhere, deep down—that seemed to recognize me.

"Sorry," I murmured, helplessly.

I chased after her.

• •

I took my time getting to the car. From a distance, through the glare of the windshield, I could tell that she was crying. Sobbing relentlessly. The moment she saw me, she shook herself to her senses, wiping away the evidence of heartbreak. Meanwhile, I took slow, deliberate steps.

By the time I reached the passenger-side door, she had collected herself.

"As my friend," she said, "can you promise me never to talk about this?"

I bit my lip. Nodded.

"I promise."

TWENTY-SEVEN

THE DAY OF *Twelfth Night* was finally upon us. Due to the performance starting at three p.m. sharp—which, on a school day, was crazypants insane—Ziggy *begged* Principal Durden to give us excused absences from seventh period. We needed more time.

Principal Durden—who was totally fangirling about her son in the lead male role—gave us excused absences from fourth period on.

We were ready. We were prepared. There was no way anything could go wrong.

Or so we thought.

It happened as I was putting on my torn "shipwreck dress"—ready to be washed ashore, like flotsam, upon the coast of Illyria.

Flash.

Suddenly, my face was pressed against someone else's face, and we were in a dim room, and I was pretty sure I was leaning against a shelf. I attempted to pull away and bumped into a long vertical stick. The stick fell over, knocking a stack of soft white cylinders off the shelf with it. Toilet paper?

I grabbed my chest. It was as flat as the earth according to acclaimed rapper B.o.B.

"Oh my god," I said, and it was my voice. Ezra Slevin's voice.

"What's wrong?" said Holden. "Are you okay?"

Holden flipped the lights on. We were in the janitor's closet. He was decked out in Duke Orsino's dark waistcoat and matching cravat. His hair was a hot mess.

"Oh my god, oh my god, oh my god," I said.

"Are you still Wynonna?" said Holden. "You're still Wynonna, right? Please tell me you're still Wynonna."

There was a distant scream of flat, low-level panic, escalating rapidly in frequency. It was the sound of Wynonna having a meltdown.

"Oh my god, oh my god, oh my god, oh my god, oh my god—" I said, with no sign of stopping. I fumbled with the janitor's closet door, opened it, and stumbled out. The handle of a mop came with me, landing with a swift crack.

"I can explain," said Holden. "You see, I told Wynonna I was nervous, and she was like, 'Oh yeah? I've got something for that,' and she grabbed me by the hand, and dragged me into the janitor's closet, and—"

"Dude, I don't care about *that*," I said. "We've got a much bigger problem."

"We do?"

Was he seriously serious?

"Viola?" I offered, hint-wise.

Holden's eyes drifted, then crystallized with realization. "Oh."

"Oh" was right. We had a Viola on our hands who—suddenly and inexplicably—didn't know her lines. And she was *only* the STAR OF THE FUCKING SHOW.

My power walk escalated into a frenzied sprint. I barreled around the corner to the hallway leading "backstage"—sliding, scraping for traction—just as shipwrecked Wynonna was blasting through the backstage doors.

Wynonna spotted me and said, "What do we do, what do we do?"

"Fuck, fuck, fuck, fuck, fuck, fuck, fuck," I replied.

"Maybe... we could get a headset or something?" said Holden. "And Ezra can read you your lines?"

"And where would we get a headset?" said Wynonna. "The show starts in, like, a half hour!"

"Viola can't wear a *headset*!" I exclaimed.

"Viola doesn't know her goddamn lines!" said Wynonna.

"Even if we *did* get a headset, that only solves half the problem. It's a performance, not just reading lines. It's practically *choreographed*."

"Ohhhhhh god," said Wynonna, collapsing to her knees, enveloping herself in the folds of her shipwreck dress. "I'm going to be sick. I think I have a hernia."

"What's going on?"

This came from Imogen—just now arriving on the scene, wearing a long-sleeve black dress and a veil pulled back over her hair. Olivia would soon be mourning the deaths of her father and brother. Provided the play didn't collapse due to the sudden amnesia of Viola.

"The show can't go on," said Wynonna. "I have a hernia."

"Ezra, are you kidding me?" said Imogen. "This thing starts in a half hour."

"That's not Ezra," I said.

Imogen glanced from me, to Wynonna, back to me, and back to her.

"Oh crud," she said.

Meanwhile, Holden was silently having an existential crisis because he had accidentally made out with his best friend in the janitor's closet.

"Someone, call nine-one-one," said Wynonna. She moaned, and rolled onto her side, and curled into the fetal position. "I have a hernia."

"C'mon, you do *not* have a hernia."

"How do you know?"

"Because I *was* you just two minutes ago!"

"Oh yeah?" said Wynonna—suddenly looking more challenging than ill. "You think just because you *were* me, you know everything *about* me? You don't know me!"

"This is ridiculous," I said, shaking my head.

"The auditorium is filling up," said Imogen. "We need to figure this out, fast."

"Really?" said Holden. "People are actually showing up to this thing?"

"What? Yes! Of course they are! Why wouldn't people show up?"

Holden shrugged. "This just seems like the Special Olympics of Shakespeare productions."

Imogen opened her mouth, appalled. "I can't believe you said that. The Special Olympics is a *wonderful* organization. That's the most offensive thing I've heard all week!"

"Look, I wasn't trying to diss the Special Olympics. I'm just saying . . . It was a figure of speech!"

"This is how I die," said Wynonna, still lying on the floor.

"Seriously, man," I said. "It was kind of fucked up. And, Wynonna, you're *not* going to die."

"Okay, I'm sorry!" said Holden, hands in the air. "I submit my official apology to Imogen, and Ezra, and the entire Special Olympics."

"Herniaaaaaaaa!" Wynonna moaned.

"What, do you want an apology, too?!" said Holden, unhinged.

"I want you to kill me," said Wynonna, sprawling onto her back, writhing like an ant under a magnifying glass. "Kill me now, before it's too late."

"Okay, okay, okay," said Imogen. "We need to figure this"—she made an ambiguous gesture to her best friend, doing a variation of the worm on the floor—"out."

"Think, think, think," I said aloud, tapping my head like I was Winnie the fucking Pooh.

"What would a *genius* do in a time like this?" said Holden, because he apparently wanted to be a part of the conversation. "What would *Shakespeare* do?"

"What would . . . Shakespeare . . ." said Imogen, breathless. Her eyes lit up like sparklers. "Shakespeare! That's it!"

"That's it?" I said. "*What's* it?"

Imogen grabbed my hand and tore off backstage, dragging me behind her like a human streamer.

"Wait!" I said. "What about Viola?"

"*You're* Viola," said Imogen. She turned and gave me a devilish grin. "You were *always* Viola."

• •

Fact: During Shakespeare's time, all the roles were played by men. The male roles, the female roles, the female-*pretending*-to-be-male roles . . .

All men.

That was just the sexist state of things at the time. After all, who could trust a woman to accurately portray her own gender? Absurd!

But it meant that Viola was initially played by a dude.

Tonight, we were going to be digging *deep* into the roots of Shakespeare.

The trick was that I had to still *appear* like a woman to the audience—even though I was pretending to be a man. This meant that the makeup was *staying* on, and it was staying heavier than ever.

Imogen was my makeup artist. She stepped away from my face with a powder brush in hand. Scanned me up and down. She seemed less than impressed.

"How bad is it?" I said.

"What?" said Imogen. "No, no, your *face* is perfect. *Everything's* perfect."

Her gaze shifted downward.

"Everything except for your chest. Your chest is as flat as Texas."

I glanced down at my chest. I was wearing the shipwreck dress—this low-cut, dirty-green thing, somewhere between algae and snot. Even though it was stretched a little tight on the shoulders, there was a definite excess of loose fabric in the front.

"You need a bra," said Imogen.

She glanced down at her own chest. Her bra would *maybe* fit around the thickest part of my thigh.

She glanced at Wynonna, who was standing nearby, watching my transformation—*miraculously* healed from her hernia! Wynonna glanced down at her own chest.

"I mean, you could *try*," said Wynonna, "but it'll probably cut off blood circulation in his entire body."

"What's going on?" said a new voice.

We all turned. It was Daisy Munk.

"Daisy!" Imogen exclaimed. "I will give you *anything* if you let Ezra wear your bra for the next two hours."

"Uh . . ." said Daisy. "Does Ziggy know about this?"

"Not yet," said Imogen. "But Wynonna has a hernia."

Daisy glanced at Wynonna, who was dressed in Ezra's trusty Servant costume. Wynonna hunched over—suddenly deathly ill—and gave a weak cough. I was 100 percent certain she had no idea what a hernia was.

"I know all of Viola's lines," I said.

Daisy narrowed her eyes, unconvinced. And then—whether to test me or to prove a point—she said: *"Will you hoist sail, sir? Here lies your way."*

Act 1. Scene 5. Line . . . um . . . one hundred and something?

"No, good swabber," I said—elevating my tone, scraping for some solid ground between masculine and feminine. *"I am to hull here a little longer."* I turned to Imogen. *"Some mollification for your giant, sweet lady."*

"Wow," said Daisy, duly impressed. "Okay, then. This should be interesting." She started for the girls' bathroom and called out, "One bra coming up!"

• •

Ziggy's failure in the art of delegation had turned him into our one and only stagehand. He was so all over the place, it was shockingly easy to step in as Viola.

As act 1, scene 1 ended, Duke Orsino, Curio, and Valentine exited the stage. Ziggy—dressed in all black, like a ninja—pushed out a blue silk curtain on a roller rack. Duct-taped to one of the vertical rods was a cardboard cutout of a capsizing ship, hand-drawn in Sharpie. Ziggy had already turned on the fan—sitting offstage, to the left—which caused the blue silk curtain to ripple and sway.

It was supposed to be the sea. A very low-budget sea.

The boy playing Captain—a chubby kid with a red, splotchy skin condition and a gray beard glued to his face—crawled onto the stage from the left. I crawled on from the right. It was then, and only then, that most of our cast recognized the drag situation. A wave of hushed whispers and what-the-fucks came from all directions, hailing together like the whistling of the wind. Ziggy turned, searching for the source of the commotion and made brief eye contact with me, sprawled across the center of the stage, wearing a dress.

He turned as white as the ghost of Hamlet's father.

I crawled to my feet. Glanced down at Captain—who was still on his hands and knees, just *now* noticing that the one person he interacted with in the whole play had been replaced by the dude who auditioned for "tree."

"What country, friends, is this?" I said.

"Uh," said Captain. He staggered to his feet. *"This is Illyria, lady."*

"And what should I do in Illyria?" My tone was deliberately sick with dread. *"My brother he is in Elysium. Perchance he is not drown'd: what think you, sailors?"*

"It is perchance..." said Captain, finding his groove, pausing to choose his scripted words carefully, *"... that you yourself were sav'd."*

"O my poor brother!" I clutched my hands to my heart. *"And so perchance may he be."*

Captain and I finished the scene. We exited, and Sir Toby Belch (Jayden) and Maria (Daisy, braless) entered. Sir Toby was distraught by Olivia's behavior—mourning the death of her brother and all. Didn't she know that grieving was bad for your health?

The moment I stepped offstage, Ziggy—still in black—materialized from the shadows like a Ringwraith.

"I'm not even going to ask what's going on," said Ziggy, hands in the air. "It's working. Just do me a solid and make sure it *keeps* working, 'kay?"

And that was that.

I quickly changed out of the dress and into my Cesario costume. Imogen helped. She insisted I keep the bra on. I needed to "emphasize the femininity of Viola" because I would spend the rest of the play dressed as a man. She lightened up the makeup but only slightly. Imogen informed me that my facial bone structure was "way too masculine, like Hugh Grant" to take off too much.

I'd never really associated "Hugh Grant" with "masculine," but still. That made me blush.

Imogen smiled, pretending not to notice.

"What"—said a voice that was unmistakably Willow—"the fuck?"

Imogen and I turned and looked at her—in full Malvolio costume, which made her look kind of like an impish goblin who had abandoned her post at Gringotts.

"They swapped," said Imogen.

"Oh," said Willow. And then her eyes widened. *"Oh!"*

She suddenly looked very apologetic for coming off so abrasive.

"Well . . . you look so pretty, Ez! And you're doing *great*."

I blushed *again*. And I was WEARING BLUSH. My face probably looked like the red planet, Mars.

"Thanks, sis," I mumbled.

Willow smiled maniacally, giving me an overenthusiastic thumbs-up.

From then on, it was like nothing had changed. Everyone was shockingly on board with the new Viola. We performed just as good as—if not better than—dress rehearsals.

Nearly two hours later, Sebastian and Imogen were in each other's arms, as were Holden and I, and Willow was storming off furiously, declaring vengeance upon House Olivia.

We exited the scene.

Tucker sang his song.

The moment Tucker stepped offstage, the audience exploded sharply in a bullwhip crack of applause. That was our cue. We flooded the stage in an arranged order. I was at the center. On my right was Holden, and on my left, Imogen. We held hands and bowed in a synchronized wave, and as we came up, threw our interlocked hands in the air.

It was very, very, very difficult not to smile. The happiness of this moment was splitting my face open.

That's when someone's embarrassingly loud dad yelled, "WHOOOOOOO! VIOLA AND MALVOLIO! THEY'RE OURS! THOSE ARE OUR KIDS!"

Willow—holding Holden's other hand—locked mortified eyes with me, and then we spotted them. *Our* parents. Mom and Dad were sitting right next to each other. Maybe they weren't holding hands or looking terribly romantic, but they *were* standing, and clapping, and cheering, and smiling with a pride that made my heart swell with the highest level of happiness: stupid-happy.

At least, I felt that way for a moment. Then I felt a phantom itch—like the itch an amputee feels in a limb that's not there anymore. Only this itch enveloped a whole body.

I looked left.

I looked right.

I didn't see Wynonna anywhere.

I knew exactly where she was *supposed* to be—to my left, between Captain and Curio—but she wasn't there. Instead, Captain and Curio were stepping together awkwardly, filling a gap that had clearly just been evacuated.

As soon as we were free to stop bowing, I made a quick, determined exit. Forced and weaved my way through the crowded stage.

"Ezra?" said Imogen. "Where are you go—"

The backstage door closed behind me.

I veered into the main hall. Searched clockwise. Heard the soft chokes of sobbing. I followed the sobs until I was practically upon them—and yet, the source was invisible.

I glanced at the two side-by-side water fountains, wedged in an alcove in the wall. Glanced down.

Wynonna was lying on her side, curled up and inserted beneath them. Her eyes were red.

"I'm not crying," she said, and sniffed.

"I didn't say you were."

"Okay, well . . . what do you want?"

"Are you okay?"

Wynonna's facade of okayness collapsed effortlessly, like a house of cards. She wept.

"Hey, hey, hey," I said.

I curled up on the floor facing her. Her hands were draped limply in front of her face. I don't know why I did what I did next—it was so uncharacteristic of me—but I took her hands. They became a ball in my own hands, and I squeezed them.

"It's okay," I said. "Everything's going to be okay."

She finally opened her eyes. Our gazes met sideways, across the plane of the vinyl tile floor.

"Carol didn't show," she said finally.

"Is that why you were crying?"

"No. But it still hurts, you know? I mean, you two were really connecting. I thought for sure she would show."

"I'm sorry."

"I was crying because of your parents."

"My parents?"

Wynonna tried to nod. The mere effort, however, was making her lip quiver and her eyes flood.

"They just love you and Willow *so much*," she said. "And it kills me because part of me thinks I was *so close* to having that again. So close. But I don't. And I know I'm the one pushing Roscoe away, and *I know* I'm the one who can't forgive him, but . . . but that doesn't mean I don't *want* it. You know? Of course I want a family! Of course I want a dad! But why does it have to be like this? Why does it have to *hurt* so much?"

I didn't say anything. Words felt inadequate—my words most of all.

She looked at me with tearstained eyes. "Does that make any sense? Am I crazy?"

"You're not crazy."

"What am I supposed to do?"

"What do you want?"

"Oh god, I don't know," she said, rolling her eyes. "I know what I *don't* want."

"What's that?"

"I don't want my motherfucking *dad* to go to Switzerland without me! I don't want to go to Switzerland *with him* . . . but I don't want him to go *without me*."

"Okay," I said, nodding—which is a weird, almost impossible thing to do with your head lying sideways on the floor. "Then let's stop him from going to Switzerland."

Wynonna looked at me quizzically, like I had proposed a non-option. "Can we even *do* that?"

"You're Wynonna fucking Jones," I said. "I was under the impression that you do whatever you want."

Wynonna laughed and cried simultaneously. It came out in a single emotional burst.

"So?" I said. "Are we gonna stop your motherfucking dad from going to Switzerland or what?"

"Yeah," said Wynonna—smiling, sniffling. "Let's stop that motherfucker."

TWENTY-EIGHT

THE MOMENT WE TOLD Holden and Imogen what we were doing, it was like we had extended each of them a formal invitation. It wasn't even a question of "Can we come?" The only question was:

"Why does your dad want to burn Switzerland?" said Holden. "Is he some sort of anarchist?"

"What?" said Wynonna.

"Oh my god," I said.

Imogen threw her long arms in the air in exasperation. "He's moving to the *city*, Bern—B-E-R-N—Switzerland. Keep up, Holden."

"Oh," said Holden, slightly disappointed. "Dang. I thought this was like a stop-the-pyro-terrorist sort of mission."

"Nope," said Wynonna. "My dad's just a chef. A *food* chef. He doesn't cook meth or anything."

Holden opened and closed his mouth during Wynonna's clarification. I swear to god, if that was his *actual* question—!

"Dang," Holden repeated. "Okay. That's cool. I was just starting to feel like Jack Bauer from *Twenty-Four*, is all."

"You can still be Jack Bauer," said Wynonna. "Think of it as a . . . um . . . rescue operation."

"Please, don't encourage him," I said.

"Rescue operation?" said Holden, totally perking up.

"Yeah!" said Wynonna. "We're rescuing him from the Evil Corporate Agenda. You know, the one that steals fathers from their homes, making them slaves to the system, while their children die of parental neglect and loneliness."

"Actually," I said, "Leif's restaurant is a small, independently owned— *Ow!*"

Wynonna punched me in the arm.

"Yeah!" said Holden, nodding his head, getting more and more pumped by the second. "The Evil Corporate Agenda! Hell yeah!"

It was like his entire existence had prepared him for this one critical moment—which was beyond stupid. But I sighed and let him have it.

Imogen massaged her temples, like this was all just a bad dream. Not the mission. Mostly just Holden.

Of course, we had just finished performing a two-and-a-half-hour play *directly* after school ended. The four of us were experiencing varying degrees of starvation. We resolved to hit up IHOP, snarf down some pancakes, and strategize. We all agreed *any form* of a game plan sounded nice, and pancakes sounded even nicer.

It was decided. I went directly to my parents to tell them we were going out for food and also to be smothered in their love and adoration.

Willow looked relieved. She'd been on the receiving end of enough love and adoration to last a lifetime.

"Hey, there he is!" said Dad. He ruffled my hair—the way I was almost ashamed to admit that I loved—and then pulled me in for a hug. "You did great, bud, real great."

"Okay, okay, Mom's turn, hand him over," said Mom.

She literally pried Dad's arms open, stole me from his grasp, and hugged me even harder.

"You were excellent," she said into my ear. "You and Willow. We're so proud of both of you."

"Thanks," I said. "Hey, my friends and I were wanting to grab dinner together at IHOP, is that okay?"

My parents looked wounded—as if I had presented them with DNA evidence that I was adopted, and this was the first they'd heard of it.

"Oh," said Dad. "Well, your mother and I were thinking of taking you and Willow out to dinner as well . . . but . . ."

"But it's fine," said Mom, in a damaged tone that indicated the opposite. "You have friends. We understand."

"Yeah . . ." said Dad, nodding sadly. "Sure . . ."

"It's okay . . ." said Mom, and I thought she might cry.

Even Willow looked devastated. Like I had just filed for my own parents' divorce.

"But . . ." I said, "um . . ."

I stole a sideways glance at Wynonna, Imogen, and Holden, standing a distance away, but not far enough to look like they *weren't* shamelessly eavesdropping.

Wynonna sighed. Nodded that it was okay. Forced a weak smile in the name of family.

"But . . . you could meet us there?" I said. "And sit and eat with us? If you'd like?"

"Oh!" said Mom, and her entire countenance changed. "Are you sure?"

"We wouldn't be intruding?" said Dad.

Wynonna strolled over and threw her arm around my shoulder. "Hey, we're family now, remember? Of course we're sure!"

As my family burbled with elation, Wynonna winked at me.

I couldn't help feeling like she was the greatest thing that ever happened to me.

• •

We did our best to endure IHOP with my family. On the one hand, it was wonderful. I couldn't remember the last time my family ate out together.

On the other hand, well . . . Wynonna.

She scarfed down her food as a sort of anxious reaction to the situation, then spent the rest of dinner twiddling her thumbs with existential dread.

As we finished eating, Mom insisted on paying for everyone's meal. Wynonna, Holden, and Imogen thanked her. As the waiter ran Mom's card, I asked if I could hang out with my friends a bit longer.

My parents—thrilled to be asked permission for *anything*—said yes.

• •

At first, Holden, Imogen, and I waited around the corner of the building hallway—peeking, of course—while Wynonna knocked on the door. After knocking for the third time, she whipped out her phone and attempted calling instead. He didn't pick up.

At this point, Holden's, Imogen's, and my attempt at hiding had kind of fizzled out.

As Roscoe's voice mail played, Wynonna dropped her arms and gave me a desperate "What now?" look.

"We could kick his door down," Holden suggested. "I've actually been studying Jack Bauer's technique. I think the trick is to become *one with the door—*"

"OH, COME ON," said Imogen.

"The door is like water," Holden continued, undeterred, "and when you kick, you want to kick *through* it, like it doesn't exist. I think it helps if your daughter has been kidnapped, and you're fueled by the fury of justice—"

A door opened—suddenly, brashly—causing all of us to jump.

It wasn't Roscoe's door.

Rather, it was Roscoe's next-door neighbor to the right. He was huge, wearing an apron dusted with flour strapped over an orange Bears jersey, and—I swear to god—oven mitts on both hands.

"Can I help you?" he said, in an irritated tone that indicated the opposite. His voice was André the Giant–deep, but his accent was embedded in the roots of Chic*aaah*go.

"Sorry," said Wynonna. "We're trying to get ahold of my dad."

"Dad?" said André the Bears Fan. "Who, Roscoe?"

All four of us nodded our heads eagerly.

André's eyes narrowed to skeptical slits. "Roscoe doesn't have any kids."

"Um, well, he *does*," said Wynonna, annoyed. "I just stopped living with him when he went to *prison*, thanks."

"No shit," said André, genuinely flabbergasted. "Damn. Well... Jesus, I don't know how to tell you this. He just moved all his things out."

"What?" I said. "When?"

"This afternoon."

My heart plunged.

Wynonna opened her mouth—wordless, breathless.

"Sorry, kid," he said, and he looked like he meant it. "Alls I know is: Some guy was helping him move, and they were talking about flight information and passports, and uh . . . Sweden. Yeah, they kept talking about *Sweden*."

It was too late. *We* were too late.

No.

No, it *wasn't* too late. There was still a chance.

"Okay, thank you, gotta go," I blurted out.

I grabbed Wynonna's hand and tore off down the building hallway—dragging Wynonna behind me like a water-skier.

"Whoa, whoa, whoa!" said Wynonna. "What are you doing? Ow, my arm!"

"Sorry, sorry!" I said, letting go. "I think we can beat him to the airport."

"*Which* airport?"

She had a point.

By the time Holden and Imogen caught up to us, I had already started the car. (That's right, *I* was driving.) When the last door closed, I peeled out of the parking lot, out of the gate just as it was closing behind another car, en route to US-51.

"What . . . is . . . *happening*?" said Holden, out of breath.

"Everyone, look up Illinois flights to Bern!" I ordered. "I'm on my way to the Southern Illinois Airport. Let me know if I need to redirect. Preferably before I hop on the highway."

There was a surprising deficit of argument. Everyone silently whipped out their phones, tapped on quiet digital keys, scrolled through pages and options.

"I think I've got it!" Imogen exclaimed. "It's the only flight to Switzerland. Thirty-two-hour trip, layovers in Detroit and London. It arrives in Zurich—not Bern—but I think that's the closest major airport. Departure is . . . oh wow, four a.m. Yuck."

"Which airport?" said Wynonna.

"Uh, let's see, let's see . . ."

Her round face went as pale as a turnip.

"O'Hare International," she said. "That's in Chicago."

"Chicago?" I said. "That's a four-hour drive!"

I glanced at the time. It was almost eleven.

Imogen scrolled through all her information. Frantically double-checked everything.

"I know, but . . . that's it. That's the only flight I'm seeing."

Holden glanced up from his phone. "I'm not seeing anything else."

Shit.

Shit, shit, shit.

Wynonna started sobbing.

"Hey," said Imogen, softly. "It's okay."

"No!" Wynonna shook her head violently. "It's *not* okay! What if he changes his phone? Don't people change phones when they move to a different country? I don't know his address. He's not on social media!"

"Relax," said Holden. "He's wouldn't just disappear from your life." He shot me a glance so I could back him up. "He *wouldn't*, right?"

"You don't know that! You weren't there, Holden. You didn't hear all the horrible things I said to him. I called him a drunk piece of shit. I told him I'd never forgive him. I told him he was nothing to me! Why wouldn't he disappear from my life? If I were him, I would!"

She looked at me—blubbery-eyed, devastated, practically *begging* me to prove her wrong.

Knowing full well that I couldn't. I was, after all, there.

"We're not gonna give him the chance," I said.

• •

It was a cold, hollow vacuum of a road trip. Endless stretches of pitch-black countryside. Occasional small towns—dead as midnight—filled the vast space in between like trail markers. The fact that I was going fifteen above the speed limit was overwhelmed by the three hundred and fifty miles between here and there.

I didn't dare go faster. If I got pulled over, any chance of us stopping Roscoe was toast.

At some point, Holden fell asleep.

Maybe an hour later, Imogen fell asleep, too. And she had quite the impressive motor on her; her initial snore was a crack of thunder.

The only thing more shocking than the sheer decibel level was that she fell asleep to begin with. She'd won the Whose Music Are We Going to Jam Out To contest, which was why we were currently "jamming out" to the *Les Mis* soundtrack (tenth-anniversary edition). "One Day More" swelled from the Subaru speakers—sad, swooning, glorious. Until minutes ago, she had been singing along at the very tippy-top of her lungs.

"Okay," said Wynonna, reaching for the volume knob. "Let's dial down the revolution a bit."

She dialed down the revolution significantly—settling on a soft, subtle rebellion.

It was only Wynonna, me, and Imogen's snoring—set to a low-key revolutionary ambience.

Even so, it felt like there were miles of silence between Wynonna and me.

"Just so you know," said Wynonna, finally, "I have lots of things I want to talk about, and a billion questions I want to ask, but they're all bouncing around in my head like bingo balls, and it's hard for me to make sense of any of it, so I'm mostly just silently panicking."

"What sort of questions?"

"Am I making a mistake? Was the mistake not doing this two years ago? Does doing this mean I forgive my dad? Can I *ever* forgive him for what happened? What *is* forgiveness anyway? How many licks does it take to get to the center of a Tootsie Pop? Et cetera, et cetera."

I laughed—a defenseless, caught-off-guard sort of laughter.

Something ignited inside her. She laughed as well. A nervous smile splintered across her face.

And then it faded.

"Do you think he hates me?" she asked.

"What? No! Of course not. He's stuck around in Carbondale for two years because of you. He was stalking you, for crying out loud! Which is weird, okay, but, I mean . . . you don't stalk people you hate. If anything, I'd say he's obsessed with you. You're his family. His *only* family."

For some reason, this didn't seem to make Wynonna feel any better. In fact, she looked worse. She folded her arms over her stomach and leaned forward like she was ill.

"I hate myself," she said.

I stared at her, silently.

"Not just now," she continued. "I've *always* hated myself. Deep down. It's like the core of who I am. This great, big, rotten, fucking core."

"How can you say that?" I said—like the world's biggest hypocrite. I was obviously the King of Hating Myself.

Or . . . I *had* been.

Now that I thought about it, everything that had happened recently was making it more and more difficult to hate myself. There was something about caring for someone—genuinely *caring* for them—that made you forget yourself. That made you realize you were part of something bigger. That you were important. That you were loved.

I realized that now. I was *loved*. By my family. By my friends.

"You wouldn't get it," said Wynonna. "You're *perfect*. You care about everyone, and everyone cares about you. But me? I can't even visit my mom's grave because it hurts too much. I can't even look my dad in the eyes. God*damn*, Ezra, I can't even hold a polite conversation with Carol! I'm not a human being. I'm a fucking train wreck."

"You think I'm *perfect*?"

"Dude. I *know* you're perfect. You're like one of the Precious Moments figurines. You're so perfect, it's disgusting, and it makes me want to hate you, but I can't because you're perfect."

"I'm not perfect," I said. "You *know* I'm not perfect. Remember when I spent a month meeting with your dad behind your back, and you almost killed me?"

"Because you were trying to *help* me!" Wynonna exclaimed. Lines of moisture brimmed in her eyes. "This is who we are, Ezra: You're the person who *helps*, and I'm the person who needs . . . who needs . . ."

She mouthed the word "help," but it came out as a choking sob.

"It's like I'm drowning," she said. "I'm constantly drowning, and there's nothing to hold on to. The water's either at my neck, or it's coming down my throat, and it's all I can do just to stay afloat. I'm kicking my arms and legs so hard—*so hard*—just trying not to die. And I'm *so tired*. And I think: Maybe dying would be easier than this. *Anything* has to be easier than going on like this, because I can't do it, I just can't do it anymore."

Finally, she looked at me.

"Have you ever felt like that?" she asked.

More than she could ever know.

More than I could ever tell her.

"You know what you need?" I said. I removed my phone from my pocket. "You need some Sufjan."

"*Soo-fawn*," Wynonna repeated, skeptically. She blinked the last of her tears away. "What the hell is a *soo-fawn*?"

"Sufjan Stevens. He's the greatest musician of our time."

Wynonna rolled her eyes. "Oh. *Awesome*."

"Close your eyes," I instructed. I unplugged Imogen's phone from the adapter. Switched it out with mine. Scrolled through the artists, to the *S*'s, to Sufjan Stevens's "Chicago."

Chicago.

Goddamn.

If ever there was a specific song, meant for a specific person, at a specific moment in time, "Chicago" was meant for Wynonna right fucking now.

I held my thumb over the play button and glanced at Wynonna. Her eyes were still open.

"CLOSE THEM," I commanded.

"Okay, okay, I'm closing them," said Wynonna. "Jesus."

I pressed play.

A series of chimes dinged, escalating like some sort of celestial elevator.

The strings came swooping in, strong and swift and heroic.

A stampede of folksy instruments paraded through the speakers. The thundering beat of new life.

And then silence—all except for a faint keyboard chant. This chant became the frame for words—Sufjan's tender words—of love, and mistakes, and re-creation.

I thought about what this song had always meant to me—about how to free myself. "Wynonna Jones, you are no longer of this world," I said. "You are giving yourself up to the universe."

Wynonna smiled at the thought of this. But she kept her eyes closed, and her comments to herself.

I spoke of disintegrating, dissolving into your surroundings. About atoms coming undone from each other, and being freed from yourself.

She was *free.*

She was free to float upward. There was nothing to stop her. She was floating up through the roof of the car, through the atmosphere, through the stratosphere, into the stars. Into outer space. Her atoms were intermingling with stardust. She was floating up here because this was where she belonged. Her atoms were weaving like thread into the fabric of the universe. Together, they formed a tapestry—a great, infinite tapestry—of stars and nebulae, of death and darkness, of life and creation. Swirling together. Endless.

She was the universe.

And the universe accepted her.

A tear seeped out of Wynonna's closed eyelid, tracing a line down her cheek.

"Whoa, hey," I said, snapping out of my narration. "Are you okay?"

Wynonna opened her eyes. Gently wiped the tear away. Nodded. "I am now."

She looked at me—a look with so much meaning, it contained worlds. A universe.

"I was wrong," she said.

"About what?"

"What I said about drowning and having nothing to hold on to."

• •

It may have been the deadest of night, but Chicago was electric, pulsating, alive. Skyscrapers jutted from the earth like the long, glassy teeth of some Lovecraftian deep-sea god monster—slowly swallowing us whole. I forced myself into high alert, navigating the jungle of concrete highway ramps, switching lanes to make quick exits.

Finally, we were on a course to O'Hare International Airport, following the signs to the Terminal 5 departure area. The quickest way to do this was to drop everyone off. From there, it was up to the three of them to make it to security in time.

Meanwhile, I would look for parking.

Yeah, it was an anticlimactic end for my leg of the journey. But what can you do?

As I pulled into the drop-off, I didn't even come to a complete stop. Doors were flying open and everyone was hopping out of the car like it was a parachute drop over enemy territory. Holden even attempted to do a roll as he landed, Jack Bauer–style.

Bad idea. He knocked his head on the concrete as he somersaulted.

"Shit," he said, cradling his skull, stumbling through the sliding doors of Terminal 5. "Shit, shit, shit."

"Holden, this is no time to concuss yourself!" said Imogen.

"Dumbass." Wynonna chuckled, clearly in love with his dumb ass.

That was the last thing I heard as the sliding glass doors slid shut behind them.

I sighed. Sank into my seat. Slowly unraveled. Every muscle in my body was a knot, taut with the tension of a four-hour race against time.

I glanced at the time display.

It was 3:14 a.m.

"Oh f—"

Flash.

"—ffffffuck!" I said, out of Wynonna's mouth.

I screeched to a halt in my combat-boot tracks.

Imogen and Holden looked at me, then looked at each other, and then just dropped their shoulders and looked disappointed.

"Come on, Ezra!" said Holden, exasperated.

"Do you think I have any control over this?" I snapped.

Wynonna's phone vibrated in my butt pocket. I pulled it out and—of course—it was "Ezra." I answered it.

"Go, go, go, go, go!" said Wynezra. "I'll catch up."

I glanced decisively between Holden and Imogen. They seemed to know exactly what that look meant—because the very next second, we were running.

I lifted the phone back to my ear. "Ditch the car," I told Wynezra.

"Really?" she said.

"Really-really. Before I change my mind."

Wynezra chuckled. "Okeydokey, Shrek."

She hung up.

Airline logos gleamed overhead—Delta, Southwest, United. We dashed past individual baggage check-in areas, each with their own conveyor belt systems and ticket kiosks. Each was roped off from the others. Customers herded *themselves* in, like sleepy, well-trained cattle.

Finally, we arrived at security.

For a quarter past three in the morning, security was impressive. The roped-off line was halfway full. Several security stations were manned, filtering people into one of many X-ray lines. These people were forced to empty their pockets, to remove their laptops from their bags, to take off their belts, and their shoes, and their dignity, and to put all this shit in plastic bins. Once a person's bins made it through the X-rays and TSA had determined they were a non-terrorist, the poor bastards could have their things back. Everything except their dignity. TSA kept that in jars and fed it to their Demogorgon who lived downstairs in the airport TSA dungeon. These were the facts.

Holden, Imogen, and I shuffled to staggered halts. Our gazes zigzagged through the lines, scouring them for any sign of Roscoe.

Heavy footsteps clapped behind us, slowing to a stop. Frantic breathing. I didn't have to look back to know it was Wynezra.

"Is he here?" she said. "Where is he?"

No one said anything. We were too busy scanning the lines for the second, third, fourth times over.

Not seeing Roscoe.

He wasn't here. We missed him.

Eventually, our intense search petered out. Our gazes drifted uncomfortably. We continued to not say anything. What could we say? The disappointment was too big, and words were too small.

No.

It couldn't end like this.

I *refused* to let it end like this.

"Holden," I said. "Imogen. I need you two to create a diversion."

"A *diversion*?" said Imogen, not liking the sound of this, not one bit.

"Wynonna and I are going to sneak through security."

Wynezra's eyes exploded in their sockets.

I looked directly at her. "If you want to, that is."

"You do realize," she said, calmly, "there's a nine-out-of-ten chance we're going to get arrested."

"I know."

Wynonna stared at me.

"Whaddaya say, Wynonna Jones. Are you 'down to clown'?"

Wynezra's mouth slithered into a great big devious smile. "I've been known to dabble in a little tomfoolery."

She turned to Holden.

"Can we count on you, Jack Bauer?"

Holden's eyes lit up with the fires of justice, and tactical espionage, and the explosions of every spy thriller he had ever seen. This was probably the single greatest moment of his life.

And then his entire face morphed into shock, and I realized he was already in a role because Holden had no concept of timing.

"TAYLOR SWIFT," Holden screamed, pointing in the general vicinity of Delta. "OH MY GOD, EVERYBODY, IT'S TAYLOR SWIFT."

"What?" Wynezra hissed. "Not right now—shit!"

Imogen—realizing the starting gun had already been fired—clapped her hands to her cheeks and exclaimed, "TAYLOR SWIFT, OH MY FREAKING GOSH."

She bolted in the vague general vicinity of Delta's baggage check-in, hands in the air, like she was on an actual roller coaster or something. Outside of Shakespeare, she was kind of a terrible actor.

The line to security reacted, all right. All sense of sleepiness was eviscerated. People leaned over the rope, ducked under the rope, abandoned the rope entirely—all for a better look.

That's when a guy the size of an offensive lineman bulldozed Imogen into the floor.

Wynezra, Holden, and I stared, openmouthed. We could barely process what had just happened. It was like watching a galloping giraffe get taken down by a dinosaur.

"Chicago PD!" said a hostile male voice. "Hands in the air!"

I didn't know when, or where, or how, but suddenly, we were surrounded. Men in blue shirts and dark bulletproof vests swarmed us. There were three of them, with three guns pointed at each of our heads—just *begging* us to give them a reason to go for the head shot.

We all threw our hands in the air simultaneously.

The officers moved in, grabbing our wrists, cuffing them behind our backs. They didn't seem incredibly concerned with our comfort.

"What the hell, man?" said Wynezra. "What are you doing? You can't do this!"

"Yeah, we have rights!" Holden proclaimed. And then, a little unsure of himself: "I mean, we do, don't we?"

"Yes, Holden, we have rights," I said.

"Are you the owner of the silver Subaru Forester in the drop-off zone?" an officer asked Wynezra. The oldest and unfriendliest looking of the bunch—craggy-faced, square-jawed, no-bullshit vibe. He looked like a disgruntled Josh Brolin *playing* a cop, which seemed to indicate there was a fifty/fifty chance he was dirty.

"What?" she said. She glanced down at herself. "Well, I am *now*, I guess, but... c'mon, guys, I was gonna come back for it!"

"Sure you were. Right after you distracted security."

In my peripheral, I noticed the dinosaur of a cop who took Imogen down peeling her off the floor like a piece of string cheese.

"I can't feel my anything," she mumbled.

"We're gonna take you kids down to the station," said Officer Brolin. "Maybe find out why you felt it necessary to visit the airport at three in the morning and leave a suspicious, illegally parked vehicle outside the terminal. So, you know... you have the right to remain silent, anything you do say can be used against you, so on and so forth. You've seen the movies."

I had seen *way* too many Josh Brolin movies to feel comfortable with this scenario. All I knew was we were royally screwed.

"Wynonna?" said a familiar voice.

The voice came from the security line.

An adult *male* voice.

But it wasn't Roscoe.

The flow of traffic had led him to our end of the retractable belt barriers. He was holding hands with two mousy-haired children—a boy and a girl—four and six years old. I only knew this because I knew *him*. He had a mustache, and his hair was receding, but not *nearly* as receded as the midlife crisis he once wore like a toupee.

It was Theo. The restaurant manager from Newell House.

"Theo?" I said, startled. "What are you doing here? Have you seen Ros—? Have you seen my dad?"

"Uh . . ." said Theo, thoroughly flustered. "He didn't . . . *tell* you?"

I stared, blankly. "Tell me? Tell me *what*?"

Officer Brolin glanced between Theo and me. "Sir, you know these kids?"

"I know *her*. I work with her father. Or . . . *worked* with her father. He actually, um . . . he helped me get my new job." He glanced nervously at me. "In Switzerland."

"WHAT?" said Wynezra.

"You're going *with him*?" I said.

"Not *with him*," said Theo, laughing nervously. "Roscoe actually . . . well, he checked himself into a rehab."

Wynezra's mouth was open so wide, I could have stuck my fist inside it.

"Rehab?" said Officer Brolin.

"For *alcohol*," Theo clarified, eyeing the officer. He ducked under the security rope and stepped out of line. "Our flight is actually a little delayed, so I have some time. I'll be glad to explain everything to you if these fine officers don't mind." Theo glared at the other officers before returning his attention to me.

"I think I know what this is all about," he said.

• •

Roscoe was in rehab, sure. But that wasn't the reason he wasn't taking the job.

Roscoe just couldn't leave without Wynonna.

After his and Wynonna's blowout, he realized he could *never* leave without her.

So, he decided to stay.

He told Leif this. But he also told him he knew a damn good chef who *hated* his job and *hated* living in Carbondale ever since his husband left. From there, things escalated very quickly. Leif was desperate, and Theo was eager to GTFO. Ba-da-bing, ba-da-boom, Leif basically agreed to fly Theo out—with accommodations—until he and his small family got on their feet.

So basically, we drove four hours to Chicago and got arrested for nothing.

But it didn't feel like nothing. In all honesty, it felt like a very big something. The sort of something you cherish because you fought for it.

To Wynonna, I knew this something was everything.

Wynezra, Holden, Imogen, and I were still taken to the Juvenile Temporary Detention Center in Chicago. Technically, it was a guilty-until-proven-innocent situation. However, the nature of the arrest had softened significantly. Officer Brolin looked only *slightly* disappointed that his terrorist arrest was most likely a sham. *Offisaurus rex*—whose name was Winston—even apologized to Imogen for pulverizing her into the earth's mantle. As a token of peace, he offered her a pink frosted donut with sprinkles.

Since it was the middle of the night, we were placed in individual holding cells—narrow things with brown brick walls; cold, sandy-speckled floors; a bed that more closely resembled a cot; and a silver sink-toilet combo. (I *so* wish I was kidding.) In my cell, however, someone had painted the narrow back wall into a pure and simple work of art. It was blue, with a hopeful-looking white bird standing off to one side, and words:

DON'T LET WHAT
YOU CANNOT DO
INTERFERE WITH
WHAT YOU CAN DO.

I read those words over and over again until I fell asleep.

I was pretty sure I fell asleep smiling.

• •

It was still dark out when we were released. Probably only an hour or so later. Wynezra, Holden, Imogen, and I were shepherded out of our cells, down an earth-colored hallway, out into the lobby.

Where Roscoe was waiting for us.

We all stopped walking, like we had suddenly run out of floor. Looked at Wynezra.

She just looked sick.

Roscoe seemed to notice this. He cleared his throat nervously.

"I've already talked to your parents," he said. "Or . . . *we* have. The police and I. I've agreed to take everyone home since I was, um . . . in the area."

I assumed "in the area" meant rehab.

"Fortunately, there aren't any charges against you four," Roscoe continued, "so there was no bail, although, Ezra, um . . . your car was impounded, so that's something you'll have to take care of."

I sighed and nodded my head acceptingly.

Then I realized I was Wynonna.

Then I realized I really didn't give a fuck.

Roscoe noticed this, too. If he thought anything of it, he kept it to himself.

"Anyway," he said, "I already filled out all the paperwork to get you guys out, so . . . you're free to go, ya hoodlums!"

I think that last part was meant to make us laugh. Or to at least break the tension. It didn't really do either.

"Thank you, Mr. Jones," said Imogen, politely. "Holden and I are going to go outside for a breath of fresh air."

"We are?" said Holden.

"Yes, Holden. *We are.*"

"Oh. Right. Of course, *we are*. Obviously."

He gave Wynezra and me the most unsubtle wink he was capable of, then sauntered outside. Imogen shook her head, perplexed, and followed after him.

It was just Roscoe, Wynezra, and me.

"So . . ." said Roscoe. "That's Holden, huh? I like him."

He didn't seem to know who to look at—so he glanced between the two of us like we were playing an invisible match of telekinetic Ping-Pong. The sheer effort seemed to be making him dizzy.

"So you got out of rehab easy enough?" I said, mostly to fill the silence.

"Yeah, well . . ." said Roscoe, shrugging. "It was an emergency. The police called the center I was staying at. Plus, I checked myself in, so . . ."

Wynezra said nothing. She was stewing. A pot of boiling silence.

"But, um..." he said, "I'll probably check myself back in once everything here is settled. The usual stint is six weeks, and that's probably what I need to get my bearings straight anyway."

He glanced from me, to Wynezra, back to me.

"We don't have to do this right now if you don't want to," he said. He was apparently using a plural *you* because his gaze was fixed in space, directly between us.

Wynezra's eyes grew misty, but her face hardened. It was a fierce juxtaposition of emotions, and they did not seem to be operating in Roscoe's favor.

"Actually, we do," said Wynezra.

Roscoe finally looked at her.

He looked *directly* at her.

"I *want* to forgive you," she said. "But I think, deep down, we both know that what you did was unforgivable. Hell, I don't even know what forgiveness means! Forgive? Don't forgive? All I know is that Mom is dead, and that's a forever thing. We're *never* getting her back. Not in this life anyway. And this life is *waaaaaaay* too fucking long and painful for me to focus on anything else."

Roscoe was speechless. Breathless.

"But I have a friend," said Wynezra. She looked at me. "And he has taught me that *I deserve to be happy*. Goddammit, man! I am so fucking sick and tired of punishing myself for something that isn't my fault! I *deserve* to have a father in my life! And I'm sorry, buddy, but you're it. You're all that I've got. So, if you're willing to give that to me, then I'm willing to take whatever you got. Just know that you have seven years to make up, so you better make 'em count. I expect the princess treatment: breakfast in bed, deep-tissue foot massages, the works. And just so you know, my feet smell like ass, so this is *not* gonna be a picnic for you."

Roscoe's eyes were wet. Overflowing.

And they never broke from Wynezra's gaze.

Not for a moment.

"Nona?" he said. His bottom lip quivered. "Is that really you?"

Wynezra's face was like aquarium glass, and it shattered—flooding with teary happiness.

"Yes!" Her voice—my voice—was soft, brittle, delicate. "It's *me.*"

"Oh my god. Oh my god, Nona!"

Roscoe and Wynezra sprinted into each other. They collided like snap bracelets, wrapping around each other, squeezing fiercely, crying. Wynezra's face was buried in Roscoe's chest as she clung to his shirt. Roscoe cradled her head in his hand, his thick fingers in her hair.

Meanwhile, I had my arms wrapped around myself. Kinda wishing I had someone to hug as well. *Definitely* wishing I had a tissue. I was a mess.

A great big happy smiling mess.

You couldn't buy happy endings like this—not from Disney, not even from the Hallmark Channel.

Flash.

Suddenly, my face was mashed in fabric and muscle, and I was clinging to Roscoe as if to a rock wall or a cliff face, and I definitely had snot coming out of my nose, and oh boy, this was embarrassing.

Not a second later, Wynonna hug-attacked me from behind. She squeezed me between her and Roscoe like the dulce de leche in a stuffed churro.

"Get in there, Slevin!" said Wynonna. "Just let it happen."

"Whoa, wait," said Roscoe. "Did something happen?"

"I'm me, and she's her now," I mumbled into Roscoe's shirt.

"Really? Just like that?"

"Yep," said Wynonna. She rested her head on my shoulder. "Just like that."

I sighed. Embraced the awkwardness. Released all the tension in my body and let myself be hugged.

I wasn't gonna lie. It felt fucking amazing.

TWENTY-NINE

THERE WAS ONLY ONE question left to be answered.

"We *saw* you packing," said Wynonna. "And your neighbor *told us* you moved out. What was that all about?"

Roscoe laughed nervously. "I could tell you. But it might be easier to show you."

Four hours later—as we fell asleep in turns—we pulled into a quiet neighborhood, in front of a quiet house. Morning had finally punctured the horizon, spilling orange light across the sky, casting everything in a dreamlike hue.

"We're here," said Roscoe, quietly.

"Here?" said Wynonna. She was just now waking up in the passenger seat, blinking desperately for clarity. "Where's here?"

"My new house."

Wynonna kept blinking because that didn't make *any* sense.

"*Our* new house," he said. "If you're interested."

Wynonna stopped blinking. Rotated her head slowly.

It was a small white thing, single story, with a tiny little porch, and a tiny little garden—all of this encased in an *actual* tiny little white picket fence.

"It's two bed, one bath," he said. "I know it's small, but—"

"You bought a *house*?" said Wynonna.

Roscoe shrugged. "It's Theo's, actually. He was selling, and I'd kind of decided I was staying here for good, so . . . why not?"

Before Roscoe could even finish, Wynonna was nodding her head desperately.

"Yes," she said.

"Yes?"

"I'm interested."

Roscoe's face broke into a smile. "Great! I mean . . . I'm still checking myself back into rehab today. But a month or so from now, if you're still interested . . ."

"Yes," said Wynonna, still nodding. "Still interested."

"Great!"

"Go check yourself into rehab already. I need you to get out ASAP."

"Okay!" said Roscoe, like this was the happiest day of his life. Which it probably was.

"Guys!" said Wynonna, turning back in the passenger seat. "Wanna see my new house?"

She was smiling so wide, it couldn't *possibly* be genuine. Except it was.

• •

After calling our parents, letting them know where we were—and emphasizing where we were *not*: aka jail—we kind of fell asleep at Wynonna's new house. The living room was filled with every pillow and blanket Roscoe owned, stacked into a soft, lulling mountain in a corner. The quantity of bedding was truly staggering. Like, did he swap them out every day or what?

At the end of the tour, the four of us just sort of unraveled into it.

Didn't wake up until late afternoon.

Even I, the broken sleeper, had sunk into an impenetrable sleep. When we woke, it was a collective awakening. We were a tangle of bodies in the den, and when one of us moved, it sent ripples across the labyrinthine human network.

Suddenly, Imogen shot up and exclaimed, "Prom!"

That caused the rest of us to splinter and unravel. We scrambled to our feet in an aimless frenzy.

"What time is it?" I said.

"Four forty-five!" said Imogen.

"WE HAVE TWO HOURS TO GET READY?" said Wynonna. She slapped her face with both hands like she was Macaulay Culkin.

"Two hours and fifteen minutes," said Imogen. "It's not exactly *plausible,* but it's possible."

"Wait, wait," said Holden. "Getting ready in two hours and fifteen minutes isn't *plausible*? What are you doing? Training forest animals to follow you around like Disney princesses?"

Wynonna rolled her eyes. "I hope you and Imogen start body-swapping. *Then* you would know."

"Please don't wish that on me," said Imogen.

The girls demanded we drop them off at Imogen's house first. Apparently, Wynonna's dress was already there. They had *planned* this. From there, Imogen told Holden and me that we could take her car.

The suits were at my place. *We* had planned this. We hopped in Imogen's car and drove.

Silently.

Holden cleared his throat awkwardly. "Can I ask you something?"

I didn't think Holden had ever *asked* if he could ask me something. He usually just skipped straight to the "asking" part.

I nodded suspiciously.

"Do you think I'm"—he hesitated—"gay?"

"Oh!" I said.

"Because I think I'm just a *little* gay," said Holden—anxious, vulnerable. "But before you go getting weirded out, it's not that I have a thing for *you*, per se. It's mostly just Wynonna *in your body*."

"Hey, Holden, it's—"

"I mean, mostly I just have a thing for Wynonna, period. But I'd be lying if I said I didn't have a thing *specifically* for Wynonna when she's *you*."

"Holden, it's—"

"And I just wanted to tell you that because, well, there was the janitor's closet thing that we never really talked about, but also, you know, it's prom, and there's a possibility that you and Wynonna will switch again, and if that happens, there's a possibility that she and I will . . . uh . . ."

"Holden!"

Holden stopped. Looked at me.

"It's okay," I said. "I'm a little gay, too."

Holden reared his head back, except for his eyeballs. Those stayed fixed in midair, practically dislodging from his face. "You *are*?"

"I think I'm a little lesbian, too."

Holden couldn't help it. He laughed. He was defenseless.

"Can I tell *you* something?" I said. "What *I* think?"

Holden swallowed, suddenly nervous, and nodded yes.

"I think," I said, "that there are so many words and labels for who we can be, and what we can be attracted to, and what we can identify as, that it's sometimes easy to forget ourselves. The important thing isn't the word or the label. The important thing is you."

"Me?" said Holden, confused.

"And me," I said. "And Wynonna. And Imogen. We're all human beings. I think we're more complicated than a single word: gay, straight, boy, girl, whatever. Most days, I identify more with a dot in the middle of a blank white page than anything else. And my life could start moving in any direction, and I don't even know what direction that is! Only that it's happening. I *identify* with the blankness. But... I think that's okay."

"Because the important thing is *you*," said Holden.

I grinned. Returned my attention to the road. "Exactly."

The important thing was me.

• •

I had been bracing myself for the We're So Disappointed in You treatment. I had, after all, gotten the car impounded. I spent an hour or two in a juvenile detention facility. I'll be honest: If I were my parents, not knowing the situation, *I* would be disappointed in me. I might have even grounded myself from prom! Which made me suddenly panic and wonder if the greatest night of my life was in jeopardy.

That wasn't what happened.

You see, my parents found out about all this from Roscoe. My parents *knew* who Roscoe Jones was. They knew who Wynonna Jones was, for that matter!

This *whole time*, they knew who she was.

And now they knew—in a confused version of the truth—my role in reuniting Wynonna with her dad.

"Hey, these things happen," said Dad.

"They do?" I said. I wasn't sure which things he was talking about: leaving your car at the airport drop-off so it could get impounded, or getting mistaken for terrorists and spending a couple hours in a juvenile detention center.

"Of course they do. The important thing is *you're okay*."

"It was a great thing you did for Wynonna," Mom added. "We're so proud of you, Ezzie."

"What am I, chopped liver?" said Holden.

"I'm proud of you, Holden," said Willow.

"Oh, you know we're always proud of you, Holden," said Mom.

"You keepin' our Ez in line, Holden?" said Dad.

"Oh, you know," said Holden, casually brushing his shoulders off. "It's a full-time job, but I do what I can."

• •

Holden and I cleaned up well. Partly because we were really, really, really *trying*. Partly because my family—who knew nothing about prom tonight or our respective dates until now—made it a Slevin family effort to pull our prom shit together.

"Imogen Klutz?" said Dad. "Who's Imogen Klutz? Do I know an Imogen Klutz?"

"She was Olivia," said Willow.

"What, the really tall, skinny one?" said Mom. "Is she taller than you, Ezzy?"

"Mom!" I said. "Seriously?"

"No, no, I'm just saying... she's a total cutie-pie. But do we need to get you shoes with a little extra... *oomph*?"

"We're, like, the same height."

"They're, like, *exactly* the same height," said Holden. "Like, you could balance a table on top of their heads and build a card castle on it."

"That is a really weird way of saying we're the same height."

"I thought it was poetic," said Willow.

"Thanks, homie!" said Holden. He extended his fist, and she bumped it.

"So she'll be wearing heels," said Mom.

"I don't know," I said. *"Probably."*

"Of course she is. That's it. I'm getting you shoes. Spiffy off-white shoes to go with your suit coat." She was already starting for the door.

"Please don't get me shoes."

"I'm getting them. Whether you wear them or not is your choice."

"Oh my god. Do you even know what shoe size I am?"

Mom shot me a look of the utmost indignation. "I gave *birth* to you! Of *course* I know what shoe size you are." And then, slightly less certain, "Nine, right?"

"Ten," I said.

"Ten? Oh lord. My children are radioactive monsters. They won't stop growing."

"Ouch," said Willow. "That hurts a little."

"I'll go with you, Mrs. Slevin!" Holden volunteered. "I think I'm going to get myself a pair of those bad boys. Then Ezra and I can match!"

Oh my god. My house had gone insane.

"What about you?" I said to Willow. "Are you not going to prom?"

"*Psh!*" said Willow. "No. Boys are stupid."

Even as she spoke, I caught the slightest glimpse of it: the tenderness of a wound that hadn't quite healed.

It vanished the moment Holden opened his mouth.

"Boys *are* stupid," he said. "Except for me."

"Except for you," Willow agreed. (And they fist-bumped again.) "No, Mom and Dad and I are doing a daddy-daughter date. But, like, with Mom, too. Is there a name for that?"

"What?" I said. And scanned the vicinity for privacy—Mom was looking for her purse, Dad was on the phone—then dropped my voice to a whisper. "Mom and Dad are going on a *date*?"

Willow smiled, knowingly. "Well, it's more like Dad's going on a date with me, and Mom's going on a date with me, too, and they'll be with each other by association. But yeah. I guess Mom and Dad are *kind of* going on a date."

She winked.

"Okay, Holden!" said Mom. "You ready to get these shoes? If you get Ezra to wear his pair, your pair is on me."

"Seriously?" said Holden. "Heck yeah!"

"Can I come, too?" said Willow.

"Oh god," said Mom. "If you must." She smiled, teasingly. "Ezzy? Do you want to pick out your own shoes, or are you leaving this valuable decision in the hands of your mother, your BFF, and your little sister?"

I sighed—barely suppressing my happiness. "Fine."

It was *more* than fine.

The four of us were on our way out the door when Dad abruptly ended his call. Stopped us in the entryway.

"Sorry," he said. "I hope it's okay, but I just rented you guys a limo for prom. The driver will be here to pick you boys up at six. I hope that's early enough to pick up your dates and get to prom in time."

Holden and I raised our hands and looked at each other like we were about to scream the highest notes our limited teenage vocal cords were capable of, puberty be damned.

But we didn't. Last second, we played it cool.

"Cool," I said.

"Awesome," said Holden.

But we were screaming on the inside.

My parents were kinda sorta amazing. When they tried.

• •

We arrived at Imogen's house at 6:15 p.m. sharp. We were right on schedule. Dressed to kill—but a metaphysical killing, with our dashing good looks as the murder weapon.

The door opened.

Suddenly, my and Holden's "dashing good looks" were equivalent to bird poop on the front steps of the Taj Mahal.

Imogen's gown was long and narrow and sweeping and white, touching the diamond texture of her glittering heels. She was statuesque, like a tree in winter, immortalized in snow. Her hair was straightened, a sandy waterfall, flowing down the heart-shaped curves of her face. Her makeup was minimalist and breathtaking.

Wynonna's dress was short and daring, strapless and electric blue. Lacy and crystallized on the top, rumpled and layered on the bottom, like the petals of a flower, pluming at the dawn of spring. Her legs were carved and powerful, showcased in cage-strap heels. Her makeup was bold, existential art that said, "I am here."

Her hair was cut.

"Cut" actually wasn't a strong enough word. It was short. Very short. *Pixie* short. Over the month that I had spent as her, her roots had grown devastatingly out of control. So, she cut her hair to the roots. Every strand of blue was gone. Her hair clung to the curve of her head, in delicate sweeping tufts, highlighting the gentle softness of her face.

I felt bad. After all the extravagant hard work Wynonna and Imogen had put into themselves, Holden and I were left staring at the top of Wynonna's head. It was unfair. It was also impossible to do anything else.

Wynonna shuffled awkwardly. Self-consciously. "Do you hate it?"

"What?" said Holden, snapping out of his trance. "No! It's beautiful. *You're* beautiful."

I just nodded my head, stupidly. Quickly turned my attention to Imogen.

"You look amazing, too," I said. "I especially like the . . . um . . ." I absorbed her in one stifled breath. "Really, the whole thing is kind of perfect."

Imogen lifted her shoulders bashfully, her long fingers interlocked, her arms twisting together. "You look pretty snazzy yourself."

Suddenly, Wynonna took two steps forward, intercepting the space between Holden and me—completely moved on from awkward prom greetings. "Is that a limo?"

"Whaaaaaat?" said Imogen. She also wedged herself between Holden and me. "A freaking limousine?"

Holden and I exchanged a look. If looks could scream in falsetto, that would be the look we exchanged. But we kept our cool.

"Yup," I said.

"Pretty sweet, huh?" said Holden. He pretended to be bored.

Wynonna and Imogen screamed at each other, then they screamed at us—at which point, Holden and I could hold it in no longer, and we screamed, too. We all ran to the limo screaming. The driver—a dapper gentleman who belonged in a '90s British sitcom—looked mildly alarmed.

But only mildly.

We piled inside. The interior was all plush white leather upholstery.

The seating wrapped around one side of the limo, while the other side was a fully functional bar.

Well, *almost* fully functional. There was no actual alcohol. (Holden and I checked.)

"Where to?" said the driver in a disappointingly non-British accent.

"To the prom!" Imogen exclaimed, giddy on limousine vibes. "And step on it!"

"One prom coming right up."

• •

"Wow," said Holden. "I feel like I'm in *Frozen*."

The Activities Committee didn't take their prom themes lightly. They Winter Wonderlanded the *shit* outta the place. Blue-tinted lights cast the gymnasium in an azure glow. Icicle lights were strung across the ceiling, filling an artificial sky with constellations. Fake, white, leafless trees lined the walls like ghostly forest sentries. An aurora borealis of sheer streamers flowed over our heads—blues and greens and purples. There were clusters of balloons, a range of every arctic hue between blue and white. White chairs with white tablecloths.

And fake snow.

Lots of fake snow. The floor was dusted in gallons of it.

We slowly immersed ourselves in the swoony atmosphere of prom. There were some surprising couples. Sebastian O'Hara, for example, was with a boy I could only *assume* was the Oscar of urban legend. I'd never seen him at Piles Fork High School. But whoever he was, he clearly *adored* Sebastian. And Sebastian's usual Dexter the Serial Killer personality melted, rendered into something sweet and innocent and nonlethal.

Even more surprising: aspiring wizard Tucker Cook and Daisy Munk.

I didn't know when or where or how *that* happened, but suddenly Tucker was completely googly-eyed for Daisy—which he had to kind of crane his neck back to do properly. She was nearly a foot taller than him. You could tell Daisy's guard was up; she hesitated to dance, to talk too much, to even *smile* excessively. But Tucker was kind of relentless in his adoration. Like a puppy.

When Daisy and Tucker finally *did* dance, Imogen pressed her hands to her cheeks, smooshing her face like a giant stress ball, swooning.

"Be still my heart," she said.

Wynonna, Holden, Imogen, and I danced ourselves silly. As a group, in pairs, by ourselves in moshing droves of sweaty bodies during the really fast songs. The ambience was magnetic. The air was pulsing, fueled by a thousand racing heartbeats. Even the fruit punch was on point. And that was to say *nothing* of the music.

DJ Ziggy Donovan was in the house. I swear, the guy had, like, a billion hobbies, and half a dozen side jobs. Of *course* he would be our DJ.

Prom was perfect.

Imogen was probably the greatest dance partner in the history of the universe. She gave zero shits about how one was supposed to dance. She just moved, and I moved, and we had fun—a blast, even—and we couldn't stop laughing, and she made me feel like I *wasn't* the worst dancer on the planet. (Which I knew for a fact that I was.) She was more than I deserved. I couldn't ask for more.

I also couldn't stop looking at Wynonna.

For the life of me, I couldn't.

When she danced, she was moving poetry—reckless, electric, alive. The more I looked, the more I felt myself fading in her presence. She was water, and I was a dissolvable tablet. I broke apart, crumbled, disintegrated in her wake.

The feeling was strange. I wasn't, like, in love with her.

I realized I was *happy* for her.

I realized I had never cherished the happiness of another human being more than I did for her, right now, in this moment.

I wasn't *in love* with her. But I did love her.

I felt a something trickle down my face.

"Ezra?" said Imogen. "Are you okay?"

I snapped out of my daze. Touched the part of my face where a tear had obviously snuck out. Wiped my face with my sleeve.

"Yeah," I said, smiling. "I'm just happy is all."

And I meant it.

"Pictures!" said Wynonna. "We gotta get pictures!"

The photo area was set up in an adjacent classroom, with poster-board signs and arrows guiding the way. The pictures were being taken against a painted snowy backdrop, framed between two fake frosted pine trees. The four of us agreed we wanted our picture taken together. Wynonna took the far end. I took the opposite end, forcing Holden and Imogen in the middle, paired with our respective dates.

"Okay, on the count of three," said the photographer. "One . . ."

Flash.

Suddenly, I was on the opposite end of our group, next to Holden.

"Oh, for fuck's sake," I said, in Wynonna's voice.

"Two . . ." said the photographer. He looked immensely confused.

Holden looked at me, and Imogen looked at Wynezra, who was rolling her head back in exasperation.

“STOP!” Imogen and Holden screamed simultaneously.

They wordlessly swapped sides so that Imogen was next to me, and Holden was next to Wynezra. Imogen grabbed my bare arm and pulled me close, smiling.

“I got your back,” she said, winking at me.

Holden attempted to follow suit, wrapping his arm around Wynezra’s waist. Except that, since Wynezra was significantly taller, he leaned into her instead.

“Okay,” said Holden, grinning. “We’re ready.”

Wynezra’s anemic complexion had turned magenta.

The photographer—perplexed but not perturbed—took our picture.

We looked great. Maybe even Happily Ever After-ish.

As we exited the room, Imogen and I were arm in arm. Holden and Wynezra were hand in hand. And then we crossed paths with Jayden and Thad—faces still swollen and purplish—and their respective dates. I didn’t know either girl, but I had half a mind to lean into both of their ears and tell them to run.

They didn’t pay much attention to Imogen and me. They were far more interested in Holden and Wynezra holding hands.

“I knew it!” said Thad. “I *knew* you two were a couple of queers!”

Wynezra unlatched from Holden’s hand. Strode up to Thad, fists compressed, arms swinging at her sides like a pair of wrecking balls.

“Oh shit,” said Thad. He turned and ran—abandoning his date, scampering around the corner.

Wynezra turned on Jayden.

“Whoa, hey!” said Jayden, lifting both hands in the air. “I’m cool. My dads are gay.”

It was a good thing Jayden’s face still looked like a sack of plums. Otherwise, I might have hunted down Mr. and Mr. Hoxsie and told them what misogynistic pieces of shit their son and his homophobic best friend were.

Back in the gymnasium, everyone was sweaty and out of breath. Even teenagers were no match for Ziggy's affinity for EDM. Ziggy read the crowd and decided to show a little mercy. He strung several slow songs together—slow songs with *just enough* innuendo and sexual tension to keep things interesting without alarming the authorities.

Imogen and I danced silently. Leaned into each other. It wasn't romantic so much as it was . . . relaxed. My hands wrapped around the small of her back, hers around my bare shoulders. But she seemed distracted. Distant.

Not *terribly* distant. Just enough for me to notice it. To recognize that it heightened every time she was facing the southwest corner of the auditorium.

We rotated slowly.

And then I saw her.

I knew her from a few of my classes over the years: Kimiko. A small-framed girl with hair the color of the darkest part of night. She was bubbly and smiley, and had a habit of whispering hilariously inappropriate jokes at the most inopportune moments of class. The sort where you either laugh or you die trying to hold it in. Tonight, however, she was wearing a bright red gown, and she was sitting all by herself, and she had clearly been sitting that way all night. She was wearing defeat like a burial shroud.

I looked at Imogen as we slowly rotated.

She was entranced.

It wasn't long before Imogen realized I was looking at her looking at Kimiko. And then she turned pink.

"Sorry," she said. "Just . . . lost in my own thoughts."

"You should ask her to dance," I said.

"*What?*" Now she was as red as Kimiko's dress. She hastily stole a glance at Kimiko, then lowered her head, embarrassed. "No, it's not what you . . . C'mon, Ezra. I came here with *you*."

"And you're here with me."

"I mean . . . I *asked* you here."

"And here I am," I said, clapping my hands to my sides. "And I've had a wonderful time."

I looked at Kimiko.

"And there *she* is. And she's really pretty, and smart, and funny, and she looks like she's had a rough night. And I can't imagine anyone in the world making it better than you."

Imogen bit her lip—practically gnawing it—in a moment of romantic crisis.

"One dance," she said. "One dance, and I'm coming back here."

"Hey," I said, hands in the air. "You do what you need to do. I'm not counting."

Imogen hugged me—a surprisingly intense hug that caught me off guard.

Then she turned, and click-clacked to the southwest corner of this perfect, fake-snow-dusted winter wonderland. She lifted a single finger straight into the air like a promise.

"One!" she said. "One, and then I'm coming back!"

I resolved to give Imogen and Kimiko a little privacy. Wandered to the northeast corner, closer to the stage, and the speakers, and the noise, and the sweat of a thousand teenagers misting the space. It was actually kind of gross, but I guess this was the human experience. Oh well.

I adjusted my dress and placed my hands in my lap and sighed.

I could already feel the loneliness setting in.

“ ’Sup, bro?” said Holden, *literally* out of nowhere. He collapsed next to me and threw his arm around my shoulder. “Where’s Imogen?”

“Um,” I said. “Dancing with Kimiko?”

“Kimiko? You mean *super-hot* Kimiko?”

I only knew one Kimiko, and she wasn’t *not* super hot, so I said, “I think?”

“Dude. You’re letting Imogen, your prom date, THE LOVE OF YOUR LIFE, dance with super-hot Kimiko? Are you crazy?”

I paused to consider this. Then shook my head. “Actually, for once in my life, I feel like I’m *not* crazy.”

Holden frowned at this. Folded his arms and leaned back in his chair.

“Well,” he said, “I guess you just need a good dance with Wynonna.”

“What?” I said. “No, c’mon. What about you?”

“No, believe me. You’d be doing me a favor.”

“How’s that?”

“She won’t shut up about you! Dude, she keeps talking about you like you’re her best friend, which, I guess you *are* her best friend—like, her *other* best friend—and no offense, but it’s getting *super* annoying. Like, I get it. Ezra’s amazing. Let’s build a shrine in his honor.”

I laughed. I actually snorted—a full-on, trademark Wynonna snort.

“Anyway,” he said, “here’s what we’re going to do: You’re going to go up on that stage and request a song from Ziggy. And you’re going to *make sure* he plays that song next because that’s when I’m going to give Imogen the ultimatum of dancing with me or super-hot Kimiko, and I’m sure she’ll pick super-hot Kimiko because, c’mon. And you’re going to dance with Wynonna, and you’re going to make that dance count because you two have something special, and I know I can't compete with it, so I might as well make room for it."

I stared at Holden, speechless.

"Okay?" said Holden. "Are we doing this?"

"You're a pal," I said. "Seriously."

"Dude. Tell me something I *don't* know."

Holden grinned and pulled me into a bro-hug—hands clasped, fists to chest, squeezing each other from the side. Then he turned me around, smacked my ass, and shoved me off in the direction of the DJ table.

He cupped his hand over his mouth and shouted, "You better pick a good one!"

Oh, I would.

• •

"This one," I said, pointing at Ziggy's laptop screen.

"*That* one?" said Ziggy. "Wow, we're going old-school, huh?"

"I need you to play it next."

"Um. Look. I can play it *at the end of the queue*. But that's the best I can do for you. Other people have requested songs. I can't just let you cut in line."

I had anticipated as much. That's why, before coming up here, I went out to the limo and retrieved my (Ezra Slevin's) wallet.

I opened it, pulled out a twenty, and slid it across the DJ table.

"Whoa, hey," said Ziggy. He raised his fingerless-gloved hands in the air. "I can't take that."

I pulled out another twenty. Slid it across the table, directly parallel to the first bill.

"This is called bribery," said Ziggy. "I could lose my DJ gig here, just looking at this."

I removed a third twenty. Pressed it into the table with a single, electric-blue fingernail. Slid it *slooooowly.*

"Dude, fine!" said Ziggy. "I'll play your song next. Just get that shit off my table before someone thinks I'm dealing nose candy!"

And not a yoctosecond too soon. The slowest of slow songs had finally come to an end. Ziggy's hands danced across the keyboard like a duet—like Fred Astaire and Ginger Rogers—ending with a show-stopping tap of the enter key.

The sound system echoed with familiar chirping guitar chords ricocheting across the metaphorical chasm separating two hearts, somewhere in the '80s.

Ziggy sighed, grabbed his mic, and waved it at me like a magic wand. "Shall I make a dedication, or would you like the honors?"

I grabbed the mic in response and pranced to the edge of the stage.

"WYNONNA JONES!" I said.

I pointed directly at Wynezra. She appeared double-startled because Holden had suddenly stolen away, lost in the crowds, and now her name was a Mach wave blasting from the speakers.

Her eyes met mine.

"This song is for you," I said.

Okay, so it sounded a little narcissistic, like I was dedicating the song to myself. But Wynonna knew. And that was all that mattered.

"Many times I tried to tell you," sang Pat Benatar, *"many times I cried alone. Always I'm surprised how well you cut my feelings to the bone."*

I tossed the mic to Ziggy—which he fumbled for and barely managed to catch. I crouched down with ladylike grace, knees tucked to one side, swung my legs off the edge of the stage, and descended with finesse.

I marched directly to Wynezra. By some miracle—fueled by the magic of prom—the crowded parted before me.

They parted all the way to her.

Wynezra stared at me, openmouthed.

"May I have this dance?" I asked.

Wynezra grinned. "Yeah, okay."

"We belong to the light, we belong to the thunder!" Pat wailed. *"We belong to the sound of the words we've both fallen under!"*

Okay, so neither Wynonna nor I was what you would call a good dancer. If anyone had been hoping for the finale of *Dirty Dancing* with Baby and Patrick Swayze, they would be sorely disappointed.

Wynezra and I proceeded to move like we belonged to the light and thunder—jumping up and down, headbanging like Andrew W.K., taking turns clumsily twirling each other, etc. Our general strategy was to "move a lot"—to expend every ounce of energy afforded to our mortal vessels. To move until we died, or Pat Benatar stopped singing—whichever came first.

When the crowd around us realized the staggering extent of our dancing inability—surpassed only by the deficit of fucks we had to give—the circle broke apart, disinterested and slightly annoyed.

But we kept dancing. Coalescing.

For three minutes and forty seconds, at least, until the song ended in a fade-out. We barely had a moment to stop when Wynonna leaned forward and hugged me. It wasn't a brief hug. She just hugged me and didn't let go.

She didn't say anything. I didn't say anything. We didn't need to.

We both just knew.

THIRTY

AFTER MY DANCE WITH Wynonna, Holden gave me a high five and praised me for my "sick moves," which was such a lie. Wynonna hugged me again. And then the next slow song started, and they were pulled into its current, lulled away.

I wandered off as well, in a sort of dreamlike haze. Out of the gymnasium. Out of the building. I sat on the curb, leaned back, and looked at the stars—crystalline, sparkling against the black tarp of the sky.

I wondered how much of me was up there. How many times I had disintegrated, dissolved into that infinite sea, become one with something so much bigger than myself.

How many times had it saved me?

"Hey," said a voice.

I arched my head back all the way. Imogen was looking down on me, upside down, but otherwise perfect.

Then the blood started rushing to my head, and things got a little woozy.

"Ugh," I said, lurching forward. I mumbled a feeble "Sorry. Hey."

Imogen sat down beside me on the curb. Her long legs curled to the side, knees pointing at me, toes pointing away.

"You kinda left me in there," she said.

"Sorry," I said, again. "I just didn't wanna crowd you and Kimiko."

"You do realize," she said, "that I asked *you* to prom. Not Kimiko."

"I know, I just . . . I saw the way you were looking at her, and—"

"Ezra . . ."

"And I want you to have what *you* want, not what *I* want, because you *deserve* that, and I don't want to just guilt you into dating me, just because everyone knows I've had a crush on you since the dawn of time—"

"Ezra—"

"And as much as I'd like to *believe* you're bisexual, I don't *know* that, and I just want to be realistic, because I know the only reason you asked me to prom is because Wynonna talked to you, and you felt bad about the past month, but you shouldn't have to feel *so bad* that you have to pretend that you like me—"

"Ezra!"

I shut my mouth. Closed it airtight.

"Wynonna didn't *coerce* me into asking you to prom," she said, clearly hurt. "She didn't *guilt* me into it. I asked you because I *wanted* to ask you. That was *my* decision. All mine. You think I'm *pretending* to like you? Ezra, have you ever even thought to *ask* me if I'm bisexual?"

I had certainly pondered the question about a billion times over the past month. But the thought of actually *asking* it was always a terrifying nonoption. I'd rather ask a reincarnated Nietzsche what the meaning of life was.

"Are you?" I said.

Imogen shrugged. "I don't know."

"Oh." I couldn't help but sound a little disheartened.

"But I'm not *pretending* that I like you. I *like* you! I just . . ." She sighed. "I *was* staring at Kimiko, and I'm sorry. But it's not like that. I just get a little flustered and discombobulated when I'm around all"—she made an ambiguous gesture toward all of me—"this."

This?

I glanced down at myself.

Or, I should say, *Wynonna's* self.

Oh.

"I like you," she repeated, "but you're also wearing my Kryptonite to prom. And I want to separate my feelings for *you* from my feelings for *her* because they're two entirely different feelings. You deserve that much."

I suddenly felt very stupid. About everything.

"I'll admit," said Imogen, "Wynonna is like an adrenaline shot, directly into my heart. She's wild, and dangerous, and exhilarating. She's like riding a roller coaster that's not up to code. But you, Ezra . . . you're someone I want to *be* like. You inspire me. You're kind, and gentle, and so sincere it hurts. You make my heart melt slowly, like an ice-cream cone on a lazy summer day. And yeah, I don't know if I'm into guys. But honestly—and I mean this as a humongous compliment, so please don't take offense—I don't feel like I'm with a *guy* when I'm around you. No matter *which* body you're in. And I'm sorry for staring at Kimiko, but I promise, it was only because I was trying to get Wynonna out of my head, and I'm sorry you have to deal with this hot mess, but it's just . . . it's *hard* sometimes. You know?"

I didn't even know if there was a word in the English language capable of digging me out of the stupid, self-pitying hole I had dug myself into. So I continued not to speak. So far, it was my best tactic.

"Can I just . . . get to know you?" she said. "The *real* you? Not the fake Cesario you?"

Those words—"the real you"—caused something to click into place. They made me realize I was ready for something. Something that I had not been ready for in the entire history of my existence.

I glanced down at myself—my lack of pockets and, particularly, my lack of a phone. I glanced at Imogen.

She had a small white purse lying at her side.

"Do you have your phone on you?" I asked.

"Uh. Yeah?"

"Can I see it?"

Perplexed, Imogen unzipped her purse. Reached inside, pulled out her phone, handed it to me.

I connected to her data and typed "Ezward Slevinhands" into the search engine. Then handed the phone back to her. Imogen accepted it awkwardly and squinted at the screen.

"Ezward... Slevinhands?" said Imogen, confused.

"It's my YouTube channel," I said. "I do Johnny Depp impersonations."

She leaned forward, trying to piece together what exactly she was looking at. Then her eyes bugged out of her face.

"Oh my gosh," she said, alarmed. "This says you have eleven *thousand* subscribers."

I nodded.

Imogen glanced from me, to the screen, and back to me. "Ezra, you're, like, a YouTube *celebrity*."

"'Celebrity' is a stretch," I said. "I make enough money to buy more costumes and makeup, and that's about it."

"You get *paid*... to make *videos*... on *YouTube*."

"It's seriously not a lot. At my peak, it was, like, less than a part-time summer job making minimum wage in Georgia."

Imogen's eyes were *saturated* with amazement. "Can I watch one?"

"No."

"Oh . . ." Her entire countenance drooped.

"Of course you can watch one! Seriously?"

"Oh!" She lit up again, instantly. "Which one should I watch?"

"Whichever one you want. Except Tonto. Please don't watch Tonto. I feel a lot of moral regret about that one. I don't know why I haven't taken it down already."

Imogen scrolled briefly, then her finger hovered—excited and a little bit terrified—over Sweeney Todd. She pressed play, and my heart did a little cardiovascular fist-pump because I knew we were starting with our best foot forward.

Sweeney Todd breathed with malice: "*I had him. . .*"

He screamed: "*I had him!*"

He sang: *"His throat was bare beneath my hand. No! I had him! His throat was there, and he'll never come again!"*

Imogen turned and stared at me with her mouth all the way open. Her eyes were radiating gleeful mania.

And then she whipped her head back because things were just getting good.

"There's a hole in the world like a great black pit. And it's filled with people who are filled with shit. And the vermin of the world inhabit it. But not for looooooooong."

Imogen glanced down at her arm, then raised it for me, just so I could see that every tiny hair was standing on end.

We watched it all the way to the end. Or rather, I watched Imogen watch it all the way to the end. Her reaction—fear, shock, elation—was far more priceless than anything I had ever uploaded to YouTube.

The song ended with Sweeney at his most unhinged.

"And my Lucy lies in ashes! And I'll never see my girl again! But the work waits! I'm alive at last! And I'm full of JOOOOOOY!"

That last note sounded like anything but joy. It was murderous rage spilling freely, pooling out into a halo of blood.

The video ended abruptly, like death.

"Oh. My. Freaking. Gosh." Imogen had both hands pressed to her head to keep the contents from exploding out. "You can *sing*."

"I really can't," I said. "I literally just mimicked Depp's whole thing."

"Your pitch is dead-on."

"*Johnny's* pitch is dead-on."

"Aaaaaauuurrghhhh!" said Imogen, grabbing clumps of her perfect, straightened prom hair. "You are seriously not giving yourself *nearly* enough credit. People don't just *copy* something this good. You and Johnny Depp don't have the same vocal cords. You had to *improvise* to make those notes work, and you made them freaking work! You *slayed* them! Like all those poor people who are going to be baked into meat pies!"

"So you liked it?"

"Did I *like* it? Ezra, it was phenomenal! Does Wynonna know about this?"

"Well, yeah, but—"

"AND SHE DIDN'T TELL ME?" Imogen practically fell backward, reeling. "That traitor! She *knows* I would've eaten this up! I can't believe she kept this to herself, that greedy little—"

"Actually, I asked her not to."

Imogen blinked. "What? Why?"

This was the part where it was difficult to put feelings into words. But I tried anyway.

"Have you ever had something that was *so special* to you, that you were afraid no one would understand it? That somehow, their words would cheapen it? Or worse, someone you cared about just wouldn't like it, and it would shatter you, because in a weird sense, it's basically like they don't like you?"

I looked at Imogen for some hint that she understood. Instead, she just looked mind-blown.

"Anyway," I said, returning my attention to my heels, "it's kinda like that."

"How many people have you shown this to?" she asked, softly.

"Um. Well, Wynonna found it because she was snooping on my computer. So . . . I guess you're the first?"

A rush of emotion flooded Imogen's face. She leaned toward me. Grabbed my hand on the concrete. Squeezed it.

"Thank you, Ezra. You have no idea how much that means to me."

I was smiling so much, my face ached. I didn't even need to look at myself to know I was glowing.

Imogen blinked the emotion away, then glanced eagerly down at her phone. "Can we watch another one?"

"As many as you can stomach," I said.

"Oh, goody," said Imogen. She patted her stomach ravenously, and said, "Get in mah bellay!"

• •

We watched all of them. Every single video I had ever created. All in one sitting.

The dinner-roll "dance scene" with Sam from *Benny and Joon* got the biggest reaction. It was literally just a pair of dinner rolls, stabbed with forks, tap-dancing. It was the picture of absurdity. And Imogen laughed so hard, she cried.

She laughed so hard, her stomach started hurting.

She laughed so hard, she thought she was going to be sick.

"Should I call nine-one-one?" I said, only halfway joking.

"It's too . . . it's too late!" she said, curled into the fetal position on the concrete, *still* laughing. "I'm already dead! Call my mom. Tell her I love her."

By the time we finished, Imogen was experiencing something of an existential crisis.

"That's it?" she said. "That's all of them?"

"Johnny Depp only has so many movies," I said.

Imogen leaned forward, grabbed me by my bare shoulders, and shook me. "You *have* to let me make one with you."

"What?" I said.

It wasn't a bad "what." I was just completely shocked.

But Imogen seemed to read it like a bad "what."

She backtracked. "I mean . . . I'm not asking to be *in it*, of course. I know this is something really special to you. I just . . . I would love to see your MO, your modus operandi. I would be honored. But, like, I understand if you don't want me to—"

"I would love that," I said.

Imogen looked like she had suddenly gone weightless, suspended in zero-g. "Really?"

"So much. Seriously."

And that's when I told her about my passion project: *Ed Wood*.

I explained to her that this was my favorite Johnny Depp movie, my favorite Tim Burton movie, and probably just my favorite movie in general. And that was going up against the likes of *Inception*!

I explained to her that it had to be perfect.

I explained that—

Flash.

Okay, so I didn't get through with the explanation, because suddenly, I was *me*, and I was in a dark classroom, on top of some poor teacher's desk, and Holden was beneath me, and I was making out with his face. Actually, that was putting it lightly because his tongue was all the way down my throat. I gagged on it.

"Sorry, sorry," said Holden. "Too much tongue?"

I was still gagging. I was pretty sure he licked my uvula.

"Oh no," said Holden, clutching his face. "Please don't tell me—"

Suddenly, the classroom door flung open. Imogen raced into the room with Wynonna falling leisurely behind her, crying with laughter.

"Sorry, Holden, I'm stealing your boyfriend," said Imogen. She grabbed me by the hand and practically whipped me off the desk. Towed me out the door behind her. "We're taking the limo, but we'll send it back for you. PS: You guys should get a hotel or something. That's Mr. Gunther's desk, and he has some scary-bad dandruff. Like, winter wonderland–themed."

She closed the classroom door behind us.

"Where are we going?" I said.

Imogen grinned. "We're doing *Ed Wood*."

"Tonight?!"

"It's the most important night of the year for teenagekind! Of course we're doing it tonight!"

Her smile was infectious. I caught it.

"Let's go angora sweater shopping," I said.

• •

We bought the outfit almost entirely at Marshalls—except for the angora sweater, which we snatched at Nordstrom Rack right before they closed, and a blond wig, which we found at a high-quality wig store and spent a small fortune on. Imogen had the gall to bring both the wig and the sweater into Marshalls but was sure to let her favorite cashier, Phoebe, know about it. She explained that I was going to walk out of this store looking like "a nineteen-fifties goddess."

"Mmm, girl, you better," said Phoebe. "I'll call security if you don't."

"Question," Imogen said to me. "If you did your own makeup in *every single one* of those videos, how are you with, like, *makeup*?"

We decided to find out. I brought the necessary makeup items into the dressing room with me. (I was going to pay for them, relax!)

Here were the facts:

- I had inherited the steady surgeon hand of Mark Slevin. This thing was as steady as Willow's relationship with My Chemical Romance.
- I knew the natural contours of my face like a fully indexed topographical map.
- I *really* wanted this.

When I was done, I was wearing black pumps, a below-the-knee pleated skirt, and the most comfortable sweater I had ever worn. Or maybe it was just emotionally comfortable. All I knew was that I dug it. A lot. The blond wig was a little jarring against my eyebrows, but otherwise, it served its purpose well, framing my art like a divine architecture. Like the Sistine Chapel.

I didn't just *feel* beautiful. I was.

Either that, or I was as deluded with myself as Ed Wood was with his god-awful filmmaking career.

I had that sudden thought the moment I stepped out of the dressing room. Felt a spike of panic. Imogen was going to turn around, and she was going to let out a little snort of laughter, and tell me I looked "adorable," and then I would be ruined. Ruined forever.

That wasn't what happened.

Imogen looked a little startled when she saw me.

"Damn," she said.

My jaw dropped. "Did you just swear?"

"No," she lied.

"That was a swearword that came out of your mouth just now."

"No, it wasn't."

"I've never heard you swear before. Not once."

"What? Whatever. I say swears all the time."

"Like what?!"

"You know? Swears. Like . . . holy dicks!"

Imogen had never said "holy dicks" once in her life either. I was pretty sure *no one* had. That was not a thing anyone had said, ever.

"But you didn't swear just now?" I said. "That wasn't a swearword?"

"Uh . . ." she said, panicking. "I'm confused."

I was smiling so hard, it was an unstoppable force, threatening to conquer my face forever.

"Oh my god," she groaned, like she had a stomachache. "Your smile is so goddamn pretty."

"YOU DID IT AGAIN."

Imogen started fanning herself with her hand. "It is hot in here, or is it just you? I mean, me. I mean . . . what? What are we talking about?"

• •

When we arrived at Slevin Manor, Willow and Dad were curled up on the couch watching *Steven Universe*. That was their thing—watching cartoons together. They lit up when they saw Imogen—aka Ezra's date—and then looked *suuuuper* confused when they saw Miss Nineteen-Fifties walking in beside her.

Slowly, over the course of ten of the most awkward seconds of my life, realization clicked in.

Willow stood up.

Started clapping.

"Bravo," she said. "Dang, bro. You look smokin'."

Don't blush, Ezra, don't blush, don't you dare fucking—

I blushed.

"Ezra?" said Dad. "Wow. You look, uh . . . I guess 'beautiful' is the word? Beautiful. Yeah. You look beautiful. Sorry. We just watched the 'Jail Break' episode of *Steven Universe* where Garnet sings and beats up Jasper, so my brain is all over the place."

And then Willow and Dad looked at Imogen, and panicked.

"You look *amazing*, Imogen!" said Willow.

"Absolutely stunning," said Dad.

"Gorgeous."

"Amazing."

"I already said that, Dad."

"I'm reemphasizing."

"Oh, you guys," said Imogen, shrugging her shoulders bashfully.

"So, uh . . ." said Dad. "Is this a prom thing?"

"Actually, we're making a YouTube video," I said. And then a sudden, very important thought occurred. "Willow, who did your Malvolio makeup?"

"Uh, me," she said. "Duh?"

"How would you like to play another old man?"

I explained the scenario: that this was essentially a highlights reel of the movie *Ed Wood*. (Willow watched it with me once, although she seemed less impressed by modern films that felt the need to be filmed in black-and-white.) I explained that she would be Bela Lugosi, the original *Dracula* actor.

Ed Wood was about friendship, after all. And besides, Bela Lugosi had all the best lines.

"Is this the one where Dracula's a heroin addict?" said Willow.

"Uh, morphine, actually," I said.

Willow grinned, and then attempted her best Transylvanian: "*Count* me een. Get eet? Because I'm ze *count*. Ah, ah, ah, ah, ah."

• •

We finished filming at about two thirty in the morning. For the first time ever, I uploaded the video directly onto my social media. On the part of the internet that knew Ezra the Person, not Ezward the Enigma.

I tagged Willow and pressed post.

"Is anyone else as *not* tired as me?" said Willow. She was still in full costume, of course. Thick emo hair slicked back. Fake, out-of-control, bushy eyebrows (leftovers of Malvolio's, dyed black). Crinkly, vaguely hostile "old man" face. She was dressed in her loosest black clothes, swaddled in a black cape.

The cape was hers. Don't ask me why or how she owned a black cape.

"I'm not ti . . . *hired*," said Imogen—yawning, and stretching like the world's longest cat, and smiling sleepily.

"Great, it's settled," said Willow. "We're watching a movie."

We watched *Splatter*. The original. I wish I could tell you that it was less terrible than the sequels, but it really wasn't. It was *so* bad. I loved it.

Jane Jenkins was still in high school. It was prom night. And she was in for a rude, gory, breathtakingly violent awakening.

About ten minutes into the movie, Willow fell asleep. Just completely conked out—head hanging, snoring violently, there was a little bit of a drool situation threatening to transpire on the bottom of her lip. It was highlighted perfectly against the glow of the TV.

"Wow," I said. "That didn't take long."

Imogen didn't say anything. I turned—expecting to find her asleep on my other side.

She was looking directly at me. One side of her face pale in the TV's glow, the other dark, all of it very intense.

"Oh, hey," I said. "Is . . . everything okay?"

"Can I kiss you?" she said.

She *literally* asked me permission for this. Like I might say no or something.

"As an experiment," she added, after I failed to respond. "In the name of science."

"Well, if it's for science—" I started to say.

And she kissed me.

I'd tell you how it was, but this was the sort of kiss that seals space and time and reality in its sphere. I was on a different planet. In an alternate dimension where anything was possible, and nothing was hopeless. When her lips finally broke away from mine, I didn't even know who I was anymore. Ezra? What's that?

Imogen smiled.

Then rested her head on my shoulder.

"So . . ." I said, "experimentally speaking . . . how was . . ."

"Further study is necessary," she said.

"Further *study*?"

"More experiments are required."

"More *experiments*?"

"Oh yeah," she said, nodding seriously. "So many experiments. A wide variety, for sure. It'll probably be an ongoing study. It could take a substantial amount of time. You know, before we come to any conclusive evidence. For science."

I could feel her smiling into my angora sweater.

• •

We stayed that way for a long moment. Long enough for Imogen to fall asleep.

For the snoring apocalypse to commence.

I lost interest in the movie. Buddy Borden's body count was already in the double digits. I instead found myself transfixed by the large living room clock on the wall. As the minute hand clicked on fourteen, and the second hand tick-tick-ticked closer to the infinite, irrational number between fifteen and sixteen.

Thirteen . . . fourteen . . . fifteen . . .

Sixteen.

I let out the breath I didn't know I was holding. Glanced from Willow to Imogen to myself. I wanted to laugh and cry simultaneously. But mostly, I just felt breathless from the anticipation.

My phone vibrated on the coffee table. From where I sat, I could see the caller.

Wynonna fucking Jones.

I quietly reached, struggling not to disturb Imogen. My fingers splayed, tracing the edges of the phone.

Grabbed it.

I gently leaned back into the sofa. Imogen stirred slightly, adjusted, then fell back into a deep snoring trance.

I pressed the answer button.

"Hey," said Wynonna quietly. Like she knew Imogen and Willow were sleeping on the other end. Or maybe Holden was asleep where she was. Who knew? "Just wanted to make sure you were still alive. Also, to hear your voice. If that's not weird. It probably is. Whatever. Fuck you."

I laughed. "Hey, Wynonna."

"Okay, well . . . that's good enough for me. Sleep tight, Slevin. If you can manage that much."

"Good night, Wynonna."

She hung up.

I set the phone in my lap.

And I fell asleep.

ACKNOWLEDGMENTS

Does it take an army to write a book? Maybe! This novel would not be the beautiful thing that it is were it not for the many beautiful people involved. For starters, my agent, Jenny Bent, who listened compassionately while I had an actual midlife crisis over the phone. (I'm only thirty-three, but I feel like I'm one hundred and three, and not in a wise, sagely way.) My editor, the actually wise and sagely Laura Schreiber, who corresponded considerately while I threw toddler-like temper tantrums about her brilliant edits and intuitive suggestions. Laura's wonderful editorial assistant, Mary Mudd, who is basically Wonder Woman and fills in all the gaps. Managing editor Sara Liebling, who keeps track of all the production schedules I'm so fond of fucking up. (Just kidding, I promise I'm not trying to!) A huge shout out to the visionary Mary Claire Cruz who designed a cover so lush, it makes me want to cry. Copy editors Guy Cunningham and Meredith Jones, who fine-tuned the inner-workings of this story like that '63 Corvette Stingray that Ezra couldn't drive. School and library marketing guru Dina Sherman, who is a beacon of sunshine to meet in person. A special shout out to my three cats, Stormy, Bagheera, and Tyson, who contributed nothing, and even walked across my keyboard a couple times and deleted shit, but they help keep the bad feelings at bay. And lastly, my partner, Erin Rene, who is just the fucking best.